Shadow Jumper

Karen Andor

DEDICATION

To Silvia
With thanks always

ACKNOWLEDGMENTS

Thank you to Sue Andor, Jan Sargeant, Silvia Galli, Kathy Duggan, and Mark Crussell for taking the time to read this book and for giving me your thoughts and opinions on it. Thank you to Erica Hutchison for the hours of proof-reading.

1

Something made a noise and I think that is what woke me up. A part of me tries to struggle through the thick molasses of sleep to see what woke me and yet another part of me wants to yield to the tenacious tendrils that pull me back towards blissful oblivion. Sleep has always been a haven, a shelter I retreat to as much as I can in order to escape the agony of life. Unfortunately, it seems that this time I am unable to fall back into the unknowing sea of blackness.

I try to open my eyes, but my vision is blurry, and my left eye does not seem to want to open. As consciousness dawns ever more fully, I become aware that my body hurts. The pain starts as a dull ache and becomes more acute and sharper as time grows. I don't think there is a part of me that doesn't hurt and it's hard to know if one part hurts more than the other parts. How is it that I am in so much pain? A memory pulls at the edge of my consciousness, but I banish it as soon as I am aware of its desire to manifest.

I can see a shaft of wan light peeking below the hem of the thick curtains. I am not sure what time it is, but it must be quite late. I hurt so much and I just don't want to get out of bed. I roll over gently and bury my face into the soft pillow. I shut my eyes again and will myself to sleep. I want to escape the pain of my body and the horrors that the day must surely hold.

My body jerks involuntarily and pain lances right through me as a loud knock sounds on the door. I am terrified.

"Get out of bed now, boy! Your mother's made breakfast and it's going to get cold. We've got work to do and it's getting late. Get your sorry, worthless ass out of bed right now! It's late and there's lots of work to get done. Do you hear me?"

"Yes, Sir."

I guess I must have heard Dad calling me for breakfast earlier and that's what woke me up. I sit up painfully. I climb out of bed and have to sit down immediately as a wave of dizziness washes over me. I wait for it to subside. When it does, I gently stand up again and turn the light on. My room is plain. Dark wooden floors meet sharply with white walls that have been turned slightly brown by the dust of time. I have an antique wardrobe that stands menacingly against the opposite wall. I feel that it knows many secrets and has witnessed many events that should never be spoken of. I am scared to open it, for fear that all those secrets will come tumbling out and smother me. I never open it. Instead I always hang my clothes on the old wooden chair by my scarred desk. I don't have that many clothes in any case. I tentatively pad across the old, worn red carpet to the desk and pick out my clothes for the day. It feels cold and so I select thick denim dungarees and a warm jersey and jacket. I go back to my bed in the corner with its welcoming white duvet and sumptuous pillows and sit down to get dressed.

Turning on my bedside lamp I can now see why I am so sore. My legs, chest and arms are covered in bumps and a slight blue is barely visible beneath the surface of my skin. I know that in a couple of days, the bruises will turn a deathly looking blue and black. The bumps are very tender to the touch and I try to slip my clothes on as gently as I can. I am sure that I have more bumps on my face and I am pretty sure that my left eye is swollen. I don't dare look at myself in the mirror. I can't stand mirrors. I never ever look at myself in a mirror, as the sight of what I will see is too terrifying to behold. Also, I would have to open the wardrobe to look at myself in the mirror and I don't want to do that.

I slowly start to remember what happened to me last night. Dad had had another of his bad nights. It always happens when he loses at poker. He likes to go to the bar in town after work on a Thursday and play poker with his friends. They all drink a lot. It's not a problem if he wins the game, but it is if he doesn't. He hates to lose at anything or to anyone. When he came home last night, we had a late dinner. We always eat as a family, because Dad likes us to be together, like a proper family should. So we had to wait for him to come home. I couldn't eat all of my dinner, as I was not feeling very hungry. That made him really angry and he said that I was insulting my mother's cooking. I apologised and tried to eat it all, but he said that I was pulling a face and eating too slowly. I am sure I wasn't pulling a face. I would never ever do that.

That's when I heard the crash of his chair, as it fell to the ground. He hit me everywhere. I just saw his large fists coming for me. I didn't really feel the pain. I just remember thinking that my father has the biggest hands I have ever seen. I tried to get under the table and curl into a ball, with my arms over my face to protect myself from his fists and feet, but he was too strong and he pulled my arms back and kept on hitting. In the end, I just became numb and relaxed in a strange kind of way. I knew it would end. Either I would die or he would stop. He stopped. I had to get up, eat the rest of my food and then clean up before he let me go to bed.

As I enter the kitchen, I see my mother staring out of the window at the grey morning sky. Mom and I ran out of words to say to each other a long time ago. I get my bowl and cereal and gingerly chew on the flakes, hoping the milk will soften them quickly. I don't have much time to eat as Dad will get angry again and I don't think I can handle another beating today. As I chew, Mom cleans the dishes without paying much attention to what she is doing. Her eyes stare vacantly out the window and she looks as grey as the blanket of clouds that are blocking out the sun.

"Boy! Are you ready?" I hear my father's voice bellow from the entrance hall.

"Yes, Sir!"

"Let's get going. I'll be waiting in the truck. Don't make me wait long!"

" No, Sir, I'm coming now."

I place my bowl in the soapy water, careful not to touch my mother's hand, which is resting in the water. I glance at her for a moment, but it feels too strange, and so I fetch my muddy boots from the cupboard in the entrance hall and carefully pull them on.

I don't want Dad to know how much I hurt today and, even though it is extremely painful, I walk as quickly and as normally as I can to the big truck. It is hard to suppress the groan that wants to escape my mouth as I swing myself into the truck's cab, but I feel proud that I don't make a sound. Before I have slammed the door shut, Dad shifts the truck into first and pulls off.

Neither of us speaks. Dad is far more communicative than Mom is, but there is not much that we can talk about. I don't have that same easy-going relationship with him that other kids have with their fathers. I always have to watch what I say, because anything can set him off and I am never sure what that might be. Some things I know for sure are bad things to mention, like if I am feeling sick, or if I talk about Bobby's Dad, who is doing really well financially. Those things really set Dad off and then I know a beating is on its way for sure. Sometimes I can talk about something that he really likes like pig farming and he's okay, and then on a different day, I can talk about the same thing and he'll just punch me in the stomach.

So we ride in silence. Eventually Dad pulls out a cigarette and lights it. I feel claustrophobic with the smoke of the cigarette filling up the cab. I don't dare open the window, as that will make Dad really mad, because then he'll say that we are wasting heat, as it is a cold day. Dad turns on the radio and we listen to the news, while the truck bumps along the road, jarring my body painfully. I try to focus on the drab fields that we pass in order to take my attention away from my body. The continuous motion of the fields passing by in blurs of yellow and brown lull me into a kind of peace and the pain slowly starts to subside from consciousness. I listen vaguely to the radio. The newscaster is talking about a woman in our county, who killed herself because she found out her husband was having an affair. They seem to think it was a suicide, but homicide is looking into it just in case. Stories like that are big around here, because no one ever gets killed. Everything is so peaceful and quiet here. My Dad says it's like living in a small piece of paradise. The newsreader drones on about the case, but I stop listening, and once again I let the motion of the passing fields alter my state of consciousness. I am an expert at doing that.

The truck pulls up to the barn with a jerk that causes every nerve in my body to shudder with agony. Dad gets out of the car and strides over to the barn. I try to keep up with him, not wanting to make him angry again. He wrenches the old barn door open.

"Fetch the rake and shovel, boy. The pen needs a good cleaning today."

I fumble around in the dim light near the cupboard in the corner of the barn. I carefully make my way with the equipment to the door, which Dad has let swing shut. My body aches as I heave the door open.

A truck pulls up next to ours in a cloud of dust.

"Morning there, Joe."

"Morning, Bill"

"It looks like it's going to be a good day today. Weather looks like it will hold for a couple days."

"Sure does."

"Heard lady luck wasn't favouring you last night."

"It had nothing to do with luck. It's Charlie who keeps cheating. I don't know why Bud invites him. If he invites him again, I'm going to quit."

My heart skips a beat as a feeling of hope floods me. If Dad would only quit poker, things might be a little better.

"You'll never quit, Bill. Poker's in your blood. Same's your old man. What happened to you, kid?"

I look up in alarm at Uncle Joe. My brain is thinking of a million things to say, but none of them seem to make sense. Thankfully, Dad jumps in.

"You know what boys are like, Joe. Always getting into scraps. He's not saying, but I reckon he got into a fight with another kid and the other kid probably got the better of him."

"You need to learn to pick your fights better, son."

"Yes, Sir."

"Your father should give you a good wallop and that would help you to keep your nose clean."

"Yes, Sir."

Uncle Joe eyes me with a mixture of pity and anger. I

feel very uncomfortable under his stare and so I hang my head and look at the dust at my feet.

"Well, get going. You've got the whole pigpen to muck out. It's late already. Too damn lazy to get out of bed!"

"Yes, Sir. Sorry, Sir. Bye, Uncle Joe." I trip over my words as I turn to leave.

"Bill, is your stomach too weak this time of the morning, or can you handle a beer?"

"Nothing wrong with me, Joe. I have a constitution made from cast iron!"

I am half way to the pigpen when I hear Uncle Joe's truck pull away. My heart feels numb with fear and I wish Uncle Joe had not swung by this morning. I try to bury my fear deep inside my mind and I focus on the happy thought of spending time with Wilbur.

I named him Wilbur after the pig in a book we read in school a couple years ago. I can't remember the name of the book for some reason. It seems like such a long time ago, but it can't be.

Dad will be away for some time, so I reckon I have a bit of time to play with Wilbur, before I have to start mucking out the pen. He is so cute. He's a little pink thing, filled with the joys of life, which mainly tend to centre on eating. I watch him trot around for a while and then I decide that maybe I should clean out the pen first, because then it is done and I can play with Wilbur until my Dad comes to pick me up.

I take off my gloves and jacket and the cold of the rake burns my hands while I grip it. My body hurts with each sweep of the rake, as I push the pig poop into a corner. It's a big pen and it takes a long time. The good thing is that my body and brain become sort of numb as I go along and so I don't feel the pain. I just concentrate on making a small area clean before moving on to the next area. When I get to the last spot, I am filled with a great deal of satisfaction. I survey the pen. It looks clean again. There is nothing better than cleaning up something that is dirty and a mess, it makes me feel reborn. I am feeling pretty tired though and heaving the manure out of the pen into a wheelbarrow hurts me everywhere. It is a different movement from the raking and it hurts. I comfort myself with the thought that with every shovelful I throw into the wheelbarrow, I am getting closer to my goal and the sooner my time will come to play with Wilbur.

I really wish I was at school. I try to stay there as long as possible, because then I don't have to come home. Weekends are always terrible. The more time I have to spend with Mom and Dad, the worse things are for me. I know other kids have a better time than me, but I guess that's the way life is. I may not be able to visit anybody on the weekends like regular kids, but I get to spend time with Wilbur, who is the best friend I have anyway.

After a long trip to the manure heap, laying down fresh yellow straw for the pigs to sleep in and filling up their troughs with food and water, I rest and sit down to eat the apple I snuck out of the kitchen when I left this morning. It's not much food, but I don't feel very hungry anyway.

I walk slowly up to Wilbur. He knows me pretty well by now, but I don't want to scare him. I want him to know that he can trust me completely. I hope that Dad will keep him as a breeder. If he doesn't, I am going to have to find a way to sneak him out of here to somewhere safe, where Dad won't find him. I haven't figured out where that is yet, but I reckon I still have a lot of time. Wilbur is too small to slaughter. I spend all my time thinking about where I can take him. I wish I was old enough and rich enough to have a place of my own then I could take him away for sure. Dad would never notice. He has so many piglets this year that he will never notice one missing.

I feed Wilbur out of my hand and he seems happy to guzzle the food up. I take some more and I feed him until he's done. I pat him really gently and I know he likes it, because he stays and doesn't walk away. For the first time today I am feeling really happy. I manage to get Wilbur onto my lap and cuddle him. I love him so much. I wish I could take him away and keep him safe forever.

"I'll teach you to sit around doing nothing all day!"

I jump up and drop Wilbur, who squeals in fright.

"I did everything you wanted me to do, Sir!"

"I did everything you wanted me to do," he says in a mocking voice. "You're a good for nothing, waste of space! Do you ever stop to think that there is more to do? Do I have to tell you every little thing to do? You're not a baby anymore, are you?"

"No, Sir"

"I didn't think so! So why do you need me to tell you what to do?"

His face is red and his eyes look blurry. It's a sure sign he's been drinking. I know I am going to get another beating.

"I'm sorry, Sir."

"Sorry! Sorry? No. I think you just say words without meaning them. I'll teach you to be sorry. You get too distracted and so I'll have to get rid of the distraction! There's something wrong with you boy! Something real bad!"

The blood in my body plummets to my feet as he walks towards me. I desperately try to grab his arm to stop him, but he shoves me backwards. I try to stay upright, but I trip over my feet and land painfully on my back.

My father stalks towards Wilbur, who is pulling on some long grass. I want to scream, "Run, Wilbur!" but nothing comes out of my mouth. Wilbur continues to eat the grass happily, as my father carefully lifts the hoe. He raises it above his head. I see him bring it down, but when I hear the screaming, I bury my face in the ground and cover my ears. It doesn't help. The screaming seems to go on forever. I keep my head buried in the grass. I wish my life was over. Wilbur can't be dead. I hope he didn't hurt too much. The silence seems deafening. I slowly and carefully look up, not wanting to see what is left of Wilbur. I see my father standing over me, the pick raised above his head, dripping with blood. His mad eyes stare down at me. He starts to bring the pick down in what seems like slow motion. I don't move and I can't feel anything. I black out, as I am thrown backwards by a huge force.

2

There is something on top of me. I scream and push it off and fall to the ground. I feel winded, but I am so scared. I manage to fight through my fear and open my eyes. I have no idea where I am. I have never seen this room before. Foreign curtains drift in the breeze and sheets I have never seen wrap around a mattress above me. I look at the ceiling. There is a plain white lampshade staring down at me. I look at the duvet in my hands. It has a small blue floral print on it. I have never seen it before either. Maybe I am in a hospital. But after a little more thought I realise that I can't be in a hospital, because this room is not clinical. It is a room that exists only in a house.

I twist over so that I am on my hands and knees. Where did Dad go? Where is the farm? There is no soil beneath my fingers. Instead I feel the texture of a thick cream carpet. I don't remember getting here. Maybe Dad took me to someone's house after I passed out. I stand up dragging a rush of vertigo after me. I realise I was holding my breath and, as I gasp for air, the vertigo passes. Well at least the horrible feeling has gone, but the after effects of the vertigo remain, because everything in this room seems a little further away from me than it should be. I am sure it will pass.

I wonder whose house I am in. I hold onto the duvet, wrapping it around me and slowly walk to the door of the room. I look down the passage, but don't recognise anything. I have no idea where I am. I have never been in this house before. It seems quiet too. There doesn't seem to be anyone around. I feel a lonely terror creep over my skin. I probably should get back into bed. I am sure Dad will be mad at me if he sees me standing up and dragging this duvet with me. It's probably one of his friend's houses and he will be angry that I am disrespecting other people's property. I walk back to the bed and lie down, pulling the duvet up to my chin.

As I look around the room, I think about Wilbur and how angry Dad was. I don't want to remember that. I concentrate on the patterns of the flowers in the duvet and try to see faces or objects in them. I make out some funny faces that make me laugh quietly to myself. Looking for faces and creatures in patterns helps to get me through the horrible times. I can spend hours doing it. But, as I continue to look at the patterns, they start to look a little more familiar.

I look around the room again. I do recognise this room. It is slowly coming back to me. I sit up. No, I am sure I do remember this room from somewhere. But where? As I look around, the memory of where I have seen all of the objects is just out of reach of my mind – a memory I can't quite grasp.

I want to look around the room, but I am scared that Dad will come back and find me out of bed and then I'll get another thrashing, that's for sure. I look at the duvet, then at the curtains, the door leading to what appears to be a bathroom and then at the ceiling light. The bedside table has a book on it. I pick it up carefully and look at the cover. It looks like a grown-up's book. There is a bookmark midway through it. I feel that I have read this book before, but that doesn't make sense. I don't like reading much and I don't think I would read something like this. It looks boring. Somehow I don't think it is boring though. That is strange. Why would I think that?

Part of me wants to cry. I feel so confused and scared and I don't know when Dad will be back and I don't know whose house I am in. I can't cry though. Sometimes

I feel sad, but tears never come. I don't know how to cry.

I know what to do. I lie down again and close my eyes. Sometimes it is hard to remember things if you try too hard. It is better to think about other things and then it comes back. I try to think of something nice. It is difficult, because this room and Wilbur both come flooding in, but I keep trying. Nothing nice comes to mind. I try to think of going for a ride on my bicycle or going to school, but none of those thoughts keep me safe from the other thoughts. Then I imagine my favourite daydream. I dream that I am a superhero and I save the school from some bad guys. Everyone thinks I am the greatest person in the world. Even Mom and Dad are proud of me and they take me out for a big meal and tell everyone how I am the best son anyone could hope for.

It's working. Slowly I can feel the memories of this room coming back. I don't pay them too much attention. If I do that they will evaporate. So I continue thinking about how Mom and Dad take me home afterwards and they have cut out newspaper articles about how I saved the school. They have made a collage and framed it and it's hanging on the wall in the dining room and we are laughing about something while we eat our dinner. The memory is there – just at the edge of my consciousness.

I look at the clock on the bedside table. It reads nine o'clock. I must have slept a long time. Do people usually pass out for this long? I don't know. There is no one to ask either. The house is very quiet. I will wait a little bit more. I concentrate on my daydream and make it more and more elaborate. I decide that I get paid a reward for being a hero and I get lots of money. Mom and Dad are so happy that I made lots of money for them. We buy a big house and Dad stops drinking. We go on holidays to the sea and Dad and I go on rides at the amusement park together. We go fishing and Mom comes with us and we have delicious dinners outside under the stars next to a warm campfire.

I look at the clock again. It's nine thirty and still there is no one in the house. Maybe I should go and have a look? I still can't remember this house properly. I think I was too absorbed in my daydream. I'll leave the duvet behind so that I can run back quickly in case Dad or someone else is in the house. I climb out of bed and slowly walk to the door that leads to the passage. Things still look out of proportion - maybe because of the vertigo. I guess lying in bed for half an hour didn't help to make it go away. Maybe after I walk around a bit, it will go. I listen at the door, but I don't hear anything.

The passage is dark. There are a few closed doors and one open one that illuminates the passage wanly. Again, the knowledge that I know this house gnaws at the edges of my mind. I tip toe down the passage and put my head around the corner of the open room. There is no one there. An empty slept-in bed is the only sign of another person. The empty bed makes me feel sad. I am not sure why.

I continue walking down the passage. It ends at an entrance hall. Two doors lead off this - one to an empty kitchen and one to a living room. All the doors to the house are locked. I walk into the living room and see that it has a dining room as well. A huge set of double glass doors look out onto a beautiful garden. I really feel like going out into the garden. I try the doors and they are locked. I find myself walking to a chest of drawers and I open the first one. There is a key inside it. That is strange. The key fits the door. How did I know this?

I open the doors and walk out into the garden. It is a big garden with a fishpond and lovely flowerbeds scattered about. It fills me with peace. I wander around it, seeing how all the flowers are doing. They look well watered and there are no weeds. I am glad about that. It is truly a lovely garden. I feel quite proud of it.

I start to feel thirsty. In fact my mouth is quite dry. I am sure that is why I was feeling light headed. I go back into the house and into the kitchen. I find the coffee and boil some water for myself. I must know this house, as I seem to know where everything is without having to look for it. I find the teaspoon and mug almost automatically and it is easy to locate the sugar. The milk is in the fridge – well I think that is fairly obvious. Milk is always kept in the fridge. But the fact that I know where everything else is seems strange and not strange at the same time. Maybe I am dehydrated? I take the coffee outside to the patio and sip it while I drink in the peace of the garden.

I eventually drag myself away from the garden and go back into the house. I take my coffee mug back to the kitchen and, as I pass the passage, I see a shadow at the end that flickers in the corner of my eye. My skin crawls with fear. Is Dad in my bedroom? Is he looking for me? I am going to be in serious trouble. I don't know what to do.

I am momentarily glued to the floor with indecision and fear. Eventually my head starts to work again and I realise that it would be worse to get caught out of bed with the coffee cup than just to be caught out of bed. Dad will yell at me for using someone else's things without asking permission. I quickly sneak into the kitchen and put the mug in the sink. I creep back to the passage.

I see a shadow dart across the back wall of the main bedroom. I am in serious trouble. It is always better to face Dad than to run away from him so I walk back to the bedroom, holding my breath. As I get to the door, I prepare myself for his fury. I walk into the bedroom. I look around. There is no one there. I walk to the bathroom and it is empty too. It must have been a shadow cast by the moving curtains. I am so relieved that Dad is not here.

I should not have been so stupid. I should have stayed in bed. That was a silly risk to take. I am standing in the middle of the room, when I hear footsteps coming up the passage towards me. I am frozen to the spot with fear. I force myself to turn around and face my father, but it is difficult. My body does not want to turn. With great effort, I force myself to turn around.

There is no one there. I am sure I didn't imagine it. I have never imagined something like that before. I look down the dark passage and there is no one there. I listen and I can hear subtle noises coming from one of the rooms off the passage. I see a shadow move across the triangle of light from an open bedroom. I am not sure if I should go and investigate or if I should crawl back into bed. I stand riveted to the spot and listen with every muscle of my body straining.

Suddenly something white comes out of the room. I scream. The white bundle falls to the floor and screams too.

"Oh dear, Miss Claire, you frightened me! I didn't know you were home today." A stout woman bends over and picks up the bundle of sheets. She looks at me and I look at her. She eventually turns around and walks back towards the kitchen. I look behind me. I don't see a 'Miss Claire' anywhere. What did she mean? Who was she talking to? She seemed to be looking at me, but she can't have been talking to me. Strange.

I think I need to lie down. This is all very strange. I

really am not sure where I am or what is going on. I think I should use the bathroom first. I walk up to the toilet and lift the lid. I put my hand inside my pants and feel around. It is gone. No. My mind is spinning. It can't be true. What has happened to me? I pull my pants down and am absolutely horrified at what I see. I run my hands up my stomach and over some breasts. There's a mirror in the bathroom. I can't bear to look in it. I don't want to see myself. I run into the bedroom and fling myself under the covers.

As I lie there in my cocoon, it suddenly dawns on me that I am Claire and this is my house. I live here. I feel sick. What happened yesterday? It was real, wasn't it? Or is this real and that not? I must have had the worst and most vivid dream ever. That must be what has happened. That is the only thing that makes sense. I have never experienced anything like this before. I have had vivid dreams certainly and dreams that linger for a long time. The vestiges of those dreams haunt my day, but I have always known they were dreams. Maybe I am getting sick because my dream seemed as real as this moment right now feels real. Or is this a dream?

The phone starts ringing. I can't face answering the phone right now. I am still feeling a little disorientated. Would a phone ring in a dream? Yes, and it would probably ring directly after you had the thought you were in a dream. That is how it would work. Maybe yesterday was real and right now I am in a dream that I can't wake up from. I continue to lie with my head under the covers and ignore it. Eventually it stops.

And then it starts again. I suppose I should answer it. Maybe it will contain some clue as to what is happening. It might help to clarify if this is a dream or if yesterday was a dream, but I lived on that farm with my parents all my life. Could I have a dream about an entire childhood and all the memories that go with that in one dream? No, this must be the dream and maybe I am stuck in it. Maybe I can't wake up from it. Maybe Dad managed to put me into a coma and I am lying in a coma on a hospital bed having this dream.

"Hello?'

"Hi, Claire. This is Helen from the office."

"Hello Helen."

"Bill was wondering where you are this morning. It is just after eleven and you had a meeting scheduled with him."

All the blood runs from my body to collect in horror in my feet. Shit!

"I am so sorry, Helen. I am sick. I woke up a few minutes ago. I am not sure what's wrong with me. I might have flu. I was about to phone you."

"You don't sound ill."

"No, it's just a headache and my muscles hurt. I think it's the beginning of the flu. I completely overslept. I really am so sorry. Please apologise to Bill. I will be in tomorrow and I will reschedule with him then."

"I will let him know."

"Thanks, Helen."

The line at the other end goes dead. She was never particularly friendly. Can't say I like her too much or anyone else at the office for that matter. Well, maybe not a good start to the day, but a day off is actually quite nice.

Where did those thoughts just come from? This seems real to me. It all makes perfect sense to me. I think back about my life and I remember lots of different moments. This can't be a dream. So I must have been dreaming about the farm.

That dream was odd though. Maybe I really do need

to get myself checked out. I might be getting really sick. It worries me. It is not a nice thing to contemplate. Firstly, why did I have that dream? It was a horrible dream to have. Why would I dream I was a little boy, whose father beat him? And secondly, why would I get so disorientated by it, to the point where I forgot who I am and what my house looks like? Certainly, I have had times when I have woken up and not remembered where I was. It has happened on occasion, but not like this.

Maybe I should see the doctor. I could get a note, which would appease the powers that be at work and I could find out what is wrong with me. It can't be good and it needs to be looked at. I think that would be best. I like to get things checked out immediately. If you leave them too long then things really develop into something terrible and you end up paying a worse price. I ring up the doctor's office and get an appointment for four this afternoon.

I check my work diary to see if there are any other appointments I need to cancel. There aren't any. I do have an entry for tonight though. It's a dinner for Bryan's boss and his wife. Bryan wants to impress his boss so that he gets a promotion. Damn it! How could I have forgotten that? Maybe I should cancel the doctor's appointment. I won't be prepared on time if I don't. Ah, but I have the whole day to prepare, which I would not have had otherwise, as I am not at work. In fact, I have plenty of time to prepare today and I can relax a little as well.

I walk down the passage and into the kitchen. I am feeling a little hungry. Maria is in the kitchen wiping the counters down. When she sees me, she starts scrubbing very hard with a look of intense concentration on her face.

"I am sorry I scared you, Maria."

"No, I am sorry I scared you, Miss Claire. I didn't know that you were at home today."

"I am feeling a little ill today, so I stayed home."

"I have put Mister Bryan's sheets in the wash. I was going to do yours next. Do you still want me to wash them today?"

"Yes, of course. Thank you. I don't think I will be going back to bed now. I need to prepare for the dinner tonight. I think we agreed you would stay on tonight?"

"Yes, I will stay until seven to do the washing up."

"Ah good. I am feeling a little hungry. I think I am going to make myself some breakfast. Are you finished here or shall I wait?"

"No, no. I will make you breakfast. What would you like me to make you?"

"Oh, that's very kind. You really don't have to."

"Please, what would you like to eat?"

"Well, I think an omelette and toast."

"The usual with bacon, onion and mushrooms?"

"Yes, thank you. That would be perfect. I am going to have a shower and get dressed, so I think in about twenty minutes if that's all right?"

"No problem."

I wonder why Maria insisted on making my breakfast when she seemed so reluctant about it. I was quite happy to make my own breakfast, but since she seemed so insistent upon it, I felt I should let her. I wander down the passage back to the bedroom to get ready for the day.

As I enter the bathroom, I catch a glimpse of movement in the mirror. I don't think I can face that. I really don't. I am not sure why, but I just know I cannot. I go back into the bedroom to think.

I know what to do. I open the door to the linen

cupboard and find a sheet. I locate duct tape and scissors in the study. I find yesterday's old newspaper and with all this, I return to the bathroom.

It is not easy to do, as I have to do most of it with my eyes closed, using touch to guide me. I manage to stuff the sheet between the mirror and the wall and then I duct tape it heavily to make sure that it will not fall off. I make sure that the entire mirror is covered. I then proceed to cover all the other mirrors in the house, which are much smaller, using newspaper and duct tape.

Maria came sometime during this process to tell me my breakfast was ready. I told her to put it in the warmer. I am sure she must think I am mad, but she walked out of the room immediately after I had delivered my instruction.

I feel much safer now that all the mirrors are covered. A tension I did not realise was there seems to have left me, my shoulders, which were rigid with stress have relaxed back into place. I have lost a lot of time with this activity, but it was important to do. I feel much better and that is worth a great deal. I enjoy my shower and my late breakfast out in the garden. In fact, I feel so relaxed, I feel as if I had been to the spa.

I better get ready to go to the shops to buy the food for tonight's dinner. I put on a lovely summery dress and am then faced with the problem of applying my make-up without a mirror. I did not think about that when I covered them all. I stand in front of the covered mirror and a flash of me putting on make-up yesterday and the day before and the day before that leaves me reeling. I saw my face in my mind and it is an image that I do not want to have. I feel sick.

The strange thing is that it never seemed to bother me before. I try to think back. No, I never was bothered by looking at myself in mirrors before. I was never bothered until this morning. In fact I think I quite enjoyed looking at myself in the mirror. But there is something in me resisting it today. I am absolutely terrified to see myself in the mirror. It doesn't make any sense to me.

Nothing happened last night, did it? It was a fairly ordinary evening. Did I have any bad experiences this week? I don't remember any. The only strange thing was the dream I had this morning when I could not wake up. Well, I did wake up, but I was disorientated. I feel my forehead. Maybe it is a bit warm. I could be sick. I could actually be sick. That would explain all of this, wouldn't it? I find the thermometer, shake it and stick it under my tongue. I leave it there for a minute. When I take it out, it reads normal. I shake it again and leave it in my mouth for five minutes this time. The reading is still normal.

All indications are that I don't have a fever. That would certainly be the best explanation here, but it has been ruled out. Well...... Maybe I am going senile. I walk back to the bedroom and fall backwards onto the bed in horror. Maybe I am going senile like my father. It hit him early. He was in his fifties. I am late thirties. Maybe I have early onset dementia like my father. Very early onset.

I need to get myself together. I need to buy the food for tonight and I am going to see the doctor later. She will be able to tell me what's wrong. I need to put it from out of my mind until then. That is best. I feel quite naked leaving the house without make-up on and I haven't been able to see if my hair looks good or not. It is a very uncomfortable feeling, but I am going to have to force myself out of the house.

I know what I am going to make for dinner tonight. I know George can be a picky eater and a lot rides on this dinner for Bryan. I will make beef stroganoff, roast potatoes, creamed vegetables, a big salad and to end, crème caramels with a cheese board and coffee to follow.

I find Maria outside in the laundry.

"Maria, where is the cooler bag?"

Maria walks back into the house and retrieves the cooler bag from the pantry. She hands it to me. I open the freezer to look for the ice packs. I find one. It is not enough. I put it in the cooler bag and walk outside again.

"Maria, where are the other ice packs. I only found one and it is not enough. Where are the others?"

Maria looks at me, but doesn't say anything.

"Are you deaf, Maria? I asked you where the other ice packs are? Have you stolen them? Is that what has happened?"

"No, Miss Claire. I didn't steal them. You told me to sterilise them yesterday. Here I'll show you."

Maria walks outside to the sink and retrieves a bucket from underneath it. She brings the bucket over. My eyes burn as I peer into the fumes of bleach to see three ice packs floating around inside.

"Maria! The bleach is too strong! Did you pour the whole bottle in here? It is going to eat into the plastic and destroy them! How long have they been in here? Why didn't you take them out after half an hour and put them back in the freezer? What's wrong with you?"

Maria stands there, holding the bucket and staring at me stonily.

"Well, speak up! I asked you a question."

"You told me to put the ice packs in here, Miss Claire."

"And when was this?"

"Yesterday."

"When yesterday?"

"When you came back from shopping."

"And why so much bleach?"

"I will bring the bottle to show you, Miss Claire."

Maria returns with a bottle of bleach that is half empty. I am not sure why she is showing me a half empty bottle.

"Why are you showing this to me, Maria?"

"To show you I used half."

"Half! Half a bottle of bleach!"

"That is what you always tell me to do."

I stare at Maria trying to work out if she is being insolent on purpose.

"You know what, Maria. I don't have time to deal with this right now. Take those ice packs out immediately and wash them thoroughly. And put them back into the freezer. This has really ruined my day, I can tell you. How am I going to keep the meat fresh with one ice pack? Never mind, that was a rhetorical question. I don't have time to explain to you what that means. I have to go. Just... just sort this out. Now!"

I am really annoyed. I angrily make my way to the shops. Why is my day such a bloody mess? I find a parking that is miles away. Of course it would be. I lug the cooler bag over to the supermarket and put it into the trolley. I get all the items on my list and then have to drive over to the garage to buy ice cubes, which I wrap in ten plastic bags, so that they will not melt and leak all over the food and my car.

I manage to just make it to the doctor on time and then have to wait twenty minutes to be seen. All the time I am worried that the food is going to go bad. I know that food can go bad very quickly.

The doctor's appointment is a complete waste of time. She tells me that there is nothing wrong with me and that I am not ill nor am I becoming senile. She informs me that these things can happen on occasion. I don't believe a word she says. I will seek out a specialist tomorrow. Well, it's always better to get four opinions, so I will make four specialist appointments tomorrow. Then I will be absolutely sure that everything is fine. I feel better having decided on that course of action. The good thing is that the doctor gave me a note for work, which I will give to them tomorrow.

When I arrive home, I lug the cooler bag and my shopping bags from the car to the kitchen. All those ice blocks are hideously heavy. I unpack the cooler bag and find that there is no room in the fridge. What the hell is in here?

And then I see. The fridge is full of the same salad items I have just bought. There is a carton of milk and a box of eggs for the crème caramel. A side of beef exactly the same weight as the one I am holding in my hand is sitting on a shelf in the fridge. I turn around. On the side of the kitchen counter is a bag of sugar and some vanilla essence. The exact same box of chocolates that I bought a couple hours ago is on the counter next to the sugar and vanilla essence.

It all comes flooding back. I bought all the food for tonight's dinner yesterday. I have had no memory of that until this moment. And I always ask Maria to use half a bottle of bleach, because of the germs.

3

After apologising to Maria for my earlier behaviour, I set about cooking dinner, confused as to why she was so stony. I am also worried about the problems with my memory. My feelings soon evaporate with the vapour coming from the pot of steamed vegetables. I love cooking. It is an activity where I have complete control. I measure every ingredient exactly as it says in the cookbook and use a timer to make sure that nothing cooks a second longer than it should. In fact, I always set the timer to go off two minutes earlier than the due time. Then I have enough time to put my oven mitts on, so that the food is not cooked any longer than it should be.

I use a ruler to lay the table so that every place setting looks absolutely identical. I stand back to admire the table. It looks absolutely perfect. I don't know why people do not take time over the little details. I have discovered that it makes a huge difference. When George and Cynthia sit down to their meal tonight, they are going to feel very happy and they will not know that it was because I paid attention to the little details. This could help to sway George into promoting Bryan and no one would know that it was actually mostly my doing. That thought makes me feel very content. I imagine that Bryan and I will have a very different life with more money coming in. Everything will change for us. It will be better, brighter and more beautiful.

I check to see that the food is surviving the warming oven. The meat is moist and the vegetables are succulent in their cream base. The salad continues to look fresh and crisp in the fridge. Feeling satisfied, I wander out into the garden to cut some flowers and sprigs of leaves. I weave this into a garland, which I place on the table. I do not like flowerpots on tables. People do not realise how annoying it is for guests at a dinner party to have to look around a flower arrangement in order to talk to the person across from them. It is far better to have something that is far below eye level that looks pretty, but doesn't obstruct the view. I try out different positions for the garland until it is perfectly placed. I then pick up the little twigs and leaves that have fallen off. I close all the windows near the dining room table so that nothing will be disturbed, but I leave the lounge doors open across the room so that the room does not become stuffy.

I open up a bottle of Merlot and pour two glasses and leave them to breathe. Carrying my glass, I walk over to the CD collection and run through the titles with my fingertip. I decide that some Satie would be perfect for this summer's evening. I pop the CD into the player and turn the volume to setting ten. Bryan always messes around with the settings, even though he knows I like setting ten. He is not terribly considerate that way. If he had a setting he liked, I would always put it back to that setting when I was finished listening. I suppose small things like that should not bother me.

I walk out onto the deck and sip from my glass of deep wine while the strains of the music waft out the door to mix with the music of the night. I feel peaceful and relaxed when the motor of the garage door starts to turn. I walk back inside and pick up Bryan's glass. I wait in the entrance hall for him.

As he walks in, I admire the efficiency and strength of his movements while he hangs his coat up. A shadow of stubble highlights his jaw and lips. He is a handsome man. I can't believe I still find him attractive after six years of marriage. I think that I don't always pay as much attention to how beautiful he is. I suppose it is so easy to get swamped by the demands of everyday life and I just don't always pay attention to what is important. He turns around and looks at me waiting for him.

"How was work today?"

"The usual. Dinner looks good. Thanks for doing this."

"It's my pleasure. Here. Come and have some wine with me out on the deck."

Bryan stares at me for a long moment. He does not come closer or make and attempt to take the glass of wine I am holding out to him.

"I don't have time. They'll be here soon."

"Not for another forty minutes."

"I need to shower and get changed."

He walks past me ignoring my attempt to kiss him hello. Well, maybe he is preoccupied and didn't realise I was trying to kiss him hello. I am sure he is just stressed about tonight. I can understand that.

I walk back outside and place his glass on the table. I continue to sip from mine as I admire our garden in the glow of the garden lights. Little night insects are gathering in clouds around the lights. I'd better do something to stop them coming in the house. I hate all these insect deterrents, but it's worse if they come in the house. We have a bug zapper located strategically close to the door, but not close enough to make a mess. I also light some citronella candles on the table. I am worried now. I don't want any flies coming in and they do sometimes come in at night. One never knows. I go into the kitchen and chop up some sweet basil and clover and put it into a container. I walk outside the house around to the dining room. I carefully sprinkle the mixture along the window sill. I know Bryan will open the dining room windows when the guests arrive and I don't want any flies coming in.

I wash the tub and dry it. I then go into the guest bathroom to wash my hands. Bloody hell, Bryan!

Bryan has left his clothes and towels lying on the floor. The basin has started growing dark stubble of its own. He knows we have guests coming soon! Why would he leave such a terrible mess? And why are there bits of ripped newspaper lying everywhere?

I look around and see that the newspaper on the mirror has been torn down, with bits of it clinging to the edges. The duct tape seems to have held. At least the mirror is covered with condensation so I can't really see myself.

Well that's one thing I should be happy about. I rinse out the basin and put everything back in order. I pick up Bryan's suit that he has thrown to the ground. It will be creased now! I look at his jacket. There is a spot of something on the cuff. Looks like some dried sauce. Why doesn't he take off his jacket to eat? It really irritates me. He knows that dry-cleaning is both expensive and time consuming. I suppose this is going to have to be dry-cleaned now. I search through his pockets so that I don't take anything important along to the dry cleaners to be lost or more likely stolen. I find some cash and a crumpled up note. I open up the note to see if it is something important, or if it is some trash that needs to be thrown away.

As I unfold the page, the words "I miss you and I love you" emerge. I turn the page over and the following conversation appears:

Bryan: This meeting is so boring. I know what I would like to do instead....

Other: What on earth would that be??

Bryan: You know exactly what.

Other: Yes, I do. I think we should have another 'meeting' like we did last week. I have a few issues I need you to look into thoroughly.

Bryan: Oh, yes, I think I need to pay a lot more attention to detail. I think we will have to book another 'meeting' as soon as possible.

Other: What about tonight?

Bryan: Can't. Have to have dinner with the boss and the old ball and chain.

Other: It's too long until you leave her. I can't stand this.

Bryan: You know I am going to. Once everything is in place we will be much happier. If I leave now, we are going to struggle. Please be patient. I love you.

Other: I miss you and I love you.

The note is snatched out of my hand and I look up into Bryan's belligerent face.

"Stay the fuck out of my personal life!"

"But I am your wife. I am your personal life! I spent all afternoon and evening making a dinner for you. For you and your bloody promotion! How can you do this to me?"

"Don't lay that crap on me," Bryan pushes past me and starts picking things up off the floor, "You need this promotion as much as I do. You've got your fancy-ass lawyers asking for half my assets, remember? My assets! That I have worked very hard for. And when they are cut down the middle - nicely in half - I am not going to be very well off, now am I? You, no you'll be fine! You'll have my money and your money, you greedy bitch! So, as I see it, this serves both of us. I get to live a better life, which I care very much about after these years of shit and you; you get to have even more money. More money for you. That's what you want. So shut the fuck up and be a good little hostess for tonight, so that we can both move the fuck on with our lives. And stay out of my damn pockets!"

"Well you left the mess here!"

"I was getting to it. Can I not put on some goddamn clothes, first? Must you control every move I make? No, no, don't answer that. That was a stupid question. Of course you have to control every part of my life!" Bryan roars in my face.

I stare dumbly at Bryan. I don't know what to say. I didn't know he was having an affair. I didn't even know we were getting a divorce. I thought we were happily married. Well, I did have an inkling that maybe it wasn't totally happy, but that things would be better after the promotion. I am sure I was thinking that this afternoon.

"And where is your face?"

"Excuse me?"

"Are you going to entertain like that? They will be here any minute now."

"My face?" I reach up and feel my face.

"Makeup you crazy, bitch! Are you not wearing any today? Because let me assure you honey, you need it!"

"I don't want to put any on."

"What? You without makeup?" Bryan clutches his chest in mock horror.

"Stop it, Bryan!"

"Just some friendly advice. Take it or leave it. Oh and what's this shit on the mirrors? Some new obsession you've developed?"

"Yes."

"Well take it off! It doesn't look good. What will George think when he comes in to use the john and sees this shit plastered all over the mirrors?"

"I am not touching the mirrors."

"Fine!" Bryan starts ripping the duct tape off the wall.

I step over the debris in the bathroom and walk outside away from Bryan's curses.   I   don't understand. I sit down, put my head in my hands and just sit there, not thinking. The doorbell rings and I ignore it.

"Here she is!"

I look up to see George and Cynthia looking with concern at me. Bryan gently helps me up and kisses my forehead before holding me close to his side.

"Claire has been feeling a little under the weather today, haven't you, sweetie?" Bryan gazes lovingly at me, "But I think she is starting to feel a bit better now, aren't you?"

I gaze dazedly into Bryan's loving gaze for a few moments until he gently squeezes my arm.

"Yes, yes I am. So sorry. A bit of a headache. How are you, George? Cynthia?"

We exchange pleasantries and small talk and I assure them that I am feeling much better while Bryan fetches the wine. He pours a glass for everyone and tops mine up. He comes to sit down next to me and Cynthia tells us how lovely our garden is. We exchange tips about what species grow best where and at what time of year and George makes us laugh with tales about some of his gardening mishaps. It all feels so surreal that I can't believe that my earlier encounter with Bryan actually happened.

We move inside to eat dinner. Bryan helps me serve and clear away each course and Maria washes up the dishes in the background while we listen to George and Cynthia tell us about the cruises they have been on. They recently went on a luxury cruise to Alaska. Cynthia tells us how well they were fed and pampered and George describes one of his on land excursions where he went salmon fishing. Bryan says that we were actually thinking of going on a cruise ourselves in the near future and that he would appreciate some advice when the time came. George says that he is more than happy to help out.

Throughout the long evening, I play the perfect hostess. I serve food and coffee. I ask polite questions and make sounds to show that I am interested. Bryan is warm and affectionate with me and I don't know how to respond to this. I suppose, to George and Cynthia, I appear to be a little shy about public displays of affection.

The evening ends with George inviting us to come to his lake cabin in a few weeks time. He tells us that some other young couples will be there and that the men will go fishing and the women can sit around and gossip. It will be fun. Bryan and I thank him and express our delight at the invitation. Everyone says goodbye with exclamations of how lovely the evening was. Bryan and I walk out arm-in-arm to the car to see them off. Once the car has disappeared from view, Bryan pulls away from me and stalks back into the house.

I walk back to the front door, but can't bear to go inside just yet. I hug myself and lean against the wall. I look across the street to the houses of my neighbours. I can see the soft amber lights glowing in the windows. I imagine that their lives must be far better than mine. I am sure that in their houses wives and husbands love each other, without pretending that they do, like we are. I am sure that the warmth of those windows comes from the genuine warmth that exists inside those houses.

I hear Bryan washing up the last few dishes that were used after Maria had left. I should help him, but I can't bear to encounter his hostility again. I feel strange that I feel safer outside my house than I do inside it. I don't know what I have done to make him so angry with me and yet I have a feeling that I do know. I just don't want to know.

A movement on the side of the garden catches my attention. I watch in horror, as I see a dark shape walking next to the hedge in the shadows. It slips behind the wall of our house.

I slam the door shut.

"Bryan there's someone in our garden! I saw him slip round the side! He must be at the back. Did you shut the lounge doors?"

"No." Bryan throws the dishcloth into the sink and stalks off to the lounge. He grabs the fire-poker and walks outside.

I am not sure what to do. I decide to walk to the lounge doors. I watch as Bryan walks around the garden. He looks angry and intimidating.

"I don't see anyone. Which side did you see him come in?"

I point.

Bryan stalks off and is gone for a long time. I hear a noise on the other side of the garden and turn in alarm, before I realise that it is only Bryan stomping back towards me.

"There's no one here. You did that on purpose didn't you?"

"Why the hell would I do that on purpose? I saw someone. Is he gone?"

"Of course he is gone. There was no one here to begin with. You know what, Claire you get loonier and loonier as time goes by. You should see a shrink, you know that?" Bryan shoves the poker back into its holder and stomps off down the passage. I hear a door slam.

I look around the garden. I still feel a little scared.

Maybe I am going crazy. I shut and bolt the doors just in case. I go back into the kitchen and then the dining room. Bryan has cleaned most of it, but there are odd items here and there that need to be put away. I tidy up, making sure that everything is put back neatly in its place.

As I pass the spare bedroom, I hear movement. The door is shut and I dare not go in there. I listen for a while and then decide to go on to my room. I guess it is my room now and not our room. I sit down on my bed. The spare bedroom door opens. I hear Bryan walking towards me.

"I am going to stay at Theresa's tonight. It's too stressful staying here with you. I think tonight with George and Cynthia went well though despite everything. I think we demonstrated the loving family stability thing. A couple more of these and then I'll have that promotion and then we can get divorced."

I watch his retreating back as he walks down the passage with his bag slung over his shoulder. The lonely silence of the house pushes against me once again as the front door slams shut.

I don't know what is wrong with me. How could I think that everything was all right when it wasn't? I remember now. I remember that Bryan has been getting angrier over the years. I remember that he started an affair about eight months ago. I remember that he asked for a divorce seven months ago. I didn't and still don't want the divorce and so I have been fighting it. He thinks I am greedy, that I just want his money. That's not want I want. I want him back. I want things to be the way they were before this mess happened. I don't feel that if we are apart it is going to fix anything. We need to stay together to fix this. It's the only way. He doesn't sleep here very often anymore. He pops in a couple times a week when he needs fresh clothes, or to keep up appearances if it is warranted. And nothing I do seems to make it better.

I suppose that was what this was all about – this little breakdown I had today. I suppose it was a breakdown brought on by stress. The past few months have been extremely stressful. It is so difficult to see your life dissolve before your eyes and having no power - no matter what you try – to stop it.

But I am not the only one at fault here. He keeps blaming me. He says I am too controlling. But he was perfectly happy before that bitch Theresa came along. I think it's because of her that this is happening. It is easy to blame me, because then he doesn't have to take any of the heat. Then he comes out of this as the poor innocent victim and I am the one responsible for that. Well fuck that, Bryan!

I get up from my bed and drag the vacuum cleaner out the cupboard in the spare room. I take it to the lounge and vigorously clean the lounge and dining room. Maria won't be in tomorrow and I am damned if I am having all these crumbs and shit from this dinner lying around my house! "The promotion is for you too Claire…" what rot! Manipulative, conniving bastard!

I survey my clean lounge and I feel calmer now. I put the vacuum away and have a shower, as I am sweaty from the activity. I climb into bed and start reading my novel. It's a great book – a real page-turner.

"Claire!"

I startle. I look around. I am lying on my bed. The book is lying face down on my stomach and has slid a little to the side. The bedside light is still on. I look around. There is no one there. It felt like someone shouted my name in my ear and that's why I woke up. I am a little jittery as I get up and walk to the passage. It's dark. I turn the light on. Everything is dark and still. I walk back and peek inside my bathroom. Nothing is out of place. I walk back down the passage and turn on the lights in all the rooms as I walk past, checking each to see if everything is safe. All the windows are closed, except for the one in the spare room. I reach quickly for the latch and pull the window closed. Someone could have gotten in through the window. Maybe there was someone in the garden tonight and now they are in my house. I am so scared, but then nothing looks out of place.

Surely if there was a burglar, then they would have taken something? Yes they would have and they would have gone into the lounge where the TV and everything is. I listen, but don't hear anything. I think of phoning Bryan, but he won't come to help me. He will tell me it's my imagination. Maybe I should call the police. That would be the wisest thing to do, but then, if it is my imagination, I will look like an idiot. If it is a real burglar though, I could get hurt. I don't know what to do.

The house is deafeningly quiet. I decide to sneak over to the lounge. I creep along until I get to the doorway and peek inside. It is quiet and empty. I turn on the light. There is no one there. I check everywhere. I check every cupboard and make sure all the doors and windows are latched. There is no one in my house. I must have had a bad dream again.

Of course I had a bad dream! That's what happens when you sleep with the light on. It is not natural. I think your unconscious just wakes you up. I feel silly for being so paranoid. I really am stressed. I think I need to calm down. I make myself a cup of herbal tea with honey and curl up on the couch in the lounge. I turn on the TV and watch an old movie on the classics channel. Those were simpler, better times. When the show ends, I reluctantly drag myself back to my bedroom.

I am not feeling scared anymore – just totally exhausted. I am not going to feel good tomorrow morning. I check that my alarm is set for the correct time. I pull the covers over myself and fall asleep instantly.

4

My alarm clock rudely disturbs my sleep. I fumble around with my eyes closed and push the snooze button.

My alarm clock once again awakens me after what feels like hours. I know it has only been five minutes that have elapsed since its last bout of annoying beeping. I am exhausted. Last night was an ordeal. I have to get up. I really don't want to. I wish I could sleep late like yesterday, but I cannot miss work again today. I will have to support myself soon, I suppose, though hopefully things will not come to that. I know that Bryan and I agreed that I would get half of what he owns, but if I don't work, that money will eventually run out. I have to learn to take care of myself now. I can't believe I have got to this point in my life. I can't believe I have lost so much. It is too much to think about all the things that I have lost. No. No, I will not go down that road! I am not going to lose Bryan. I am going to make it as difficult as I can for him to divorce me and then he will be forced to stay with me and work things out. We are meant to be together. Deep down I know he knows that too. I need time to remind him.

I turn on the bedside light, so that I will not fall asleep again. My eyes burn and I shut them tight. I rub them and stretch. I really wish I didn't have to get up. A cold bath would help to wake me up. I wish I could just lie in bed all day and catch up on the sleep I have lost over the last two nights. Yes, I did sleep in yesterday, but it came at the cost of a horrible dream. I need a good, solid, peaceful night's sleep.

I sit up and hang my legs over the edge of my bed. I flop back down on the bed and close my eyes. I just can't get up. I feel so lonely and miserable and grumpy too. But if I keep lying here, these feelings are not going to go away. With a groan, I force myself into a sitting position. I stand up and walk despondently to the bathroom.

A cold bath is not a pleasant experience, but sometimes a necessary one. It is quite torturous actually, but if I don't do it, I will not wake up and I will be late for work. Today it is necessary. I run the water and look in the closet for something to wear. I once heard that the colour you wear affects your mood. I want to feel cheerful, so I pass over my beige and black suits and choose a lilac one. I lay it out over the bed and select a white blouse and white pumps. See, I am feeling better already. Maybe there is something to this.

I walk back to the bathroom, turn the water off and undress. My breath catches in my throat as I step into the cold water. I force myself to continue and sit down. I am well and truly awake now. My skin tries to shrink away from the cold and cling onto my bones. This is really unpleasant. I scrub myself vigorously and quickly and then climb out of the bath to dry off. The towel scratches harshly against my cold skin. The cold bath worked though. I rub cream onto myself and spray perfume into the air. I walk through it to the bedroom and put on my suit. I brush my hair and arrange it into my customary work bun. Satisfied that I look nice, I go into the kitchen to make myself a cup of strong coffee.

I feel better now that I have had the cold bath and the coffee. I would feel better had I had the day off, but that is not going to happen and it is not good for me either. Too much time sitting around imagining things is not good for me. What I need to do is go to work. My career is the only thing I have right now that is a safe constant. I need to go to work. I will feel better and then I can deal with Bryan later. In fact I may call my lawyer and see if there is anything else I can do to make it even harder for Bryan to divorce me. He really needs to come home. It is better. It is better for both of us. We belong together. We are meant to be together. Yes, the more I think about all of this, the more certain I feel about it. I wonder why I doubted myself. I really shouldn't. I always know what's best.

Yes. I feel better. Today is going to be a good day. I am a woman in charge of her destiny. The other idea I have been toying with is to get pregnant. I am sure I could manage that. We have had sex a few times over these last few months – granted it has not been terribly satisfying, but getting pregnant is possible. Having a baby would bring us back together. Bryan loves children. We wanted to wait, but I think this is the right time.

I walk into the kitchen and set about making another cup of coffee and some toast for breakfast. I take out my box of pills and sit outside on the deck. As I eat breakfast I look at the pills. Should I do this? I have heard that it can take a long time to fall pregnant after coming off the pill. I think that is true for some people. So even if I stop taking it now, it does not mean that I will fall pregnant right away. So that's good in case I don't want to be pregnant, right? No. No. I think a baby is the solution. I knew I would get there in the end. It was just a matter of time before I figured out how to solve this situation. It's for the best.

I feel much better now that I have a two-pronged plan for dealing with our situation. I will continue to make it difficult for Bryan to divorce me and I will get pregnant and then we will go back to where we were and there will be no more Theresa.

I take my plate and cup to the sink and wash up. I pop one of the pills into the sink and watch it dissolve in the moisture there. Then I rinse it away. Bryan may check the box to see if I am still on the pill, so it's better if I dispose of them one at a time. I don't want him to think I have stopped taking the pill. I go to the bathroom, give my teeth a quick brush, so I don't have a stale coffee smell on my breath, grab my briefcase and drive to work.

My welcome at work is rather dismissive. Everyone seems disinterested to see me. I greet Michelle, who sits in the cubicle opposite me, but she just looks at me and goes back to work. Well, they are all nasty self-invested people, so what did I expect?

They certainly do not have the life that I do. I have the husband, the high-powered career, that is going much further than theirs, and I will have the baby too. I will have it all, so I do not care what they think of me or how rude they are to me. They are little people, who are behaving as small people do. I really do not need to trouble myself with the thought of them. My head will be better employed on moving ahead in my job.

I put my briefcase down next to my chair and sit down. Oh for fuck's sakes! Someone must have used my chair when I was not at work yesterday. This is my chair. Just because I wasn't here to guard it doesn't mean it's a free for all. What must I do to have my property respected? Put a sticker on it saying "Claire's property. Keep off!" No, that wouldn't work with this bunch. I would have to literally lock it away every night when I left the office. That would be the only bloody way to ensure that my stuff was left alone.

Now I have to waste time adjusting my chair again. I glare around the office to see if anyone looks guilty. No one is looking at me. I stare at Mike's back. He always uses other people's chairs. He is sitting hunched over his desk. Does he usually sit like that? No, he doesn't. I am sure he is sitting like that, because he doesn't want me to see him. It's him. I am no idiot! I can spot a guilty person a mile away.

I roll my chair over to my desk. Yes, it has been sat on. The arms are too high and bang into the desk. My legs are not at the correct height and that is going to cause me backache. It is also tilted at the wrong angle. I feel as though I am reclining, as I stare at my blank computer screen. Why didn't he just sit on it and not mess with the position? It's spite. He is a horrible spiteful man. I slowly drop the seat's position, so that the arms slide exactly under the desk. I slide in and out a couple times to test it. Then I adjust the back. This is the difficult part and it takes me a good ten minutes to get it exactly right. It has wasted a good part of my morning. I am not going to let this go!

I turn on my computer and, as soon as my email comes online, I type out an email to the entire office requesting that people not tamper with other people's desks or chairs or anything else for that matter, as it is both disrespectful and a nuisance. I would have preferred to write it to Mike, as I know he did it, but that will just cause a fight between him and me and then it will be his word against mine and no one ever believes me. In any case, the whole office could use a lesson on respect. It makes my blood boil!

I survey the rest of my desk to see if anything else has been tampered with. Everything looks in order. I open my drawers and my hole punch and stapler are there. Those are known to grow legs and walk off. I bet he used one of my pens! I open the second drawer and take out my box of pens. I count all the pens inside four times. I believe that if you check things four times it leads to better accuracy. It is easy to make a mistake, so you have to check again. And you can make a mistake while you are checking your mistake and you would not know it. So the third time you check will then just verify one of the mistakes you made. So checking three times, which is what most people do, is not enough. It has to be four times. More than that is wasteful and less than that is incompetent. I count four times. They are all there. That is good.

People waste pens. They have no respect for them. They pick them up from other people's desks and forget to return them and then leave them behind somewhere and they get lost. I believe that we all need to respect our property. It is better for the environment too.

I check my in-tray. And there are no reports in there. I wasn't even in the office yesterday, so Debbie has had a full day to get them into my in-tray. How difficult is it for someone to get up from their desk, walk a few meters and place the documents in another person's in-tray? I think even an ape would manage to do it. What is even more mind-blowing is that is what the dumb woman is being paid to do. We should let her go. It would be far more efficient for me to get up and get them myself. In fact, if they let her go, we could all get a pay increase. She is totally superfluous.

"Debbie, where are my reports that I asked for?"

"Sorry, Claire, they are here." She hands them to me.

I stare at her.

"Is there anything else I can do for you, Claire?"

"Yes, actually there is, Debbie," I say raising my voice. I want the rest of the office to hear this. Maybe if the rest of them hear how inefficient she is, they will do something about it. "I would love it if you would please explain to me how come it was so difficult for you to walk across and put these files in my in-tray where they belong."

"You weren't in yesterday, Claire."

"Just because I was not in, does not mean that you get to not do your job properly."

I walk back to my desk and I am pleased to note that a number of heads have turned and were listening to us. Good. Maybe she will get the axe and we can have more efficiency around here.

I make space on my desk by pushing everything neatly to the edges and then open up the reports. There is a lot to go through today. I really wish they would make these desks a little bigger, so that I had more space. I push my previous annoyance away, pick up my red pen and start to read through the reports.

I start to feel light-headed. I glance up at the time on my PC. It's 2:30pm. I have forgotten to get lunch. That's why I am feeling a bit dizzy. I reluctantly close the report I was working on. I place a tab inside it, so that I know where I was and write down the line number I had got to, so I don't have to waste time rereading information I have already looked through. I neatly pile the reports on my desk and make sure that everything is in order. I want to continue working, but the hunger pangs are disturbing me. All I had was one slice of toast for breakfast. I need to eat. I don't want to. I wish I could stay here and work all night. I can't though. Security ensures that everyone leaves at 11pm at the latest. I will take it home with me. It will give me something to do tonight and I will be on top of things tomorrow. I pick up my cell phone from the desk and fish out my wallet from my briefcase.

As I walk past Mike's cubicle, I swear that I see him hunch over even more. Well, he cannot hide from me. It confirms my suspicions. I know it's him. The inconsiderate prick!   And he knows that I know it's him otherwise why else would he scooch down even more in his desk? Well the whole office knows that I know and we will see what happens to the arrogant fucker. I bet his day of reckoning is coming sooner rather than later. Also his productivity is appalling. He'll be out of a job soon enough.

Jose is working at the canteen today. He must have changed shifts to the afternoon. I ask for a meat pie and a coke. He doesn't seem too interested to see me either and doesn't acknowledge my thank you. Well, when I get to management level, I will fire Jose. It's important to have a friendly attitude towards the other staff and he needs to work on his manners. I sit at the end of the canteen with my back towards him in my usual spot. The meat pie is ok. Not too healthy. I guess my diet of these, as well as the candy and coke, is the reason for my weight gain. I don't care right now though. I have other things to focus on at the moment, so my eating habits are low on my list of priorities. I am just a little overweight, not fat, and it's good to get a little more padded if one is going to fall pregnant.

I look out the window. The street outside is busy with people. There are shops and restaurants outside my office. There are even a couple of fast-food chains, but I always eat up here in the canteen. I don't want to go out. I usually eat as quickly as I can and then get back to work. Also, I dislike crowds. There are too many people and they are all so rude. People these days will walk into you and not apologise. I prefer to stay up here and watch them instead as they scurry about tending to their daily affairs.

There's a couple, who seem to be meeting for a late lunch. They look so happy together and so engrossed in each other. I can't look. There's a man sweeping the streets. I try to make myself feel better that I at least have money and a good home and an interesting job. I am in a much better position than he is in. But maybe he has a happy marriage. No. He is a street sweeper. There is no way any woman would be content to marry a man with no prospects. I feel better again. I am in a much better position than he is and it is only a matter of time before my marriage is on track as well. So I will have it all – the high paying job, the nice house, the doting husband and soon a baby. So many people are not as fortunate as I am.

I spot a good-looking man walking hurriedly down the street, talking on his cell phone. I stare at him until he is out of my line of vision. There is no harm in looking at what's on offer. I think about the man – is he as handsome as Bryan? No I don't think so. I wonder what Theresa looks like. Well, whatever she looks like, I am sure she isn't terribly intelligent. That note I read didn't indicate that she was a bright woman. Bryan likes intelligent women. He will tire of her soon enough and will be very happy that he can come back to me. It must be some soon-to-be-midlife crisis for him.

I finish the last of my coke. I need to finish all those reports by the end of the day. It would have been much easier had I come to the office yesterday. I need to meet all my performance indicators so that I can get a raise. I see an old lady walking slowly across the street with shopping bags hanging off her walker. She seems as lonely as I am feeling. I never ever want to be that old and not have anyone to look after me. I don't want to be the sad old lady trying to cross the road alone. I feel even more determined to have a baby. I am not going to die all alone in this world. A couple of students walk past her, laughing and chatting in high spirits. I follow them until they disappear into the mall and I lose sight of the old woman. That is a good thing.

But I continue to think about her, as I walk back to my desk, until I sit down and become engrossed in my work. I check the figures in the reports and cross check some of the references. It lulls my brain into an almost meditative state and it is all absorbing. Time flies by.

My office line rings. I wish I could be left alone to get on with this. Every interruption takes me off track. Then I need to reread what I have already read to help me remember where I was. After the third ring I pick up.

"Hello, Claire Bellevue speaking."

"Claire, this is Helen. Bill wants to see you in his office at 5pm. Can you make it then?"

"Um, hang on, Helen, let me check my schedule."

I know there is nothing on my schedule today, but it sounds better to say that. It is never ever good office politics to admit that you have lots of free time, as then it seems that you have not done any work at all the whole day. Well that's what I would think if someone said that they were free.

"Helen?"

"Yes?"

"5pm is good. I can see Bill then."

Helen hangs up.

"Bye," I say to the silent receiver. I put the phone down.

I know why Bill wants to see me today. It is happening sooner than I expected. Clearly today is not as bad as I thought it was!

Bill must have heard about Debbie this morning and I am sure he read my email too. Some people in this office are going to get chopped or at least get a warning and a warning always leads to being fired. It is just a matter of time. I knew it! People can treat me anyway they like, but I am the one, who is moving forward and they are the ones, who are going to be looking for a new job. Good luck to them! I hear it's tough out there these days.

I return to my report in a happier state of mind than I have been in all morning until I realise that I have completely lost my train of thought. That really irritates me! That is why I hate being interrupted. Now I have to reread what I have already read in order to get back to where I was. It is such a waste of time. Before I get down to that, I set my alarm for fifteen minutes before the meeting with Bill, so that I have ample time to finish up what I will be reading and get organised before the meeting. I pick up my pen and scan through the report until I remember where I was. So annoying!

As I pass Mike on my way to Bill's office, he turns around and stares at me. I stare back, but I find it very disturbing. He sniffs the air and a slow smile spreads across his face, but it is the look in his eyes that scares me. I have never seen him behave like this. It's very creepy. I hurry away to Bill's office.

When I arrive at Bill's office, Helen motions for me to sit on a chair and wait, which is really disrespectful. I made certain that I was on time for Bill, so he could at least pay me the courtesy of being on time for me. Helen is typing something up on her computer. The clicking of the computer keyboard keys continues unabated for ten minutes. In this time I could have finished another page instead of sitting here doing absolutely nothing. I am glad that he wants to meet with me to discuss this morning's issues, but I really would appreciate not being kept waiting. And the weird thing is that Bill is always punctual, so I wonder what is keeping him today. Eventually his door opens and he says goodbye to Pete, shaking his hand jovially. Pete walks off and Bill turns to me. The smile fades from his face and he looks serious as he motions me into his office. I guess they are getting the axe then.

I sit across from Bill at his desk.

"Claire, we need to talk."

"I know what this is about, Bill."

"You do? Well that will make this easier then. This is never easy, as I am sure you must know."

"Of course, Bill. I am sure it was a difficult, but necessary decision."

"Yes it was difficult. Very difficult. But I am surprised that you feel that it is necessary. I didn't expect you to feel that way at all actually."

"Well it's always about improving overall efficiency."

"Yes. That's exactly what it is. We need to have company moral as high as is possible, whenever and wherever possible."

"I have always felt that."

"I am glad that we are on the same page, Claire. This is so much easier than I thought it would be. There's something you're not telling me. Have you got plans that you have not told me about?"

"Well, Bill. Nothing conclusive, as I wasn't sure what was going to happen, but I have some ideas that I think are going to create a very constructive future."

"That's good to hear, Claire. That makes me feel so much better. I have never been terribly good at this. I like to give people as many chances as possible and … well, it gets to a point where I suppose giving chances is not enough if there is no change in behaviour. I have given you as many chances as I can, Claire. We've discussed you being a team player and you have really tried, Claire, after the last warning. In fact, I felt things improved a great deal until today. I am not sure what happened yesterday and how it has affected you today, but I have had several complaints today about your behaviour and I am afraid that, as agreed, I am dismissing you with immediate effect."

"You are firing me?"

"I am afraid so, Claire."

"I thought you'd brought me in to talk about Mike and Debbie."

"I am sorry for the misunderstanding, Claire. I understood from our conversation a moment ago that you knew I was letting you go."

"You can't, Bill."

"I can and I am, Claire. I am not going to go over this again. We have had meetings and written warnings. I have given you ample opportunity to change your behaviour, and you really did try, Claire. I was so hoping that things had changed. You are one of my most efficient employees."

"So why are you firing me then, Bill?"

"Because you bring down the morale of the rest of the staff, Claire. People here don't like you and they don't like it when you bring them down. I cannot deal with continual complaints about you again, Claire. That was the agreement. You can read it here. You agreed to this, Claire."

I read through the agreement and look at my signature at the bottom of the page. How could I have forgotten this? My heart seizes in my chest. I start to feel dizzy. The talks, the warnings, my efforts to stay out of everyone's way over the last two months all comes flooding back to me. This job is so important to me. I have been here for six years. It is my second home. I really tried to keep my irritation to myself. How could I have forgotten something so important?

"Please, Bill. Don't do this. I wasn't well yesterday. I really am not okay today. I am not sure what is wrong with me. I can't lose this job. I have given everything to this company for the last six years. I have helped to develop and grow this business."

"You have, Claire, and I appreciate what you have done more than you know. That is what makes this so hard, but I cannot lose the rest of my staff, who are good people too, over one person. I would rather lose that person. I will write you a good resume, Claire. You need to sort yourself out. Make a fresh start somewhere else. I really do wish you all the best. Can I get security to help you pack your desk and carry your stuff to the car?"

"No, Bill. Please, please, I am so sorry. It will never happen again. I swear, Bill. Give me one last chance. I need this job."

"I am sorry, Claire. You have just used your last chance."

The door opens and Mike comes in with a gleam in his eye. He is sniffing the air and looking at me.

"Mike, this is a private meeting. Will you leave immediately!" Bill roars.

Mike looks at Bill for a moment and then turns to me and continues to sniff as a smile spreads across his face.

Bright lights flash before my eyes. I try to stop them, but they flash even more intensely. My ears start to whoosh and I can vaguely hear Bill's concerned voice in the background, but the whooshing is too loud to make out what he is saying. I don't understand what is happening. Bill's desk starts moving up towards me. I try to put my hands out to stop it, but they are moving too slowly.

5

"Wake up, Cher! Wake up! Are you all right? Must I call a doctor?"

I feel disorientated and my head hurts. I am sitting in a chair and someone is shaking me. Bill is shaking me. It makes the dizziness feel worse.

"I'm okay. Stop shaking, me! Sorry. I am okay."

"I was worried when I couldn't wake you. I thought you were dead."

"I am fine, Bill. I just passed out. I am not dead - just feeling a bit woozy."

Silence. I try to open my eyes, but they are all blurry and I shut them again.

"I think I should call the doctor."

"Really, I am fine. A bit embarrassed. Sorry to have passed out like that."

"You missed tea so I came to see what was wrong. Are you sure you are all right, Cher?"

"I did? I missed tea? Since when do we have tea?"

Silence.

"Have you had a stroke, dear?"

"What?" I open my eyes again, but they are still blurry. Oh, my god. Have I panicked myself into having a stroke?

"Maybe. Maybe you should call the doctor, Bill. Maybe I have had a stroke. Oh, dear! I can't see. Everything is all blurry and I can't hear properly. Oh my god! I am not feeling okay at all! What's wrong with me? My whole body hurts when I try to move. It's not working properly."

Silence.

"Hello?" I open my eyes again. It is hard to see through the blur, but I don't think anyone is there. How could Bill leave me like this? What's wrong with me?

Maybe he went to get a doctor. Why did he just not call from his office desk? Probably didn't want to scare poor mad, Claire anymore than he had already. I am a grown-up for god's sake, why do I have to behave like a ranting lunatic? And now I have had a stroke. I feel sore. I can't see and I can't hear properly. Bill's voice sounded all odd. It must be from the stroke.

I want to cry. I was just getting my life back on track and now Bryan won't come back to me. He won't want a blind, deaf and paralysed woman. Why is this happening to me? What have I done to deserve this? No..... No..... I won't be able to have a baby now. My whole life is falling apart. I won't be able to have a baby...

No! I must stop panicking. Maybe it's not as bad as I think. Maybe I hit my head and the effects of this are temporary and I am okay. Yes. I must think of the positives. I will be fine. This is temporary. My head will clear and I will be fine!

I can't believe Bill would be such a coward as to run away and leave me here. Well that is something I will take up with my lawyer. I am not going to let him fire me and then run away like a coward when it didn't turn out the way he wanted it to.

Soon I hear hurried footsteps.

"Cher, are you okay?"

"No, actually I am not okay! You just fired me without any warning. I am in shock. And you will be hearing from my lawyers! And if I do not make a full recovery, you will be hearing from my lawyers a lot!"

"Just calm down. Shush. It's okay. Let me check on you, okay?"

"Calm down? Calm down! No I will not calm down! I have worked harder for you than anyone else in this shit

hole company. I have gone above and beyond for you
time and time again, Bill, and this is how you reward me?
I do not deserve to be treated like this!"

"Shush…. I am just going to take your blood
pressure, so you are going to feel something tight around
your arm. Don't get a fright. I am just unbuttoning your
sleeve. There we go. Now I am going to push it up. Is
that comfortable?"

"You are not Bill."

"No, Cher, I am not Bill. Just take some deep
breathes in. I am sure you are fine. Okay, I am going to
take your blood pressure. You are going to feel a little
squeeze. Just relax and breathe normally."

"Are you a doctor?"

"It's me, Lindsey. Just relax and breathe in and out
slowly and gently. Breathe in…."

"Lindsey? I don't know any Lindsey. Who are you
and how come you know all about me? Oh! Oh, that's
what's going on here! Bill has already replaced me! When
did you start working here? Today, I suppose?"

"Cher, I need you to calm down, please."

"I can't calm down. Get your hands off me! Why
can't I see?"

"I am not taking your job. I have been working here
for four years now."

"How come I can't remember you then? Why can't I
see? What's wrong with my hearing?"

"Please let me do my job and take your blood
pressure. I am sure there is nothing to worry about.
Please just sit back, close your eyes and breathe. It will all
come back to you when you are feeling relaxed and calm
again. Okay?"

I nod.

"Good, now let's see….There we go. Blood

pressure's a little low, but that's normal for you. You missed tea, so your blood sugar's probably fallen."

"What tea? We don't have tea at work. Is this something new that's been brought in now that I am fired?"

"Shush… you are just fine. You are a little disorientated after missing tea. I think that's the problem. Looking at your photos again, I see. You probably lost track of time and fell asleep."

This lady is batty. Why haven't they called the paramedics? Where is that bastard, Bill? Maybe they have sent me off to some loony bin.

"Oh, look, you glasses have slipped off. Here, let me put them back on for you and you will be able to see better. There you go!"

I don't wear glasses. I can feel the Lindsey-person putting the glasses onto my face. I want to push the stupid things off my face! I lift up my hand to pull them off and open my eyes. The blur has gone away. That doesn't make sense. I don't wear glasses.

"I don't wear glasses. How come I can see with these on?"

I pull the glasses off and the room immediately goes out of focus. I put them on again and the blur disappears. I do this several times. But I don't wear glasses. Am I dreaming? I don't feel like I am dreaming.

I look up into two concerned faces. Both are women. One is young. The other is old.

"Is that better, Cher?"

"Who are you people?"

"Just relax. Everything is fine."

The younger woman pulls out a walkie-talkie. I bet she is going to call security on that damn thing! I try to get up to pull it out her hand, but my body doesn't work properly and I collapse back into the chair with a groan. What have they done to me? A feeling of dread prickles through my skin. Has Bill done something bad to me and sent me here. Does Bryan know where I am?

"Hi, could you bring up some tea with lots of sugar and some biscuits to Room 8A please. Thanks."

They want to poison me now.

"Where am I? Who are you people?"

"Shush. Just relax. Everything will be just fine."

"Don't you shush me! Why won't you answer my questions?"

"Cher, I want you to relax. Just give yourself some time. The tea is coming soon and you will feel much better."

"I can't hear properly." I want to cry. Who are these people? Where am I? I can see that I am not in Bill's office anymore. Where did he take me? Suddenly I hear a high-pitched noise that makes me jump, which makes my bones ache.

"Sorry, Cher, I didn't mean to give you a fright. I was just adjusting your hearing aid. It seems to be working just fine."

Hearing aid?

"Have I just had an operation?"

"No, dear. You are fine. You just fell asleep in your chair and missed tea," says the older woman.

"Where's Bill? Did he bring me here?"

"I am not sure who Bill is? Is he someone you knew once?"

"No! I was in his office before I fainted and now I am sitting here. How did I get here?"

"Cher, you haven't been anywhere but here. You have been here all morning since breakfast, I assure you. There is no Bill here. Maybe you had a dream about the past? Did you know a Bill once?"

Did I know a Bill once? I was with Bill not more than a few minutes ago. This doesn't make any sense to me. I start to feel very panicky. I can feel my heart rate pounding in my chest. I have no idea where I am. I don't know who these people are and I don't feel well. I am intensely scared.

There is a knock on the door and I startle.

"Don't worry, Cher. It's just your tea. Thank you. Let me put it on the table here. Lift your arms. There we go."

The woman has pulled a table over my chair and the warm fragrance of tea drifts up towards me. The biscuits look inviting and I realise I am feeling hungry. I am not sure this is all laced with poison or some kind of tranquilliser. I hesitate. There is another thing that is bothering me.

"You are not pronouncing my name properly. It's Claire. Not Cher."

"Here you go. Drink this and you will feel much better."

She lifts the teacup up and tries to give it to me. I don't want the tea. I am sure there is something in that tea. There is something about this whole situation that doesn't feel right to me and I do not trust these people. I try to the push the tea away from me and I am horrified by what I see.

I can't quite comprehend what I am seeing. My brain just does not want to work properly. It just cannot be true. I must be seeing things.

I withdraw my hand and look at it. It's not my hand.

It moves when I move it and the fingers stretch out when I make them. They curl in when I make a fist. I flex and relax the fingers. But it is not my hand. The birdlike claw is covered in brown spots. The joints are swollen and the skin looks so thin and fragile. My gaze travels up from the hand to the arm, which is covered in pink cardigan. I move the other hand that looks similar and pull the jersey back to reveal more brown spots on skin that has been stretched too much. Where did my life go?

"I am old."

"That's stating the obvious," says the older woman.

"Please drink your tea, Cher."

I take the cup and drink the tea. It tastes good and I feel better physically, but otherwise I feel completely bewildered.

"How can I be old?"

"It happens to all of us, dear."

"But I was in the office just a moment ago."

"You were dreaming. You worked in an office for many years remember."

I nod my head, but I don't remember.

"Were you looking at your photos? That always upsets you, dear. Let me take that from you."

"No!" I hold the photo album, which is still on my lap. I have no idea why I feel so protective of it, but there is no way this woman is going to take it away from me.

"Let's leave that for now, Jenny. Don't worry no one is going to take that away from you, Cher," but I see the meaningful look she gives the old lady. I don't trust these two. They are going to take it away from me and they can't. If they do I will be devastated. I am not sure why.

Lindsey reassures me that I am fine and tells me she will check on me again at the end of her round in the evening. She tells me to call her if I feel worse. I am left alone with the old lady, who has taken a seat in a chair across from me.

"Lovely weather today, isn't it? We should go for a walk in the garden, if you are feeling up to it. Once your blood sugar is normalised of course."

"Yes, I think a walk would be lovely. Thank you. That is very kind."

"Don't be silly. I love to go for walks, as you know. I love the company. And with all the old coots batty as hell…. Well, Cher, please don't go senile on me. Not like poor Henry. You know what happened to him. Never was the same man again. You are the only friend I have here. "

We look at each other and then look away. The silence starts to feel a bit uncomfortable. Since I can't remember her or what she is talking about. I can't contribute to the conversation.

"It is a lovely day. A walk sounds like a good idea," I say to try to ease the awkwardness.

"Yes. After your tea, and once you have regained some of your strength." She looks out the window and seems to be lost in the scene outside. I take the opportunity to look around.

I am sitting in an armchair, a light blue one that matches the one Jenny is sitting in. A sky blue bedspread drapes cheerily over a bed to my left and a lamp, half-full glass of water and a book adorn the otherwise sparse bedside table. Glass doors open airily onto the balcony in front of me and to the left are a battalion of white doors. I am not sure where they lead to. I have a television and a writing desk. The desk is bare apart from one long stemmed red rose in a vase.

"You alright now, dear?"

"Yes, thank you, Jenny. Sorry to have caused such a fuss."

"No trouble. No trouble at all. Just don't scare me like that again." She gets up and pats me on the shoulder, "I am going to listen to my show. I will see you afterwards. Call Lindsey if you are feeling worse. Or I can stay if you want. If you think it's better if I do?"

"No, I am fine. Thank you. Go ahead and enjoy your show. I will see you in a little while."

I do not know where I am and what has happened to me. Did I dream about my life as a young woman? I am not sure. If I did, why don't I know who I am? It is easier to not think about it right now. I look out the window and sip my tea and nibble on my biscuits. All this makes me feel good and at peace and I lose track of time.

With a jolt I realise that Jenny is going to take the photo album away from me and hide it. I have a vague recollection of her doing that to me before when I was upset. It made me more upset. I need to hide it.

I turn and place the cup and saucer on the bedside table with shaky hands. I try to get up and fall back into the chair with a groan. I think I did that too quickly. I need to take it more slowly. I place both my hands on the armrests of the chair and place my feet firmly on the floor. Then I push very slowly and firmly. It hurts and it is really hard to do. I feel like I have lost all my strength. My left knee and hip ache, but I need to hide that photo album. I keep going. I know I can do it. I know I can get up. Eventually I am standing. I try to adjust to the feeling of stiffness in my joints. I stand like this for a while, letting the blood flow through my body after sitting for such a long time. I am impatient. I want to get this done before she comes back, but my body won't obey me.

I look around the room and see my walking stick. How fortuitous! I hobble over and get it and hobble back to my chair. I sit down in the chair, which is not easy and I end up falling backwards into it at the last moment, which jolts my whole body. I don't have time to dwell on this, however. I need to get this album under the bed. I lean forward and try to place the album as carefully as I can onto the floor. I lose my grip and it thuds to the floor. No time to lose, I take the walking stick and push the album as far under the bed as I can make it go. I then lean back in my chair exhausted but also triumphant. Let that old bag try and take my album away from me now!

"Wake up, Cher! Wake up, dear. We are going to miss the light and then we won't be able to go for a walk."

"Huh?" I look around and blink my eyes. Jenny is looking at me with her hand resting on my shoulder.

"Oh yes, that's right. I must have dozed off again."

"Are you feeling alright?"

"Much better dear. Much better. No need to fret. I think I fell asleep after that lovely tea."

"Good to go for a walk though. Loosen up the joints a bit."

"Yes. Yes. I am looking forward to it."

"Shall I call Lindsey to help you get up?"

"No thanks, dear. I am not an invalid yet. It might not be easy, but I can get myself out of the chair."

"Can I help?"

"No, I am fine."

Jenny walks away as I struggle to get myself into a standing position.

"Where's your photo album?"

"Mm? I have no idea." I pretend to look around for it. To make my act more   believable I say with a distressed voice, "Where is it?"

"It's not here."

"Isn't it? Maybe Lindsey put it away while I was dozing."

"Maybe."

I hold my walking stick and wait for Jenny. She looks

suspiciously around the room, but to my relief seems to let the idea go and leads the way out of the room. I don't say anything and my face is a blank mask, or so I hope. It is certainly the look I am going for.

"How's your leg today?"

"A bit stiff."

"Growing old is not for the feint-hearted."

"That is most certainly true."

"Shall we take the lift today instead of the stairs?"

"If you don't mind, I would prefer that."

"Not at all."

Jenny walks over to the lift and pushes the call button. I envy her. She seems to be able to manoeuvre a lot more easily than I can.

"How was your afternoon?"

"It was alright thank you. I went to see Simon. He's not well."

"Is it serious?"

"Oh, he is fine. Just a big baby, really. He has a cold and so he feels like he is dying. Men never change, do they?"

"No, they don't."

"His daughter and son-in-law came to visit him this morning and spent three hours with him, so he really can't complain and his grandson is coming tomorrow afternoon."

"He is extremely fortunate."

"Fortunately his cold has dampened his ardour."

"Is he still asking you to marry him?"

"Yes, it is so ridiculous! Getting married at our age, I ask you? And I have told him I am not interested. I have been married once. I have no desire to repeat the experience again. Ah, here's the lift. You go first, dear."

"Thank you. How's your daughter?"

"Very well, thank you. She called this morning and said that she is up for a promotion. They want her to be a creative director at the advertising firm. It's a great achievement. Though I don't know when she will have time to spend with her children."

"That's wonderful news. Please send her my regards."

"I will. Young people these days are always so busy. After you dear."

"I suppose it is the nature of modern life. She seems to have time for her family and she does see you three times a week."

"Yes, she is a good girl. I am very lucky. Oh, isn't this day beautiful?"

"It is indeed."

I realise that this is how it has always been. I am not sure how I could have been so disorientated. I must have been dreaming about being Claire. I suppose when I thought I was dreaming about being the boy, that was a dream within a dream. Maybe it is a sign of senility?

We walk out of the wooden doors in the lounge area into the garden, which is painted vivid green with splotches of dazzling colour in the late golden afternoon sun. Thankfully, Jenny seems as taken by the beauty as I am and she has stopped talking. I am glad for her company, though. We amble around the ample garden and stop every now and then to appreciate the beauty of the flowers. I must say that the walk is doing me a lot of good. My left leg is feeling a little bit less painful and at my age a little less painful is a good thing.

I also feel less confused and know where I am and who I am. I have been living in this retirement home for the past three years and Jenny is my very dear friend. My brother paid for me to come to the retirement home and then left enough money for me to stay here in his will after he died. We were always very close, my brother and I. I really miss Bobby very much. His wife visits me every two weeks. Her driver brings her to see me. I wish I had a driver. Then I could get out of here and see the world. The home is lovely, but it gets a bit much staying cooped up here day after day. Like a very nice prison, but a prison nonetheless. That is what it's like here. Sometimes my sister-in-law will get her driver to take us out somewhere for tea and that is always a treat and once a month the staff take us on an outing to the theatre or the cinema or out for tea. I wish it was three times a week instead of once a month, but I can't complain. I could be living in a shack or someplace worse. I am very grateful to Bobby for putting me here. I thank him every night.

Lindsey comes up to us and inquires how I am feeling. I tell her I am feeling better. She is pleased and rushes off before Jenny can ask her about the album. I am so happy that she has to rush off. I am not sure if Jenny remembers about the album, but I am glad Lindsey rushes off before seeing her jogs Jenny's memory.

We sit on a bench in the garden and I get lost in the beauty. I am glad it's summer time. When winter comes, everything is dead. It's lovely to come outside for a walk, but it's not as pretty. I just sit and try to soak up the summer sights and smells and the feeling of the gentle cool breeze on my skin.

"It will be dinner time soon. Shall we make our way back inside. I want to see the six o'clock news before we eat. If I don't get to see it at six, then Roger will be watching a documentary at eight and he refuses to change the channel for the news. I like to know what's going on in the world. So much happening all the time."

"Yes, I'll join you. No need for me to go all the way

up to my room and then come all the way down again for dinner."

I manage to get up with a little less difficulty, though it hurts. I cannot believe that I live with this much pain every day of my life. It's arthritis. Not a nice disease. We walk slowly back to the lounge. I say goodbye to the garden in my head. I hope the weather will be good again tomorrow, so that we can go for a walk again. I hate being cooped up indoors.

"Thank you for the company, Jenny. It was a lovely walk."

"Isn't the garden at this time of year simply divine?"

"It is splendid. I hope the weather will be as good tomorrow."

"Well, let's see what the weather man says on the telly tonight."

We make our way to the TV room. Albert, Roger and Ethel are there already waiting for the news.

"Good evening ladies."

"Good evening Roger, Albert, Ethel."

"Had a good walk did you?"

"Yes, it was lovely. The garden is so beautiful this time of year."

"Yes it is. That oak tree has really taken off with all the rain we had earlier in the season. Ah, here we go."

I sit down in a lovely soft armchair and watch the news avidly. There was a terrible accident and twenty schoolchildren died. Such a tragedy! Prices of food are going up and some lucky lady won the.......

"Cher, wake up dear."

"What? What? Where am I?"

"You fell asleep as usual."

"Oh yes, dear me! Did I miss anything?"

"Not much. Prices are going up on food."

"Yes, I saw that bit. Ridiculous!"

"It's the way things are these days."

"What did the weatherman say?"

"It will be a lovely hot day tomorrow again."

"Oh, wonderful!"

I struggle to get out of my chair and hobble after Jenny to the dining room. Sadly we are not seated with Roger and the others. Jenny and I share a table with Sally, Jim and George. Sally cannot feed herself anymore. She has a helper, who places food in her mouth with a spoon. The helper doesn't really talk. A middle-aged, sourish woman, who does charity work. Jim and George are both completely batty and everything that comes out of their mouths is complete gibberish, which they insist on foisting on one. What nonsense! If I had nothing intelligible to say, I would keep my mouth shut. I cannot even talk to Jenny. She gets so irritated with Jim and George that she cannot concentrate on maintaining a decent conversation herself. I concentrate on savouring my meal and trying to ignore Sally dribbling across from me. It's not her fault, poor thing, but it's very disgusting, especially when one is trying to eat.

Dinner tonight is good as usual. They really make an effort with our food here. Jenny was in a different home before she came here and the food they served there was terrible. So that is one thing I can't complain about. Tonight we are having cottage pie and a lovely fresh salad. I thoroughly enjoy each mouthful. My appetite is not what it was when I was younger. I don't eat much and so decline a second helping when Edith comes round to offer more food. I think I will save my appetite for pudding.

With not much in the way of conversation, I tend to drift off a bit until pudding arrives. It's fruit salad with vanilla ice cream. A lovely pudding in my opinion on a hot summer's night.

After dinner, I hobble back to the lounge and take my tea in front of the telly. I watch a documentary about lemurs in Madagascar. Fascinating animals. It seems that these islands always have unusual animals. Australia also has strange animals. I always wanted to go to Australia to see the kangaroos and the koala bears, but I have not been able to do everything I wanted in my life. Just after ten o'clock, I say goodbye to everyone and make my way slowly and painfully back to my room.

I go through my usual night routine. I wash my face, take out my teeth and put cream on. I put on a thick nightie and a pair of socks, because I always get cold at night, no matter what time of year it is. I have always been like that ever since I was a child. Bobby was always hot and I was always cold.

I like to look at my album at night. It gives me so much comfort, even though the light is not bright enough for me to see properly. They think it upsets me, but it doesn't. It upsets me more not to see my photos. They won't even let me have a photo on the wall or on my bedside table. People have strange ideas sometimes. Just because I show emotion, does not mean that it is bad for me. I very painfully get down on my hands and knees and try to fish under the bed for the album, but I have pushed it so far under, that I can't reach it. Now I am starting to get upset. Let them see me now! After a rather painful crawl across my room to retrieve my walking stick and then a painful crawl back to my bed, I try to fish the album out with the walking stick, but I can't seem to hook it over the album and it's too dark to see properly under the bed. At first I start to giggle at the thought of what someone might say if they saw an elderly woman crawling around her room in the middle of the night in her nightdress, fishing under her bed with a walking stick, but as my attempts prove increasingly more futile, I lose my sense of humour and a heavy depression starts to fall over me. I eventually give up and painfully stand up. I will have to try again tomorrow.

I can't imagine a night of not looking at my photos. I wipe the tears away from the corners of my eyes and climb into my bed. I turn off my lamp and arrange myself on my right side with a pillow between my knees. The only way I can get some decent sleep is if I lie in this position. I know what I will do. I will take a photo out of the album and hide it in my bedside table. Then in emergencies, at least I will have that photo available.

I feel a bit better. I pray and then I say thank you to Bobby for his kindness and I say good night to Jack, Jessica and Michael.

6

I wake up early in the morning as usual. I don't sleep long these days. I suppose it could be worse. Jenny and my sister-in-law wake up continually throughout the night. I can sleep through. I am lucky that way, but I only manage to sleep from eleven o'clock at night to four o'clock in the morning. A good solid five hours, but it is annoying to wake up so early in the morning. There's not much one can do at four o'clock in the morning. I set about my usual routine.

I make my way to the bathroom and painfully lower myself onto the toilet. One good thing about living in a retirement home is that they provide for old people and their toileting needs. There are lots of silver handles everywhere to help me pull myself off the blasted contraption once I have finished my business. Once I have finished, I pour a glass of water for myself and make my way back to my bedside table. I open the curtains and the balcony doors and let the fresh early morning air into my room. Then another stiff walk back to my bed. I prop myself up with my pillows so that I am in a semi-reclining position. I sip my water as I gaze out my window, which is dark at the moment, but I will get to see the sun rise, which is one of my favourite things in this world. I also let my memories slip back to the good times. I don't think about the bad times. I have put those on a shelf at the back of my mind. I just think about the good times. This is how I always start my day.

Then the worst part of my day arrives at six in the morning in the form of Beauty. Beauty is not what I would call her. I am very tempted to call her Beast, but I wouldn't dare. But I do call her that in my mind. Beauty comes to give me a bath, well, at least half a bath. She washes the bits I can't get to and she helps me in and out of the bath. The home insists on this. They say that they will not be held liable if I slip and hurt myself in the bath or if I drown. I say it is my own business, but they won't hear it. I don't have much choice in the matter, because where else would I go?

It was so humiliating the first time. It is hard to lose one's independence. It is hard to have some strange person seeing your naked, wrinkled, old body and washing it because it is their job. There is no tenderness and no meaning in your body for them. But life is not always easy. No one ever said it was.

The Beast is friendly enough. She greets me and helps me to the bathroom. She is as respectful as she can be and she lets me take my nightgown off myself. She helps me get into the lovely warm bath that she has already drawn for me. Gone are the days when I could sit and luxuriate in a lovely bath. Now baths are very functional affairs. I do my part and then I pass the cloth over to the Beast, who proceeds to give me a thorough rub down. It hurts. My skin has always been sensitive and it has gotten worse as I have gotten older. I try not to make a sound. I asked her once if she would mind being a bit gentler, but it did not seem to make a difference and I don't like to make a fuss. It's not that she doesn't care, it's just that her approach is rather clinical, I suppose. She has to wash a number of us and I suppose washing old people early in the morning is not a lot of fun. That's why I am happy to do it myself, but they insist on this. Who is going to sue them if I get hurt or if I drown? No one. So why can't they leave me in peace?

After my short and unpleasant bath, the Beast helps me out and dries the bits I can't reach. She then leaves me to dress myself, which takes a while. I am not so good with buttons. My fingertips have lost most of their sensation and so I can't really feel the buttons so well. It's a fresh blouse – that's the problem. Usually, I leave the top button undone, so I can get my head through and then I only have to do one up, but when I have to undo three, it is very tedious. It's a good thing I am a patient person. I like to wear elasticized trousers. I have black ones and blue ones and they look elegant. The material is a good quality. It makes it easier to put on. I then slip on a pair of comfortable shoes and brush my hair. I am too old to wear make-up. I think it makes one look like a clown, if one is putting make-up over one's wrinkles. Anyway, I can't face looking in the mirror. I am sure I look fine.

I make my way down to breakfast. Jenny looks up and says hello, but I can see from her face that is she annoyed with Jim and George - so another meal with no conversation. Sally seems to be struggling with her yoghurt. It is oozing around the sides of her mouth. I greet her helper and sit down. I am not much of a breakfast person. I like my tea and a slice of brown toast with butter and marmalade. I eat this and try to think what's on the schedule for today. Oh, yes, we have craft this morning. It is so patronising. It's like we are in kindergarten again, but there is nothing else to do so we just go along with it, so we don't lose our sanity. The others, who are senile, seem to enjoy it, so I guess it does the trick all round. You would think they would be able to come up with something more interesting for the elderly. I would knit if my hands had sensation and didn't ache after five minutes. Knitting is the right thing for someone my age, not craft.

Once I finish breakfast, I enter the craft room and sit next to Jenny. Today we are making greeting cards. I am not sure what we are supposed to do with the greeting cards once we are done with them. Usually when we do greeting cards, I take mine upstairs and throw it away. I know that Jenny uses hers as birthday cards for her grandchildren. I look through magazines and then awkwardly cut out some pictures of flowers. I feel like a kindergartener and my cutting out is probably as bad. I then stick my jagged cut-outs onto a card. It looks terrible. Jenny is doing a better job. Her hands don't hurt as much as mine and she has more use in them. She is seven years younger than me and I suppose that makes a big difference at this stage. She is very sweet and comments on how nice mine looks. I don't reply. The pro to craft classes is that we can always chat and it gives Jenny and I some time to talk. I love to hear about her two daughters and her grandchildren. Her eldest grandson is in Grade 10 this year. It's worrying that young people today have so much to do. He has extra murals and sport and on top of all that, hours of homework. In my day, we had less to do, but then I suppose we did not have all these technological things to keep up with all the time. I cannot manage these bank machines on my own. Someone from the home has to come and help me to draw money. And the machines keep changing how they display the information so I can never keep up with how to use those blasted things.

At long last craft is over and I retire to the lounge to read the newspaper. There are always so many fascinating things happening in the world. I like this time of the day, because I can relax and not be disturbed until lunchtime. The weather is as lovely as the weatherman predicted and so all the doors and windows in the lounge are open and the breeze carries in the lush smells of summer.

Lunchtime is not worth thinking about much. It's the

same routine. Jim just stares into space while feeding himself. Sally dribbles. Jenny glares and George mumbles endlessly. The egg mayonnaise sandwich is delicious; nice and soft and a bit of a tang to it, which I always like.

And then for the best time of the day. I go up to my room and I can spend time looking at my photos. There is no one to disturb me. It's just me and them. My precious ones. I use the bed to help to lower myself down onto the floor. The light is better now that it is daytime. I push my walking stick under the bed and then I peer underneath. Yes! I can see the album, I carefully manoeuvre the walking stick until I get the handle hooked around the end of the book and then I carefully pull the album towards me. Yes! I have it. I put the album on my bed before I get up and then I lower myself into my chair.

I take the album and open the first page. I spent a lot of time making this album. I used to have a number of albums in my room, but it was difficult to look at them all at the same time and I wanted one that would capture each important moment. I wanted all the important moments in one place. My other albums are at the top of my cupboard. But this one is special. It took a long time to make it. It kept me busy for a very long time, because I had to decide which pictures captured my Loves the best.

I open the album and tell myself my favourite story about the people who made my life beautiful. The first photo is of Bobby and me with our parents on the farm. It is such a happy photo. Papa is looking jolly. I remember he told us a joke before the photograph was taken. He always did that so that we would all look happy. It worked and I am so glad he was so wise. I love looking at all of us. Mum is laughing. I love her open smile. My mother was a beautiful woman. She was always there for me. I can't believe it has been so long since they both passed away. Bobby has his arm around me and we are both laughing. We were a happy family. Not one of those families that looked happy in photos, but were unhappy behind the scenes. We were genuinely happy. We did not have much, but we had each other. And what more does one need? Young people today are so concerned with getting things and that is not what is important. Family is important.

The next page is Bobby's graduation from university. He studied accounting and he did very well at his job. I think he was happy. He managed to support his family. That is all a man can hope to do in this world is support his family. Mum and Papa and I are all looking very proud of him. The other page shows Bobby and Jane's wedding. I love this photograph, because the whole family is there. I spend a while looking at each of them. Their faces are a bit small, so I use my magnifying glass so I can see the details. It's not the best pose for Aunty May, but everyone else looks good.

I flip the page over to a picture of Bobby and Jane and their two boys, when they were young. They are nice boys both of them. Well brought up and caring people. Both are married now. They come with their families to visit me when they can, but it is difficult for them. They have so much to do, just living their own lives and, of course, they also need to see their mother and their in-laws. The next two pictures are of James and Ben's weddings. Bobby and Jane both look so proud. Bobby approved of the girls his sons married. He got on with both their families and there is nothing more that one can ask for then to get on with one's children's in-laws.

I turn the page to two big photos of James and Ben with their wives and children. I am very fond of Ben's youngest, Catherine. She is such a sweet, caring little girl.

She is eight years old now. She always brings flowers for my room when she comes to visit. It's amazing that a child so young can be so caring. She has always been like that. The others are lovely children too, but I have always had a special place in my heart for Catherine. The opposite page is the last photo I have of Bobby. It's a picture that James took. Bobby and I and Jane are all standing arm-in-arm outside Bobby and Jane's house. We all look so happy. Bobby taught his sons the joke trick and I remember James told a joke to make us all laugh. I can't remember the joke now. I miss Bobby so much. We used to see each other every week and we would call each other at least twice a week. I am very fond of Jane and she is good to me, but I don't have the same relationship with her as I had with Bobby. He was such a good brother.

I turn the page to my wedding photo of Jack and me. He was such a good-looking man; well at least I thought so. I remember being so nervous on my wedding day and at the same time so proud to be his wife. I look at Jack and try to etch every line of his face into my mind. I always do this. I can never get enough of looking at this picture of him. Reluctantly, I look away from the photo and look at the wedding picture with everyone in it. Mum and Papa and Bobby and Jane are in these ones again. Despite being so nervous, it was a good wedding. I remember that everyone said that they had a good time.

I turn to our honeymoon pictures. There are pictures of Jack and I together at the beach and of Jack and I having dinner. We didn't have enough money to go overseas, so Jack took me to a swanky hotel down at the coast. It was the first time I ate lobster and crab and we both felt like the two richest people on the earth. There's a picture of Jack painting a landscape. He loved to paint. I am sure he could have been a good artist.

I turn the page and there's my baby. There's me with Jessica, the day after she was born. She was such a tiny, delicate baby and I remember being so scared I would hurt her in the beginning. She seemed so fragile. Jack was much more confident with her. That was unusual for a man, but he was a special man. He was so keen to be a father. He was very involved in our children's lives - unusual for a man in those days. He loved our children. He couldn't wait to get home from work and then he would spend time playing with them and reading to them. I had to fight him for reading time. We used to take turns. One night he would read to Michael and I would read to Jessica and the next night we would swap.

I selected pictures of Jessica's first year. The best pictures of her. I have a picture of her sitting by herself and one of her being bathed. There's one of her with her favourite teddy. She never did outgrow that teddy. Papa gave it to her when she was born and she never would sleep without it. Papa liked to give all his grandchildren a teddy bear when they were born and I think all the children loved theirs very much, but Jessica never outgrew hers. Michael, James and Ben I think lost interest in theirs around the age of five or so. They kept them, but they didn't have the same attachment to them as Jessica did.

There's the photo of Jessica at her first birthday. Jack's parents are there and so are mine and Bobby and his family. I remember Jessica grabbed the cake and ended up with icing all over her face. And there's the picture of her looking rather full with icing everywhere. She was such a sweet child. I laugh as I look at her.

There's a series of photos of Jessica's first holiday at the beach with us. Jack had to keep an eye on her, because she always wanted to run into the sea. She was totally fearless. There are some more snaps of the proud grandparents with Jessica and then her second birthday. I remember spending the whole day before making her cake. It was a Humpty Dumpty cake. It wasn't easy to make.

Then there's the birth of my sweet boy. He was also such a beautiful, bubbly baby. I have a series of him in his first year. I decided I was going to have pictures of him all by himself so that he could have a set when he was an adult. Second children often have to endure being in photos with their siblings and never have ones of themselves on their own. I have those too of course, but I just wanted photos separately of both of them, so that when they were adults they could have their own pictures of themselves. I am glad I did that, because I can look at each of my children separately. I thought they were the most marvellous beings. They were the most amazing things I did with my life. I would spend hours marvelling at their accomplishments. The first word. The first sentence. The first step. The first day at school. Probably to other people it wouldn't seem so important, but to me each moment was the most magical thing. All I wanted to do in life was to be a mother.

I look at the pictures of my two babies as they grew up through the years. Michael's fourth birthday was so much fun. Jack was doing much better financially. His business was starting to take off, so we hired a pony. They brought it to our house and all the children rode on it. Both Michael and Jessica are beaming from ear to ear. No jokes needed to make them smile in these pictures. These are my favourite ones. I spend a long time studying each feature of each of my children. Jessica favoured Jack's family more and Michael was a bit of a mixture of the two of us. They both had Jack's big feet, which was a bit unfortunate. Jack said he could ski on those feet. I well believe he could have had he tried it.

I have put the pictures of the children's first year at school next to each other. Jessica loved school. She was so lucky. She had good teachers. Poor Michael did not have a good first year at school. His teacher was very strict and was not a good fit for him. Jack and I were discussing moving him to another school the following year. I then have Jessica's Grade 2 and 3 photos on the next page.

The last page is a very special page. It was Jack's idea to get a professional photograph made of the four of us. It's in colour and I chose the best one of the lot. The photographer took so many pictures. It was hard to decide, but I thought this picture captured each of them the best. My babies. I miss them so much. I don't know why it hurts so much now. I start to cry. For years I was resigned to the loss of them. I have always missed all three of them every single day of my life, but I have not been so emotional about it for so many years. Maybe, it's because I am at the end of my life.

I have had so many years of them not being in my life. I would have liked to have grown old with Jack. That was our plan. I would have liked to see the people my children would have been. I try to imagine what kind of people they would be like. What kind of jobs they would have had, who they would have married. I would have liked to have met my grandchildren. I would have loved to go and visit my children and their families. I would have liked to have spent more holidays with them. I don't have any regrets about the time we did spend together, but I have missed the time we have never spent together. I have missed them all so much. I lost half my heart when they died.

I let the tears fall onto my lap as I stare out at the trees through my open balcony doors. It has been so many years without them. I have lived for forty-three years without them. I like to believe they are with me all the time. I talk to them all every day. I tell them what has happened.

I gather myself together and turn to the last two pages. I have pictures of Jack's parents and me and of my parents and me. They were all so good to me. Jack's father employed me after the accident. Jack did have a policy, but it wasn't much and I had to work to survive. They only had Jack. They didn't have any other children. They weren't able to and so Jack and the children's loss was as bad for them as it was for me. I wasn't qualified to do anything, so I worked as a receptionist in the firm. Mum, Papa and Bobby also helped me out when they could. I miss them too, but it doesn't hurt as much or in the same way as missing Jack and especially my babies. The last photo is of the house I lived in with Jack and the children, but it is too much to look at anymore and I shut the album.

I am feeling so tired, but I mustn't let Jenny or Lindsey take this album away from me. I need to think of a way to keep it safe. I must never fall asleep with it in the afternoon. As emotionally drained as I am feeling, I get up and look around the room. I know where I want to put it. I have a brilliant idea. At least my mind is still working well. I open my cupboard. I am going to hide the album between my cardigans. First I carefully take the photo of the four of us out of the album and then I slip the album in between my cardigans. I pull the cardigans over it so that the album is concealed. I look carefully at my handiwork and am pleased with the result. You cannot make out that there is anything concealed there.

I take the photo and slip it under my books in the drawer in my bedside table. As tired as I am, I make my way down to tea. Nobody notices that I have been crying. I am lucky that way. My eyes don't really go red for long and they never swell when I cry.

Jenny and I have another lovely walk in the garden and I feel much better afterwards. The weather is holding and it is lovely. We retire to the lounge to watch the news before dinner.

Dinner is slightly more eventful tonight. Jim jumps up and starts arguing with an imaginary Ronald Reagan, before being led off elsewhere by one of the staff. At least it is a bit more interesting than most meals.

The documentary tonight is about the Egyptian Pyramids. They were such a fascinating culture. Roger and I play a game of checkers, which we often do if there is not too much of interest on the telly. The other documentary is about fighter jets and neither of us is very interested in that. I lose as usual, but I don't mind. Winning has never been that important to me. The important part is playing the game. I say good night to everyone and make my way upstairs.

I perform my usual night routine, but tonight there is a new aspect to the whole affair. I open my cupboard and feel between my cardigans to see if my album is still there. I am relieved to feel that it is there, snug and secure. It is safe from Jenny and the others. She didn't ask me at all about it today. Good thing about getting old. Your memory doesn't always work so well. And in this case it's not such a bad thing after all that Jenny's is not so good!

I get into bed and take out the photo of the four of us. I say goodnight to Jack and my babies. I give them each a kiss, before I put them back in the drawer safely under the books. I turn out the light, turn onto my right side and place the pillow between my knees. I pray and say thank you to Bobby. I say goodnight to Jack, Michael and Jessica.

7

I open my eyes. The room is very dark. I am not sure what woke me and then I hear it.

There is someone in the room with me. There is someone bending over my bed and looking at my face. I can hear his ragged breathing and feel the coolness of his breath on my face. I know he is staring at me. I cannot see in the dark, but I feel the burn of his stare as it bores into my unseeing eyes.

I am terrified. Malevolence radiates off his body in waves. I want to scream for help or push him away, but I can't. My voice is caught in my frightened throat and my limbs are paralysed by panic.

As fear pumps its way in a buzzing rush through my body, I lie on my bed – an easy prey for my assailant. My mind freezes in place and I black out.

8

I open my eyes to find I am sitting in a room. The walls are white and the dust of many years has etched itself into the pores in the wall, making the paint look mottled in places. Did someone kidnap me last night and bring me here? Is that what happened? I don't know this place. I have never been here before. I don't think I have. I am a little afraid to move in case I alert my captors to the fact that I am now awake. Who on earth would want to kidnap a little old lady? I don't have any money or relations. It doesn't make sense. I look around carefully.

In front of me is an open window. I see trees swaying in a gentle breeze, their branches heavy with verdant leaves. If I was kidnapped, why would they leave a window open for me to get out of? Probably, they think I am too old to escape out of a window. The drop doesn't look high at all – maybe a meter high. I may be old, stiff and sore, but I am sure I could manage it.

I keep my head in the same position it was in when I woke up and very slowly shift my eyes to my immediate surroundings. I seem to be sitting at a table. There is nothing on the table. The table is a greyish metal colour. It is one of those very practical utility tables. There are metal-framed folding chairs set around the table. I am alone at the table.

I suddenly become aware of talking. I get a fright, but I don't think my body betrayed my reaction in any way. Maybe it is the kidnappers. Maybe that's why they left the window open. They aren't worried that I will get out, because they are sitting in the same room as me and would be upon me before I even reached the window. Silly me!

I need to listen to them, so I can get an idea of what

is going on. I don't move. I close my eyes and still my body and just listen.

They are playing a game of checkers it seems. Two of them are playing and a third one is watching the game. The third one is commenting on the game continuously, which seems to be annoying the other two, because they keep telling him to shut up and go away, but he is ignoring them and continues with his commentating. They are on my left and a little away from me.

Three people here to guard one little old lady? I think that is absolutely ridiculous! What do they think I am going to do at my age? Overpower them all with my stiff, weak limbs and make a run for it? I don't understand why they would kidnap me in the middle of the night in the first place.

I hear a shuffling coming from my right hand side. I sit still and breathe quietly. The person shuffles behind me and continues to my left. This person walks very slowly and heavily. It seems hard for him or her to walk normally. Do they have another senior citizen taken hostage besides me? What on earth is going on here? Who on earth would kidnap the elderly? It is utterly preposterous! What on earth for? Can't we be allowed to live the last of our days in peace and quiet? What could they possibly expect to gain from all this? I mean really!

The person is walking past the other three people playing checkers. They don't seem to notice that a hostage is walking past them and carry on with their arguing. Well, they don't seem too concerned that we old folks are going anywhere. They just let that other person walk past quite unnoticed. I think it will be okay to open my eyes and move around. I should be all right.

I take a deep breath and open my eyes again. There is no one in front of me. I glance to both sides and I can't see anyone immediately near me. I just couldn't stand anyone being too close to me right now. It appears that all is clear and I am alone in my part of the room and that no one has noticed me.

I take a deep breath and let it out. I am feeling a little stiff. I roll my shoulders and shrug them slightly. I can feel the tension ebbing out of them a little. Yes! That feels a bit better. I rotate my head in a slow clockwise movement and then repeat the rotation in an anti-clockwise movement. I feel so much freer. How long have I been sitting like this?

I shift in my seat and look at the checkers players. The two players are both middle-aged men and the commentator seems to be a little older than they are, but not as old as me. Maybe mid-sixties, I am guessing. They are all dressed very casually. The one man is wearing a tracksuit and the slightly older man seems to be wearing a pair of beige trousers and a purple-striped pyjama top. That is really odd! Who would want to kidnap the elderly, while wearing a purple-striped pyjama top? This really is a very strange situation!

I shift my gaze to my right, wondering if there are more pyjama-clad people, but I see that there is a small passageway, which leads off the room I am in and at the end of the passage there is an open door leading outside.

It really is an exquisitely beautiful day outside. The sun looks so warm and inviting. I really would love to pick up one of these chairs and go and sit outside. I would love to feel the sun gently bake some warmth into my skin, while the gentle breeze acts as a soothing balm. That would make me feel so much better. I am sure I would be able to handle my situation much better after a little sit outside. I just need to drink in the beauty of this garden for a little bit. Then I will be able to deal with my kidnap situation far better, I am sure. They don't seem to be very worried about people walking around or so it seems.

I think that is what I should do. A sit outside will be good. I just need to make sure that no one will hurt me for going outside. I don't want to make any silly decisions. A thorough appraisal of the situation will be best before taking any action. Just to think that I have to reason like a soldier at this time in my life!

The board game players appear completely absorbed in their game and have not noticed me. That is good. Well, it could be good, because I could go outside and they would not notice me, but it could also be bad, because if they don't notice me leave and then notice later that I am missing, they will come after me and probably hurt me. Maybe, I should ask their permission to go outside. Yes. I think that's the best solution. Then they won't hurt me and if they say I can't go outside, then I will move my chair to the window. That is not quite the same as actually being outside, but it is better than nothing. At least I will be able to see the trees and the flowers. It really does look so pretty and inviting.

I'd better check if there is anyone else in the room. I turn around in my seat and look behind me. The room is quite large and goes on for quite a bit. There are many tables – two rows of four tables and each table is surrounded by the same cheap folding chairs. This place is odd. There is a young teenager sitting at a table reading a book and a lady, who is knitting a pink jersey. Neither of them notices me. Are they kidnappers too? The boy seems a bit young to be in that kind of business. Or is he a hostage too? I really wish I could ask someone what was going on here, but at the same time, I don't want to provoke anyone's anger. Behind the boy, against the back of the room, is a row of bookshelves littered with an untidy assortment of books. There's a prefab cupboard against the left wall. The overhead neon lights are on. It makes the room look less dark. There are no windows in any of the three walls of the room and no pictures on the wall. It's quite a practical room. The only source of light is coming from the windows that I was facing when I woke up.

"Oh my God! Look! Look! The statue is alive! Alive! Look it's moving!"

I jump in my chair and turn around. There's a wild-eyed dishevelled young man with limp untidy hair staring at me and pointing.

"The statue is moving! Look guys!"

What is he talking about? And why on earth is he looking at me? The checkers players have ceased their game and are staring at me. I look behind me and the other two are looking at me too. I shouldn't have moved. What have I done? I am getting a bad feeling about this. It's better not to move. I shouldn't have moved. Why did I move?

"I saw the statue move first. I am going to tell. I am the first one. Hooray! Yippee! I am the first! I am the first! And none of you wankers saw a thing. I am going to tell!"

'Oh, for christsakes, shut the fuck up! Go and tell! Just get the fuck out of here!" This is from the one middle-aged checker player. He seems the most normally dressed in a light jacket and jeans.

The black-haired youth takes off skipping and yelling, "The statue is awake!" in the same direction that the shuffler took earlier. The others stare at me for a while. I feel like an animal trapped in a hole with predators all around me. I want to run, but I know that I won't get anywhere fast. I can't run at my age. I just put my head down and stare at the floor. I hope they will lose interest. I wait a long time. There is no sound. I am so scared. I don't know what they are going to do to me.

After what seems like a very long time, I hear the men resume their game. I hesitantly look up. They seem involved and don't notice me at all. That is good. That is very good. I take a deep breath. I didn't notice that I was holding my breath. I am too scared to look behind me. I need to run, but I can't. I need to get out of here, before someone does something terrible to me. Who has that young man gone to tell? Is it the head of this kidnapping cartel? Did they tell me not to move and I forgot? I wish I hadn't moved. Why did I do it? I am always so stupid. I never listen. I never do as I am told!

I am starting to panic. I can hear my breath is coming out in short gasps. I am also aware of an intense feeling of wanting to go to sleep. Why on earth would I want to go to sleep at a time like this? Then I will really be vulnerable. Then they could do anything they wanted to me and I would be defenceless. Why on earth do I want to go to sleep? I want to slap myself across the face to stop this insane feeling! I am too scared to do this, because I will draw attention to myself again and then what would happen? I shouldn't have moved. The desire to fall asleep is so intense and seductive. I need to fight this off. My mind feels like it is slipping into sleep, just like it does before I fall asleep at night. I know I am going to fall asleep. I just know I am. How do I stop this?

Are the two people behind me still looking at me? The thought is unbearable. I don't want them to be looking at me. It makes the back of my neck and head burn. I want to turn around and look at them, but I can't, for the life of me, move my head.

I need to think. Clearly, I am panicking. This is doing no good. Panicking will get me nowhere. I need to settle down and not fall asleep and not panic. How am I going to do that? The feeling is so overwhelming. Okay, just breathe. That will help. I have done that lots of times before and I know it helps. Just breathe in and out. Yes! In and out! There you go, old girl. You can do it! In and out.

No! Oh, no! I can feel I am getting sleepier. This is bad. This is very bad. I can't go to sleep. Okay. No breathing. The panicking was at least keeping me awake even though it made it hard to think. But at least I was awake. Okay. I cannot go to sleep. That is not an option here. I wonder if they are pumping a sleeping gas into the room? Why else would I feel so sleepy at a time like this? It makes no sense at all. Who goes to sleep when they are in danger, I ask you?

I take a look at the three on my left. They seem unaffected by this sleeping thing. In fact they seem quite alert and rowdy again. It's just me. Why on earth would I want to go to sleep? I focus on the rowdy group. They don't notice me. As I focus on them, I feel a bit more alert. Good! This is helping. I listen to them arguing. The jacket man seems to be beating the tracksuit man and the pyjama man is commenting in the jacket man's favour and against the tracksuit man. The tracksuit man is getting irritated by this and is snapping at the pyjama man instead of making his move, which in turn is irritating the jacket man, who clearly wants to win.

Wow. I feel so much better now. I did it. Distraction here is the key. Focusing on breathing needs to be avoided at all costs.

Should I try to slip out? I need to check if the two behind me are still looking at me. Maybe they are keeping an eye on me and that's why the others are not paying attention to me. The last time I moved, I seemed to get into trouble and I am yet to see what form that trouble will take. I don't want to get into worse trouble for moving again, but at the same time, I might have a chance of getting out of here.

Okay, of the two options, I think I should take a chance and look behind me. I am sure it won't make things any worse than they already are, right? I mean I am in trouble for moving so how could it get worse for moving again. It could get so much worse. No it couldn't. Absolutely not! I must not be silly!

Okay, here goes. I try to move my head, but it seems as if my body is resisting each move. Despite this, I persist and very slowly and painfully, I manage to turn around and look behind me.

Fantastic relief floods over me. I feel so much freer. The boy is reading again and the lady is concentrating on undoing her row of knitting, no doubt she missed a stitch during the commotion.

They are both distracted and so is the group of men. I could very quietly slip out and maybe no one would notice me. Do I dare? I am terrified, to be absolutely honest. But maybe I could hide somewhere in the garden and then get out of this place. It would be better than getting into trouble.

Okay, I have convinced myself to do this. I need to move quietly and carefully so as not to draw anyone's attention. It will be hard, because my movements are not as agile as they were when I was younger. It's going to be hard going, but I can do this.

I slowly slide my chair back until I can stand up. This seems to take forever, because I don't want the chair to scratch the concrete floor. I am proud of myself for not making a noise. I very slowly stand up using the table to support myself. Again, I do this slowly so as not to draw attention to myself. All the time, I sneak glances at the people in the room to make sure that they haven't noticed anything and they all seem very involved in what they are doing. I also check both doorways, but no one seems to be near them.

Good. I am doing well. Stealth! I just need to move slowly and quietly and get to the door, and then I will be home free. My body is sore and stiff, but it is not letting me down. I am not going to take this lying down, so to speak.

I very carefully edge my way around the table. I get to a point where I am very visible to the three men, but they are still arguing, so I reckon I am safe and I will know immediately if they see me, because they will stop arguing. The other two are preoccupied.

The fight behind me is getting louder and louder. They are really getting irritated with each other. In fact they have got to a point where they are shouting. The other two look up and I hold my breath. They don't even seem to notice me. They are both staring at the fight.

What should I do? I don't know. If I don't move, maybe they won't notice me standing up and leaning on the table. If I do move, maybe they will notice me, so maybe I shouldn't move. On the other hand, if I don't move, surely they will notice me eventually. I don't know what to do.

Suddenly I hear, much louder than the group of men fighting, "Look, I told you, the statue is moving! You didn't believe me! You thought it was make-believe, but I told you! I told you! I was right! I was right!"

Oh god, they've caught me at it. There's no denying that I moved. Bloody hell! I am standing up! They can see

I moved. I was sitting and now I am standing. That's hard to miss. I want to fall asleep again. It is so overpowering, my head swims with the need for it. I can't. I absolutely cannot. I need to concentrate. Okay, last time I just needed to distract myself by focusing on my surroundings.

The telltale is saying that he told everyone that the statue could move. The two people at the back of the room are still focusing on the group of men. I think that a woman is telling off the pyjama man. She is telling him that he is supposed to stay away from the other two men when they play checkers and that they have had this discussion before. It seems that there is another man in the room, because I can hear him talking to one of the men in the group. He is telling him to calm down and he is telling him to come with him.

I am confused as to what is going on. I am trying to figure out who is who. If the three men were kidnappers, why is the new woman telling them off? Is she the kidnapper? She and the other man? I really am baffled. The good thing is that the sleepy feeling has been taken over by a feeling of curiosity and confusion.

The commotion seems to be simmering down. Suddenly the young man is standing next to me at the table. He stares at me and then shouts, "The statue is alive! Look the statue is moving. I can see the statue's eyes moving. Look!"

He grabs hold of my arm. As a reflex, I twist out of his grip and shove him away from me. He falls backwards onto the floor in a sitting position. He looks at me in confusion and then bursts into tears. The woman comes running up to him and soothes him. She looks at me warily. I obviously don't know my own strength. It must be the adrenaline.

"What happened here? We do not tolerate violence at all."

I am confused. Kidnappers, who are non-violent? What is going on?

"I can see you are conscious today. That is a good sign, but I don't approve of you shoving people, do you hear? Am I going to have to give you something to calm you down?"

"No, Ma'am," my voice comes out in a harsh rasp. It seems like I haven't used it forever. Maybe I have been sleeping a lot longer than I thought. It seemed like it is morning, so surely I went to sleep last night, was kidnapped and now it is morning, the next day. So my voice should not be this raspy. I try to clear my throat.

"Good. So you promise me that you are calm. I am not going to have to call Edward to help me with you?"

"No, ma'am." I think I am going to need some kind of throat lozenge and maybe some water to sort out my voice.

"Good. Now why did you shove Bradley?"

"I thought he was going to hurt me."

"I understand. He gets very excitable, but I promise he won't hurt you. Bradley, are you all right?"

"Yes."

"Good. Go and ask Martha for a glass of juice."

"All right."

The woman looks at me again as Bradley slouches off with far less energy than he displayed earlier.

"I am so glad to see you are awake today. That is a good sign."

She seems kind now that she is not so angry anymore. She seems to be genuinely concerned. Maybe she is not a kidnapper. I want to ask, but I am a bit scared.

"What happened to make you wake up? Anything? Or did you just wake up?"

"I am not sure. It's morning, so I woke up. Don't people normally wake up in the morning?"

She laughs, "Yes, you are right. I am not making sense here. I am sorry. I am just so surprised to see you conscious and alert."

"I am confused. Someone took me out of my bedroom last night at my retirement home. You people. You kidnapped me and brought me here. I am just a little old lady. I don't have many years left. Why would you do this to me? I don't have any money and I don't have a family, who will pay my ransom, so you are wasting your time, do you hear? What kind of people kidnap the elderly? Not very intelligent ones! That's for sure! Come in the middle of the night! Scare me half to death! Bring me here. I don't even get a glass of water, that's how inhumanely you treat people. I need a glass of water. Listen to my voice! And then I demand that this rubbish end right now and that you take me back to my home!"

The woman looks at me for a bit and then says, "You are not a little old lady. No one has kidnapped you. You have been here for the past five months. Your family brought you here, remember?"

"No, I don't! I remember going for a walk in the garden in the home I live in just yesterday with my friend, Jenny, and looking at the photos of my children and my husband. I was not here, I can promise you that."

"Richard, you were here yesterday. I saw you. I know you are feeling confused."

Richard? What? My name is Cher. I look down at my hands. They are big strong hands. There is a dusting of light brown hair on the back of them. They are man hands. They aren't my hands. I have man hands at the

KAREN ANDOR

end of my arms. Do I have man arms? I pull my sleeve up. My arms are hairy and strong, with veins roping under the skin. I feel my chest. It is flat. No breasts. I look down and see a slight bulge at my crotch area.

I am a man. How did that happen?

"I am a man."

"Yes, Richard, that's right, you are a man."

I look at my hands again.

"How did I become a man?"

"Richard, you have always been a man."

"But yesterday, I wasn't a man."

"Yesterday, I saw you sitting here with my own eyes and I promise you that you were a man then too. You were a man before that also. You have been a man ever since you got here."

"For five months"

"You have been here for five months, Richard, but I am pretty sure you were a man even before then."

"How old am I?"

"You are twenty five."

"Really? I thought I was old. Yesterday, I was old."

"How old were you?"

"Really old. Really, really old, like about to die old. I am not old?'

"No Richard, you are a young man."

"I don't understand. What's going on?"

"Richard, you were under a lot of stress and you had some difficulties and don't........."

96

9

I wake up slowly. The kind of waking up that can only happen when you have nowhere to go. My body feels nice and warm and relaxed. My bed is very comfortable. I crack an eye open and can see a sharp slash of light forcing its way between the curtains. With some effort, because I am feeling so comfortable, I turn over and roll away from the light. I fold the pillow over my head so that my head is almost fully encased in its softness.

Someone knocks at my door. Bloody hell! I make a deep groaning sound. Maybe that will scare them away. Nope! The door opens.

"Morning Richard. Are you awake?"

"Does it look like I am awake?"

"No, it looks like you want to sleep some more. You've been out for a day. Would you like some breakfast?"

"No. I want to be left alone to sleep."

"I am sure you do, Richard, but I think it would be better for you to get up. If you lie in bed, you are going to feel grouchy."

"I am grouchy already, because you won't leave me alone."

"Yes, I can see that I am irritating you, but I need for you to get up. Also Dr. Tsakonas will be here at 11am. He is coming in especially to see you. I am sure you will want to talk to him."

"Who is this guy?"

"He is your psychiatrist. He's been dealing with your case since you got here. I am sure he will be able to help you now that you are awake."

I groan. I can see I am not going to sleep now and

even if I wanted to get back to sleep it's too late. I unfold my pillow and sit up.

"I am awake. So he can help me now."

"I can see you are in a bad mood today."

"I just had a really hectic fucked up experience yesterday. First I am in an old age home, living out the last years of my life. Then I wake up not as a little old granny, but as a young guy who has a psychiatrist. It's a little hard to get my head around. So I was hoping to have some time to process all of this in bed sleeping."

"I understand what you are saying, Richard…."

"I really doubt that."

"Okay, Richard, this attitude is not helping. It's not helping you in particular. Hopefully talking to Dr. Tsakonas will help you to sort this out. Okay? So will you come to your appointment today?"

"Sure, whatever." I rub my eyes with my thumb and then run my hand over the stubble on my jaw. I am sure it's not too bad. I am really not in the mood to shave today.

"Is there any way I can get a cigarette around here? And where do I go for breakfast?"

"Richard, are you sure you want to start smoking again? You haven't smoked for 5 months."

"Sorry, who are you by the way?"

"I am Sister Jean."

"Nice to meet you Sister Jean. You've obviously met me, so I don't need to introduce myself, but I am afraid I haven't met you until today. Fucked up, man!" I have an urge to laugh, because this is whack, but I hold it in.

"Yeah. I am pretty sure I would love to have a cigarette. Maybe I have been sleeping for five months, but I need a drag now."

"You weren't sleeping, you were catatonic."

"Sure, what is that? A disease caught from patting cats?"

"No, Richard, it means that your eyes were open, but you were none-responsive for five months."

"Shit, that is heavy man. I definitely need that cigarette. Fuck, what would cause that? What would make someone act so fucking weird?"

"Dr. Tsakonas can discuss that with you, Richard."

"Great. Well if you are not going to help me in that department, can you at least tell me where I can get a smoke, a shower and some clean clothes, because," I take a whiff of my shirt, "these aren't too fresh and I need directions to breakfast. I must have not been paying attention when I was cat-eyed."

The sister sighs. I can see I am irritating her, but I don't give a shit. I'm in a really pissy mood this morning – probably because I didn't get to wake up nicely.

"Your parents have put you in a private room and so the shower is that door to your right. Your clothes are in the closet over there. There's a vending machine for cigarettes down the hall to your left. You should have money in your wallet. It's in your closet. And breakfast is also down the hall to your left."

"Thanks Sister Jean. I'd better get to it then."

Sister Jean closes my door and I slide back down into a reclining position. Fuck. I really wish I could go back to sleep, but she's ruined that for me now. What's the time anyway? I look to my left. There's a bedside table, but the surface is clear. I turn to my right, but that bedside table is also uninteresting. I roll over onto my stomach and check the drawers. All empty. I roll over to the other side and find my wristwatch in one of the drawers in the other bedside table. It's 9am. Jeez. I could have slept another hour and a half. Man!

The bathroom is nicely appointed. Not bad for a whacko joint. I have a shower and a bath. They are separate from each other. Not bad. My toiletries are arranged on a shelf above the sink. Not bad at all.

I need a leak. I pull down my tracksuit pants and let rip. God it feels good! Whoa! I didn't realise I needed that. I suppose I have stored up a small dam over the past 24 hours. I look at my dick. Yep it's a dick that any guy would be proud to own.

"I missed you, big guy! It was weird not having you around. Way too weird. I must have some serious issues. I guess so, because now I am talking to parts of my anatomy. Right…."

Okay, I am not really a bath kind of guy. It's not really my thing. Shower should be good. I turn the faucet and hot water sprays forth. Fantastic, this shower has really excellent pressure. I hate showers that limply spit at you. This one is hard and the spray is going to be aimed directly between my shoulders. Yes!

I get undressed and then decide to shut the bathroom door. It might be my own private room, but it seems people feel just fine to come right on in if they so choose. Holy fuck! There's a mirror on the back of the door. Thank Christ I didn't really see myself - just a lot of pink skin. I need to see a bit of sun.

Now what? I stand with my back to the door. There must be something here. I look around. Yes! Great, there are two bath towels. I grab the one off the rail. It's big. I think it should cover the mirror. I hold the towel in front of my face and turn towards the mirror. I lean forward and feel around the edges of the mirror. Great! It's not fixed at the edges, so I should be able to get the towel behind it. I just have to be careful that I don't pull it off the door. Not that I'd care. I don't want the damn thing in my bathroom, but I'd probably get into shit for pulling it off.

I can't really get the towel behind it properly. I am going to have to figure out a plan B, but hopefully plan A will hold until I am done showering. I back away slowly from the mirror but keep my hands hovering close by in case it slips. Yeah. I think it will hold for a bit.

I step into the hot shower. God it feels good. I get the spray to hit me between my shoulder blades just where I imagined it would be. I put my hands on the wall in front of me and let my head hang down. It feels so good. I must have been sleeping in an awkward position.

I wash myself and check through the shower door to see if the towel is still over the mirror. It looks good. I step out of the shower and grab the other towel. I am not going to stay in the bathroom with the door shut in case that towel slips off the mirror. If someone comes into the room and sees me in all my naked glory so be it. They will have to deal with it. That concerns me a lot less than the mirror.

I towel myself dry and pad through the bedroom to the closet. I pick out a pair of black boxers and jeans for Sister Jean. I made a joke. Not a good one it's true – and a brown shirt. I locate my sneakers at the bottom of the closet and a pair of socks in a drawer in the closet.

I must say I am feeling better than I have in a while. I grab my wallet and flick through. I have a few bills and some coins. I should count myself lucky that no one snuck in here and nicked it while I was out of it. I would have done. I shove the wallet in my back pocket and return to the bathroom.

Yes bathroom. I have returned to face you once again! Yeah, I am being truly corny today, but I kinda feel happy. I guess it's that appointment with my psychiatrist.

Maybe at long last I will learn what the fuck is wrong with me, because waking up every day or so as a different person is really starting to get to me in a really bad way. I don't think I can cope with it for much longer.

Yes! There's a tub of hair gel. My mom doesn't miss a beat! I scoop a glob out and run it through my hair. I then mess my hair up. It's out-dated I know, but I like the messy, I-don't-give-a-shit look. I wash the gel off my hands in the sink and slap on some aftershave – not that I have shaved, but you never know who I might need to impress today and I need to smell my rosy best.

Yep, it's another bright sunshiny day. The corridor outside my room is lined with windows and they are all open to let the summer air in. I locate the vending machine at the end of the corridor and select a pack of Marlboro's. I slip the pack into my shirt pocket. I don't want these bad boys to get crushed. I am looking forward to my after dining smoke. I grab a box of matches from the machine as well.

I enter the dining area. I recognise the three checkers guys from yesterday and there's my little buddy, Bradley.

"Hey Bradley."

"You're a mean statue, man."

"Yeah, sorry about yesterday. You Okay, buddy?"

"Yeah."

I walk over to the self-serve. I feel like having a big breakfast today. I get two eggs over easy, some toast, bacon, a sausage, fried tomatoes, mushrooms and hash browns. It smells great. I start to salivate as I make my way to the coffee counter. Some serious shit comes out of the coffee machine. It's as thick as mud. Holy crap! Well if that doesn't stop me from 'falling asleep' nothing will. It smells good, but I am sure it tastes like cow turd.

I am not really in the mood to chat today, especially

since I don't know anyone and Bradley will get on my tits, so I find a table at the back of the dining hall where I can sit and observe.

I tuck into breakfast and its good, but my prediction about the coffee was right. I have to wash it down with mouthfuls of food. I am too busy eating to pay attention to those around me, but once I am done, I sit back and survey my 'home'.

Most of the people are really weird. I don't know how I am going to fit in here. I look at each of them. There's a mixture of men and women of different ages, sitting at tables. Some of them are talking to others, some are staring into space, and others are making repetitive movements. One guy is poking his food and the rest of his food is dribbling down his chin and onto his shirt. Gross, it's really disgusting. I am glad I ate before I saw that. I need to get out of here. I grab my tray and stack it. I make my way down the corridor, past my room and eventually meet up with another corridor. I follow this one and end up in the common room I was in yesterday. Well at least something already looks familiar. There's not a whole lot to this place.

I look at the table I was sitting at yesterday. It's weird how I was in a totally different frame of mind yesterday to now. Hey, I am a totally different person today, well not really, but in my head I am. As I am not a kidnap victim, I can safely pass out through the door into the garden.

Man, the sun is bright. I hope mom packed my shades. I could really use them. I will have to call her and ask her to bring some when she visits if they are not in my room somewhere already. I squint and look painfully around the garden for a bench under a tree or something. It's a very pretty garden, but I am sure I'd appreciate it through my shades a whole lot more. There are a lot of buildings around here. I guess they are different wards or something. There are a couple of trees, but none that I can see with a bench underneath. I spot a low wall that runs part way under a tree. That will have to do. I make my way there. I take a seat and cup my hands to light my smoke. There's a breeze today so it is not so easy to light up. A lighter would be easier. I keep inhaling and lighting matches. When the cigarette catches, it takes me by surprise. I end up coughing. Man! It must have been a long time. I feel like my lungs are going to come out. It will pass though.

"What the fuck?"

I look over the wall and see a pair of angry eyes staring at me.

"There's nowhere you can go in this hell hole to get some peace."

I just stare at the girl. She is hot! She has got pale skin with long, dark hair and piercing blue eyes. She has piercings through her eyebrow, nose and lower lip, as well as several in both of her ears. A tattoo of a dragon winds its way along one of her arms and up the side of her neck. She is dressed in black - a black top, skirt, stockings and boots. There's a tattoo on her left forearm, but I don't get to see it, because she stands up and stalks away from me.

I feel so embarrassed to be coughing in front of her like a newb. Fuck. That is no way to make a first impression. I watch as she walks away and eventually disappears behind a building. This place may not be so bad after all.

I look at the time. I have an hour to kill before I have to try to find out where I have to meet this psychiatrist. I am looking forward to seeing him. But it can also wait. I sit in a comfortable position; drag slowly on my smoke and think of nothing.

10

I take a look at my watch. It's 10:45. It's a little later than I would have liked, because I don't want to miss this appointment. I notice a vending machine stacked with soft drinks under the shade of the roof of the building across from me. I walk over a select a can of coke. I crack it open. Boy does it taste good! I don't think I have had one of these either for a long time - probably not for five months.

I make my way back to my building and it takes some time for my eyes to adjust to the dimmer light after the glare of the day. I walk through the common room, but there is no one there. I walk along the corridors and pop into my room, but I don't see anyone. I make my way to the dining room and notice there's a short corridor leading off to the left just before the dining room door. I hadn't really noticed that this morning. I walk down it. There are several office doors. I knock on the door marked Sister Jean.

"Come in."

I turn the knob and push the door open.

"Oh, hi Richard, what can I do for you?"

"I have that appointment with that doctor guy."

"Yes, right. Do you know where to go?"

"Nope."

"Okay. Follow me, I'll take you there."

"Thanks."

She closes the file she is working on and steps out of the office. I follow her back outside and we walk past two buildings before entering a third one. The first thing that greets me is a waiting room fronted by a receptionist.

"This is Richard Carter. He is here to see Dr. Tsakonas at 11am."

"Sure no problem. Thank you, Sister. Richard, you can take a seat. Dr. Tsakonas will be with you shortly."

"Bye, Richard."

"Bye."

I sit down on one of the blue waiting-room chairs. There's a bunch of magazines on the table in front of me. They all look pretty mundane. There are a lot of chick mags – I bet that girl I saw today wouldn't be caught dead reading one of these. I push them aside and find some car and sport magazines. Neither of these genres are really my scene. I find an old Rolling Stone magazine at the bottom of the pile.

That's more like it. I sit back and flip through it. It's from three months back. I check out all the movies and music I have missed. Pretty sad really. I don't have long to wait.

"Richard Carter?"

"Yes."

"I am Doctor Tsakonas."

A shortish man – well he is a couple inches shorter than me – greets me. He has dark hair with a bald patch making its way increasingly known at the back of his head. He has a goatee and his sideburns are turning grey so I guess he is in his forties. He is wearing black-framed glasses, a white shirt, grey pants and loafers. He has a nice expression in his dark eyes. I think I am going to be okay with this guy.

"Hi."

"Please follow me. Do you recognise me?"

"I am sorry, I don't."

"I have been treating you for the past five months. I see you once a week."

"Okay."

"I have been treating you with different

antipsychotic drugs and I guess we have found the one that works, or the drugs you have taken have finally left your system, or both. Please take a seat."

He stands at the doorway to his office. I walk past him and sit in one of the chairs that are arranged in the middle of the room. At the other end of the room is his desk and rows of bookshelves overflowing with books. The carpet is a light grey and the walls of his office are a teal colour. It wouldn't be my choice of colouring. He has some abstract art paintings on the walls and a coffee table with four chairs around it. A large rubber-leaf-type plant sits in a pot in the corner.

"Taking in my office, I see."

"Yeah, it's okay. The colour-scheme is not my scene though."

"Nor mine," he says as he takes a seat across from me. He picks up a file from the table and leafs through it. I notice my name is on it. He grabs a pen.

"So, Richard. Tell me how you are doing?"

"Fine, I guess."

"You guess?"

"Yeah, well I apparently woke up for the first time in five months yesterday and I am here and I don't know how I got here."

"Your parents brought you in after you had taken an overdose of barbiturates."

"An overdose? Was I trying to commit suicide?"

"No, we don't think so. It seems that you had been taking them for a number of years and you obviously were growing accustomed to them, so you probably misjudged how many to take."

"Was I in a coma or something?"

"No, you came to fairly quickly after appropriate interventions were administered, but you remained in a catatonic state until now."

"A what?"

"A kind of waking sleep is the best way to describe it. You were awake, but completely unresponsive."

"Whoa! That's heavy. I don't remember any of that. Nothing. How did I eat?"

"Sometimes you would eat and at other times we fed you and administered various anti-psychotic medications to you through a drip. It seems that the latest dosage is more effective. Did you take your meds today?"

"No, no one gave me anything."

"It's not good to miss your meds. We don't want you to slip back again. I am sure the staff weren't sure what to give you since you woke up. Let me write a script for you and just hand it in to the sister on duty and she will make sure you get what you need. I think I am going to keep the dosage at what it is for now. It seems to be working well for you. I don't want to stop medication for the moment."

The doctor hands me a script. I fold it up and put it in my pocket.

"Have you been to a psychiatrist before? Do you know how things work?"

"Yes, I've been seeing one for five months now, but the mechanisms of the process seem to have slipped my mind."

The doctor laughs, "I see you have quite a sense of humour. Let me ask you a question: do you have any memories at all or thoughts from the past five months?"

"No, but I have had some vivid dreams that are so long and so detailed that it seems that I have been living them. They are as real as sitting here with you right now is and they are fucking long and detailed and really boring and mundane for the most part, with some horrible parts thrown in."

"Tell me what you mean by long, boring and mundane."

"Okay, for starters I will end up going to the toilet in my dreams and getting dressed and I don't know, picking out what I am going to wear and what I am going to eat and shit like that. You know like stuff in ordinary life. It's really weird, because in the dreams that I have had in the past they are sort of more, what can I say........ they are more symbolic, I guess. They are not so detailed. It's not like I can remember every little thing that I do to get through my day."

"And you have never had dreams like this before?"

"No. Never. And they don't feel like dreams. They feel so real. Like when I move from one dream to the next it's really confusing, because the last dream seemed so real and then the next one seems so real that it takes time to adjust between dreams. And I am different people in each dream, but I don't realise this immediately, so I still think I am the person I was, but I am not anymore. I am someone else, but it takes time to realise that. Like, I have to wait for other people in my dream to tell me who I am, or it takes time to get my bearings and then I start to remember who I am by looking at things. I don't know if I am making sense?"

"Yes, you are. You are saying that you have been having extremely long dreams that seem so real and each time you wake up, you are a different person, but you don't know this initially and it is very confusing for you. Am I getting this?"

"Yes. Like even now, Doc. Sorry, do you mind if I call you Doc, your last name is really hard to pronounce?"

"Doc is fine. Go on."

"Like right now, Doc, this doesn't feel any different

from the dreams, so how can I be sure I am not dreaming?"

"Because you are awake and talking to me right now, Richard. I have seen you in a catatonic state for the past five months. You have been here the whole time and you have been nobody else but you?"

"Can you explain this catatonic thing to me, Doc?"

"It's a state of non-responsiveness. It can manifest in different ways for different people and there are different causes for it. We think that yours was brought on by prolonged drug abuse. Generally, you would wake up in the morning. You would have to be dressed and then led to the dining room. If a plate of food was placed in front of you, you would sometimes eat it. Sometimes you wouldn't eat it, but you would let someone else feed you. At other times you wouldn't eat for days and then we would feed you through a drip. You would generally spend your day sitting in one position until someone took you to use the toilet, eat, bath or sleep."

"For five months?"

"Yes, for five months. I am going to be frank with you, Richard, we weren't sure we would be able to help you, because everything we tried, didn't seem to work. Your parents were insistent that we keep trying. You are on very high doses of antipsychotic medication and we have also had to use ECT."

"ECT?"

"Yes, basically passing a current of electricity through your brain."

"You fried my brain?"

"Yes, it sometimes helps to rewire the circuitry so to speak. We don't fully understand how. But in your case it seems to be working. I wanted to fill you in on what's been happening to you. I don't believe in keeping things from my patients. In any case, you will end up hearing it from one of the other patients and I would rather you heard it from me. How are you feeling about all this?"

"Man, it's a lot to take in."

"I know it is. I have been seeing you once a week, but since you've come out of that state, I'd like to see you every day this week, if that's all right with you?"

"Sure, I have wanted to know what is wrong with me and if you can help me... yeah, absolutely, I'll be here every day this week. Sure."

"Tell me if you can. When did these dreams start? I know it is hard to give a time frame for a dream, but if you can that might be useful information."

"That one is a real easy question, Doc. Excluding yesterday, which is/was reality, five days."

"So it feels like you have been having these very vivid, yet mundane dreams for the past five days?"

"Yep."

"Right, that might be useful...... Mmm, I will ask the nursing staff if they saw anything unusual in you over the past five days. It may have been that you have been coming out of this state over that time. Have you had any periods of lucidity in between the dreams?"

"I am not quite sure what you mean. I felt pretty lucid for all the dreams."

"No, what I mean is did you have any moments when you were aware of the hospital around you?"

"This place?"

"Yes."

"Nope. I don't recall seeing it during my dreams at all."

"That's fine. I am just trying to understand what has happened here."

The Doc scribbles notes in his file. I watch him for a

while and then stare into space. The sound of his pen on the page is kind of soothing and for the first time in a long time, I feel safe and that the world makes sense. At last someone is taking the time to find out what is going on with me. I like this Doc guy. He seems cool. There's something about him that I feel I can trust. I hope that we are going to figure things out and I can get my life back on track.

"Sorry about that. I just don't want to forget anything about what you have said. How are you feeling so far?"

"Okay, well, pretty relieved actually. I have been so confused the past couple of days and it's just really good to have someone at last who I can talk to about all this."

"We are going to figure this out together. You and me."

"Great."

"Tell me about your dreams. Maybe we can figure out what has been going on in your head the past few days."

"Okay, they are long and well, long. I don't know where to start."

"Are they kind of confusing, like bits and pieces here and there?"

"No. They are quite separate. Um, I guess I'll start with the first one."

"Go on."

"Well, I kind of woke up and I was this kid with shitty parents. Well, my mom was kind of dozy and my dad was an asshole."

"Try to go into as much detail as you can."

"I guess we were living somewhere rural and we had a farm – a pig farm. And my dad would beat me. In fact when I woke up in the dream, it had been after he had beaten me and I was really sore. He didn't seem to give a

shit though and I didn't want him to know I was sore –
you know, to show him how much he had hurt me – but
it was really hard, because he had hurt me a lot. And my
mom didn't seem to care much. She was kind of switched
off. Then I had to go with my dad out onto the farm and
he made me muck out the pigsty while he went drinking
with a buddy of his. I did everything I had to and then
had time to play with my favourite little pig. I had named
him Wilbur. When my dad came back, he had gone mad
with rage and he killed Wilbur. He came at me with the
pick and I…….. I thought he was going to kill me and
then I woke up into another dream as some neurotic
lady."

"Go on. I hope you don't mind if I take notes while
you are talking?"

"It's okay."

"I don't want to miss anything. Everything you say is
important and if we can get to the bottom of all this then
maybe we can make you feel better."

"Sounds good, Doc."

"Please go on. I am not going to go into the meaning
of these dreams today. I would rather hear all about them
and then we can look at them and how they relate to your
life tomorrow if you can hang on until then."

"It's fine with me, Doc. I am just glad to be awake
and to know who I am and to not be dreaming or be
catatonic again."

"So tell me about the neurotic lady."

"Well, she was kind of out of it. Well, I guess I was
kind of out of it, because I wasn't really sure who I was
and I ended up missing work the day I woke up in that
dream. I was married to an asshole. But I couldn't
remember this or know that I was married to him, until
he called me to remind me that his boss was coming for

dinner. Then I was freaked out because I didn't remember his name until the maid told me. Then I got really involved in trying to make the best dinner on earth for him and his boss and he was such a shit to me, but in the end it turned out that apparently I was a shit. But it was really confusing, because I was so nervous all the time and everything would scare me. Then the next day I was really out of it, but I was trying to work hard and be good at what I was doing and then my boss fired me and I kind of went hysterical and then I passed out."

"This was the second dream then?"

"Yes."

"How long did it last?"

"I think two days."

"And the dream of the boy?"

"That I am not sure of. I don't know if I had been dreaming that one for a really long time or if it was just one day."

"That's fine, and after the dream of the lady?"

"Well, after the dream of the lady, I woke up into another dream, where I was an old lady, which really freaked me out. I was getting really confused. It was like one of those dreams where you think you have woken up only to find that you were dreaming and that you weren't awake in the first place. You know - the never-ending cycle. Anyway, so I am now freaked out because I don't know I am an old lady, I still think I am the neurotic chick and I think that my boss is talking to me after I passed out, but it's another old lady, who fetches a nurse, because she thinks I passed out and they decide that I passed out, because I missed tea. And I am this really sad, lonely old lady, who has lost her whole family and she is all alone in the world, with no one to really care for her. And she hangs onto these photos of her family like they are the most precious things in the world. It was really sad. Anyways, she goes to bed one night and then she thinks she is being attacked in her bed. Then she woke up here and thought that the attacker was a kidnapper, who had brought her here and then she or I was trying to escape. Then Sister Jean explained to me that in fact I was not a little old lady and here I am talking to you – well after I passed out again. It was quite hectic to find out that I wasn't a granny anymore."

"And how long did that dream last, about two days?"

"Yes."

"That's all very interesting. I think we will stop for today, if that's all right with you? I am going to think about this and we will meet tomorrow again, once I have given it some thought."

"That's great. Thanks, Doc."

The Doc grabs his diary.

"Let me see. We can meet at 2pm tomorrow. Is that okay?"

"Yep. I am not going anywhere."

"Great. I'll see you then. Don't forget to hand that script to the nurse and please take it easy. Don't get too stressed out. We have done good work for today."

"Great. Thanks, Doc."

"Enjoy the rest of your day, Richard."

"Trust me, I plan to. See you tomorrow, Doc, and thanks."

"Bye, Richard."

"Later."

As I walk out the office, I feel so much better. Yes, I am in a messed up situation. I obviously screwed up my mind, but at least I am awake and not dreaming anymore and I know exactly who I am. It is the most amazing feeling. It's like I was carrying a heavy sack around with me and now all of a sudden it's gone and the world seems so much better and I feel so much better.

I really don't want to mess things up now, so I decide to follow through with what the Doc ordered. I walk back to my ward and hand in my script to Sister Jean. She assures me that she will sort out my meds. One bonus of being in a psychiatric hospital is that I don't need to take care of myself. It's all done for me. I just have to show up and follow instructions. It feels so much better than having those dreams where I felt I had to fight to survive. I need some much needed rest, even if they were just dreams. Dreams can be intense like that sometimes. I remember when I was a kid and having fever dreams, where I thought I was awake and seeing things, so this is no different.

One thing's for damn sure. I am not going to take any more drugs unless they are prescription.

I wonder back to the wall in the garden, but that chick is not there. In fact, no one is around. That's okay too. I sit down and light up another cigarette. This one is a lot smoother and I relax and enjoy the view of the garden and the taste of the cigarette.

After a while, I walk back to my ward. Some guy is sitting in the common area reading a book. I take a chance that he is not too loopy and ask him what people do for fun around here. He mentions a number of things, but the only option that appeals to me is going to watch TV in a ward across from us. TV sounds good; I don't feel like eating lunch.

The TV room is comfortable. There are couches and beanbags scattered around. The windows are open, so it is not too stuffy. A middle-aged woman is sitting there staring at the screen and rocking back and forth. She seems to have a glassy look in her eyes. She is watching infomercials, but she doesn't seem to be taking them in. There's no fucking way I am watching infomercials. I wait a bit. She just keeps on rocking, so I take the remote from the table and flick through the channels. I find a movie channel that seems to be showing some cool stuff. I choose a cop thriller and settle into a beanbag and put my feet up on the table. After a while the rocking lady takes off. That is great, because I have the TV to myself until I get called to dinner.

That's my kind of day.

11

I stroll out into the garden for a smoke after breakfast. I seem to be establishing a routine. I go over to my wall and that chick is there. Boy is she hot! Maybe there is some bonus about being in this place and going through all this after all. I get to meet someone new. I check her out. She is petite but fiery. She does not seem to notice me as she gazes off into the distance and smokes. She is wearing leggings under a mini-skirt and high lace-up boots. She has a vest on with no bra and everything she is wearing is black. She has a lot of black eyeliner on, but it looks really cool. It makes her brown eyes stand out from her pale skin. Her hair has been died black and is kind of messy. She is so sexy. The sexiest part about her is that she has a blue dragon winding up her right arm and its head is resting under her chin. Did I mention she isn't wearing a bra? She has great tits – about a size C (I never get this wrong) – and I can see the soft outline of her nipples pressing against the fabric of her vest top.

"What are you looking at asshole?"

"That's a great tattoo."

"Didn't look to me like you were looking at my tattoo."

"So what are you here for?"

"Don't you think that's a little personal, pervert?"

Yes definitely fiery!

"Just trying to make conversation."

"Do I look like I want to have a conversation with you?"

"Actually yeah, you do."

"You are arrogant and a pervert."

"I am a package deal."

"A fucking comedian too I see."

"But yet here you are still talking to me."

"Yeah, whatever, maybe I am bored."

"Yeah? Well, I am bored too."

"I haven't seen you around here before. Not till you came to disturb my spot."

"Looks like we like the same things."

"Did I mention that you are annoying as shit too."

"Nope, but I am enjoying your appraisal of my personality. I have been here for five months."

"Really? This the first time you dared to come out into the garden? What do you have a fear of the wide open scary outdoors?"

"Nah. I OD'ed on drugs and have been in a sort of coma. I just came out of it now."

'Heavy. Do you have any on you?"

"No, firstly, how would I have managed that in a coma? And second, I don't want to mess my brain up anymore."

"Speak for yourself. This place is no fun without a bit of help."

"Is that why you are here?"

"It's none of your god-damn business why I am here."

She gets up.

"Stay away from my fucking spot!"

"I like this spot so I don't know if I will."

She storms off.

I am intrigued. I like hectic chicks. In fact, I think they are the only girls I have ever dated. They seem so tough on the outside, but when you get to know them they aren't tough at all. They just give everyone else a hard time, but not me. I am definitely going to get to know this chick. She doesn't know this yet, but I will. I think she can be really deep. Anyway, I need someone to talk to besides the Doc, otherwise I am going to go crazy with all the loonies around here. This chick seems pretty sane. But now that she's gone, there is not a whole lot I can do.

I sit on the wall and light up my smoke and chill. Then I wonder around the garden. It's a nice day. The garden is cool, but I get bored after a while. I decide to explore the layout of the place. It's pretty okay for a loony bin. I find an old rusty hoop at the back of some kind of tool room. I wouldn't mind shooting some hoops and so I go back inside my ward to the common room to see if there is anything around there. Nothing. I ask the young guy, who was reading a book when I first woke up, and he tells me to ask the sister so I go round back to Sister Jean's office.

"Hi Richard. I've been looking for you. Take a seat. We need to talk."

"Okay….. What's up?"

"Dr. Tsakonas wanted me to inform your parents that you are out of your catatonic state now and so I gave them a call. They would like to see you. Would you be up for seeing them this afternoon after your appointment with Dr. Tsakonas, or would you like to wait until tomorrow?"

"I am good. They can come after my appointment with the Doc. I haven't seen them for five months, so yeah."

"Great. I will tell them that they can come at around 4pm. That will give you a bit of time in case anything hectic comes up in your session with Dr. Tsakonas."

"Sure, great. Um, Sister Jean, is there a basketball around anywhere? I feel like shooting some hoops."

"Yes. I hang onto the ball, so that it does not get

lost. You need to sign a form saying that you are taking the ball and will replace it should anything happen to it."

"You run a tight ship here, Sister!"

She doesn't respond to my comment. She goes to her cupboard and pulls out a form, which I duly sign.

"Thanks! I'll treat it as if it were my own. Don't worry I will return it."

The woman has no sense of humour, but besides that, she's okay.

"Thank you. And Richard?"

"Yes?"

"Please take it easy. You haven't exercised in a really long time."

"Don't worry."

I walk back to the patch of cement with the hoop and shoot some hoops. I get most of them in, which I guess is not bad for a guy who has been sitting on his ass for five months. The exercise makes me feel good. I like the feeling of the ball in my hands and the blood circulating at a faster pace through my veins. I can feel that I am not in top form, but it is amazing to move. I feel alive and it feels damn good!

I run around the small area and toss the ball into the hoop until I am too tired to go on. I am not sure how long I have been doing this. I squint up at the sky and the sun is pretty high up so I guess it must be near noon. I definitely want some lunch today.

I take a quick shower before I head to the dining room for lunch and loony-watching. Some people watch TV while they eat. I like to observe the crazies around me.

There is a guy staring at his plate and not eating or moving. I must have been like that. There's another guy, who looks like a hobo. He is wearing really tattered clothes and talking to himself. My favourite is the lady, who sits in the corner and just wrings her hands. Okay, there aren't many people to watch. Most of the people around here just look bored or depressed or both. Watching them, however, is not fun at all, so I would rather look at the guy talking to himself or the lady wringing her hands. I wonder why she does that? The only explanation I can come up with is that she used to be a washer woman until they brought her to this shithole and now she is still sitting there washing her clothes like she used to back when she was free.

The hobo guy; I think must have had a really good job as the CEO of some major corporation. I reckon he then got involved in some seriously shady deals and made a small fortune for himself. He took his two kids and his wife away on some bling holidays and did a lot of drugs and alcohol on the way. Then one day, the alcohol and drugs start to fry his brain slowly, like on a slow roast and so he doesn't realise this is what's happening to him. He thinks everything is peachy, but his wife is unhappy and she is sleeping with their landscaper and the five year old and three year old have found his secret stash of booze and drugs and are dealing at their kindergarten. So, his life is starting to rot away on the inside, but he doesn't even know it. Then one day, some police officers arrive at his door, say during family dinner, and take him away. They arrest him for corruption and fraud or whatever. He gets sentenced to ten years in the slammer. Then his wife remarries – it's to the landscaper of course. His kids don't want to see him now he's broke. He gets out of jail and he is flat broke. No one wants to hire him, because they all know he's a crook – they've read the papers – and he has no money at all. Well, just a little stash that they never found out about, but now he's so depressed that he doesn't know what he wants to do with himself anymore, so he starts drinking and lives on a bench in the park until one day, by sheer chance, one of his kids finds him and recognises him, despite his filth. They take pity on him and bring him here and so there we are. Yip, I reckon that's his story.

Now for the guy staring at his plate and not eating, um, I think he had a shock. Yes, that's what happened to him. It must have been at dinnertime and now he associates all eating with that one event. He came home to his wife and she made him dinner like she always does, but this time there's no wife, just dinner. This is unusual. She is always there. But not tonight – dinner, but no wife. He wonders around the house looking for her and hears something in the bedroom. Just a muffled sound, not very distinct. He doesn't know why, but his suspicions are aroused, so he walks slowly and quietly to the bedroom. The door is ajar, but it's not wide enough for him to see anything. He quietly pushes the door open and is greeted by the sight of his wife getting it on with their German Shepherd!

I kill myself, really I do! I burst out laughing. The people at my table scowl at me and continue eating. Fuck, I should be a comedian! I can't stop laughing and it's bad, because everyone looks so serious. That makes me want to laugh more. I can't look at the guy, who isn't eating. I grab my plate and my glass and head outside. I am sure I am not supposed to do this, but I can't stay in there. Maybe I am going as nuts as everyone else here. I finish off my lunch, but my stories, which I made up just then, don't seem so funny anymore. I am glad that chick is not in my ward with me. If she had seen me just then, I'd never stand a chance. Nope, not a snowball's hope in hell.

It'll be time to see the Doc soon. Oh shit, I forgot to

hand the ball in. I take my plate through to the kitchen and retrieve the ball and hand it over to Sister Jean. I make my way down to the Doc's office and stop for another smoke. That girl is nowhere to be seen. Bummer.

The Doc seems very happy to see me and I feel really comfortable with him already. His office is already starting to feel familiar and I select the same chair I sat in yesterday.

"How are you feeling today?"

"Good, Doc, thanks, apart from being in this crazy place. Well, I guess I belong here what with all the catatonic stuff and that."

"Do you feel like you are crazy?"

"Ah… yeah. Why else would I be here first off and second off, I have never heard of anyone who clocks out for five months and then clocks in again after having some weird dreams where they were a chick. Yip, I definitely think I am crazy, but maybe not as crazy as some of the folk here."

"Are you feeling isolated?"

"Sure, a little, yeah."

"I hear your parents are going to come through later for a visit. How are you feeling about that?"

"It will be good to see them. You know, they are parents and parents can be difficult, but they are still my parents, so I am glad they are coming through."

"Is there anyone here you could talk to – you know – hang out with?"

"Well, there is this hot Goth chick that I kind of dig, but she thinks I am scum right now so it's more of a chase."

"Do you like the chase?"

"Sure, what guy doesn't?"

"Some guys don't."

"I like the chase."

"Do you get bored once you have made your catch?"

"No, not really. I guess after all the chasing, it's worth holding onto what I have pursued."

"Well, let me know how things go in that department – good or bad."

"Thanks, Doc, I'll keep you posted, if anything comes up."

"How do you get on with your parents?"

"Does anyone get on with their parents? My Dad has always put a lot of pressure on me to achieve and my Mom has always been kind of social, but otherwise my parents have been as good as anyone else's. They've done a lot for me"

"Explain to me what you mean by social?"

"Well, my Mom was one of the really popular girls at school and she hasn't changed really, I suppose. She always wanted to have a family and only managed to have me. She lost three other babies after I was born. I guess that was hard for her. She also really likes to socialise. She is always going to parties and hanging out at the bridge club and the tennis club and she also belongs to a charity organisation. They help homeless kids. It's really good work. They have raised a lot of funds for them to go to school and to improve the home and assist with adoptions and stuff like that."

"So she mainly is involved with the fundraising side of things?"

"Yeah. They have raffles and socials and approach corporations for sponsorship and stuff like that."

"Do you spend much time with her?"

"Doc, I am in my early twenties. What guy in his early twenties wants to hang out with his Mom all day?"

"Point taken" The Doc Laughs. "Did you spend

much time with her growing up?"

"Like, was she involved in my life?"

"Yes."

"Yeah, I guess she was. She always came to the Little League games that I played in when I was a kid and tennis games when I got into senior school. We went on holidays together. She read to me at night. So yeah, I reckon my Mom was a good Mom. She was always there."

"So both you and your Mom enjoy tennis?"

"My Mom enjoys tennis. Me not so much, but I had to do some kind of sport growing up. All kids do Little League and tennis was the best option for me when I got older. I really didn't see the point of busting my neck and back chasing a ball around a pitch and being all superficial like the jocks. I am not a jock. That mucho crap is not my style."

"Do you play any sport now?"

"Nah, not really. I shoot some hoops occasionally. It works off stress or boredom. Actually, I shot off a few today."

"Stressed or bored?"

"Bored. There's not a lot to do round here – just eat, sleep, shoot some hoops, read or watch the tube."

"Do you have any hobbies that you like? Maybe you could work on those while you are here."

"Nah, I am not really your stamp-collecting kind or your model-building kind."

"What do you like to do in your free time?"

"Honestly, Doc?"

"Yes, honestly?"

"I like to smoke dope, pop pills and listen to music."

"What kind of music?"

"Metal. Any metal. I am not fussy in that regard."

"And studying?"

"I was studying. My father wanted me to do a business degree."

"What happened?"

"I started out as a freshman, but never saw the year out. It was really boring. I couldn't imagine doing that for the rest of my life."

"So what did you do after you dropped out of school?"

"I have been taking the last, um, let's see, three years off to think about what I want to do"

"Any ideas"

"Nope, not yet."

"Who supports you?"

"My folks do. I still live at home."

"What have you been doing the last three years?"

"Hanging with my loser friends and doping."

"Would you classify yourself as a loser?"

"Totally."

"Why do you say that?"

"Come on, Doc. I don't have a job. I mooch off my parents. I think that classifies."

"Have you felt depressed?"

"Over the last three years?"

"Yes."

"Over my whole life more like. I think I have always been depressed."

"Do you know why?"

"Not really. I just am that kind of guy. That's why I like to hang out with the dark kids – the Goths. Life is depressing."

"Are your parents depressed?"

"I have never really thought about it. I don't think so. They are both really busy. I am not, so I have time to be depressed."

"What does your father do?"

"He's a Chartered Accountant. He is one of the bigwigs at a big accounting firm. He worked his way up there. It's really a huge accomplishment."

"How would you describe your relationship with your father?"

"He's a good guy. He works really hard. He deserves every cent he has earned."

"That's describing your father, Richard. What is your relationship with him like?"

"Oh, right. He is a busy man. He's not home much. You know, he gets home late from the office and then he's really tired. He works Saturdays, but he has always tried to be around on Sundays."

"Did you spend time with him on Sundays growing up?"

"Sure, my Mom and Dad and I would always have something going on on a Sunday. My parents like to socialise. I think it's how my Mom helps to support my Dad and he supports her that way too, so we would always meet people and go for lunch and dinner and hang out. It's really good for business."

"So the three of you would never do much together, just the three of you?"

"Yeah, we would. Sometimes we would have breakfast together and sometimes dinner. Sometimes we would go to a movie. Sometimes my Dad would come to my games."

"How have your parents reacted to you taking the last three years off and doping, as you call it?"

"They are not happy and we fight all the time, but it's not like I want to do this. Seriously, Doc, if I could find what I wanted to do, I would go for it. I would be happier if I could figure out what I wanted to do, but nothing appeals. I don't like the arts, I don't like business and I don't like sports. That rules out pretty much everything."

"So you are saying that you are stuck and there's no way to get out of this. What is going to happen in the end?"

"My parents will probably get fed up with me and kick me out of the house and I'll be a bum on the street."

"Have they said that they would kick you out?"

"They have threatened me several times, but nothing has happened so far, but I am sure they will get there eventually."

"Are you pushing them to kick you out the house?"

"Now why on earth would I do that? It's great there and being a bum is not so great. I don't think so, Doc."

"I ask, because they have threatened to kick you out, unless you start working towards your career, but you aren't."

"What am I supposed to do? If I start something that I do not like, then I end up wasting the old man's money and he doesn't enjoy that."

"What would you need from your parents, Richard? What do they need to do to help you out?'

I can't think at all. What would they need to do to help me out? What would I need from them? My automatic response would be to tell the Doc nothing. That I want nothing from them, but I don't think that that is true.

The Doc just looks at me. We sit in silence for what seems like ages and nothing comes into my head. I don't know what I need from them.

"I don't know what to say, Doc. I want to say that I want nothing from them, but I don't think that that is true somehow. I don't know why. I just know, but nothing is coming into my head."

"That's fine. I am going to leave it here today and I will see you the same time tomorrow."

"Sure, my diary is pretty booked up, but I reckon I could squeeze you in then."

"Your parents are coming round this afternoon. Maybe that will help you figure out what you need from them. I'll see you tomorrow. Take care of yourself. Don't forget your meds as well."

"No problem. Thanks, Doc. See you tomorrow."

I have an hour to kill before my parents arrival. I go back to my favourite wall to see if the Goth chick is there, but disappointingly, she's not. I guess I am more than she can handle right now. I walk to the vending machine, grab a coke and then walk back to the wall for a soothing smoke. The act of inhaling and exhaling cigarette smoke is somehow very soothing and almost meditative, especially if it's done outside. Maybe that's why the Native Americans used to smoke tobacco. They were a very spiritual people.

I amble back to the common room, where apparently, I find out, is where we meet our visitors. No visitors are allowed in bedrooms in case people decide to slip patients dope or have wild sex. My parents would do neither. Actually, that's a really gross thought!

The three original checkers players are playing their game and arguing as usual. Otherwise, the common room is empty. I am glad. I don't want people to overhear my conversation with my parents. And I think the three guys are too involved to pay any attention to me. They didn't even notice when I walked in the room.

I get bored waiting for my parents and so I walk over to the bookshelves. I am not really in the mood for reading a book. I actually don't have the energy right now. I don't have enough energy to start a whole book and nothing really grabs me. I find an old Batman comic. He's one of my favourite cartoon characters – really dark and tortured – so I take that over to the couch to read.

"Richard, my darling!"

"Hi Mom. Hi Dad."

My mother grabs me in a huge hug. Even the old man gives me a big bear hug. I want to cry. I never want to cry, but just seeing them makes me want to cry. My mother starts crying for me. I swallow my tears back.

My father starts the conversation, because neither my mother nor I are able to talk.

"How are you, son?"

"I am good, Dad."

"You feeling okay after what happened?"

"Actually, I feel fine. I am not in top form, but really not bad, considering."

"That's good…. That's really good."

"Mom, I am okay."

My mother is hysterical. She does not seem to be able to stop crying. I sit down next to her on the couch and hold her. My father continues to stand. He looks around the place.

One of the nurses comes past and hands my mother a glass of water, which she drinks in awkward gulps. I feel a bit embarrassed, but the nurse moves on and I don't really care what the loonies think. My mother blows her nose, dabs her face and then starts to compose herself.

"I'm okay, Mom."

"I know, my darling. I just didn't think I would ever speak to you again like this."

"I am really okay."

"We didn't think you would ever come right again.

132

The doctors told us that the damage was so bad that you would be like this forever. I made them try everything. We even paid for specialists to come in and see you and they all said that you would never be the same person again. They all said that you would be this, this vegetable forever. I made them try everything. I made them give you every medication. They said that the medication could do further damage, but that was not possible. You were so bad. You didn't know who you were. You didn't know your father. You didn't know me. I thought I lost you. I thought you were gone."

My mother starts crying again. I hold her and she cries into my shoulder. My father looks at us and then walks around the room inspecting everything. At that moment, I don't feel anything at all. I have never seen my mother cry like this in my whole life. I don't remember my mother crying ever. Maybe she did cry, like when she lost the babies, but it was never in front of me. I feel very awkward, but I hold her anyway. It seems like a long, long time, before my mother calms down enough to pull away from me, blow her nose and stare at me with her red, puffy eyes. My father stops his pacing and returns to us.

"I am okay now, Mom."

My mother just looks at me.

My father comes to the rescue during the stare. "What have you been doing since you came out of the ah, state thing?"

"There's not much to do here, actually. I have been sitting in the garden. Not many people to talk to round here, really. They're all a bit crazy. I shot some hoops today. Oh, and I have this really cool psychiatrist, who I am talking to. I'm seeing him every day. He is going to try to help me figure out what happened to me."

"That's good. Maybe he can help you figure out how

you got yourself into this mess in the first place."

"Please, Jonathan. Not now!"

"It's okay, Mom. I want to figure that out too. It's been really frightening. I had some really scary dreams before I woke up and I really just want to figure out what has been happening. I don't want to do this again. I really don't. I swear you don't have to worry about me using again. I'll never do it again, I swear."

"I believe you, my darling. I didn't before, but I can see something has changed."

"I swear, Mom and I swear, Dad, that I will never use any drugs again. I won't even drink again. This has been really messed up. I am glad to be me again and I don't want to lose that. I don't want to lose big chunks of my life. I'd never have thought I'd say that, but I don't."

"Are you going to do something with your life, now?"

"Dad, I really want to. I am just scared that I am going to try something and I'll hate it and then you are going to be mad at me for wasting your money."

My father sits down next to me and looks me intensely in the eye. I am feeling a bit nervous. He puts his hand on my shoulder and gives it a squeeze.

"Your mother and I will do everything in our power to help you, Richard. I just want you to get better, get out of here and find something that you like. I may have put pressure on you before to be something you are not and for that, I am sorry. I don't care anymore. Your mother doesn't care anymore. Neither of us cares anymore what you do with your life, Richard, as long as you do something. You can clean windows, if that drives you wild, son. As long as it makes you happy, your mother and I will support you. Things should never get to this point. I don't know what went wrong, but it went badly wrong. We need to pick up and do what needs to be done to move forward from here. Dr. Tsakonas has recommended a therapist for your mother and I to see. Now that you are back to your normal self, we are going to go for therapy and see what we can do to support you. We are there for you, son. Never forget that."

I feel a pressure building from my solar plexus and it pushes up into my throat. I find myself overcome with sobs, as I cry against my father's shoulder. My mother holds me from behind and she is crying too.

I haven't cried since I was a very small boy. It is very strange. It just doesn't feel like me at all, but I let it happen. When I have cried myself out, my father tells me that we will sort this out. That we can get through it.

"When will I get out of here?"

"You've been sick for a long time, Richard. I know it is boring here, but we need to make sure that you are all right before you leave. Can you hang in there a bit more?"

"It's really hard with all the loonies around here and there's nothing to do."

My mother asks, "What can I bring for you, sweetie? Would you like your DVD player or some books? I can bring something through for you tomorrow."

"I wouldn't mind if you brought through my comic book collection."

"Is that all you want, my love?"

"Yeah. I think that's it for now. Thanks Mom. Thanks, Dad. I am sorry I put you guys through this."

"Don't worry about that, son. We are moving forward. We are going to put this behind us."

I say goodbye to my parents. I am so emotionally exhausted. I eat a few bites and then go to bed. I lie down without even getting undressed and fall into a deep sleep.

12

I feel hammered this morning, almost like I have a hangover, but I haven't been drinking. It was all that crying. I am so glad they are all loonies here; otherwise I wouldn't be able to go out my room ever again. It was so weird to cry and to cry as hard as that. I seriously can't remember the last time I cried. I can see why I haven't cried. I feel completely rotten. I will try never to cry again - if I can avoid it.

Breakfast is the same old routine as yesterday. I can't get enthused about making up stories about other people today. I don't bother to look up from my plate. I just eat and leave. I don't have the energy to shoot hoops and I don't have the energy to spar with Goth chick today. I grab my pack of smokes and the Batman comic that I didn't finish yesterday and head out to the area next to the basketball hoop. There are a lot of trees around and it is quiet. No one bothers me. I sit until lunch and read and doze and smoke. I don't think about much at all.

I am keen to skip lunch, but I know that they will worry about me if I don't eat, so I manage to force down a few mouthfuls before retreating back the garden, where I sit until my appointment with the Doc.

"Hi, Richard. How are you doing today? You look a little down."

"I had an intense session with the folks yesterday."

"Do you want to talk about it?"

"Honestly? Nope, I don't."

"It might help you figure things out."

"Ummm, I think that's bullshit."

"Why?"

"What's there to figure out, Doc? I OD'ed and now I have to recover from what I have done. End of story."

"True, I agree, but some of your symptoms, such as your dreams, are worth exploring."

"Worth it for you or for me?"

"For you, Richard. What's going on today? What is making it difficult to talk today?"

"You are what is making it difficult. You fucking shrinks are always digging, digging, digging. It gives me a headache!"

"This is quite a change from yesterday, because the past two sessions you were very keen to talk and sort things out and today you are so angry."

"I don't know why I am angry, but you are right, I am angry."

"Tell me what happened yesterday. Please try. I think it would help."

I sigh. I don't want to relive the whole experience again. I put my head in my hands. I wish the world would just go away for a while. I know I have to deal with this shit and the sooner I do it, the faster I'll be out of this place, but to go through that all again – I just don't think I have the energy for it.

"I saw my parents and I cried."

"I think that is a very healthy and normal reaction under the circumstances."

"Then why do I feel so rotten?"

"Because you have been through a really rotten time."

"And I have put my parents through a really rotten time."

The Doc doesn't say anything. We both just sit here and say nothing. The silence hangs between us. I feel worse. I really have stuffed up badly.

"Why do you think you started using?"

"I guess, because there was nothing else to do,

Doc."

"What do you mean?"

"Well, I didn't and I still don't know what I want to do with my life."

"Is it hard to make a decision?"

"Hell yeah! Nothing appeals, Doc."

"Have you thought broadly about what you would like to do with your life?"

"No offense, Doc, but you really don't know me and you don't know how hard I have thought about what I wanted to do. I have been thinking about it since the Eighth Grade. My parents had suggestions and wishes as to what they wanted me to do as a career, but they aren't the pushy kind and they are not the conditional kind, before you ask me that question. I think they just want me to be happy. I think they just want me to be successful in whatever I do. We would chat about different careers a lot. I have thought about it all."

"Have you considered things out of the mainstream?"

"Let's think: Architect, archaeologist, artist, acupuncturist, bead-worker, babysitter, beekeeper, botanist, bible-basher, butcher, baker, candlestick-maker, carpenter, clairvoyant, chiropractor, chiropodist........."

"I get the point. Have you tried any of those?"

"What is the point, Doc, of trying something that doesn't really appeal and then wasting my father's money on it and my time only to move onto the next thing that appeals and then finding out the same thing?"

"Why do people work?"

"To earn a living."

"Is that the only reason?"

"Pretty much."

"But then I am finding it difficult to understand

what the problem is, because you could then do any of those jobs and you would earn a living."

"Well, it also has to be satisfying."

"So what do you enjoy?"

"Nothing."

"Nothing?"

"Nope, nothing."

"Is that why you started using drugs?"

"Yip."

"What was it like on them?"

"You seriously want to know?"

"Yes, I do."

"Well, it was a rush sometimes, like I had all this energy. Well, that was if I took something to give me a high. I took different kinds of drugs. Some would make me feel really mellow, like the world was just so cool. Some would take me on the most mind-blowing trips. I had some cool trips. I had this one, once, where I was at a house party and the music was really pumping and I took some E. And then I could see lights around everyone and then I was floating around everyone. I could see all these beautiful lights and every person had their own individual light. Like their light was telling me some secret about them. Then I have had some weird stuff that was kind of funny, like when my friend Dave and I took some acid and it looked like his face was all messed up and he looked so weird. I couldn't stop laughing. He kind of looked all deformed."

"You are so much more animated when you talk about your experiences on drugs."

"It beats reality hands down any day, Doc."

"What is the difference between your drug world and your real world, if I can put it that way?"

"Well, the drug world is so much more fun and alive

and how can I put this? Um, let me think...... It's more colourful. Like the colours are brighter and the sounds are more detailed. It's the difference between watching an old black and white TV and a high def TV. It's as different as listening to music on an old record player, where the music is crystal clear, to a cassette tape, where it's all muted and vague. It's an adventure. You never know what is going to happen. It's alive. It's energy."

"And real life?"

"Real life is dull and boring. You know, you have to do dumb things like get up, do the same thing every day, like brush your teeth, go to work, do the same repetitive thing at work every day, come home, eat, watch the same shit on TV every night, sleep. And the next day it cycles all over again. I think you have to be pretty mindless to enjoy that shit."

"You explain it well. I understand how different it is for you – ordinary reality and drug-induced reality. It is interesting how your dreams were about everyday life - I mean the dreams you had before you came out of your catatonic state. Were they different in any way to your drug trips or ordinary life?"

"That's really interesting, Doc. It's kind of weird that I had that kind of dream. It's weird that I dreamt about ordinary life, when I took drugs to get out of ordinary life and I have never had a drug trip that was about ordinary life. Were they different from my ordinary life? Totally! They were so much more hectic."

"I have a question for you and I ask it in the spirit of understanding, rather than as a criticism....."

"Okay."

"Do you think your life has been too easy? I ask this, because you say that your parents have done everything they could for you and you have no problem with them as parents."

"True."

"And I get the impression, though your life has not been perfect, it has not been too bad."

"Well, excluding this current episode, I agree."

"Yes, I want to talk about this episode in a minute."

"Okay."

"I am wondering, Richard, because I am trying to figure out how these dreams fit it. I am wondering if your life has been too easy? Because in those dreams, there has been a great deal of pain and struggle, which, apart from the struggle and pain about not knowing what to do with your life, you have not really experienced. Am I correct? I am just trying to work this out with you."

That is a really interesting question. My life has really been okay. I try to think about things that were horrible and apart from your usual stuff like the occasional fight here and there, it hasn't been too bad.

"I guess you are right, Doc. I haven't really had to struggle and life hasn't really been difficult till now."

"I want to leave you with that thought. I will see you the same time tomorrow."

"Okay, thanks, Doc."

I leave the Doc's office feeling heavy. I haven't really thought about all this stuff before. It's intense. I think the Doc has a point. In those dreams, there was a lot of angst and pain and suffering. I haven't really had that. Well, I haven't had those feelings really except about life in a way. Like life is just dull and that is hard to bear and drugs are just so exciting. I feel more alive when I am drugging than when I am living in reality.

Have I ever really been deprived or had to struggle? No. Not until now and this doesn't feel so great either. I don't really know what to do. I wish I could go back and continue sorting this out with the Doc, but I know he has other people to see besides me. I'll have to hang on until tomorrow. I need to do something. I can't sit around all day and think. I need to be busy. I need to shoot some hoops.

I fetch the ball and walk over to the rusty ring. I pay attention to the bouncing of the ball and the feel of its rough texture in my hands. I love the feeling as my arms snap to release the ball. It's satisfying to get the ball in and frustrating to miss and it keeps me occupied until I am too tired to continue. I wish I could keep going, because it stops me from thinking, but I am too out of shape. I lie on the ground panting and sweating. My throat burns and my legs and arms are stinging and twitching. I lie like this until my body calms down.

I walk over to my wall for a smoke. I am glad that that chick is not there. I don't really have the energy for banter today and I am also all smelly and sticky, so I am not looking my most attractive. I love smoking. It is just so peaceful.

I return the ball and take a nice long shower. It feels great to have the water pounding on the back of my neck and then streaming down my body. I don't even bother to dry off. I wrap the towel around my waist and lie down soaking wet on my bed. I drift off to sleep with the prickling feeling of water slowly evaporating from my hot skin.

13

I wake up slowly and deliciously. That hasn't happened for a long time. I pick up my watch. I have an hour before breakfast. I pick up a comic book to read. One of my old Batman comic books. I am not a great fan of books. All that writing is so boring. I like comic books, where you can see the action unfold. It's like watching a movie. I like ones with lots of action, but also with a deep story and Batman definitely has a deep story.

Mom came round yesterday for an hour and she brought my comics. We sat outside and chatted. There are a bunch of chairs and tables round the corner and I could sit there with her. It was much nicer, because no one was there and it was a lot more private. She just told me about what she and Dad had been doing while I was in the hospital. She tried to keep it light and keep me up to date with news about my friends and family and her and Dad's friends, but I could tell that it has been a really difficult five months for her. I feel really bad about that. Mom brought my cell phone and Dad phoned to check up on me. He doesn't like to talk too much. He just told me there is a game on this weekend and that maybe he could come through and watch it with me. I said that would be great and that I would ask if it would be possible for my father to watch the game with me if no one else wants to watch anything on TV at that time. I will speak to Sister Jean about that today.

Breakfast contains the usual suspects. The staring guy is still thinking about the German Shepherd and wondering if maybe he should have joined in. The washing lady is very busy today. It looks like a tough bit of wringing out that she's doing there. I reckon it must be a really heavy flannel shirt or something. The hobo guy is also staring into space. I reckon he is wishing he could get his hands on a good cheap bottle of wine. Just another boring day in the loony bin. We don't even have any newcomers to spice things up a bit. Ummm, I wonder......

I haven't paid much attention to Bradley. I think I could get a bit of a rise out of him. That would certainly make things a bit more fun. I pick up my stuff and go and sit opposite him at the table. He is busy mumbling to himself as he picks at his food. I put down my tray and sit dead still and just stare at him. Now I know that if you stare long enough, a person will eventually stare back at you. I think a loony may take a bit longer to realise this, but I am a patient guy.

Bradley keeps mumbling and picking, but eventually after a good ten minutes, he realises I am there and looks up at me. I continue to stare at him and he continues to stare at me. I am good at this game. I used to play it a lot with my friends when I was a kid and I am pleased to see that I haven't lost the knack. I just don't blink and I keep staring. He keeps staring. I let this go on for a while and then I whisper loudly, "Boo!"

Bradley jumps and falls backward off his chair. He lands like a tortoise with his arms and legs up in the air. He scrambles up and runs screaming from the dining hall. This is too good. Everyone else has turned to look. I was hoping that he would run screaming around the dining hall instead of screaming out of it, but it was great while it lasted.

It doesn't create the chaos I was hoping for. Everyone just returns to what they were doing. I was hoping everyone would run around and scream and shout, but they don't. They just return to their eating. I guess they must be used to it.

If he had run around and around the room, it may

have been better. I wonder if he has gone to tattletale on me? That would provide a bit of amusement as well, because then I could deny it. I don't think anyone heard the 'boo'. Well, I guess they didn't otherwise they would be here in the dining hall giving me a good talking to. Sadly, life just carries on.

I walk to Sister Jean's to get the ball again and ask permission for my Dad to come through and watch the game with me. She says it's no problem, because most of the loonies will want to watch as well. Well, that will be a whole different take on father-son bonding.

I walk out to do my normal routine. I reckon I was able to shoot a whole lot more than yesterday. I walk to my wall and score! That chick is there looking as fine as ever.

"Hey."

"I thought I told you to stay away, Perv."

"As far as I can tell, this is a public place, and I like this spot."

"Why are you all sweaty? Had a nice session wanking about me?"

"Nah, I tried that this morning for a good 3 seconds, and then I got bored, so I decided to shoot some hoops instead."

I light up my cigarette and inhale deeply. I let the smoke slowly stream out of my mouth and nose. She doesn't leave. Cool. We sit there is silence for a long time. It feels okay not to talk. We are both just sitting and smoking and despite her not saying anything, I reckon she feels as comfortable as I do. I don't look at her, though. I just stare off into the distance.

My phone rings. I look at the screen. It's Spec.

"Hey, Spec!"

"Hey, buddy! How are you doing?"

"I am doing good."

I walk away from the wall. As much as I dig Goth chick, I don't want her to listen to my conversation with my best buddy. Spec and I have been friends since we met at a friend's party when we were fifteen. I used to call him Inspector Gadget, because he loves gadgety things and he probably has every new gadget from MP3 players to espresso makers. Inspector Gadget is a bit long, so it got shortened over the years to Spec.

"I honestly never thought I'd talk to you again, man."

"I know. To me it seems like we spoke a couple weeks ago, but I guess it's been longer than that."

"Yeah, a lot longer."

"I know."

"I spoke to your Mom yesterday. She says you are doing okay."

"Yeah, I am. In fact, I reckon, I am one hundred percent, but I guess I need to work through some shit, so I will stay here a bit longer. They need to make sure it doesn't happen again."

"Good idea."

"Yeah."

"I thought you were going to die and then you were okay. I thought you were okay. Then I came to visit you and you just weren't there, man. It was scary shit. I haven't used anything since then. Fucking scary!"

"I can imagine. Of course, I don't remember a thing."

"Yeah, well maybe it's better that way."

"I am not going to use again either. I have a good shrink. He's really cool. So, hopefully I can stay off the stuff. I don't want a repeat performance, so to speak."

"Yeah, that shit is heavy. Um, do you want to hang sometime?"

"Here?"

"Sure."

"At the loony bin?"

"Sure."

"There's not a helluva lot to do here."

"Nah, it's okay. We'll just hang."

"Sure, you want to come Friday?"

"Yeah, I'll come after work in the evening. I'll let you know what the guys have been up to. Benjy's got a girlfriend!"

"You are shitting me?"

"Nope. Will let you know all when I see ya."

"Cool. Later."

"Later."

Well, at least, I still have my best buddy. And he is clean. That's good. I always heard that you have to drop your friends if they are still using, because then you start using again too. I walk back to the wall, but she is gone. I feel disappointed. Well, fuck her. She seriously doesn't know what she is missing out on and what else is there to do in this shithole?

Bradley is not there when I get to the dining hall. Damn. That's disappointing. What a wet. With a gay name like Bradley, what do you expect anyway? After lunch, I grab a comic book and head out to read and smoke under the trees until my appointment with the Doc.

"Hello, Richard, take a seat. How are you doing after yesterday's session?"

"I thought about what you said, Doc, and I think you have a good point. I think everyday life is too boring for me and maybe it's because I have had it easy for the most part. I mean nothing major has ever happened to me. I have had fights and arguments, but who hasn't? I have gotten through school without really trying. I never got fantastic grades, but my grade point average was passable enough to get into an okay school. I have pretty much had whatever I wanted. I'm not like one of those poor people who have to live in a box under a bridge or something like that. Maybe it's been too easy, but what the hell am I supposed to do about that? I can't wish that my life were harder."

"You have already made it harder."

"What do you mean? By being here?"

"Yes."

"Hey, Doc, I wish that would help. Truly, I wish this would be the bit of struggle to make me sort out my life, but I feel just as bored here as I generally do when I am not here. I feel as bored now as I did before this happened. There is nothing to do in this loony bin."

"Have you thought of anything at all?"

"Nothing really comes to mind."

"I see you have a comic book."

"Yeah, well, I have been reading comics and shooting hoops and trying to talk to this girl."

"How is all that going?"

"Well, the comic books keep me occupied for a little bit and the hoops are good, but there are only so many I can shoot. Five months of sitting in one position, does not do much for a guy's level of fitness, if you know what I mean? As for the girl, I am working on her."

"How are you working on her?"

"I like the chase, so I am giving her a hard time."

"Is that satisfying?"

"A little, but when I don't see her, then there is nothing to do again."

The Doc looks at me.

"What?"

"Richard, there is something I want to talk to you about."

"Listen, Doc, if it's about this morning with Bradley, I was just having some fun."

"What happened this morning?"

"Oh, I thought one of the staff had come to tell you about Bradley and me."

"No one has told me anything about that. What happened?"

"Ah, it was nothing. Just a bit of fun. I gave him a fright, because I wanted to get the loonies fired up about something. Everyone is so quiet there."

"Are you feeling lonely?"

"I guess and I am just bored. What did you want to speak to me about?"

"The nursing staff has brought to my attention that you cover your mirror up in your bathroom. Apparently, you cover it with a towel and if they take the towel off the mirror, you put it back on again. I was wondering if there was a reason for this."

"It's a great place to hang my towel."

"Better than the hook?"

"Absolutely."

"Well, that's different."

"What can I say? I don't like to fit into the mould."

"It seems to require a lot more work than using the hanger."

"Sure."

"It just doesn't seem to fit for me. It doesn't go with all the things, you've been telling me about yourself. Have you always done this?"

"Um, I don't think so."

"When did this start? Before the catatonia or after?"

"Um, that's a good question. I think.... after. But I

remember doing it in my dreams."

"Tell me more about it."

"Well, yeah, this is really weird. I remember in all my dreams not wanting to look in the mirror and spending a lot of time trying to cover them up so I couldn't see myself."

"Why do you think you did that?"

"I didn't want to see my face, because I didn't recognise myself, because I didn't know who I was. It was scary."

"I can imagine that it was very scary, but you know who you are now, don't you?"

"Yes, I do."

"How are you sure?"

"Well, I can remember my entire childhood. I know who my parents are and who my friends are. I have been here for a long time now and those dreams were really short so this must be reality and not a dream. Also, I was really confused in those dreams and I am not confused now."

"Exactly, so I am wondering why you are still covering the mirror?"

"That's a good, point, Doc. Maybe I am scared that after what I have done to myself, I won't look the same anymore. Like maybe I have scarred myself or my skin is all messed up."

"I would imagine you have probably lost a bit of weight, because you didn't eat much over the past five months and you are probably a little paler from being indoors, but I can tell you from sitting over here, Richard, that there is nothing wrong with you."

"You sure, Doc? Is that your professional opinion?"

"Absolutely, after my many years of study I can offer that to you as my professional opinion."

We both laugh.

"I am here for you and I know this may sound weird, but I do have a shaving mirror here and we could look at you together. Then you wouldn't have to do it alone."

"You make me sound like I am five years old."

"That's not my intention. My intention is to support you."

"Do you think it's important?"

"I do. I really do. It's part of your identity and I don't think that it's healthy to avoid it. I think those dreams were important, because they helped us to understand a part of you that you may not have been aware of before. I think what they were communicating is that you find life too ordinary, because it has been without struggle."

"Agreed."

"I think that part of it also is about forming an identity and that was why you did not look at yourself in the mirror in the dreams. I think is hard to say who Richard is, because Richard is still trying to figure that out."

"You are right, Doc. I don't know where I fit in. I don't know what to do with my life. I guess I am lost."

"Nicely put. I think a way to help us find the path for you is to start on a symbolic level and looking at yourself in the mirror is a start."

"Okay."

"I am just going to fetch it. I'll be with you shortly."

"Sure."

The Doc gets up and leaves the room. What he says makes a lot of sense. One's face is part of one's identity for sure and how hard can it be to look in a mirror. Jeez, I am a tough guy. It's kind of embarrassing to not be able to look in the mirror. What am I going to do when I go home? What will I tell the old man? Gee, Dad, I am scared of my own reflection. No, when I leave this place, I am not leaving it as a nutter. The Doc is right, I have to do this. What will my friends say? It's bad enough that I have been here for five months, but then to have to go out into the world still acting like a weirdo. No way, man! No, he is right. I must face myself in the mirror.

I burst out laughing. Excuse the pun – face myself in the mirror. The laughter dies away and I feel really nervous. What the hell is wrong with me? It's not that scary. Bloody Hell! Maybe I am psycho?

The Doc returns. He has the mirror clasped to his chest. He sits down and then places the mirror face down on the table next to him.

"How are you feeling?"

"Really nervous."

"I can see that, you have gone pale. I am here with you. You are not going to do this alone. We are going to do it together, one step at a time."

"I feel so dumb."

"It's not dumb and thinking that is being too rough on yourself. It's not helpful. You have been through a really tough time for so long and there are always repercussions. This is one of the repercussions and we can deal with it. It is one more step that we are taking in moving forward. You have already beaten the odds. That was far harder and less possible than this is. This you can do."

"Okay, Doc. Let's do it."

"Fine, but we are going to do it slowly."

"You aren't going to tell anyone about it, are you?"

"This is a psychiatric hospital and so I do discuss you with other relevant professionals, but everything we discuss is held in confidence, I promise you that."

"Okay. Let's get on with it."

"We are going to take this slowly, step-by-step. We are not going to rush into it. I am going to explain the process to you. First, we are going to do a relaxation exercise together just to help you calm your system down. Then I am going to sit in that chair next to you. After that, I am going to turn the mirror to face you. You will look at yourself in the mirror and we will talk about what you see. Do you understand the process?"

"Sounds doable," I laugh.

The Doc goes through a relaxation exercise with me. I can feel my body relax from my toes up to my head as he makes me relax each part of my body.

"How are you feeling now?"

"Actually, much better. Thanks, Doc."

"Good, I am going to come and sit next to you now."

The Doc picks up the mirror and sits down in the chair next to me. He keeps the mirror face down on his lap. He shifts the chair a bit closer to me.

"How are you doing?"

"I am nervous, but not as nervous as I was before. I can do this."

"I am here with you. What do you expect to see?"

"Well, I guess, I'll look thinner and paler as you said."

"Do you remember what you looked like before you came here?"

"I don't really have a clear image in my head. It's not something I have been thinking about a lot."

"Fair enough. So you expect that you may look a little different, but otherwise much the same."

"Yeah, I guess so."

"Right, I am picking up the mirror. I am going to put

it in front of you and then when you are ready, I am going to turn it to face you. Remember, I am here and we can do this together. Just take some deep breaths for me. In and out. In and out. Just keep doing it while I turn the mirror. Are you ready?"

My heart is beating so fast, it feels like it is going to hammer its way through my chest. I am so nervous. This is ridiculous. It's my own damn face, damn it! I try to breathe deeply, but it's not helping.

"We are not in a rush. I am going to keep the mirror in front of you, facing away from you and I am going to do that relaxation technique again. This time, keep your eyes open and look at the back of the mirror."

"Okay. I just feel stupid."

"It's not stupid, please don't judge yourself."

"Okay."

The Doc runs through the relaxation exercise. I focus on the back of the mirror and I feel much calmer. The anxiety is still running like an electric current, fizzling below the surface, but it is not so overwhelming.

"I want you to keep breathing deeply. Just breathe deeply and slowly and hold onto your breath like an anchor."

"Okay."

"Tell me when you are ready for me to turn the mirror. If you can't do it today, I am pleased with what we have done already. You have been amazing. We can try again tomorrow."

"Okay. Just give me a moment."

"There's no rush."

I try to relax my body and continue to breathe deeply and rhythmically. I like the Doc's analogy of holding onto my breath like an anchor. I can use this to hold onto, to support myself. I am feeling calm and this is no big deal. I keep my eyes closed, as I tell the Doc to turn the mirror round.

"I am with you, Richard."

I open my eyes and stare into the mirror. The face inside the mirror stares back at me. The face is staring at me. It is looking right at me. It sees me. I can't look away.

"I don't know who that is! I don't know who that is!"

I can't look away. It's like it has pulled me into the mirror and I can't break free.

"You are fine, Richard. That is you. Just breathe."

The face stares at me with a knowing hatred and malevolence. I cannot look away from those snake eyes. My breath becomes light and fluttery and I start to notice that it is getting dark around the edges of my vision. Lights prick the space between me and the face and still I can't look away from those evil eyes boring into mine. The Doc is talking, but he is very faint in the background. The darkness seeps further into my field of vision.

14

Ow! My back hurts. And I am fucking cold! Man is it cold. I am definitely not lying on a bed and what the hell is that sickening smell? My back aches. Ow. What did I do? Did I fall?

I open my eyes and it takes a bit of time for them to adjust. I look up and see a muddy midnight sky above me. How did I get outside? Surely the Doc wouldn't have left me outside? Maybe he took me back to my room and then I walked outside at night? Maybe I was sleepwalking and now I am lying on one of the benches in the garden? I turn over, nope, not a bench. I am lying next to a grey wall that has been besieged by damp. Where could that possibly be?

I can hear people talking. I can't really make out what they are saying. They seem to be talking really softly. I turn painfully onto my other side and notice that I am sleeping on a bunch of newspapers. Weird. I squint across from me and see some people huddled around a fire of some kind. Am I at a party? Are we having parties at the loony bin now? This is really weird.

I painfully get up into a sitting position. I look down at myself. I am wearing the filthiest clothes I have ever seen. With a feeling of rising horror, I realise that the awful smell is me. How did I get to be so damn filthy? I smell like I haven't bathed in weeks. Very weird. I seem to be wearing what looks like a thick brown jacket. It's hard to tell in the dark. I smell so bad that I want to vomit. I retch a couple of times. I feel really embarrassed about this, but no one seems to pay any attention to me. I look around. I seem to be in some derelict building. There are no doors and the windows bear the scars of having been attacked once upon a time. The roof is missing in parts. It doesn't look too safe. Where on earth could this be?

Granted I did not walk around the entire psychiatric hospital property, but this place seems a little strange. I am sure they wouldn't have a place like this on the property and if they did, I am sure that they wouldn't let people have a party here.

I look around my area. I am sitting, after I was obviously sleeping, on some newspapers. There's a ratty blanket over my legs. Next to me is a cardboard box. I look inside it. There's a photo of a man and a woman on the top of the pile. There's a grubby, mangled book. It doesn't have a cover, so I don't know what it's about and I don't really care. There are some mangy clothes and that's about it. What else?

There's lots of trash in the 'house'. Must have been some party. I spot a box of wine a little way off from me. Cool! How long has it been since I had a drink? Over five months. Too long for a guy to go without a drink, I reckon! Far too long! I hope there's something left in there! I crawl painfully over to retrieve it.

Sleeping on the ground is obviously not great for me, especially since I haven't been moving much lately. I guess that makes it worse. I have been known to pass out regularly and many a time it has been upon the floor, but I guess I have lost practice.

I look around for a clean glass, but there's nothing but trash. Oh, well, I am not above taking a swig right from the source. I shake the box and hear the delicious swirl of alcohol inside. I purse my lips around the tap and squeeze it and a rather cheap trickle of red wine fills my mouth. Damn that's good!

Oh shit! Shit! Fuck! I swore I wouldn't use again and that includes alcohol! Fucking hell! Okay, I am sure I can withstand one swallow of alcohol. I throw the box away from me. It lands with a thump ten feet away. I sit and look at it. Nothing. I am okay. Cool. Do I feel weird? No. No, I feel just fine. Okay, I don't really feel fine. I feel like I have the worst hangover. I feel like a herd of buffalo trampled over my head, followed by a barrage of trucks and then a whole bunch of Chinese torturers. How the hell did I get such a bad hangover? I don't remember drinking.

Shit! Did I get together with that Goth chick? Did we end up sneaking out and getting fucked and now I am somewhere where I don't know, because I drank too much and blacked out. That's happened before - on more than one occasion. I know that the only thing that will get rid of a hangover is another heavy dose of alcohol. I stare at the box of wine. It stares unflinchingly back at me. I painfully shift around so that I am facing the wall and the wine can't see me anymore. Well, I can't see the wine anymore. Much safer this way.

How could I do this to my parents? How could I let this happen to me? I was supposed to turn over a new leaf. Bloody hell, Richard, you never manage to turn over a new leaf. You just grab a whole load of newly turned over leaves and chuck them into a huge pile. Then you piss on them before spraying gasoline all over them and then watch them go up in flames. That's my version of new leaves.

I could cry. I really could. I am just getting my life on track again after five months and now here I am hung over, drinking already after obviously getting thoroughly wasted and I don't know where I am. I am lost.

I turn around and ignore the wine, which seems to have crept closer to me. I scan the area for any sign of the Goth chick. That is the only possible way, I reckon, that I could have arrived in this hellhole. I don't think any of the other loonies would have tried to make it here. I think they have enough entertainment in their own heads, without needing to drink or drug to get any more.

What to do? I am going to get into shit for sneaking out of the loony bin. That's just what I need on top of everything else. I never fucking learn. You would think that five months of being in a catatonic state would cure me of my sins, but no. Here I am just a few days out of the worst period of my life and I am chucking it back again. Who knows what else I have taken? Fuck! Fuck! Fuck! You asshole, Richard!

Okay, let's get this together. I have fallen off the metaphorical wagon. Obviously. And it really hurts. When I decided to fall off the wagon, I must have done it when the wagon was travelling at at least 200mph. I made sure that my entire body would get battered in the process. Way to go, buddy! Okay, and there are going to be repercussions for this. Not that I need them. I think I have had enough percussion for one night, but that more will come is inevitable. Okay. So that's what is coming. I need to get to what is coming. How am I going to do that? I need to stand up for starters. That would be a good first step. One small step for mankind, one giant leap for Richard. Yeah, yeah....

Ow! It really hurts. I am a wanker! I use the wall to assist me on my journey to uprightness. My back hurts. My head feels like swirling slush, with small ice shards in it. My feet hurt. My eyes hurt. My ears hurt. My face hurts. Everything hurts. Way to go guy! Richard, the superhero, here at your service! Can he stay sober for more than a few days? No, he can't! What does he go and do? Ladies and gents, he goes and gets himself wasted all over again. Let's bring on another state of catatonia. Cat,

cat, cat-cat-cat-a-toe-knee-a. I wonder if that could, in another universe, be a disease that affects cat's toes and knees? Interesting questions, I pose. Indeed. Very interesting. I am not a professor for nothing. Okay, I am currently a professor of nothing, but that doesn't really matter, because matter matters.

Shit! Am I still drunk? I stare sharply at the box of wine. It stares back at me. Little fucker! I'll show you! I am bigger and stronger than you are and I can keep my mouth closed so you can't come in. So what are you going to do, you little shit? Huh? I shuffle painfully over to the box and kick it. I kick it hard. Showed you, you little shit! Do not mess with Richard, the mighty, the superb. The super-caller-fragalistic-espialidocious Richard. Richard the Lionhearted! Yeah, you little fuck! Don't mess with Richard the Lionhearted.

Okay, that was a pathetic kick and it didn't really move very far. I could reach it in a couple steps and suck the sweet nectar from its throat, but I won't! Nope! Not me. I don't need that! Fuck no! I am stronger than you are. Strong like an ox. No strong, like a lion. I am the lionhearted. Braveheart is nothing on me. He was a little pissy, weenie Scotsman, who would never be able to take on Richard, the Lionhearted! Braveheart, my ass!

Did the box move? I glare at it. You stay put, you little shit! I don't fucking need you. Oh, I do, I do, I do. I could marry you. I would always be true. Well, until you run out of dew. Then I would have to seek one anew. Ha! I crack myself up, I really do. I am a regular old cracker jack. All right, I am a poet and I do know it. Okay, well, not really a poet, more like a person with a deep appreciation of the art of poetry. What label would such a person have? Um, let's think? An apprecipoet. Nah. That's lame. A poet-lover. A poem-lover. Also, lame. Ah,

an amore la poem. Sounds like a beautiful fragrance.
Maybe I should sell the name to a perfume company and
make my millions! Yes! By Jove, I have it George, a way
to make some cash! It is strange to use such an antiquated
oath. Jupiter died out a long time ago. I should be saying,
my God. It's more relevant and up to date. One must
stick with modern times and not dwell on the past. What
is past is passed. I passed on my way to the now and
hereness of it all. That is rather profound, if I don't say so
myself.

What's that? I can't hear you whining, little box. Your
whimpers and sweet cajoling mean nothing to me old
ears.

Old ears? What am I saying? I don't have old ears.
Mine are fresh and new twenty four-year old ears.
They've barely been used. Like the rest of me. I can't
really see the rest of me. Firstly, it's dark and secondly, I
am covered in a brown coat that looks like and smells like
a dead animal. At least it's dead. It would be rather
alarming to be wearing a live animal. Thank Minerva that
I am wearing a dead one. But then again, a live one may
smell so much nicer. I am also wearing a pair of
elasticised grey pants that have not seen a soap sud, not
even a nano-soap sud, for many a day. And my sneakers
should sneak away, because they are so gross. They are
grey too. Now that's different. At least the dead animal is
brown. I like a bit of variety in my attire. Why go for a
uniform grey, when you can mix it up with a splash of
smelly brown? A man of fashion, I am. Stand back, ladies
and gentlemen, Richard has stepped foot upon the
catwalk!

Okay, maybe being hung-over and still possibly a
little drunk is not too bad. It beats those serious sessions
with the Doc. Nice to get out of the loony bin for a while!

Indeed! What's that I hear? Another sip? Mmm, so, so tempting, but I cannot. No, I must persist in retaining the dubious virtue of my liver.

I decide to go over and chat to the group huddled around the fire. I am sure I will be able to garner some clues from them to help me get back to the loony bin. The blood is circulating more freely through my cramped veins and so movement is less painful. Small things to be grateful for, indeed. I shuffle over in my smelly clothes. Shit! Maybe, I shouldn't get too close, because I totally reek and they are going to pass out from the stench of me when I come nearer.

Fuck it! I need to get back to the loony bin. The longer I stay here, the worse it will be and the more shit I will get into. I need to find out where I am and then get a lift or something back to the loony bin. I need to have a major shower and then I need to go to bed. Hopefully, they'll never notice I left and if they did, I can just say I left for a brief stroll around the lawns at midnight. It is good for the constitution, I hear.

I take a deep inhalation, as I shuffle closer to the group, steeling myself for their disgusted reaction towards my odorous self. The fire gently illuminates their faces and it really shouldn't. I think darkness would suit this lot far better. I think darkness would show off their features to a much greater advantage. They are a filthy and grizzled lot. A life of hard living has gouged itself into their faces. Who are these people? I have never seen them before. I think that I am in even more trouble than I thought I was in. Shit!

Woo-wee! They smell as bad as I do. Well, at least the potential embarrassment about my body humours has now evaporated. I can concern myself with that when I get back to the loony bin and if I can sneak in undetected,

I'll be just fine. However, the stench may give me away as loudly as if I had triggered a fire alarm, but one step at a time.

"Excuse me?"

"Hello, old boy! You finally managed to sleep it off?"

"What?"

"What?"

"Sleep what off?'

"The little purple friend."

"Yes. Indeed it was a delicious vintage!"

"I thought you would like it!"

"It was the ambrosia of the gods!"

"I wish you would quit talking like that. I never understand what you mean."

"It was a damn fine bottle of wine."

"Now that I understand!" And with that, the grizzled man slaps me painfully on the back.

I think the fool has winded me! The pain of it! I blink back a tear. Okay, I am being melodramatic! I must have been in top form last night. All these people seem to know me. They smile at me and it's a familiar smile – not the awkward smile of someone, who is trying to be polite to a stranger.

"Well, gentlemen, we must be off! We'll be seeing you."

"Same time tomorrow?"

"Same time as always."

The three men and one of the women turn and walk away, but the other woman hesitates briefly. She looks at me for a moment and then says, "Bye, Michael. Bye, Joe." The man next to me says goodbye. I look around for the other guy she mentioned, but don't see anyone else around. She looks shyly at me and then walks away. We watch her walk through the ruin and out onto the street.

"She really is sweet on you, Joe. I don't know why you have to be so unpleasant to her. I know you like playing hard to get, but I think you've been playing that game too long and it's going to bite you in the ass."

"Who is Joe?"

The man bursts out laughing.

"You crack me up, Joe. You really do. I am glad we are friends. It makes this miserable life much better having a friend like you around."

He gives me a big bear hug. I feel like all the air has been crushed out of me and with just a fraction more pressure all my ribs would shatter.

"Easy there, tiger!"

"Sorry, Joe. I get carried away sometimes. Are we going to call it a night? Sorry, man, just realised you got up. I am beat. I can stay up with you a little longer, but then I think I am going to turn in for the night. This fire sure is warm though. Maybe we should sleep a little closer to it tonight. What do you think? I reckon it's safe. This bin is pretty sturdy and I reckon if we feed it a bit more, it should keep going for another hour."

"That sounds great buddy, but my name is not Joe."

"Huh? Come on, Joe. It's a little late for your pranks."

"This is no joke. My name is Richard Carter. I am an inpatient at a psychiatric ward and I am lost. Please tell me where I am. I need to get back; otherwise I will be in serious shit. Did you see me with a girl? Tallish, black hair, broody look. Really hot actually."

The man just stares at me.

"Hello, anyone home?"

"Are you serious?"

"Yes, very serious. I know it's a lot to take in and

you probably think I am some kind of freak or something, but I swear I am serious."

"Um...."

The man walks away from me. I watch him. He walks to the wine box and picks it up. Dear god! I had forgotten about that little minx. I try to look away, but she has trapped me in a stare and I cannot look away. The man holds the box up and looks at it intently. He appears to be reading it. I think he may be a little crazier than me. He shakes the box and then holds it to his mouth and takes a swig. Like an accomplished wine taster in a very bad outfit, he swirls the mixture around his mouth. Then unlike a wine taster, he gargles with the wine and then swallows it. Very odd. He pours some into his hand and sniffs it inelegantly, before licking it up. He stares at me as he walks back to me. My eyes leave his stare and drift to the wine box, which has cunningly made its way closer to me now.

"Please take that away from me, I am trying to quit."

"Since when?"

"I have been clean for over five months now!" I say with great pride.

He stares at me before doubling over with laughter and dropping the wine box on the floor in the process. She hits the cement with a thud, which indicates that her belly is still pregnant with that seductive liquid. She rolls and lies with the tap facing away from me. I long to pick her up and comfort the both of us, but I must be strong.

I wait patiently for the man to stop laughing. He eventually does after annoying eons of time.

"You are being serious about all of this now, Joe? Or should I call you, what was it again?"

"Richard, you ruffian."

"Right, Richard. So man, you say you've been sober

for five months."

He tries to stifle a giggle.

"Yes, that is correct."

"And you are a patient in a psychiatric ward, you say?"

"Indeed."

"I love this game, Joe. You always were the eccentric type. Okay, I'll play. I was worried there for a second. You almost had me going. I thought the wine was off or something, but it ain't. So I know you are pulling my leg, but let's play. Okay, so you are Richard from a psychiatric ward. Tell me about yourself?"

"I have been in a catatonic state for five months."

"I have never heard of that state."

"It's not a state you imbecile! It's a state of mind. It's where you are disconnected from reality."

"Sounds like bliss. I try to get a good dose of 'disconnected from reality' as many times a day as I can. Yeah, I guess that's what we've been doing since we've been here. Yeah, I get that. I see what you are doing; you are playing one of your mind games, Professor. One of those meta-things."

"Metaphor, you buffoon. When will you ever learn?"

"Yo, Prof, I try man, I try. Cat-a-what?"

"Catatonia. It's like a cat, which has a disease of the toe and knee."

He bursts into laughter again. This is going to be a long night. It will be like Moses leading the tribes of Israel through the desert. It will take months. I sigh and wait for him to finish.

"Done now?"

"Yip."

I can see he is not taking me seriously.

"You say you came here with a hot woman, that

right?"

"Well, that's what I think at least. It's the only plausible way I would have ended up in a dump like this."

"Now listen here! This place is the best place we've had in ages."

"I apologise. I don't mean to insult this place; it's just not my place."

"Sure it is. This is our place. You are my best buddy in the whole world and this is ours to share."

Whoa there Bessie. What? I have never seen this guy before, not ever. Maybe we really bonded last night. I'd better be polite for now.

"Thanks, man."

"You know I mean it."

"I know you do. Did you see me with a hot chick?"

"Nope. That is a term I have never heard you use before."

"Hot chick?"

"Yes. How old was this woman?"

"About my age, I reckon. About twenty three to twenty six, I guess."

"You are a scream!"

"Why?"

"You think you are twenty five years old! Give me some of that wine. I want to be eighteen again. I really enjoyed being eighteen! That was a good time!"

He bends down and takes a swig from the box and holds it out to me. Oh the torture! One sip wouldn't hurt, just one little teeny tiny one. What is the worst it can do to me? I am a big man and one mouthful is so small. What harm can one small, delicious taste, one little sip, one little whetting of the tongue, do? Before I realise it, I have the box in my hands and the open tap to my mouth. Oh, it tastes so good. It's medicinal really. Actually, that's what it is. I have fowl breath and it will help to resurrect the animal that died in the back of my mouth. Yes, resurrection needs a lot of fuel and so I need quite a few sips. Steady there, I need to save some for later.

"How old are you now?"

"I am still twenty four."

"Damn, thought you would drink yourself even younger. Me, I am still eighteen."

"Glad that worked out for you, you don't look eighteen."

"You don't look twenty four."

"Sure I do."

"Well, maybe you just look mature for your age. Must be the beard and the grey hair."

"The what…….."

I feel my face. Holy shit! I do have a beard. It's long too…. There is no way I could have grown that overnight. I feel my hair. It is greasy and longer then it was yesterday. Oh dear. I look down at my hands and I have liver spots. I run my tongue around my teeth and I am missing a lot.

I am missing teeth. I had my teeth yesterday. There are gaps of lumpy gum, where teeth should be, and the teeth that I do have jut out here and there like desolate monoliths in a desert.

I sit down hard on my ass and a jolt shoots up from my posterior through my spine to whiplash my head. I feel like I am about to lose consciousness for a second, but it passes quickly. I reach for the box and have a few fortifying sips. Boy, do I need them and if it's a stressful situation I am sure it has absolutely no effect. Not like if I am drinking, because I am bored. Then I would have a drinking problem. This is medicinal. I am stressed and it will just help to take the edge off the stress and then I should be fine and I won't need to drink again. So, this is okay and actually it's good for me.

After having received my panacea, I look up at the man in front of me.

"I am not Richard."

"He comes round. You shouldn't stop drinking, man, it messes with your head."

"I am Joe."

"Yes, have another sip. I think it will bring back the rest to you too. Man, you gave me a fright there."

I take another swig. Maybe this guy has a point.

"How long have I been here?"

"On the street? I don't know for sure, but I reckon it's been five years."

Five years. Five months. There's a connection there somewhere. I know it. I take another few gulps. It will help me think better and I need to think better in order to solve this situation. It is just engine fuel to power the machine that nestles in my skull. I need it for that. If I don't, I will be in a fierce pickle. Hey, maybe that's why my brain works better bathed in the warm embrace of alcohol. Alcohol is a preserving fluid and I am just preserving my brain. That makes sense.

I am dreaming. I am dreaming!!!! I knew the alcohol would help. And I can drink as much as I like, because this isn't real! I knew there was a connection somewhere there between the five years and the five months. This is just what happens in dreams. Things get distorted. That's right.

What happened to make me dream? The mirror! That was it. It made me black out, because I got so freaked out. I am still in the loony bin. I didn't mess up. I am not Joe. I am Richard and I am asleep in my bed, safe and sound. This is a dream.

This is great, actually. Maybe there are some benefits to being catatonic. Maybe this is a side effect and if I can control it, I will be able to have any dream I like. It seems to be stress induced, I reckon. I would rather have dreams where I am drilling that hot chick. That would beat this dream any day. Oh, yeah. That is what I need!

Okay, but these dreams can last a long time, as I have experienced before, so I need to figure out how to make this one stop.

Mike - I guess that must be his name, if I am Joe, because that was what that woman said when she said goodbye - is staring into the fire.

"You are a figment of my imagination."

"Please, Joe, it's enough now. Enough games, man. I am beat. I want to go to sleep."

"I am going to prove it to you."

"Right now?"

"Yes."

"Can't it wait till morning? I think you have drunk too much now."

He grabs the box, but I snatch it back from him and down the contents in one shot.

"What has got into you man? You asshole! We were supposed to share that."

"It doesn't exist. You don't exist. This is a dream. I told you that I am Richard and I am fast asleep dreaming this right now. Watch, I'll prove it to you. I am invincible, nothing can happen to me."

I get up and look around for something to help me prove that I am invincible.

"Come on, Mike, help me out here. I need to show you I am invincible."

"You are not invincible, Joe. You need to sleep this off. Come let me get you into bed and we will talk about this in the morning."

I ignore him and look for something with which to do myself harm, because no harm can come to me. This is a rush. I feel a rush of power surging through my body. It doesn't hurt as much anymore, which indicates to me that I am getting better at controlling the dream.

I don't see anything in the ruined house that will demonstrate adequately how invincible I actually am. I stop to think. Damn, I wish I hadn't finished all the fuel. I can feel that the gas tank is running low and it won't be long before the engine stops running and then I won't be able to demonstrate how truly all-powerful I am. I love these dreams. Well, I love them now that I understand them.

As I stop to think, I hear a drone, and what must that drone be, but the drone of the freeway. It is music to my ears. That's the perfect way to demonstrate my invincibility.

"Come on, Mike. I have the perfect solution to this perfect problem. A remedy that will blow your mind, my friend."

"Joe, can't it wait till morning?"

"Time waits for no man!"

I head out in the direction of the noise. At first, I have to navigate by the noise of the cars, but suddenly, the layout of the land filters clearly into my head and I know exactly where I am. I know exactly where the freeway is. It is not far from here at all.

Mike is shuffling along slowly behind me.

"I thought you wanted to go to sleep."

"That's exactly what I want to do, so why are we here walking around in the middle of the night?"

"Because this whole thing will take five minutes from now till you are snug back in bed. That's not very long now, is it? So stop dawdling!"

"I guess not," Mike says very reluctantly.

"Stop acting like a petulant child. This will be great fun, you'll see."

"Ra!Ra! I can't wait. It's cold and I want to be home by the fire."

"You are a moaning Minnie! This will be fun and we need a bit of adventure in our lives, do we not?"

"Can't we have an adventure in the daylight?"

"Night-time is far more mysterious, my friend. It adds a bit more drama to the whole affair, don't you think?"

"Whatever. Just prove your invincibility and then let's go to sleep."

"Invincibility lies in wait right around this corner."

I clamber awkwardly over a crumbling wall, painted silver in the moonlight. Mike follows sulkily. We make our way through an overgrown piece of land, before climbing through the hole in the fence that leads onto the freeway. This is our short cut through to the other end of town. It makes getting around without transport far easier.

"Please don't tell me we are walking all the way to the east end? You said it would be five minutes, Joe!"

"Don't worry, it stops here."

"What are you going to do?" Mike looks at me suspiciously.

"Wait and see my friend."

The cars are whooshing past me and I can feel the air tug enticingly at my body as each car speeds by me. There is a fair amount of traffic on the road, but there is enough time to get across the lanes without getting hit. A feeling of exhilaration passes through me. This is awesome!

I let a few more cars pass me. Savouring the moment

is part of the high. You have to build it up so to speak, before the climax, because if you rush towards the climax, it is over far too soon. Goth chick was right, I am a total pervert!

"I am a pervert!!!!!" My words get sucked away by the passing cars.

"Okay, Joe, you have shown me that you are invincible. Well done. I am not sure what being a pervert has to do with being invincible, but maybe you'll remember in the morning and let me know. Five minutes are almost up. Can we go back now?"

"Just one more minute, I promise."

I can see a cluster of cars hurtling towards me. I have to time this just right, because I don't want them to stop or swerve at the last minute. I think I need to get to the other side, because the lane closet to me is empty and by the time I hobble out there, they will have passed me by.

I stroll across the highway; I still have a bit of time.

"What are you doing, Joe?" Mike shouts at me.

"I am going to show you how I can fly!"

"No! Joe! Stop this! You are drunk! You have been drinking since yesterday! You are going to die! You are my best friend in the whole world, Joe! I can't live without you! Please, Joe! Just stay there. I'll come and fetch you."

"I am not drunk, because this isn't real. I am not real, you are not real. This is just a dream and I can't get hurt."

And with that, I step out in front of the car.

"No! Joe!"

It doesn't hurt. I was right and I get to fly. I have always wanted to fly!

15

I find myself standing on the ledge of an open window. It is night time and city lights have turned the grey clouds above me an insipid brown. The night time light outside the window has coloured all the buildings and the streets a velvet blue. Little yellow lights here and there add some cheer to the otherwise quite night. I see the beams of the occasional car track a lonely path along the road below me.

I look behind me and I seem to be standing on the window ledge of an office. The computer is on and the computer screen fills the otherwise dark room with an eerie blue light. The office is neat and small. The computer rests on a desk next to a very neat paper organiser. A jacket hangs over the back of a high-backed plush chair. I look down at myself and see that I am wearing a white shirt and a blue striped tie that flutters in the breeze. The office is bare, apart from a metal filing cabinet and a stack of well-organised shelves. A corkboard is mounted on the wall and seems to have some papers affixed to it, but I can't see what they say, as it is too dark to read.

What am I doing here? I feel really miserable. Oh, I remember now. I was dreaming that I was a bum and then I tried to wake myself up and now I am here. So I must still be dreaming. I am not enjoying this. I really want to wake up now. I thought being hit by the car would wake me up. Isn't that the way it works?

Normally you wake up just before you hit the ground when you are falling in a dream. I am pretty sure that's how it works. Why didn't I wake up? I must talk to the Doc about this. Maybe it's a symptom of my condition or maybe it is a side effect of the medication, which I am on.

I am not sure. To be totally honest, I don't have the answers to these questions and since I am still asleep, I cannot go and talk to the Doc and ask him what I should do. So it's a bit of a problem.

I have to figure out a way to wake up. Standing on a window ledge is not going to help. I get down and look for a light switch. I see one next to the door and turn it on. I should open the door and look out. It scares me a little, because you never know what is behind closed doors in dreams. It could be the most amazing thing I have ever seen or it could be something absolutely terrifying and then how will I get out of the dream this time if it is something frightening? Then again, if I don't sort it out, I might be stuck in this dream forever.

The thing that scares me is that I am not able to control the content of my dreams. It seems to be given to me by my unconscious mind and I have no conscious control over my dream environment. I can control my actions. I seem to have total freedom in that regard, but I have no control over my dream surroundings.

But the thought of being stuck like this also scares the shit out of me so I should open the door. I guess it can't hurt me. That is what I have to hold onto. I mean I am still here after being hit by a car travelling at a seriously high speed, so I can't get hurt. I am sure there was an urban legend going around that if you died in your sleep you would die in real life. Well, I have thoroughly disproved that one. If I can ever get myself to wake up again, I will be sure to write in to some magazine and dispel that load of rot.

Okay, so I can't get hurt. I am brave. I have dealt with plenty recently and I have managed to cope with it so I can open this door and I can deal with whatever lies behind it. I take a deep breath and open the door. I am greeted by a passage lit by a barrage of bright fluorescent lights. The entire passage is guarded by a row of regularly spaced fake wooden doors on either side. Each door has a white plastic plaque with a name written on it in black. There is no one in sight. I listen, but all I can hear is the faint hum of the fluorescent lights. The passage continues on either end making what appears to be a U-shape.

I walk across to the door opposite me and knock. No one answers. I try the door and it is locked. I try the one next to it and it is locked. I try a couple more. They are all locked. I guess that happens in dreams. Maybe they are different compartments of my mind that I cannot access. The Doc will love that one, I am sure. I walk down to the end of the passage and find another passage with locked doors. I turn at the end of that passage and find a set of glass doors that are firmly locked. An electronic card reader is set into the wall by the side of the glass doors. I feel in the pockets of my shirt and trousers, but they are empty. I continue walking in the same direction until I come back to my office door. I know it's mine, because it's the only one that is open.

I read the name on the door. It says Jack Carlisle. It's weird that I come up with names for myself in my dreams that have nothing to do with my name. Well, hang on, both my dream surname and my real surname start with a C but that's about where the similarities start and end. I wonder why I don't stay Richard Carter? I am sure I have had dreams in the past where I dreamt I was Richard; where I dreamt I was myself. Weird. The good thing, though now, as compared to the dreams I had before, is that at least I know who I am. I can retain my sense of self. In the dreams before I woke up, I thought I was the person, who I was in the dream. Now I know I am not that dream person, but Richard, so that has helped a lot. I will get through this, I am sure of it. I just need to figure out how to wake myself up.

I go back into my office. The cold air from the window hits me, but I don't close the window. The cold air helps me to think. I see a set of keys and a key card lying behind the computer screen. I didn't see them before from my vantage point at the window. So that is the way out of here. I can at least get out of this building, but then where would I go? I guess I could figure out where I live. It eventually comes back to me the longer the dream persists, but I really don't want to keep this dream going. I really don't. I want to get back to the loony bin. That is really ironic. I don't think I would have ever had that thought before in my entire life, but I really do want to go back there. I want to regain control of my life. Right, so leaving the building is not an option, because then I will continue being stuck in this dream. And that is something I do not want.

I look at the desk. There is a phone, which I didn't see before and there is an answering machine. It indicates that there is one message and the machine is not blinking, which indicates that the message has already been heard. I push the play button for fun, to see what the message says. It is interesting to see what my unconscious will come up with and I can always relay this info to the Doc. I am sure he will be impressed with me for thinking of this. My friend, Lisa, is taking psychology at college and she has explained some of this stuff to me, so I know a thing or two!

"Hey Jack, it's Sam. Haven't spoken to you for two months. I'll be back home next Sunday and then I will tell you all about Africa. It has been amazing here. Incredible. I have so much to tell you. I am so glad I got out of the hospital and came to practice medicine here. They need it so much. Anyway, buddy, hope you are doing well and I'll call you when I am back in town. I'll be home for two weeks, so I am sure we can schedule in a couple pints at the pub!"

Maybe the Doc can figure that out. Very strange indeed! I have no idea why I would think of something like that. I have never really thought much about Africa. I know it exists and that it's poor and that's about it really. And I am still here in the dream world.

I decide to check the computer screen. I sit down in the black chair. Wow, this is a nice chair! It moulds exactly to my body. That is so awesome. I wish I had one of these in real life. I get up and have a look at it. I have never seen one of these before I am pretty sure. I wonder if they exist. Maybe I could patent it when I wake up and make some nice dough to live off for the rest of my life. Maybe these dreams are not so bad after all.

I pretty much remember the other dreams in a lot of detail, so I reckon I can remember what this chair looks like if I put my mind to it. I take the jacket off the back of the chair and lay it on the desk next to the computer. I then spend a good five minutes examining the chair minutely. I try to remember how all the mechanisms work and where they are placed. When I feel that I have got the whole arrangement fixed in my mind, I sit back down in my chair and move the mouse to get the screensaver to switch off.

I see a text document on the screen in front of me. I am not really keen to read it, but I am sure it will provide a clue as to how to get out of this dreaming thing I do. I think the more information I can give the Doc, the more likely he will be able to help me. So, even though I could think of better things to do than read some page-pusher's work, I do.

"To everyone,

I am sorry that I have done this, but I just can't live anymore. I know that you will think that I have it all and from the outside, it probably seems that way, but the outside can be deceptive and what is happening on the inside is something completely different.

I know that some of the blokes envy me, because I have always been a bit of a lady's man. I have never struggled with meeting women and I have always been able to charm them and get what I want from them, but I have never been in love and at the age of forty-five, I don't think that will ever happen. Believe it or not, the fun moments only last a moment and then life continues. There are not enough of them to fill every second of my day. Yes, I would like to have the ordinary life. I would like to come home to a house full of the noises and upheavals of a wife and kids. I feel so depressed coming home to an empty house that is devoid of everything but me.

I know that I make a good salary and that I can buy anything that I want. There are so many people in this world, who do not even have a fraction of what I have. I do not want for anything and for this, I should be grateful, but I find that every purchase I make rings hollow after a few minutes. At first, it is exciting and new and different, but after I have had it for about ten minutes, I find that I do not get any joy out of it anymore. This probably makes me sound spoilt and I probably am, but owning and acquiring things doesn't make me happy anymore. I wish they did.

What about work? I have worked hard and I have worked my way into a high position and I could work my way higher. I know it accords me a great deal of status and that people would love to get where I am, but that status is superficial. It does not make me feel happy at the end of the day. It does not bring me genuine friends. Instead, I feel empty, because I have chosen a job for the status, which no longer fulfils me and for the money, which no longer fulfils me either.

What about friendship? I think the good friends, who I once had, have long passed me by into obscurity or into self-actualisation. Some of my friends have become so boring that I can no longer tolerate a second in their company and others make me feel so small. I don't think that they realise that, but I am the master of bullshit and I can make it seem that my life is very glamorous, when in fact my life is like a fake gold watch. It looks great on the outside, but has no substance on the inside. On the inside, it is cheap. And those friends who have gone on to do what they are passionate about, they may not always have material wealth, but they do have experiential wealth and that makes their lives far richer than mine.

My life is poor. I have so little. Have I tried antidepressants? Yes, I have for many years now and I find that I still feel the same deep down. They don't seem to be able to cover up that hole adequately enough for me. I can still feel its gaping maw at the edge of my consciousness.

I feel that this is the logical next step. I hope that life on the other side is far better than life has been here. Wish me luck!

Jack"

Wow, man, that is heavy stuff. Makes me think a little. Maybe I need to do something different with my life? Maybe I need to go to Africa like Sam says and make a difference there? I don't know. Maybe that would be an idea, once I leave the loony bin. But then would I want to hang around the poor and destitute? Nah, not really. I read the letter again just to make sure that I remember everything for the Doc and that I read it correctly.

Now what? I look around the office. Not much else here. I am stuck. How am I going to wake up? I don't have even one small idea. Not even a teeny tiny one. I look out of the window and then I remember that I was standing on the ledge when I began this dream.

I have an idea. If I was about to commit suicide, which it looks like I was, because who stands on a window ledge after writing a note like that? Maybe that is at the very least how I can get out of this dream and into the next one and then I can maybe figure out how to wake myself up in the next dream and at the very best, the jolt will wake me up now! Hey, I didn't fall in the last dream and I reckon I can do quite a bit of falling in this dream. I walk to the window to check. Yes, it is quite a few storeys before I will make contact with the tarmac. Hopefully I won't make contact and I will wake up before I hit it like a normal person does when they dream of these things. I can only hope. In the last dream, a car hit me and maybe that doesn't wake people up. But falling wakes people up. Well usually, it does, or so I figure from what I recall.

And since this dream is so vivid and I have always wanted to fly a bit, I guess I can fly for a while. It's my dream after all! I may as well make the best of it. Right, my friends would think this is so lame, but I won't tell them about it. It's my dream, but I reckon I need a cape. The only thing here that will do is the jacket. I tie the sleeves around my neck. Okay, it's very lame, but it's all I have. I really need to learn to control my dream environment if I am going to have dreams like this. Then I can make a cool Batman cape for myself and fly around Gotham City instead of this boring old town.

I try to imagine a black cape hanging from the door, but nothing happens. Damn. Well, maybe it takes time. I definitely do not want to wear my underpants over a pair of tights, but I like the cape idea. I would be the Dark Knight. That would be cool. I don't know how into the crime fighting I would be, but I definitely would swoop over the city and I could fly anywhere I wanted. I think then I would try to stay in the dream as long as I could instead of trying to get out of it. But the dreams I have are so fucking morose, who would want to continue in them? I need something different.

So the jacket will have to do. At least it is a dark navy colour. I climb back onto the window ledge. The cool breeze teases my hair and wraps itself around my body. I feel like I am ready to take flight; to fly like a bird and I am not scared. This is not real. I just want to savour the moment for a while.

The occasional car passes below me. Maybe I should try to hit one. That would make this a bit more fun. It would make it far more challenging. But the movement of the cars are not as regular as that on a TV game, so it is hard to judge when to jump. I eventually decide that if I hit a car it will be a bonus.

The street is quiet for a while and I enjoy the breeze playing over my body. Then I see a car turn into the street. It is not driving fast and I try to calculate when to jump. In the end, I just go with my gut. I take a huge leap off the building and start hurtling down.

My jacket gets whipped off from around my neck. There goes that idea. I can feel the wind pushing against my body. It is quiet a force and it feels almost as if the wind were trying to push me back up and stop this journey downward, but the pull of the earth is far greater on my body than the push of the wind and I continue down. I can see the car coming. I wonder if the occupants can see me coming?

It is a rush. I think I will start parachuting or base-jumping or something. It really feels like I am totally free and it doesn't last long, but I guess that makes it feel more special. The pattern that the windows make as they rush past me is somehow mesmerising. They started slow and now they are going faster and faster. I can almost hear the whoosh as I pass each storey.

The ground is coming up fast now. It is a horrible feeling. It feels like every organ in my body is repulsed by the ground and that they are trying to crawl deeper into my body to get away from it, but they know that there is nowhere for them to go and that their efforts are futile.

It feels like the opposite of vertigo. I don't know what to call it. I guess closigo will have to suffice for now.

I miss the car and I feel disappointed. But it doesn't last. I can't look at the ground, which is too close so I close my eyes as tight as I can and curl my body up to protect it from the impact.

16

I wake up. I feel all squashed up. I can't really move. I seem to be lying on the ground and I can't stretch out. It feels like there are weights all around me and there is nowhere to stretch my body out to. My legs and arms and head all seem to be against something and I can't straighten them. I feel something against my back and my front. I seem to be enclosed everywhere except for my one side. It feels a bit claustrophobic. I want to get up and, at the same time, I really don't.

I feel sleepy. I just want to go back to sleep. Maybe I am back in the loony bin and they have strapped me down or maybe I am lying all squashed and am still 'alive' on the street. I hope that's not the case, because I am not yet powerful enough to control my dreams and then I could be stuck for the rest of my life inside a dream that I can't get out of and I will be a cripple in that dream, which will be terrible.

I could not think of anything worse than being stuck inside a dream and then being a cripple in the dream I am stuck in and not being able to move at all. I would be like one of those people, who can't even talk or move their arms. I would just be able to blink my eyes and nothing else. And that would be all I could do for eternity.

That thought scares me and I really want to wake up to check that that is not the case, but I don't seem to be able to open my eyes or move my body. My eyes remain tightly shut and my limbs remain stubbornly inert. This scares me even more, but at the same time, I feel very calm and peaceful, which is strange and all I want to do is fall asleep again.

I decide to let the sleepy feeling take over and I slowly drift off to sleep despite the panic I feel. It is very weird. I feel like I am awake still and that I am watching myself fall asleep.

It feels as if my consciousness has been split into two. I listen to my deep breathing and it sounds like it is being echoed all around me. It starts to sooth the panic and I can feel the two parts of my mind beginning to merge into one.

17

"It's time to get up."

I don't want to get up. I can feel someone shaking my body gently and stroking my face. That feels nice, but at the same time it feels annoying, because I don't want to get up. I want to stay fast asleep.

I drift off again and am awoken by the shaking, stroking and a voice singing gently, "It's time to get up. It's time to get up. The day has begun. It's time to get up."

Oh, go away and let me sleep. Despite wanting to continue sleeping, I find myself waking up.

I feel a bit disorientated initially and then I start to remember last night's dream. I remember falling from the building and being so scared that I could not move my body. I stretch out and find that everything works just fine. That is such a relief!

Am I back in the hospital? Suddenly, I get a very creepy feeling. Why is Sister Jean or one of the sisters stroking my face and singing to me. That is seriously creepy.

I open my eyes and stare into the eyes of an elderly woman. She stares back at me and the warmth in her eyes dissolves into something hard and unreadable. She takes her hand away, but continues staring at me and I continue staring at her.

Eventually she gets up slowly and painfully. It looks like she has arthritis in her hands. They look all knobbly. From the way she is getting up, I reckon she has arthritis in other parts of her body too.

When she is upright, she stares back at me again and I realise that I am sleeping on the floor. We just keep staring at each other and it is very odd.

"Get up. You need to wash and milk the cow before you go to school. If you do not get up now you will be late and your teacher will hit you."

I get up and notice that there are other people on the floor with me. They all seem to be getting up too. There are two men and a woman, besides the old lady, and a teenage boy and a toddler.

It looks like we were all sleeping on the floor together. This is a very odd dream! The old lady has not taken her eyes off me and I feel very uncomfortable, so I decide for now just to follow what everybody else is doing and to find that cow and milk it. I am a little intimidated by her and until I can figure out what to do about getting out of this dream, I just need to stay low. I am sure she can't hurt me for real, but I am scared of her anyway, for some reason.

I notice that everyone is folding their blankets and putting them in a corner. We must have all been sleeping on the floor together. I stand up and fold my blanket and put it in the corner with everyone else's. I notice, as I stand, that everyone is taller than me and then I figure out that I am a kid. That may explain why I am so scared of granny over there.

I look around me. We seem to be in a very small room and there is not much in it. There is a small chest of drawers and everyone seems to be busy finding clothes from inside its drawers. I guess that is where mine are as well.

Suddenly, everyone starts taking their clothes off. I want to die of embarrassment. Why are they doing this? The lady notices me staring at her naked breasts and smiles at me.

"Good morning, my son."

"Morning."

She doesn't seem to be worried about me or anybody else seeing her naked. The men are naked too and the one catches my eye and smiles at me.

"Are you going to get dressed today? Or are you going to risk the teacher's stick and go in your nightclothes?" The man laughs at me.

For some reason the thought of the teacher's stick brings fear into my body. I can feel it rushing through me, so I go over to the chest of drawers and rifle around in there for my clothes.

"I think you have forgotten that Granny washed your school uniform last night."

"Oh yes."

I open the door and walk outside. My eyes take time to adjust to the harsh sunlight. When they stop watering, I look around me. The ground underneath my bare feet is a rich red-brown colour. It feels soft and clingy. The area seems to be tropical and I can see trees, shrubs and ground cover sprouting up from the earth in a haphazard way. I look back at the building I have just emerged from and it appears to be a very small, white hut of sorts. I locate my school uniform hanging up on a piece of wire that stretches from the roof of the hut to a pole that has been driven into the ground.

I take the pair of red underwear, the white shirt with a badge sewn onto the pocket, the pair of grey shorts and the pair of grey socks, which are all hanging together. The teenage boy emerges from the hut. He looks like he is in a bad mood and he doesn't look at me. He grabs the other uniform hanging on the wire. He goes back into the hut and I follow him.

I am a bit embarrassed about getting undressed in front of all these strangers, but they don't seem to pay me any attention. The men and the Granny have left the hut.

The younger lady is sweeping the hut and the toddler is playing next to the door. She must be a girl, because she is playing with a doll, which has been made out of sackcloth. The doll's face has been drawn on and she is smiling.

I put my uniform on and the lady comes to do my hair. She is very gentle. I like her. She keeps smiling at me. She makes sure that my uniform is on correctly and then I leave the hut. I find a pair of highly polished school shoes outside the hut and I slip them on before walking in the sand.

I somehow know where to find the cow. I find a bucket and I slip it under her. She seems to be used to this and someone has already given her some grass to eat. She munches the grass complacently while I squat and gently, but firmly draw milk from her.

I have never milked a cow in my entire life, but in this dream I seem to know what I am doing, which is great. I don't know if I would like to milk a cow every day for the rest of my life, but it's kind of cool to do it once, even if it isn't real. I probably saw a programme on milking cows when I was a kid and so have brought it to life now in my unconscious. I am not sure why I have created this dream, but I have.

Killing myself in my dreams obviously is not working out for me and, as I have no other ideas as to how to get out of these dreams, I feel a little frightened. I do not want to be stuck in a dream like this forever.

But for now, I will go along with the story my unconscious has scripted until I can figure out something else that will wake me up. If the dying thing is not working, there is no point in doing it again. I was so sure that falling would work. I feel disappointed and at the same time really worried. What happens if I cannot wake myself up?

I do not want to be stuck in a dream forever and none of the dreams I have are terribly amazing.

If I was a superhero, who had superpowers and was super rich and had women falling over him left right and centre, then that is a dream I would happily be stuck in, but none of the dreams I have had so far have been dreams that I want to stay in forever.

I take the bucket of milk around the side of the hut. Some concrete has been laid here and everyone is gathered there. There is a fire to the side of the concrete. It is crudely built in the sand from bits of stick and two black pots are been arranged over the fire. I place the milk a little way from the pots but not close enough to the fire to melt the plastic bucket. I can see why I did that, because flies are already gathering at the edges of the milk. It is so gross I want to retch, but I don't. The fire seems to have halved the fly population, which I guess is a good thing.

I peer into the pots. The big one seems to contain water and the little one seems to contain a white porridge of some kind.

There seems to be nothing for me to do so I sit down with my back against the wall of the hut and watch the people around me. The old lady seems to be stirring the porridge every now and then. The younger lady is putting out bowls and cups and a box of sugar and tea. The men are sitting and smoking. They seem to both be looking far out into the distance.

The teenage boy is nowhere in sight. The little girl is still playing with her doll. She is pretending to give the doll something to eat and drink. I get bored and find a stick on the ground. I use it to doodle in the sand.

"Come and get your porridge."

I get up and fetch a bowl. The old lady scoops a big clump of porridge into my bowl. I follow the others as they ladle some milk into their bowls and then sit down again. The men don't budge from where they were originally sitting and the young lady brings both of them their bowls of porridge. She then serves them both tea before bringing me mine.

By the time I get my tea, my porridge has cooled a little. I don't have a spoon, but I noticed earlier that the others were eating with their hands. I use my fingertips to grab a lump of stiff porridge. I wet it in the milk and then shove it into my mouth. It could do with some sugar, but I didn't see anyone else putting sugar on their porridge and I feel too intimidated to get up and spoon sugar onto my porridge. The tea at least is sweet and I take a sip between mouthfuls of porridge to help the thick mixture to go down my throat.

I notice that the others take water from the pot to rinse their bowls and then use it to rinse their mouths out. I do the same. It is not super-hygienic, but I don't see any soap or toothpaste around. I go around the back of the hut to relieve myself in some bushes and then come back to the front of the hut again.

"Here, my son."

The young lady hands me a khaki-coloured satchel.

"Thank you, mama."

Interesting, I seem to be piecing the dream together now. It is coming back to me. This is my mother and the old lady is my father's mother. One of the men is my father and the other is my uncle, my father's brother. The teenage boy is the son of this uncle. His wife died many years ago. He has had many women, but has never married again. The little girl is my sister. She is six years younger than me. I am eight years old. My mother had many stillbirths after I was born. I remember her crying for many days after each baby was lost. That is why there is such a big age difference between my sister and myself. My grandfather died many years ago. He died of a coughing sickness. My father has a sister, but she lives with her husband's family in another village. We see her when we have festivals. My mother's family also does not live in this village, but we see them once a month. The journey there is expensive and long and we cannot afford to go there more often than that.

I feel as if a cloud has lifted. At least the dream makes a bit more sense to me now. I know who I am. My name is Amani Kibaki and I am in my third year at school. I live in this village with my family and the walk to school every day is long and dusty and on the way home it is hot and even longer and dustier.

"Amani!"

My friend, Waweru waves at me. He greets my family and I say goodbye to everyone in the family. My grandmother is still looking at me warily. It hurts my feelings, because we are close and I have never seen her look at me like this before.

But there is nothing I can do about it. I need to be on time for school or else, Mr. Chipende will thrash me with his stick. I remember him doing that to me at the beginning of the year, when I did not understand what I was supposed to do in maths. I still do not understand what I am supposed to do, but he does not hit me if I am quiet.

I am very afraid of Mr Chipende. He is a big man and his belly bulges grotesquely over his belt. His eyes are yellow and they stick out a little bit, almost as if they are trying to escape his eye sockets and come and attack you. And he is so strong. I could not sit for a week after I tasted the kiss of his cane. Well, actually I had to sit. If I had stood in class, he would have beaten me again. So even though my bottom ached, I had to sit on it. Mr Chipende likes to hit children. I don't think a day goes by where he does not apply his cane to one of the children in my class. When he does not hit us, he shouts at us. He says that we are very stupid children and that we don't learn anything.

He is right. I don't understand anything he tells me. I am lost like a baby elephant, who cannot find his mother in the dark. I guess I am a stupid child. My father wants me to be a doctor when I grow up. I can help all the sick people in my village. If I was a doctor when my grandfather was sick, he would not have died. My grandfather lives in a hole in the ground now. I hope he can breathe. Mama says that he does not need to breathe anymore, but I am not so sure about that. If I was a doctor, grandfather would still be here today. I would have saved him. But now I will not be a doctor, because I am too stupid and only clever people become doctors. My father says that doctors and teachers make a lot of money. If I was a doctor, I could give all my money to my family and we would not be poor anymore. We could have a car! I want a big red one. Then everyone will think I am the best person in the village, if I have a big red shiny car! But I won't have a car, because I am a stupid boy. I don't understand anything in class and I am ashamed to tell my father and my grandmother. They would be so disappointed in me.

Waweru and I don't ever talk much on our way to school. I guess neither of us is very happy about going to school. We talk more on the way home. The journey to school is a sad one; the journey home is a joyous one.

Waweru finds a stone on the dusty road. He kicks it.

I run and kick it before it stops rolling. He then runs and kicks it and so we go. It is fun and I am glad he started our favourite game. It distracts me from the day ahead, which will have to be endured.

We don't enter the school until the bell rings. We have an unspoken agreement to not enter the school grounds until we have to. We line up in front of Mr Chipende. Each class has to line up in front of their teacher and then the headmaster greets us. We are very quiet and listen to the headmaster. He announces that we will have soccer matches at school in two weeks time against another school. It will be on a Saturday so that all our parents can come and watch. Every class will play. I like playing soccer, so that will be something to look forward to. I wonder if my cousin will lend me his soccer ball to play with. As moody as he is, he doesn't mind if I borrow it as long as I clean all the dust off afterwards. It is a real soccer ball. It is made from real leather and it is very expensive. My uncle bought it for him as a present for his birthday after his initiation ceremony two years ago. I love going to the petrol station to pump it up. Mr Tikolo lets me pump the ball until it is as firm as a green mango. And then we can kick it so far. When it loses air, it is difficult to kick it far. But when it is full of air, it can fly through the air like a bird. It is like the air inside the ball is the same, as the air outside the ball and it doesn't know that there is a ball in the way.

I wasn't paying attention to what the headmaster was saying. I hope it was not important. He has finished speaking and we follow Mr Chipende back to our classroom. I am glad that I sit in the middle of the classroom, because he mainly stands in the front of the classroom and he is scary and he spits when he talks. I would be too scared to wipe the spit off me and then I would have to sit there with it on me until it dried.

We start the day with writing exercises. Mr Chipende writes a 't' on the blackboard and we have to copy it very neatly. If it is not neat, he tears the page out of your book and you have to do it again until you get it right. I can barely move when he comes past my desk. I force myself to keep on writing when he stands over me and stares at my book. I am so nervous that my hand shakes, but I write very slowly, so that I won't make the 't' look all wobbly. Thankfully, he eventually moves past me without saying anything. I can feel my shoulders relax a little bit.

Some of the other children are not so lucky. He shouts at them for being messy and not caring about their handwriting. He tells them that only stupid people don't care about their handwriting. He says that if you have messy handwriting, you will not get a job. He tears out their pages and throws them in the tin dustbin in the front corner of the classroom.

I finish my two pages of handwriting exercises. When you are finished, you have to sit very still with your arms folded. I do this. It is hard to sit still though, but I am getting better at it. The bite of the cane is worse than sitting still and I know I will get it if I don't sit still. There is not much to look at in the classroom. The walls are bare. The walls look like fake grey bricks. There is a green board at the front of the classroom. We each have a day to clean it and I hate cleaning it, because the dust from the chalk makes my throat hurt and my eyes sting. All the desks are brown, including Mr Chipende's desk. He has the biggest desk in the room. We each have our own desks. It's part of growing up. Last year we shared a desk with one other child and the year before we sat four at a desk, but now we have our own desks. I am not sure I like having my own desk. I feel like I am stranded on a rock and if danger comes it is too far to get down and run to another rock for moral support. I have to face the danger on my own. Maybe that is part of growing up.

I am bored, so I think about the soccer match that I will play in. I imagine my father and my uncle coming to watch me play. I imagine that I score all the goals in the game and everyone is cheering for me. My grade wins because of me. I am the best player in the whole match. The headmaster shakes my hand and I get a beautiful ribbon that I can take home to show Mama and Granny. They will tell the whole village about how good I am at playing soccer. My father and uncle will be so happy with me. Maybe father will buy me a soda to celebrate and then I will sit under my favourite tree by the waterfall and I will feel all the bubbles exploding on my tongue, as I slowly drink each drop. I will only drink half. Then I will go to the river and let the water flow over my body until I am nice and cool. I will go back and sit, still dripping river water, under the tree and drink the rest of the soda until I am dry. When I come home, my family will still be happy that I am the best soccer player for my age and they will not think about how stupid I am at learning.

My Chipende tells us to put our books away. It is time for reading. I hate reading. We only have two books for the whole class and Mr Chipende sits at his desk with the one book and we all have to take turns to read from the other book. We go row by row and I get more and more nervous as it gets closer to me. Eventually it is my turn to read. I stand up and walk to the front of the class. I pick up the book that was left on Mr Chipende's desk by the last learner and I walk to stand in front of the class. The book is about a dog that can talk and goes to school. I open it to page five as Mr Chipende instructs me and I start to read, the thing is that I really don't know how to read. I know all the letters and I try to put them together to make words, but they don't make words at all. They don't sound like words and I am not sure what I am reading. I hate reading. I just can't do it. I get to the end of the page and return the book to Mr Chipende's desk, before returning to my seat.

At least that was over and I can relax as the rest of the class has to read their pages out loud. The bell rings for break time.

Mama packed some bread in my satchel and I take that out to eat. It's just plain bread. If we have extra money, my family will buy jam to put on the bread, but there is no money for jam this week. I sit and eat my bread and then I go into the playground to play with my friends. Waweru and I play tag with some of the other children and all too soon, the bell rings again. We line up to go to the toilet and to drink some water and then it's another line up before we go back to class.

I hate maths too. In fact, there is not one subject that I like at school. I wish I did not have to go to school to learn. I wish there was a different way to do things, but there isn't. We all have to do it. My cousin has been going to school for many more years than me and he seems to have managed to do it and if he can do it, then so can I.

We are adding sums with three numbers in each row. I try to remember the way we were taught to do it, but it doesn't make sense to me. I am not sure what to do if the number is bigger then 9, because there is no space to put the answer and then I end up with an answer that looks bigger than it should be. If I ask one of the other children to help me, Mr Chipende will hit me and if I ask Mr Chipende to help me, he will hit me, because he will shout that I don't listen to him. After what seems like many years, and I must be an old man by this time, the maths lesson is over.

Then it is time for history, the last lesson for today. We learn about the history of our country. Mr Chipende tells us about all the important people who have lived in this country. I can't remember all of their names. There are too many of them and I am not sure when they lived, but I think it was a long time ago.

Mr Chipende writes up a list of words on the board for us to copy and take home to learn. We will have a spelling test tomorrow. I write down the words and check them many times to make sure that I copied them down correctly. If I get less than five words correct tomorrow, I will have to walk to the field at the back of the building after school and cut down the grass. The teachers make us do that if we don't do well, because they say that it will help us to learn to not be lazy. I have cut down many fields of grass, because I am not good at school. I don't think that I am lazy, but maybe I am.

The bell rings and we are dismissed and then my day begins. Waweru and I walk home together. He finds another stone for us to kick. We laugh and try to make each other run the furthest. I get a very good kick and Waweru has to run many steps down the road. I laugh and chase after him before he kicks the stone and makes me run fast. I catch up with him before he kicks the stone. We have to keep the stone rolling. The person, who lets the stone stop, is the loser. Neither of us loses today and we arrive at my house.

Mama is there and I can smell plantains are cooking for lunch. Waweru and I make a plan to meet after lunch and homework to swim in the river. The plantains are delicious and I eat them like a hungry jackal. I find a shady tree to sit down under and open my schoolbook. I try to get the words to go into my head. It is hard work and I keep forgetting.

"B-U-T-T-E-R"

I say the word over and over again. It just won't go in. I keep mixing up the order of the letters and I know I need to get them in the right order so I don't get into trouble.

"B-U-T-T-R-E."

No that was wrong. I do it again and again. I don't know what the word is saying. But I try to remember the order. Maybe father can tell me what the word is when he gets home. Mr Chipende did not tell us the meanings of the words when he wrote them up, but even if he had, I don't think I would have remembered them.

I can see that the sun is at the right place above the tree at Mrs. Gikonyo's house, so it is time to go for a swim. I put my book back into my satchel and take off my shoes and socks. I run on the clinging red sand down to the river. It is not a far run. I have never counted how many steps it takes to get there, but it is not too far.

When I arrive, Waweru is there and he is already in his underpants. I take off all my clothes except my underpants and we both step into the river.

The warm brown water is flowing strongly today and I can hear from Waweru's laugh that he is as nervous as I am. Neither of us knows how to swim. We do not have a swimming teacher at our school and my family does not know how to swim either, so no one has ever taught me how to do it. No one has taught Waweru either. I don't know if anyone in my village has learnt to swim, come to think of it.

It is fun to get wet and to splash each other with water. I jump up and down and then jump up in the air and land on my haunches and make a huge splash, but Waweru manages to make a bigger one. I do not like to be beaten by my friends at games like this so I wade a little deeper into the river, because the more water there is, the bigger the splash will be.

I jump up and pull my legs underneath me to make my body as big as I can. I make a huge splash. Waweru will never be able to beat that.

Suddenly my feet are swept out from under me and I can feel that the river has caught me in its arms and is going to take me away to die. I struggle against it and find that I have made it to shore with far more ease than I thought. The last time that had happened to me, father was there to pull me out. But this time, I did it by myself.

I am shaky, as I pull myself back up onto the riverbank. I lie in the sand and get my breath back.

"Amani! You were swimming!"

"What?"

"You were swimming."

"I don't know how to swim, Waweru."

"But you were. You were moving your arms like this." He rotates his arms in two circles.

"I don't think I did that."

"You did! I saw you. You were just like the swimming men I saw on my uncle's television. I saw it last summer, so I remember it very well and you were doing the same thing." He rotates his arms again.

"You are talking nonsense, Waweru and you look funny. You look like a fly that has hit his head and is going around in circles." I burst out laughing. Waweru does not laugh with me.

"You were swimming, Amani. Who taught you? Please teach me."

"I wasn't swimming, Waweru and so I cannot teach you how to swim."

"You are a liar, Amani!"

Waweru runs back to the village. I do not understand why he is so angry with me. I almost died and my father will be angry with me for being careless and Mama will be angry too. I am lucky that I am alive and have not been swallowed up by the hungry river. I lift myself up onto my elbows and look out at the river. Yes, the river is very hungry today. I must be careful or else the river will have me for dinner. I do not want to be anyone's dinner.

I feel fine though. I am happy to be alive and I let the river pull gently on my feet, which are still in the water. I just lie on my back, propped up on my elbows, watching the river. It feels nice.

I eventually notice that the sun is getting low. I need to dry off before I put my clothes on again and I want Father to help me with those words. I think we will have some chicken for dinner tonight. I remember Grandmother mentioning it last night. I think she had enough money to buy a chicken for dinner tonight. I can feel my stomach is growling when I think about the chicken.

I move up onto a rock next to the river. The rock is dry and warm, after being cooked by the sun all day. I roll onto my stomach and drift off into a light sleep. I am not worried about being late. I never sleep for very long.

When I wake up, I can see that the sky is turning the purple and red colours of evening. I get dressed and walk slowly back to my hut.

I can see the cooking fire has been lit and I imagine a delicious chicken cooking in the pot with plantains and herbs. Maybe we will have some beans tonight as well. I can see my family gathered on the concrete outside. They are all sitting quietly and appear to be enjoying the evening. My father is not yet home. My homework will have to wait, but maybe I should practice some more before dinner.

Then I notice the old medicine woman has come to visit us tonight. She is sitting next to Grandmother and talking. I don't like her. She is a scary lady. She has yellow eyes to match her few yellow teeth and her eyes are crazy. When she looks at you with those eyes, you just feel scared. But it would be rude to not greet her and the family, so I walk up to everyone to bid them a good evening.

"Hello, my son."

"Hello, Mama."

"Waweru came to ask us if you had learnt to swim today."

"I am sorry, Mama. I was careless, I was caught by the river, but I managed to free myself and I am fine. Waweru imagines that I can swim, but I do not know how to. I am lucky. I suppose I will not be able to go to the river tomorrow."

"I think that the river taught you a big lesson today, Amani," my uncle says, "I don't think you need more punishment than that."

"No, Uncle."

"Why are you talking to this boy?"

"Please, Mama, stop this," my mother says.

"I can tell that this is not your son. I have brought the medicine woman to get your son back."

"Mama, you are getting old now."

"Do not disrespect me, Daughter. I have lived many years and I have seen many more things than you have seen. I know what I am talking about. The medicine woman will not hurt him."

"Come here, boy."

I look at my Mama. I am not sure what is going on.

"It will be fine, my son. Go."

I walk to my grandmother, who still stares at me distrustfully.

The medicine woman walks up to me and crouches so that she is looking at me at eye-level. Her breath smells bad, almost rancid and she stares at me. I am scared and I can feel my heart rate and my breathing increase.

The medicine woman starts to shake a type of rattle and she starts to sing a song I have never heard before. She does not take her eyes off me and like a small rabbit trapped in the hypnotic stare of a snake, I cannot look away from her. My family is silent and they don't move. They seem to be as caught in this woman's magic as I am.

Suddenly the woman starts banging the rattle loudly in front of me.

"Be gone! Be gone! Be gone!"

I feel myself drifting backwards; I must be falling. I feel like I am falling asleep, which is very strange. Then I realise that I am not Amani. I have been dreaming this whole time. I had forgotten I was dreaming.

I am not falling asleep. I am falling awake.

18

I open my eyes. I am lying in a bed and I can see the familiar curtains of the hospital room. I look around. I am back in the loony bin. I never thought I'd be back in the loony bin again. I thought I'd be trapped in my dreams forever. Thank you weird witchdoctor lady for waking me up! That seemed to work so well. I guess I have learnt something for the next time this happens, but I am not so sure there will be a next time, because I am sure as hell never going to sleep again, if I can avoid it. But if, and that's a really strong if, there is a next time, I am going to try to think of that witchdoctor lady and get her to wake me up again.

My watch is on the bedside table. I pick it up and look at the time. It's 6:30am. I have time to have a shower before breakfast. I really need to clear my head. I hope I am going to see the Doc today. I really need to talk to him to sort this out.

Man, am I hungry!

I get out of bed and stumble to the shower. I am not fully awake, but I really am very hungry. My stomach feels like a void. I pat it to make sure it's still there – it feels so hollow.

The shower feels good. My head feels clearer and I towel off and get dressed. I make my way to the dining hall. The food smells great. I could be eating offal right now and I am sure I would think it smelled great.

I help myself to four large spoonfuls of scrambled eggs. There is some bacon and I scoop a few slices onto my plate. I help myself to generous portions of fried mushrooms and tomatoes. There is a pan full of sausages, which are leaking fat, and I grab three of those. I see that there is a jug of fresh coffee and I pour myself a mug full.

I don't bother with sugar or cream. I need a straight shot of coffee.

I sit down to eat at an unoccupied table. I don't think about anything other than eating and drinking and once I am finished I feel slightly ill. I think I ate more than I should have, but I am sure I will feel fine. I sit and stare into space while I think about the dreams I have had. I wonder if I was in a catatonic state again while I was having them? I wonder if they lasted a couple days or just one night? I run my hand over my face. The heavy growth of stubble indicates that it may have been more than one night.

"Richard?"

"Yeah?" I look up to find a nurse I have not met before, looking down at me.

"Sister Jean would like to see you in her office as soon as you are ready."

"Okay, sure. I'll go there now. Thanks."

I put away my tray in the rack and walk to Sister Jean's office. I am so glad I am no longer dreaming. Everything is exactly as I remember it. It is good to be awake. I remember where her office is. I get there and knock on the door.

"Come in."

"You wanted to see me."

"Richard. Please come in and sit down. How are you feeling?"

"Okay, I guess. How long was I out of it?"

"You became very anxious in Dr. Tsakonas' office. He felt really bad about it. You seemed just to drift back into a catatonic state and then he called for some aides to take you back to the ward. We brought you back and you were like that for the past two days. Are you feeling alright today, Richard?"

"Yes, I feel fine. I was really hungry and I felt a bit light-headed, but I feel better now. Well, now that I have eaten."

"Dr. Tsakonas will want to see you today. Are you up for that?"

"Yes. I really want to talk to him. In fact, I have a lot to talk to him about so the sooner I could see him, the better."

"I'll arrange an appointment for you as soon as I can. Richard, we as a staff have decided that maybe things have been going a bit too fast for you. We were thinking that perhaps you should take things easy and not stress yourself out. Dr. Tsakonas will talk to you more about it, but in the meantime, we have decided that perhaps it is better if you don't have any visitors just now."

"That is fine by me. I am happy to do whatever it takes to stop this from happening to me. So if you guys think that not having visitors is better for me, then I am fine with that. No problem."

"That's good. We have also taken away your cell phone for now. We will communicate with your parents and they can update your friends."

"That's also fine, Sister. If you all think I am not ready for this stuff, then I am fine. I really don't want to freak out like that again."

"We also removed the mirror from your bathroom as that seems to have been the trigger. After treatment with Dr. Tsakonas, I am sure that we will be able to get you back to normal."

"It's weird. I didn't even notice that it was gone. Huh! I remember now. I looked at myself in the mirror with the Doc and then I feel asleep, well went into a catatonic state. Yeah, I am happy with operation no-mirrors."

"Great, Richard, I will let you know what time Dr. Tsakonas can see you. Where will you be?"

"I think I just need some quiet time. I'll be in my room reading or sleeping, I guess."

"I'll come to your room to let you know when he can see you and if you are sleeping, I'll wake you half an hour before your appointment, if that's alright."

"Yeah. Sounds great. Actually I will probably end up reading and not sleeping so just let me know."

"Alright, Richard. I'll let you know."

"Great. Thanks. Later."

I walk back to my room. I don't feel like any human interactions today, so I am glad that no one can contact me. I am sure that my mother is probably freaking out again and I am not in the mood to deal with that. I don't feel like hanging out with the loonies and I am happy not to talk to my friends. I just want to talk to the Doc.

Those dreams were so vivid and I am so glad that they weren't real, especially the drinking one. I am so relieved that I didn't fuck up. It would have been so dumb if I had ended up getting trashed after five months in a catatonic state and this latest episode has made it quite clear in my mind that I have no intention to drink or drug for the rest of my entire life. Man, I have totally screwed up my mind.

If someone had told me that that would happen when I started using, I probably wouldn't have cared at all, but the thing is, it is easy not to care about something that is not real and does not seem a possibility. This is different. Now it is real and I am screwed up - probably for the rest of my life and it's too late. I wish I could go back in time and tell myself not to do all that shit, but we can't go back and now I am stuck with this condition. I am going to have to treat myself like a kid and be careful about every move I make. This totally sucks, man!

Anyway, I can't sit and think about this all day, because it will end up stressing me out even more, so I should just lie down and read for a while. I find my stash of comic books packed neatly in my bedside table. I grab them and then roll over and start at the beginning. This stuff never gets old.

Sister Jean tells me the Doc can see me at 11am and lets me know that she will come through at 10:45am to remind me. That's cool, because then I can get lost in my comics and I don't have to worry about keeping track of time. For a while, I enter the world of Batman and forget my troubles.

Sister Jean interrupts me in the middle of a really good fight scene, which I am reluctant to leave, but I do want to see the Doc. I pull on my sneakers and make my way down to his office.

"Hey, Doc."

"Richard, please sit down. How are you?"

"I am just glad to be awake!"

"I am glad that you are feeling better, Richard. I was so worried. I am sorry that I pushed you too far."

"Well, I guess it was worth a try."

"Yes, but I don't think we will try it again. I really want to slow things down a lot. We will get there. We don't need to rush to get there."

"Listen, Doc. I want my life back. I have had some really weird dreams these last two days that I want to talk to you about, but they made me think. They were a real wake up call. I have totally fucked up my mind and I want to be normal again, well as normal as I can be again and I do not want to make things worse. I have absolutely no intention of ever drinking or drugging ever again. If I need to stay in the loony bin for a whole year, I am prepared to do it. I will do whatever it takes to make my life better. I just want to be normal. Well, I guess, as normal as it is possible to be."

"You and I are going to work together to get there. There are no guarantees in life, but I promise you that I am going to do my best by you and if I can't help you, I will try to find help from other people. So, I may end up having to talk to people outside the hospital for help. Do I have your permission for that?"

"Absolutely, Doc. Absolutely. Whatever it takes."

"You mentioned you were dreaming when you were in your catatonic state."

"Yes, is that normal for someone to be in a catatonic state and to dream? Because it seems to happen to me all the time."

"We do not understand everything there is to know about the human psyche. I prefer to view each person individually and try to meet their individual needs."

"I was just wondering."

"Tell me about the dreams."

"Well Doc, the first dream was seriously freaky. I woke up and thought I had gone out drinking and ended up in some derelict house. I thought I might have gone out with one of the other patients here. I thought that she had taken me there. It felt so real. I was so angry with myself for having fucked up. You know the drinking and drugging got me to this point in the first place and then I find myself drunk and passed out. I was really pissed off with myself. I thought I was lost and wanted to find out where I was and how to get back to the hospital and the people in my dream didn't know that I was Richard and then I realised that I was dreaming and since it was a dream, I could do anything I liked. The one guy in my dream kept telling me that it wasn't a dream, but I knew it was, so I wanted to prove to him that nothing could happen to me. I walked onto a freeway and go hit by a car. I thought I would wake up then, you know, the impact and all, but I didn't."

"What happened then?"

"Then I found myself up on a window ledge in an office block. It was weird to end up there and it took a bit of time again to figure out what was happening. I ended up jumping off the window ledge in the hopes that falling would wake me up. You know sometimes you have those dreams when you are falling and you wake up before you hit the ground?"

"Yes."

"Well, I was hoping that I would wake up before I hit the ground, but I didn't. I hit the ground and then it felt like I woke up and I was all squashed. I thought that I had damaged my body, but I hadn't. I was still dreaming. I ended up dreaming that I was a kid living in a hut in Africa. I went to school and then I went swimming and I almost got washed away, but I managed to save myself. Then my grandma in the dream got some witchdoctor lady and told me to get out and I woke up. It was great! So I have learnt that falling or impacts don't wake me up. I need to imagine that witchdoctor to help me wake up."

"Very interesting. What do you make of these dreams?"

"Well, I guess the one about the drunk was about me. I am glad I had it. I ended up drinking again in the dream and I guess it is really easy to start drinking and drugging again. I was so disappointed with myself in the beginning and then that passed. So I started drinking again, because I knew I was dreaming, I kind of thought it was okay, but at the same time it was scary and I am so glad I didn't drink in real life. I am going to do whatever it takes to never drink or drug again, because let me tell you, Doc, it is seriously scary to not be able to wake myself up."

"I agree with your understanding of your dream. I think your unconscious is trying to process what has happened to you and what could have happened to you. I have another thought, which I would like to add, if I may?"

"Sure."

"I was thinking that you were drinking and using drugs and maybe you didn't care consciously about what could happen to you, it seems to be that you were scared of going nowhere and about being destitute on the street, as happened in this dream. What I am saying is that your attitude may not have been as carefree as you may have thought."

"Yeah, that is possible, Doc. But I'll tell you now, that I ain't going to drink or use ever again. That was scary."

"I believe you. What about the second dream? Tell me more about it and what you understand about it."

"Well, I was very rich and successful. I was a real player. I had loads of chicks that liked me. I had a good position in my company and I had loads of money, but I wasn't really happy. I guess that it is kind of like my life – not my life now, but my life before this – I didn't really have to worry about anything, but I wasn't happy, just like the guy in my dream."

"I think you have a good understanding."

"Thanks, Doc." I knew he would like all this stuff. I feel pretty proud of myself.

"And you said that you found yourself standing on a window ledge when the dream began and you ended that particular dream by jumping out of the window to your death?"

"Yeah, that's about what happened."

"What does that mean for you?"

"I think that when I walked onto the freeway in the previous dream, I was trying to get hit by a car. I think in part I was doing it to have a bit of a power trip, because I knew I couldn't get hurt, because it was only a dream, but the other reason is that I really wanted to wake up. I guess that maybe it felt like suicide and oh yeah, the dream guy kept yelling at me to stop, so it may have felt a bit like suicide, and so maybe I had an unconscious link to the next dream about suicide and that's why I ended up on the window ledge about to jump when the dream began."

"That makes sense. I want to explore that theme more with you, but not today. Today, I just want to hear about your dreams and what you understand about them."

"Sure, you're the boss, Doc, or should I say, you are the Doc, Doc."

"Tell me about the dream in Africa. That seems very different to your other dreams. Why did you dream about Africa? Have you been there before?"

"No, I have never been there before and I have never really given it much thought, to be honest. I have seen stuff about Africa on the news sometimes, but it's not a place I think about."

"So why did you have a dream about Africa?"

"I heard a message in the office dream on my answering machine, where a buddy of mine in the dream had gone to work in Africa. I think he was a doctor. So I guess that was why I had gone there."

"That sounds plausible, but is there any other reason, on a psychological level, so to speak, that you would end up dreaming about Africa?"

"Well, the kid in the dream was living with his family and going to school and stuff, so maybe it was about living an ordinary life and I am not living an ordinary life right now."

"Was the kid in your dream rich or poor?"

"He was definitely poor."

"What I am thinking is that maybe it provided a juxtaposition in your mind to the previous dream where you had it all and you were not happy and then you have a dream where you have nothing, the complete opposite of what you have in this life."

"That is interesting, Doc. That's a lot to think about. It's weird, because all the doors in the corridors in the passage were all locked and maybe going to Africa in my head, you know, going to the opposite of what I have, was the only way for my mind to go."

"That is interesting. Maybe you had to experience the opposite? What was the opposite like for you?"

"It was okay. It wasn't as bad as I would imagine. Life just sort of carried on. If I think about being poor, it scares the shit out of me, but it wasn't as bad as I imagined. You know. The kid had a good family and they got on with life. It was weird."

"He didn't have much?"

"No, he didn't have anything really, but he was okay. He had a horrible teacher, who he didn't like, but otherwise he was okay without anything."

"So maybe not having much is all right."

"Maybe. It wasn't too bad. It is not what I would choose though."

"I am not saying you have to choose that at all. I am just saying that maybe you need to think about not having stuff. Just think about if it is that scary or not. Just think about that for now. We can explore it all at a later time."

"Sure."

"You mentioned a horrible teacher. Tell me about this person."

"Well, he didn't really care about any of the kids he taught. It was just a job for him. Something to do to make money, but it wasn't something he liked. He was super strict as well."

"Maybe it worries you that you will one day take a job that you will hate."

"Totally, Doc. It seriously scares me and then I am stuck in that career for life."

"I am glad you had these dreams. I know that they are not pleasant, but I think that they are all giving us ideas as to what is happening to you and, if we can understand them, then I am hoping that they will point the way to helping you."

"That's kind of what I thought, while I was having them."

"Were you aware that you were dreaming?"

"Totally aware, though I sort of forgot in the Africa dream. I only realised when the witchdoctor came."

"So if you are aware, what do you feel?"

"I feel confused, because I don't know that I am dreaming usually in the beginning and then I feel scared, because I want to wake myself up and I can't.'

"And you say nothing helped you wake up until the witchdoctor came."

"Yeah, I tried all the standard dream-waking stuff, Doc. People always say that they wake up before they are about to die. That's totally not true. I am living proof of that. And it totally didn't work. I would just wake up in another dream."

"Why did the witchdoctor help?"

"I am not sure. She just told me to get out."

"Do you think that would work? Would you be able to tell yourself that in a dream? Would you have that much control?"

"Yeah, I think I could control that part of the dream. It's weird, because the dream is kind of given to me, by my unconscious obviously, but I can't control the content of the dream, only how I interact with the content of the dream."

"People have different kinds of dreams. Some people dream about stuff that they have no control over. They just remember it like a movie afterwards. Some people have some control over their dreams, like you do, and some people are able to control every aspect of what they dream about."

"I want to be part of the last group."

"Why?"

"Well, because then I could control every part of my dream. That would be awesome."

"What would you dream about?"

"What does every guy dream about? Getting laid by hot chicks and being able to do stuff that he can't ordinarily do, like fly and stuff."

"When you figure how to do that, let me know!"

"Will do, Doc. Will do."

"But for now we know that if this happens, you need to think about getting out."

"Yeah, maybe I need to just think the words 'get out' and that will make me wake up. It's the only thing that worked."

"Well, if it happens again, you will try that. Is there anything else you would like to talk about?"

"Well, yeah actually there is. I don't think I can go to sleep again, Doc."

"This doesn't happen when you sleep. You slept fine for a few nights after you came round last time, isn't that true?"

"Yeah, come to think of it, it was fine."

"So I don't think it is sleep related. I think it is stress related. I think I stressed you by putting you through the mirror exercise, Richard, and for that, I am deeply sorry. You have been through a great deal and I pushed you too far. My working plan with you now is to keep stress down to a minimum, until you are ready to deal with more. Is that all right with you?"

"That is fine with me, Doc and in fact, I am glad to hear that, because I am exhausted and I really just want to go to sleep."

"Then I think that is what you should do and I will see you again tomorrow morning. We can do an eleven o'clock appointment again."

"That would be great."

"Fine, I want you to get your medicine before you go to sleep now. Have some lunch, take your medicine and have a good rest and I will see you tomorrow."

"Thanks Doc. It was good talking to you."

"Keep well, Richard, just relax."

I follow the Doc's instructions. I am not really hungry at lunchtime so I have a mouthful of pie and swallow my meds before falling fast asleep.

19

I find it hard to wake up. I look at the time through my bleary eyes. It says it is eight. I look at my windows. Light is shining through them. It must be 8am, because it is not dark. That means I have slept through pretty much the whole of yesterday. And I still feel tired. That is weird. I have never slept that much. I must have really needed it after the dreams and the catatonia. Maybe it took a lot out of me. I don't know. Man, am I hungry!

I sit up and startle. Out of the corner of my eye, I see someone walk into my bathroom. I get up and look around the bathroom. There is no one there. I look around my room. The curtains are flapping in the breeze and casting shadows on the walls. That must have been what I saw. Still a bit woozy, I guess. I just have enough time to shower and go for breakfast before they close up for the morning.

I feel better after breakfast and so I wander into the garden. I see the Goth chick. I sit on the wall above her. She is sitting on the grass leaning against the wall.

"I was getting hopeful that you left this place, Perv. Sadly, I see that you are still here."

"Yeah. I have had a bad couple of days."

"Oh."

We sit in silence.

"How have things been for you since our last scintillating conversation?"

"Boring as usual."

"Ah."

"You ok, Perv?"

"You are enquiring into my well-being?"

"Listen, if you are going to be an asshole, I'm leaving."

"Okay, sorry. Thanks. I am glad to be awake and able to think, you know, but otherwise no, my life is really fucked up."

"Mine too."

"I'm sorry, man."

"Me too. Life sucks!"

"Yeah, you don't realise it till it's too late. I think I have totally screwed myself up and I will never be the same again. That scares me, to be honest."

"I have always been screwed up, so nothing new there, but I guess we get to the same end point."

"You are so optimistic."

"As are you."

"Point taken. How long have you been here?"

"About three weeks. I had a bit of a nervous breakdown at school."

"Sorry man. What are you studying?"

"Art. I am studying fine arts. What are you studying?"

"Nothing. I am a screw up, who never bothered to do anything. Just spent my time using and drinking and now I am here. I was kind of in a coma for five months."

"Hence why I have never seen you out and about."

"Yeah, and I went back into it a couple days ago. It seems that when I get stressed, I totally freak out. I never used to be like that. I have always been such a laid-back person. You know. Nothing would get to me, ever. Now, I do a simple exercise with my shrink and I lose it."

"Bummer. I know what you mean though. I just couldn't cope with school. I totally lost it. I just totally freaked out and ended up stuck in my dorm not doing anything. I can't remember too much about it. Then my mom brought me here. It's totally lame being here, but I guess I have to stay."

"Was it school stress?"

"Nah, just stuff from the past that I kind of remember. Just suddenly came flooding back."

"Bummer."

"Major."

"Do you want a smoke?"

"Sure. Thanks."

We both light up and sit there in silence smoking. I like this girl. There's something about her. I also like that we can just hang and we don't need to talk or anything. And did I mention that she is totally hot? I did. I did. Yeah, we'll see how things progress. I have a lot of time in the loony bin and she probably does too, so maybe one thing will lead to another and this place won't be so bad after all.

"I gotta see my shrink now. Will I see you later?"

"Yeah, sure, there's nothing better to do here."

"Cool. Later."

"Later."

I walk to the Doc's office. I reckon things may turn out okay after all. It may not be so bad. If I end up with a really hot girlfriend at the end of this experience, I can deal with that. Also, if I can sort myself out maybe I will be better off at the end of all this. That would be worthwhile. Maybe I haven't screwed myself up that badly after all. I've just got to watch the stress and that I can do. We get too stressed in this day and age anyways.

As I walk along the passage to the Doc's office, I get a creepy feeling. A shiver runs down my back and I think I see a shadow at the end of the corridor. When I look again, there is nothing there and I feel fine again. It's going to take time to get right again. I tell myself this over and over, as I open the Doc's door.

"Hi Richard, come in. How are you doing today?"

"I slept like a log, Doc. As soon as I hit the sack, I was out like a light, man and I felt really woozy this morning when I woke up. I felt better after breakfast and a shower though. It seemed to have cleared my head for the most part. Also I got a chance to hang with that girl I really like."

"I am glad you are feeling better, but remember to take everything slow."

"Yeah, I know Doc. Don't worry. I don't want another episode like that again."

"Good and take it slow with this girl as well. Relationships, as much as they can make us feel good, can also be stressful. I presume you met her here."

"Yes, Doc."

"Just take it slow. Look after yourself."

"I know, Doc. I hear you. I am going to take real good care of myself. That's why I keep pitching up at your office right on time."

"I am glad. Did you have any dreams last night?"

"Nope, I felt fine actually. I felt reassured after talking to you and I fell asleep – no problem. I pretty much slept from after lunch till this morning."

"That's good to hear. I am glad you slept well. How are you feeling on your medication?"

"I am feeling fine. I am actually almost one hundred percent fine on it. I think it is doing the trick."

"That's good. I will keep it as it is for now. I want to talk about what helps you to relax."

"As in stress management?"

"Yes, something like that."

"It's weird. I was just telling that chick that I never used to get stressed out by anything and now here I am having to manage my stress."

"Nothing bothered you in the past?"

"Not a lot. I guess the thing that bothered me most was that I wasn't bothered and that there was nothing I wanted to do. I know I should have been bothered about getting an education and finding a job, but I wasn't really bothered by it at all."

"But now stress tends to send you into a catatonic state. It is probably drug-induced. But we still have to figure out how you are going to manage it."

"I know."

"What helps you to de-stress?"

"Well, Doc, I know this is probably a bad way to de-stress, but having a smoke really helps."

"I am not in favour of smoking for a physical health perspective. But it's not a good time to cease smoking, so we will leave it for now. When you are stronger and have developed better coping skills you can always consider giving it up, but for now, I think you need to continue."

"That is something I never thought I'd hear from you, Doc. Just kidding. I understand what you are saying."

"What else works for you?"

"Well, I have recently been hit by the desire to shoot some hoops."

"That is excellent, especially for a young man. We all need to de-stress via physical exertion and I believe it is particularly important for young men. I am glad you are doing that. Do you think you could build it into your daily routine?"

"Sure, I think I can."

"But I want it to be structured, so you do not forget to exercise every day. Maybe you could shoot hoops before lunch."

"Yeah, that would work. Then I could work up a good appetite and keep my figure."

The Doc laughs. "I am glad it will have added benefits for you, Richard."

"I am a big fan of added benefits, Doc."

"Good. What about sleep? Do you find you get more stressed out if you don't get enough sleep?"

"I wouldn't know, Doc. It has never been a problem in the past."

"Well, for now, I want you to make sure you get eight hours sleep a night, just to make sure that we are keeping stress down on all levels."

"No problem, Doc."

"Good, I think we have covered a lot of areas. What about….."

I notice that some kind of black shadow is creeping out of the floor near the Doc. It looks like it is materialising from the carpet. It is sort of vague. Maybe I am imagining it?

"Richard?"

"Sorry, Doc. I wasn't listening."

"What is the matter?"

"Nothing."

"Richard, I am your psychiatrist and I am here to help you. Please tell me what is happening."

"I am sure I am imagining things."

The black shadow is more defined. I still can't tell what it is. It has no definite shape. It's like smoke, but it's not and it gives off a horrible creepy feeling.

"Whether you are imagining it or not, please tell me what is bothering you. This is important."

"Well, Doc, um, there's a shadowy thing rising up from the floor next to you."

"Where?"

"On my right side, um, your left."

The Doc turns to look. "I don't see anything."

"I told you it was my imagination."

The shadow is stroking the Doc's arm. Oh my god! This is seriously freaky.

"What's happening? Are you getting stressed?"

"Yes."

"Tell me what's happening?"

"It is stroking your arm and now it's kind of surrounding you."

"I don't feel anything and I don't see anything. What has made you feel stressed this session?"

"Nothing. I was feeling happy and positive, but this is stressing me. Well I did see shadows today, or thought I saw shadows, but nothing like this. Is this normal?"

"I am sure it is a panic attack. I just want you to breathe deeply. This thing you are seeing does not exist. Let's beat this together. I want you to breathe in and out, slowly and steadily, like this."

I watch the Doc breathe in and out. I copy him and I try to ignore the shadow that is surrounding him completely now. It is all in my imagination. I keep breathing in and out. In and out. In and out. The shadow makes its way to the Doc's mouth and I watch in horror as it is sucked little by little into his mouth, as he breathes in. Then it all disappears inside of him.

"Thanks, Doc. That worked really well. It's gone. I was just freaking out, I guess.

The Doc doesn't say anything. He just looks at me.

"Doc?"

Nothing.

His eyes are unfocused and slowly they come to life. I don't like the way he is looking at me – like an eagle about to kill its prey. His eyes are alive with an evil malevolence. I can feel it from every part of his being.

"I have been chasing after you for a very long, long

time." His voice sounds cracked and gravely, like it has not been used for a very long time.

"You are a slippery little fish. A slippery, slippery little eel that keeps slipping away. Slipping and sliding away." He drags the 's's' out in a very creepy way.

He does not blink and he stares at me. I try to retreat into my chair, but I can't move any further back into it. My heart is hammering in my chest. I can hardly breathe. In fact, I don't think I am breathing and I can hear the blood pushing its way through the blood vessels in my ears.

The Doc leans forward. He sniffs and folds his hands in his lap, as he spears me with his eyes.

"Yes, my slippery eel. I have been searching everywhere for you. Your scent was so subtle, but it has grown stronger now. It has been easier to find you this time."

He stares unblinking at me and his nostrils flare as he sniffs the air in my direction.

The edges of my vision start to blur with blackness and I feel as if my whole body is beginning to vibrate at a high frequency. I feel myself losing consciousness. I feel like I am falling asleep. I don't want to fall asleep now, with this evil man staring at me. It is dangerous and I need to get out of this chair and run, but I can't. Instead, I find myself drifting off to sleep.

Stop it! Wake up, you moron! Wake up!

But I can't.

20

Where am I?

I look around. This place is very familiar. I am sitting with my back leaning against a wall. I have a cigarette in my hand. The ash on the cigarette is fairly long. I flick it. It lands in the long green grass. It slowly erodes, as the wind catches it. I watch it until it's gone.

I look around and realise that I am sitting by the wall in the loony bin. I look down at myself and I am wearing long, black stretch pants with a short black dress over them. I look at my arm and see a tattoo of a dragon winding up my right arm.

Oh, shit. I am the Goth chick. How did that happen? I wanted to get to know her better, not be her. Am I dreaming?

Was I dreaming in the Doc's office? His office is across from the wall behind the trees. I crouch and slowly peer over the wall. I don't see anything. I must have been dreaming in his office, but it was seriously freaky. But it wasn't a dream to begin with or was it? No, it was real. So what happened? What happened to the Doc? Maybe he is a weird guy, who is into some seriously creepy voodoo stuff. I don't know what the fuck is going on and why am I suddenly the Goth chick? How the hell did that happen? It can't be real. No, it must be a dream. I am asleep again. I dreamt I was seeing the Doc today. I am in bed asleep right now!

I look down at myself again. I am definitely not a guy. I look down the front of my dress. No bra. Yip. Those were not there earlier. Damn. I really would like to get to know her better.

But I am just dreaming. Let me take a second to think about this. Right. I was in the Doc's office and we were having a good discussion about stress. And I know that stress makes me go into a catatonic state and then I saw a shadow and then the Doc went all weird. Now is it not possible that I am dreaming again? Maybe I had a hallucination about the shadow and about the Doc. Maybe I got stressed about talking about stress. That is possible, isn't it? I am pretty sure that can happen. I mean, look at me already. I have a disorder where I kind of fall asleep and then have very vivid dreams like this one.

I peer over the wall again. Nothing and no one. See, Richard, you dope! You are dreaming again. There is no one here. Okay, so wake up!

Get out! Get out!

Okay, that's not working. Right, I need to imagine the witchdoctor. I concentrate on what she looks like and will her to appear. Nothing happens. Maybe I am not doing this properly? I peek over the wall again and see that there is no one around. I am not sure why I am so edgy. I guess it was that whole thing with the Doc. It was so creepy that it is hard to shake right now. I am sure it was my imagination, but I still feel totally weirded out.

I sit down on the grass and lean against the wall. I take a couple slow drags of my cigarette and then grind it into the ground. I close my eyes and will myself to relax and think about the witchdoctor.

I remember exactly what she looks like with her colourful cloth dress wrapped around her body, a white t-shirt underneath. Her yellow eyes look into mine and I can see her sporadic yellow teeth, as her mouth moves to say get out.

Again, nothing happens. Damn it! I open my eyes. I am still in the hospital grounds. I am dreaming, aren't I? This feels exactly the way it has felt every other time, so I must be dreaming. There is only one way to check this out. I need to get back to the Doc's office. If I am dreaming I will not still be there, or will I? I am not sure and I am not sure what I will find. If I find myself sitting there, what does that prove, because that could be part of the dream and if I don't find myself there, what does that prove? Just that it is still a dream. I am not sure how much time has elapsed.

I peer over the wall again. I see the Doc standing under the trees across from me. He is a way off, but I can see him clearly. He has his hands hanging by his sides in a relaxed manner and he appears to be sniffing the air.

Okay, this is not a dream; this is a fucking nightmare, where I am being pursued by my psychotic psychiatrist! I duck behind the wall and crawl on my hands and knees as fast as I can along the length of it.

I end up at a parking lot. I look behind me. I see nothing. I then peer around the other side of the wall. I see the Doc walking slowly towards it. The fact that he is so relaxed is very scary. It is almost as if he does not have to rush, because he knows he will find me.

I wait for him to reach the wall and then I sneak to his side of the wall and run behind a car. I scuttle to the front of the car and look around it. I can see the Doc's back far away by the wall where I was sitting. He is leaning over the wall and looking down at exactly the spot where I had been. He appears to be sniffing the air again. I watch in horror as he climbs over the wall and starts walking leisurely next to the wall following the path I have just taken.

The good thing about the leisurely pace he is keeping, is that it helps me to out-distance him. I keep low and move from car to car until I get to another building. I stand up, when I am behind it, and run to the back of it. I hope it is not a dead end. There is a wire fence that I manage to climb over, but I get my dress caught in it and part of it tears off. I just keep going. I have the feeling that the evidence of a bit of dress is not going to make one bit of difference to the Doc, who seems to be following me by scent.

This must be the worst nightmare I have ever had in my entire life. I follow the building to the other side. The fence is higher here and it is going to slow me down, but hopefully if the Doc is following my exact path, it will slow him down too. I tuck my dress into my leggings so it won't catch on anything. It doesn't look too becoming, but I don't give a shit right now.

I struggle up the fence. It is not easy. The thin wire cuts into my hands and it is hard to find a hold for my feet, as the gaps left in the wire weave are very small. I start to feel panicky, because I am sure I am losing time. If I was a guy, I could rely on my upper body strength to get me over, but since I am a woman, I need both my arms and my legs. The Doc is a guy. This is going to be so much easier for him.

That thought makes me panic more and that is not helping me. I push the thought of him from my mind and I concentrate on pulling myself over the fence. I cut myself a little on the top as I clamber over to the other side, but it is minor. Once I am hanging on the other side, I let go and land on the ground with a thump.

There are a lot of trees back here and I run from one to the next making sure that I can't see the Doc and that, more importantly, he cannot see me. I run behind two more buildings, always looking around me, but he is nowhere to be seen. Hopefully he is stuck on the fences smelling for me.

That thought is so creepy. It makes me feel totally

invaded. I don't want to think of him smelling his way towards me. No. I can't think of that right now.

I make my way back to his office. At least he is not there, because he is following me and hopefully he is a long way off. I remember just in time, before entering reception, to pull my dress out of my leggings, though in this place, they are probably used to stuff like that. I hope the secretary knows me.

"Hi"

"Hello, Helen. Hang on a sec." The receptionist scans through her diary. "Your appointment is not until 4 o'clock."

"I know. I am desperate to use the restroom."

"Oh, well, you know where it is."

"Yeah, thanks."

Right now, I don't have the first fucking clue where it is. I am sure if I think hard enough I will find it, but I take a chance that it is somewhere in the direction of the Doc's office. I feel like a naughty school kid, as I take off in the direction of the Doc's office, but the receptionist does not seem to notice. That's a relief!

I hope the door to the Doc's office is open or else I will have to look through a window and I would prefer to go into the office. I want to see for sure that there is nothing there. Of course, if there is nothing there, that doesn't prove anything, because maybe I am in my room sleeping, so I will have to check that afterwards. And what if I find myself there? What does it prove? What does it prove? I don't know. I have no idea if it proves anything at all, but I don't know what else to do. I am so confused. I don't know what the fuck is going on. Oh, fuck!

The one person, who was trying to figure this all out with me, is now a creepy human bloodhound, who is pursuing me. I am not so sure I feel comfortable to talk to him ever again. I mean, I know I am probably dreaming all this and it's not real, but I still can't shake the thought of the Doc being like this out of my head and I don't know if I will ever see him the same way again. This situation is so totally fucked up!

I get to his door and turn the knob. The door opens.

I push the door and stand back in case the Doc came back to this room before I got here. With a huge feeling of relief, I see that he is not there, but in the chair nearest the door, sits a young man. He is not moving. I can see the back of him and his tousled brown hair. He does not react to the door opening. He does not move at all.

Is that me?

I walk slowly towards him. He still does not move. Is that because, he, or should I say I, am still asleep? I walk around to face him and jump back.

His eyes are open and his hands are up in a gesture of trying to push someone away. He does not blink. There is no expression in his eyes at all. I wonder if he is alive. I look carefully and watch his chest rising and falling. He is breathing.

"Richard?"

No response. It feels a bit odd to talk to myself, but I have to give this a try. I mean, what else can I do? I don't have a fucking clue what else to fucking do! Fuck! I want to cry. I want to sit down here and cry and cry and cry. I don't understand what is going on. I don't understand. I am in danger. I know I am and I have to get myself to wake up. I have to wake up and get out of here and find someone who can figure out how to help me. Someone has to know what is going on. I cannot be the only person in this whole fucking world with this problem.

I feel the tears running down my cheeks. I wipe them

away angrily. I cannot fall apart right now. I have to wake myself up. I have to get out of this nightmare. Maybe I never woke up in the first place. Maybe I thought I woke up in the hospital and that everything was back to normal, but actually, I am still asleep. I had dreams like that occasionally when I was a kid. I would wake up in the dream, only to discover when I actually woke up that I was just dreaming I was awake. Maybe that was what has happened. That is the only thing that makes any kind of logical sense to me right now.

Right, so the witchdoctor did not wake me up, but here I am in my dream staring at me and, even though I look like the Goth chick right now, I know I am me and maybe this is me looking at a dream version of me and maybe this is how I can finally, at long fucking last, wake myself up.

That must be it, because there are no fucking shadows and weirdo sniffing shrinks in real life. I am still dreaming.

That makes me feel much better. At least that is what is going on. But it is still a very scary dream and I want to wake myself up right now.

I shut the door, because I don't want the receptionist to hear me and then come in here. That kind of thing does happen in dreams.

I walk back to myself.

"Richard."

Nothing.

I try it a bit louder, "Richard!"

Still nothing. Not even a blink or a flinch. Nothing.

This is the key, I know it. If I can just wake myself up! I try shaking myself. I grab both my hands and tug gently. My arms are stiff, but they still give way to my movement. I let go. They stay where I left them.

"Come on!"

I tug harder. My body moves forward and then stays there. Nothing. Still not a blink or a change in facial expression. Not even a change in the rhythm of my breathing.

This calls for more drastic measures. I lean forward and say, "Wake up!" into my ear, as loud as I dare, without being too loud and calling attention to myself. At the same time, I shake myself vigorously. Still nothing.

How difficult can this be?

The Doc will smell his way back here soon. I don't think I have much time left. I need to wake up and wake up soon! Right, there is only one more thing I can think to do and then I am going to have to run away and come back later when the Doc has gone home and try again.

I stand in front of my non-moving, non-blinking body and hit Richard as hard as I can back and forth across his face. I actually don't care if the receptionist can hear me. Hopefully it won't matter, because I will wake up, but I don't think she will hear me. I am quite far away from reception. I keep on hitting myself. I swing my arm and my hand lands with a stinging slap on his face. I feel the sting on my hand, but I don't feel it on my face.

I keep slapping and saying as loud as I dare, "Wake up, you fucking moron!"

Nothing. This is not working. He doesn't move.

I look at him. His cheeks are red from the slapping, but he still sits there unmoving in the same position.

Suddenly, I notice that the door begins to open slowly.

I cannot move. I am rooted to the spot and all the blood drains from my body to collect in my feet and make sure I am more deeply rooted, unable to move.

I stare at the Doc. He has that same predatory gleam

in his eyes and he is smiling.

"You can't get away from me, my slippery, slimy eel. I can smell you. It's such a lovely strong deep smell. I can find you anywhere now."

I just stare at him.

"I was watching you from the window, little fish. That is one of the funniest things I have seen in a long, long time. I would have come in sooner, but it was too much fun. I love a bit of fun and you have provided with me with a great deal of fun. Fun. Fun. Fun."

He stares at me unblinkingly, as he says this.

"Maybe, slippery one, maybe if you wrap your hands around his neck, maybe that will accomplish what you are aiming for?"

I drag my eyes away from the Doc and look at Richard's unmoving body with its red cheeks. I can see the red outline of my hands on them. I quickly look back at the Doc.

He is still smiling at me. There is mirth in his eyes, but also at the same time an underlying malice. It's the look of a cat enjoying playing with its prey, before the final swipe of the claw to seal its death.

The Doc looks around and closes his eyes in ecstasy for a moment. He takes a deep breath in and sighs it out again. When he opens his eyes, he is looking directly at me.

"I can see why you like this place so much, my fishy eel. I like the feeling of this place. No wonder you have been here for such a long time. Absolutely delicious! But it is time for you to come to me. There are a few things we need to discuss. When we have finished, you can come back here. I would. Oh, yes, I would."

The Doc walks slowly towards me. He stretches out his hand as he comes and never takes his eyes off mine.

My body starts to vibrate again. My vision blurs. I see the ground coming towards me.

21

A shelf of tin cans comes hurtling towards me. I put out my hands to protect my face from the oncoming wall of cans. It hits me with a bang and I scream involuntarily as I am pummelled by a wall of falling cans. They are heavy and they hurt. I end up collapsing on the floor in a heap and burst into tears.

I feel bruised from where the cans made contact. I just can't take this anymore. Where am I? Am I still in the loony bin? Who am I? Am I Richard or am I the Goth chick or have I become the Doc? Why am I sitting in the middle of a pile of cans of fish? I am surrounded by cans of tuna, salmon, sardines and anchovies. I pick up a can of tuna and look at it. It looks normal to me. Why fish? Who gets attacked by a wall of canned fish?

"Are you all right, Ma'am?"

"No!" I can't stop myself from crying. I don't know what is happening to me. Nothing – absolutely nothing makes any shred of sense to me at all. How long will I be sitting here in a heap of fish before I find myself somewhere else? What is the point? I just want to curl up in a ball and go to sleep forever.

"Let me help you up, Ma'am."

"Leave me alone! Let go of me! I don't want to get up! I just want to stay here forever!"

"Please, Ma'am."

"Leave me alone!" I shout.

The man who was trying to help me lets go of me and steps back. He looks at me for a while as I sob and then he turns and walks away.

Good! I just want to be left alone.

"Hey there."

Bloody Hell! Not another one!

"Let me help you up."

"I just want to be left here on the floor alone. Is that so hard for everyone to understand?" This comes out in gasps between sobs.

The woman holds my face and turns it firmly towards her. I am forced to look at her through the blurry veil of my tears.

"You know me, I know you. We are not strangers. I am here to help you, okay? Let me help you up and let's go to the bathroom. I can help you get cleaned up."

"I don't know you. I have never seen you before in my entire life. Get your hands off me."

The woman lets go, straightens up and stands there staring at me. I feel like some specimen on a Petri dish. I am being watched closely. It feels so uncomfortable that I stop crying. My chest heaves with the after-spasms of having cried so much. I look around me and find a handbag. I open it, hoping to find some tissues. I have to rifle through many pockets before I find a pack in a plastic wrapper. I open the tissues and blow my nose and wipe the tears from my face. All this time, the woman keeps staring at me. She is very quiet.

I chance a quick glance at her and she is staring at me with a great deal of concentration on her face. I notice other people around me. There are two other woman. They seem to be feeling uncomfortable, but are not moving from where they are. The guy who tried to help me returns with another man.

"Hello, Ma'am. Don't worry this can all be fixed up. It is not that bad."

Oh yes, it is very, very bad.

"We can clean this up in no time. But we do need you to get up so that we can clean this so that our other customers can continue with their shopping. You also seem to have a little bump on your head that we need to attend to. It's not serious, so don't worry."

I feel my head and find that it is a bit damp. I look at my hand and there is some blood on my fingers.

"We can sort that out easily, Ma'am. If you will let me just help you up."

I let him get me back onto my feet. I don't see any other option. I would love to sit on the floor there in peace and just cry, but it seems that there is no peace to be had. I should have slid under the produce shelf and then no one would have been able to get to me and I could be left there alone forever.

"Who saw what happened here?"

"I did," one of the women says, as she hands me my handbag. "This lady was walking up the aisle and pushing her trolley. Then she just stopped moving and stood there. That's why I noticed her. She just stood there and did not move for a long time. She seemed to be staring into space, but it was like her brain switched off. Then she turned around and walked with her arms out into the shelf of cans and screamed when they fell down."

What? I wasn't pushing a trolley or walking down an aisle. I was in the Doc's office trying to wake myself up and then the Doc, who was all psycho, came in and tried to scare me.

"It's okay. I am just dreaming right now. I am still asleep and I can't wake myself up and you are all just part of my dream."

"I think we really need to get your head looked at, Ma'am. You know that sometimes, if you get hit on the head, you can get a concussion and that can disturb your thoughts. Maybe we should call an ambulance?"

"I am fine. I can think just fine. This is just a dream."

"Of course, Ma'am. It's just a dream, but I think we should get you cleaned up. Joseph, will you please clean up all these cans. Ma'am, please come with me."

"I would like to come with too."

"Do you know this lady?"

"We met yesterday."

Yesterday, I was in the loony bin, but I guess this is just all part of the dream.

The store manager leads me to his office at the back. People stare at me as I walk past. The lady trails behind us.

"Please sit down, Ma'am."

The manager rifles through a cupboard and comes out with some disinfectant, a plaster and a pair of gloves, which he dons.

"This will sting a little bit, but it is very minor, just a little scratch really."

He dabs at my head and it does sting. I don't move. I don't care. I don't care what happens to me anymore. I don't understand what is happening to me. I don't know when I am awake or asleep. I don't know who I am. I don't know where I am. I don't know anything. My head hurts, and not just from the cut, it hurts from not knowing anything. I just want to die. I just want this all to end right now. I want some peace and quiet. I want to stop thinking about things. But it seems I am stuck and this is not ending. Some nice blissful sleep would be very nice indeed.

"I think we need to call someone to fetch you, Ma'am. I am not comfortable to let you go out on your own. The scratch is not bad, but I think you have given your head a nasty bump."

"There is no one to call."

"No husband, boyfriend?"

"No."

"A friend, perhaps?"

"No."

"Oh." He looks worried. He probably thinks that he will have to deal with me for the rest of his life - that he will never get rid of me.

"I will be fine. Thank you for your help."

"I am not comfortable letting you go on your own like this. Maybe you can sit for a while. Can I get you a glass of water?"

"Thank you." I can see that he has a great need to help me, so I let him. I just really want him to shut up and leave me alone, but if this will give me some peace and quiet for a while, then I will do it. He leaves the office to fetch some water. I notice the woman still standing there, staring at me.

"You can go now. I am fine. Thank you for your concern."

"I am not going anywhere."

"I told you I am fine."

"Yes, I know, but I don't think that is the case."

"Well, again thank you for your concern, but I am fine and I would prefer to be left alone."

"I am afraid I can't do that."

"I am sure you can. See those two things attached to the end of your body? They are called legs and you can use them to turn around and walk out of here." I am not usually so rude, but this lady is extremely irritating.

"Normally, I would, but not today."

"Well, if you are going to hang around me, could you at least stop staring at me?"

"Yes, sorry, I was thinking."

"About what?"

"Here you go, Ma'am." The store manager has

returned and he hands me a glass of water. I drink from it dutifully. I am not really thirsty, but it seems to make him feel better so I do it.

"Are you sure there is no one for me to call?"

"No one."

"I know her. I will make sure she gets home safely."

"Are you sure?" The manager seems weary and relieved at the same time.

"Yes, don't worry. Here is my card."

He looks at the card quizzically and looks back at the lady, uncertain.

"I met this lady yesterday. She had an appointment with me. I have all her details in my shop. I will take her there with me now. It's just around the corner. I can find someone to fetch her."

The manager still looks distrustful, but at the same time, I can see that he wants to get rid of me, so he doesn't need to take responsibility for me.

"Alright. Ma'am, you are going to go with Ms. Palmer here and she is going to assist you. If you don't come right, please come back and I will do what I can. I am sorry about this unfortunate incident. You go home and make yourself some nice tea and maybe have a little rest. Just watch out for any signs of concussion. I don't want to worry you, but that can happen some times."

"I will be fine. Thank you for your concern. You have been very kind."

He helps me out of the chair. We say goodbye and I follow Ms. Palmer. I can always make a run for it, but for now, I will see what she has planned for me. She certainly is not as scary as the Doc, but she is a little scary. It's hard to explain why she frightens me. I try to think about it. I guess the best way to describe it is maybe how a schoolchild would feel in front of an austere headmistress.

My head is throbbing and I don't think it is just from the cans. I feel so weary. My whole body just feels really irritable. I would like to scratch my way out of my body. That is how irritable I feel. Of course, I can't do that and it wouldn't help, but I want the feeling to end.

I walk out the store and past a few shops, behind Ms Palmer. She seems to be sure that I will follow her. She never turns back to see if I am following. This woman is very strange and my suspicions that she is strange are confirmed when she stops outside a shop called, 'The Mystical Emporium.' She stands by the doorway and starts to make some strange hand gestures and seems to be muttering under her breath.

I thought I was weird. I thought I was in the loony bin, because I was crazy. Now I see it's all wrong.

"Wow! Did you choose this name? I would have chosen something else entirely. It's really cheesy. I can see the cheese dripping off the letters. Is Ms Palmer your real name? Do you do palm readings? Is that your speciality? I really don't have time to waste. You know I have been in a psychiatric institution for several months, but I think that they got the wrong person here. I really do."

She ignores me and continues to do her little fake ritual.

"Oh, I am so impressed. Doing magic are we? Bye, I am going now."

She turns to look at me. "Come inside."

"All right. I have nothing better to do and this should provide a little amusement for a while. Why not? But as soon as you get too freaky or want to fleece me of my money, I am outta here."

She stares at me and unlocks the door to the shop. There is a chime as the door opens. The cheese just gets cheesier. I am really wasting my time here, but at the same time, what else am I going to do?"

I follow her into the shop. The shop smells of incense. It is faint, not very overpowering. The floors of the shop are wooden. There is a little entrance hall, as you enter, with a bunch of flowers on a table and opposite that table, is another table with pamphlets on it. The entrance hall opens into the shop, which is tastefully decorated. It is not gaudy at all. The walls are a deep green and wooden bookshelves line the walls. Books are stacked neatly in alphabetical order. There are some tables and chairs and a coffee counter. At the back are three doors. Each door is labelled: toilet, private readings, and staff. Shafts of afternoon light from the big picture windows at the front of the shop slide along the polished wooden floor.

It is strange, because I feel both comfortable and uncomfortable here. The shop is warm and homely, but there is an undercurrent that runs through it, that runs a chill just under my skin.

Ms Palmer is standing in the middle of the shop watching me intently. She is a very strange woman. She beckons to me.

I move forward to climb the two steps from the entrance hall into the shop and I can't. I look and there is nothing there. I try again and I can't move any further into the shop. This is bizarre. I try again. Nothing. I stretch forward to see if there is some kind of barricade. There is nothing but air. I try to lean over the stairs, but that doesn't work and I am met with resistance again.

It is not hard, like walking into glass. It just won't. I can't make any more sense of it than that. It just won't.

"What is happening?"

"I have not given you permission to enter my shop.

You will be able to open the front door and come in as far as you have, but no further. You will find the same effect if you try to come through any part of the shop."

"Right. You are a very strange lady. Why did you invite me to follow you if you won't let me into your shop."

"That is a good question."

"Yes?"

"I don't have the answer for you. In part, I understand, but in part, I am very confused. I get a very strong impression that you have not been ready to understand, but you are almost ready. Very soon, you will have a meeting and it will all be explained to you. When you know, find me and I will try to help you. I normally would not get involved, but I have a feeling I should and I always trust those feelings. I wanted you to see my shop, so that you will know where to come to find me. You can only find me here and you will never be allowed to enter my shop. You will only be able to come as far as the beginning of the stairs."

"You are a welcoming sort aren't you? What if I need a cup of coffee or to use the toilet?"

"You may only come as far as the beginning of the stairs."

"Yes. I got that part. You said we met yesterday. Why was I here?"

"You came for a reading."

"Right, and in that reading did you pick up that we would meet again today?"

"No, I did not."

"You are not very good at what you do, are you? You should have picked up that we would meet again – like the next day."

"Firstly, it doesn't work that way, secondly, for

reasons I cannot explain to you, I would never have known this would happen and thirdly, I am very used to people mocking my skills. There are more charlatans out there than people with true gifts and I am very used to attitudes like yours. I merely offer my help, which I have a feeling you may need, but it is entirely up to you whether you want to accept my offer or not. I have a feeling that many others will not be able to help you or will refuse to do so. I am not sure why I am helping you, as I say. Normally I would not, but I feel compelled to for some reason. Maybe it will become clear to me later, but for now, it is not. I have laid down the terms under which we may meet. You have no choice other than to adhere to them. If you want to speak to me further, you may come and find me when you are no longer lost."

"Wow, thanks for that. When I am no longer lost? Don't people come to you when they are lost? Aren't you supposedly there to guide them back onto the right path?"

"Those are the terms. If you choose to use them or not, that is up to you. I would like you to leave now. I am opening my shop in three minutes time and I have a business to run."

"You know, Ms Palmer, you really frighten me." I don't know why I said that.

"I am glad that the feeling is mutual. It is time to leave."

I don't want to overstay my 'warm' welcome from this strange woman, so I turn around, open the door and walk out into the street again. She is right I am lost. I don't know where I am. As usual.

My cell phone rings in my bag. I really don't feel like answering it, but maybe it will be useful. I dig around in my bag, as I walk away from the shop. I don't want Ms

Palmer watching me anymore than she has. What a rude, socially inept, strange and scary lady!

I finally locate my phone. The name on the screen says Isabelle. What the hell? Let me answer it.

"Hello, Isabelle."

"You forgot to fetch me from school, Mommy."

"Oh dear. Sorry sweetie. I am coming now."

"Why did you forget me?"

"I didn't do it on purpose. I had a little accident. Nothing to worry about. I am fine. Just bumped my head. Silly Mommy. But I am fine. I will come and fetch you right now."

"I am sitting in the office with Mrs. Scheepers."

"I will be there in twenty minutes. Sorry, darling. Bye."

"Bye."

I find myself walking off determinedly to my car, which I locate with ease. How on earth would I know where my car was if I was not dreaming? Things always happen like that in dreams. You think of something and then it either appears or it just comes to you.

I find my way to the school with ease and locate Isabelle. She doesn't talk to me on the way home, despite me showing her the bump on my head and apologising profusely. I have never left her behind anywhere in my entire life and so I suppose she has a right to be cross and upset. She must have been very scared. I allow her time to get over it.

We arrive home and I park the car in the garage. It suddenly dawns on me that I didn't bring the shopping home with me. I left it next to the pile of fish tins. Great. Just great. This day couldn't be any worse.

I open the boot just to check if the food miraculously appeared there while I was driving, in the same way that I miraculously found my car, but there is nothing there. Sadly, it is empty. I slam the boot shut and push the button on the wall to close the garage door.

I am tired. I really need an early night. Miriam is sitting at the kitchen table. She looks annoyed.

"I am sorry Miriam. I hit my head at the shops today and I forgot to buy the groceries. I am sorry to keep you waiting. Please have the night off and thanks for watching Jamie. I will order takeaways tonight."

"Thank you. See you tomorrow."

"Thanks, Miriam. Have a good evening."

"Jamie?" I shout. "Mommy's home. Sorry I am late."

I walk through the house to drop my handbag in our bedroom. I walk back to Jamie's room. He seems unconcerned that I was late. He is lying on his tummy and seems completely absorbed in building a fort with his building blocks. I sit on his bed and watch him. One doesn't have many moments in life to do this. Time moves so fast and children grow up so quickly. He is in his pyjamas. Miriam must have given him a bath. His hair is tousled and his big brown eyes are focused intently on what he is doing.

I can't resist the smell of freshly washed boy. He smells so good and he is mine. I love him so much. I get down on my hands and knees next to him and give him a big kiss.

He stops what he is doing and looks at me, "Mommy, you smell funny."

I laugh. "Sorry, sweetie. I hit my head. See. And then they put disinfectant on it, so that probably smells a bit funny and, oh yes, I went into a weird shop and they had been burning incense there, so I probably smell like that too."

"What's incense?"

"It's a smelly thing that people burn to make the air smell nice."

"I don't think it smells nice."

"That's because you are not used to it."

"When are we eating, Mommy?"

"Soon. Mommy got so distracted today, she forgot the groceries, and so we are having a treat night!"

"What's for treat night?"

"Guess"

"Pizza!"

"That's right! So let me go and order."

"Yay! Yay! Issie! Issie, we are having pizza!" Jamie runs out of the room to tell his sister. I hear them both running back.

"Mommy, is Jamie telling the truth?"

"Yes. We are having pizza tonight. Am I forgiven for leaving you at school?"

"Yes! But I don't want bacon. I don't like bacon anymore."

"Right, bacon-free pizza it is!"

"Thank you, Mommy!" Issie hugs me. "Mommy, you smell funny. Not like you normally do."

"Yes sweetie, I think it's the alluring smell of incense and disinfectant."

"What does alluring mean?"

"It means it smells nice."

"But it doesn't."

"I know that, darling. I am joking. Have you done your homework?"

"Yes, Mommy. We finished everything in aftercare."

"Good. Can I see your diary?"

She rushes to fetch it. "See Mrs Watson signed it. I did everything."

"Good girl. And how was tennis?"

"Fine."

"Good. So you and I both need a shower and I need to get the pizza. Go shower, Issie and then you can watch TV. Jamie, are you going to carry on with your fort?"

"It's not a fort, Mommy. It's a lair."

"Where did you hear that word?"

"On TV."

"Of course. Well, you carry on with your lair."

I know exactly where I am, where everything is, what I am supposed to do and say and when my husband will be home. It is strange, but I go with it. I check the money in my purse and have enough for pizza, thank god; otherwise, I would have to lug the kids with me to the pizza place. I order two pizzas and am informed that it will take half an hour to arrive.

I walk back to my room and get into the shower. I need a shower and I need to wash the smell off me, which my children seem to find so offensive. I decide to wash my hair for good measure. I am not in the mood to dry my hair, but if I smell more like me, I am sure they will settle down. Hair traps so many smells – quite disgusting actually.

I can't be sure, but through the pelting of the shower spray, I hear a cupboard in the bathroom opening.

"Issie? Jamie? Peter?"

No response.

I rinse the shampoo out of my eyes and poke my head out of the shower. There is no one there. One of the bathroom cupboards under the sink is open. I am sure I must have left it open. I have had a long and confusing day and I am sure I am hearing things. I shut the door and resume rinsing my hair before I reapply more shampoo. I massage it into my scalp. It feels so relaxing. I wish I could get my hair done by an Indian Massage

Therapist every day. That would be the height of pleasure.

Slam!

Fuck!

"Hello?"

Silence.

I furiously rinse the shampoo out of my eyes again and pull open the shower door. My heart stops and it feels as if all the blood has left my body. The bathroom cupboard is shut. I shower with the door open, even though the floor is getting soaked, in case I need to vacate the shower in a hurry. I am fast. I turn off the shower and grab my towel.

There is no one in the bathroom, but my skin prickles with energy. The mirror has misted up and in the middle of the mirror, the word, 'hello' has been written.

I run out of the bathroom and look around the bedroom. I don't see anyone. I grab my gown and wrap it around me. I run down the passage.

"Jamie!"

"Yes, Mommy?"

"Are you all right?"

"Yes. When are we having dinner?"

"Soon."

"Where's your sister?"

"She's in the shower."

I hear the shower water running in the kids' bathroom. I open the door.

"Issie, are you all right?"

"Yes. Mommy what's the matter?"

"Nothing. I just thought I heard someone in my bathroom."

"Maybe it's Jamie's imaginary friend again."

"What?"

"You know Jamie has an imaginary friend."

Jamie comes out into the passage and shouts, "He's not imaginary. He is real and he was with me in my room the whole time. He is good. He is not naughty and he wasn't in Mommy's bathroom."

"Stop it you two. I believe you, Jamie." I shut the bathroom door.

"You do? But you told me that it was all in my head and that Jethro isn't real."

"I know. What I meant to say is that I am sure that Jethro wasn't in my bathroom."

"I know that, Mommy. Look, he is still in my room."

Jamie takes my hand and leads me into his bedroom.

"Look. He is sitting there." Jamie points to a spot on the carpet next to his building blocks. I don't see anything there at all. Suddenly Jamie pulls his hand out of mine and stares at me.

"What's wrong?"

"Jethro doesn't like you. He liked you before, even though you were mean and silly to him and said that he doesn't exist. Why doesn't he like you now?"

"I am not sure, sweetie, but I am sure he'll get over it."

I walk back to my room. I am so tired. I sit down on my bed with a heavy grunt and put my face into my hands. I rub my face and flop backwards onto the bed. It never stops, does it? One thing after the next. Nothing makes any sense. There is not even one clue as to what is happening. All of this is strange and bizarre and crazy. I don't know who I am and where I am. Well, I do now, but it may not last. Who knows how long this will last before I black out and end up somewhere else as someone else? Am I a man or a woman? Am I old or young? Am I Richard, wasting away in a psychiatric care centre with some rare disorder, where I become other people in my mind? I don't know and no one will help me. Well, that psychic lady said she'd help me for what it's worth, but what she said was so cryptic and unhelpful it could mean anything. She is probably a figment of my imagination, just like everything else.

I just want to sleep for a thousand years. I don't care about slamming cupboards and misty words. I don't care that I am suddenly a mother of two children, when not so long ago, before being hit by a wall of tinned tuna, I was a confused young man. I don't care anymore. I just want to sleep. I just want to lie here on this nice soft bed and just be. Just be forever. My entire body feels so heavy. I can't even pick my arms up from where they have fallen and my feet are still resting against the floor. My head feels like a giant ripe watermelon that is just too heavy to move.

"Mommy!"

Oh god.......

"The pizza guy is here."

"Coming."

So much for that. As much as I do not feel like getting up, I feel compelled to get dressed and pay for the pizza, which I arrange neatly on plates and take through to the TV room.

"We are eating in front of the TV?"

"Yes."

"You said that's not allowed."

"I know, but tonight we are having a treat to make up for me leaving you behind at school."

"Yay!"

Issie runs in and chooses a kid's channel on TV. She grabs a slice of pizza and is instantly glued to the TV set. I suppose this makes me a very bad mother, but right now, I don't care. I notice Jamie standing reluctantly in the doorway.

"Jamie, come and have some pizza."

"I'm not hungry."

"Well, you were hungry not so long ago."

"I'm not hungry anymore."

"Jamie, what's wrong?"

"Jethro doesn't want to come and sit here with you."

"Right, well, Jethro can stay outside. I want you to come in here and have your dinner and then it's bedtime."

"No."

"Jamie, right now!"

"All right."

"Here is your plate. Sit next to Issie."

The next hour passes peacefully enough and I get lost in the mindlessness of this cartoon. Jamie is so absorbed that I blessedly don't have to hear any further bleating about Jethro. I get the kids ready for bed with very little fuss. I tuck Jamie into bed and he is very quiet. As I pull his door halfway closed, I hear him whispering, I presume to his imaginary friend. Well, at least he has company tonight.

Issie is reading a book.

"Sweetie, it's bedtime."

"Can I just finish this one paragraph. Please?"

"Just one paragraph."

"It's the last paragraph of the page."

"That's fine. Read it and then I want you to close your book. Deal?"

"Yeah, deal."

I sit on her bed while she finishes reading. I tuck her into bed and give her a kiss goodnight.

"Mommy."

"Um-mm?"

"Why do you still smell funny?"

"I don't know, sweetie. Go to sleep. Sweet dreams."

I collapse in front of the TV and I must have dozed off, because I wake up when I hear a thump.

I open my eyes to see Peter walk past the door. He walks to the study. I check the time. It's 9:30pm. That's about right. He walks past again and remerges with a cardboard box, which he carries back to the study. He returns again.

"Hi. What's for dinner?"

"Pizza."

"Pizza? You're kidding. Why?"

"I knocked my head at the shops and forgot the food."

"Oh."

"Yours is in the oven."

"I was looking forward to a real dinner. I live off pizza at the office."

"I know. It's just this once. I am sure you'll live through the experience."

"Great. I'll be up late. Major deadline at the end of the week. Probably will sleep on the couch in the study - if I get any sleep at all."

"Sure. Well, I'm off to bed."

I pad through to our bedroom. I feel too awake now to sleep, so I start reading a novel. I don't remember what it was about, even though the bookmark indicates I was quite a way though the book. I flip to the beginning and start again.

The book is so riveting that I lose track of time until I hear a subtle noise. Thinking it's Peter I put the book down and look up.

It's not Peter. I see a black shadow forming by the

edge of my bed. It is very clear. I can feel my body starting to undulate with waves of energy. My vision starts to fade. Here I go again.

22

I wake up. I can feel someone feeling their way along the edge of my bed towards my head. At first, I think it's a dream, but then I find myself fully awake and I can definitely feel it. It is pitch black in the room and I cannot see anything. I can feel the pressure as it moves towards me from the foot of my bed, like an evil blind man carefully probing his way towards me.

I am too scared to move or breathe and I just lie very still and listen. I cannot hear footsteps to accompany the pressure on my bed and I cannot hear any breathing.

I have to be brave. I swing around and slam on my bedside table light, but it won't switch on. I jab at the button and my hands are sweaty so they slip off the switch, but it doesn't turn on, even when I do manage to hit the button.

I can feel the pressure has reached where my thighs are. I have to act fast. I jump up and shoot off the end of my bed. My bedroom door is shut. It's never shut. Mommy always keeps it open. I tug at the handle and my sweaty hands slide off, I try to hit the light switch, but the light won't turn on. I can feel it coming for me. I desperately grab the handle and manage to pull the door open. I can feel a breath whisper over the perspiration on the back of my neck.

I run down the passage. I need to get to Mommy and Daddy. The passage is dark and so I run blindly, but it's my house. I know where I am going.

Their door is shut. I push it open and run into the bedroom. It is dark.

"Mommy! Daddy!"

Nothing.

I run to their bed. I see a shape lying on the bed. In

the dim light, I can see Mommy's dark hair curling over the pillow and her face. I shake her.

"Mommy! Mommy! Wake up!"

She doesn't stir. I grab hold of her arm and pull her over onto her back. She doesn't respond. Her eyes are open.

"Mommy."

"It's all right now. Mommy's here. Come sleep with Mommy."

Her mouth is moving, but nothing else. She doesn't even blink. I back away from her. There is something wrong with Mommy. I knew there was.

A black shape starts to rise up from the floor on Daddy's side of the bed. It grows bigger and taller, almost like it is a man standing up.

"Daddy?"

Suddenly I hear ragged breathing. It sounds like a vicious dog. I slowly back away and then I run out the bedroom. I run through a thick patch in the air in the passage. It makes my skin crawl, but I keep on running.

I am so scared. I don't know what has happened to my Mommy and my Daddy. I try to turn on the passage light, but it won't work. I run into the entrance hall, but I can't get the light on there either. I open the door to the kitchen and try to turn on the light. Nothing works. All this time, I can feel that dog-thing coming after me.

I open the door into the lounge and try the lights. Nothing. I can hear it breathing behind me and so I run into the lounge. I have nowhere else to go. But now I am trapped in the lounge, in the dark, all alone with something very bad.

I can hear the breathing right behind me on my neck. I can hear the ragged growling under the breathing. I can feel the terror curdling up from my stomach, shooting through my chest and exploding out my throat and mouth. I scream and scream and scream. I cannot stop myself.

I think I have been screaming forever. Suddenly the lights come on in the lounge.

"What's wrong, Issie?"

"Daddy!" I start crying and heaving. My face feels like it is on fire with pins and needles and I find it hard to breathe and cry at the same time.

"I've got you. What are you doing here? Why aren't you in bed?"

"There's a monster in the house."

"Issie, monsters aren't real. You know that. It's all in your head. You were having a bad dream. Let me take you back to bed."

"No!"

"Issie, it's late. I still have work to do and you have school tomorrow morning. I don't have time for this right now. I want you to be a good girl and go back to bed."

"No! The monster's in my room and it came here! It was chasing me!"

"Well, let's have a look around. I don't think there is a monster here, but let's check."

I wrap my arms and legs around Daddy as tightly as I can and I half bury my head in his chest, just in case the monster tries to grab me. I peek at the surroundings with one eye as Daddy checks the lounge. The other eye is tightly shut against his chest.

"See no monsters here. It's just a dream. Let's go back to your room."

"No! I don't want to sleep there by myself."

"Issie, you are a big girl now. Too big to be scared of monsters."

Daddy carries me back to my room. He turns the lights on as we go. Why do they work for him and they wouldn't work for me? He turns on the light in my room and puts me on my bed, but I don't let go of him.

"Issie, I have a lot of work to do. I need to finish it."

I can hear he is getting cross with me now, but I am more scared of the monster than of Daddy getting cross.

"I don't want to sleep here by myself."

"Look there is no monster here."

"It's hiding."

"But it can't be hiding. We looked everywhere and we didn't see it. So it's not hiding anywhere."

"We didn't look under the bed."

Daddy makes a cross sound and looks under the bed.

"Nothing there. No monsters."

"Maybe it is in the cupboard."

"Issie. There are no monsters."

"I don't want to stay by myself. Stay with me Daddy."

"I have work to do."

"Can I come with?"

"No, Issie, I need to concentrate."

"Don't leave me."

"I have an idea. You can sleep with Jamie tonight."

Daddy picks me up. I am still half attached to him, so he doesn't have much choice. He walks into Jamie's room and turns on the bedside light. Jamie is still asleep.

"Let go of me, Issie. I need to move Jamie, so you can sleep next to him."

I let go and stand next to the bed. I stand as close to Daddy as I can. Jamie shudders awake as Daddy moves him.

"Sorry, Jamie. I am just making space for Issie. She is going to sleep with you tonight. She had a bad dream and she is feeling scared."

Jamie suddenly looks wide-awake and he looks at me, as he moves over to allow me space to sleep next to him.

"Don't be scared, Issie"

I get into bed with Jamie and Daddy covers both of us with the blanket.

"You both go to sleep now and you are safe. There are no monsters. Night, guys."

Daddy bends down to turn off Jamie's bedside light.

"Please leave it on, Daddy."

"Fine. Get to sleep now."

Daddy leaves the room and I can hear him walking back to the study. At least he didn't turn off the passage light.

"You smell funny, Issie. But don't worry, Jethro's here. He says that we mustn't worry. He will make it better. He will keep us safe. The baddies can't come in my room while Jethro's here. He says that there have been baddies here all night, but they can't come in. He says my room is like a fort even if the door is open. He is sitting at the end of the bed. See?"

I don't see anything.

"He says it is safe to go to sleep."

I lie on my back and I look at the ceiling. I am too scared to go to sleep. Every little noise makes my heart stop. Soon I hear Jamie's breathing deepen and turn to look at him. He is fast asleep.

The rhythm of his breathing makes me feel sleepy, even though there is a prickly feeling by my feet, I don't seem to be able to keep my eyes open. Just as I am drifting off to sleep, I feel a firm pressure on my chest.

23

I am catapulted towards the stars. I look down and I can see a frozen silvered sea of cloud floating below me. The air is so clear up here. The sky is alive with pinpricks of undulating light that stretches as far as I can see. I realise that the universe is alive and pulsing, just as our planet is alive and pulsing. It is so quiet and still up here. It is so beautiful and there is so much to look at. It's overwhelming. I watch the Milky Way as it swirls towards another part of the universe. I suppose I am swirling too, but it doesn't feel like I am moving at all. I am so used to the slow reliable rotation of my planet that I don't notice it.

This is the first time I have felt at peace in a long time. I feel as if I am lying on a frozen frothy sea of silver and that I am covered in a dark blanket, alive with billions of tiny lights. I am not cold. I feel no sensation of temperature or movement. The only feeling running through me is awe at the beauty before me. I feel no fear, no anxiety, no confusion and no worry. I just feel blissfully peaceful.

This is impossible and so I know that I am dreaming.

As I float above the clouds, I get lost in space until I notice the clouds on my right slowly starting to blush as the sky lightens. It is just a touch of colour on the horizon that catches my eye.

I would love to watch the clouds, as the rising sun warms them, but I notice that the stars are going out. That is not possible. The sky is starting to go darker as if someone is turning out each of the pinpricks of light.

I start to feel heavier and heavier and I realise that the shadow I saw earlier is up here with me and that is what is darkening the sky. I feel a force, which scares me, but which I cannot fight, coming towards me and I fall through the clouds - though I don't feel them touch my skin - before I lose consciousness again.

24

I wake up in my bed. In the room that I went to sleep in before the... I don't know. I am so tired. I just want to bury my face in the pillows and sleep and never ever wake up again. That is what I would like to do.

"Are you awake?"

"What?" I look up and see Peter staring down at me. He looks like he did not get to sleep last night.

"You overslept."

"Oh. You look like you didn't sleep at all."

"I didn't. You need to get the kids to school."

"Right."

I swing my legs out of bed and, with a groan, gather myself reluctantly into a seated position. I watch Peter's back as he walks out the room. I really don't want to take the kids to school. They are not even my kids. Why should I care? None of this is real. I don't know what is going on and I am too tired to care anymore. This has been going on too long. Why don't I just fucking well wake up? I never will.

I just want to sleep all day, but if I have these kids here, they are definitely going to interfere with this plan. So maybe I should get them up and to school and then I can come back here and sleep. I will get someone else to fetch them, so that I can sleep a really long time. I wish I could sleep forever and never wake up again.

I stand up and walk to Issie's room. She isn't in her bed. She must be up already. Well, that is one less thing to worry about. I open Jamie's door and am greeted by the sight of two large pairs of eyes staring at me.

"Morning kids."

Nothing.

"Look, you guys are going to be late for school. I

want you both to get up now and get ready. It's late already. Come on now. Get going."

"I'm not going to school with you."

"Well, Issie, there is no other way to go to school, other than with me, and I want you to get up right now or else."

"I am not going to school with you. You are not my mother."

"Um, well you can go to school with me or you can stay here with me all day long."

Issie and Jamie exchange a glance and they both get up.

"Good. Get dressed and I'll go make breakfast."

I walk to the kitchen and put on a pot to boil for porridge. I fill the kettle and switch it on. I walk back to my room to get dressed and return to the kitchen to make breakfast. This is so mundane and boring and not really what I feel like doing, but if I don't do it, I will have them hanging around me all day, which I don't want and I don't want to fight with Peter either to be frank. I make tea for the kids and coffee for Peter. I take his breakfast through to him. He doesn't acknowledge my presence. The kids come through to the kitchen and we all eat in silence. I notice them glancing at me every now and then and then exchanging looks afterwards, but I don't really care.

The kids go back to their rooms to finish getting ready and I pack lunches for them and for Peter. They bring their bags and I make sure they have packed everything they need for school. I don't want any calls from the school today for forgotten things. Peter comes through to get his lunch.

"Daddy, please take us to school."

"I don't have time. Mommy will take you."

"She's not our Mommy."

"Issie, I don't have time for this. I don't know what's up with her. Last night I found her wandering around the house. I think she had a nightmare. Maybe you should take her to the doctor."

"I'm not sick. Mommy is a bad monster."

"Issie, I will not have you say things about your mother like that! Do you hear me? I don't know what's going on with you. I don't have time for this nonsense right now. I want you to go to school. Your mother is going to take you and that is final. Do you understand me?"

"Yes, Daddy."

"She's right, Daddy."

"Jamie, don't you start now too. I am warning you!"

Jamie looks like he is about to open his mouth and then he sees Peter fiddling with his belt and so he closes his mouth again. Peter holds onto his belt and gives both kids a meaningful stare.

"Good. Have a nice day at school, kids. I'll see you later."

Peter walks out the kitchen and I hear him walk through to the garage. The kids both stare at me warily.

"Right. Take your bags and I'll see you at the car."

I retrieve my handbag from my room and find the kids sitting in the back of the car with their seatbelts on. Good.

The journey to the kids' schools is quiet, which I don't mind. I am not in the mood to make idle conversation with children. Neither of them says goodbye when I drop them off. Part of me is hurt by this, but for the most part, I just don't care.

I guess I can now go home and sleep. The problem is I am not really feeling very tired anymore. If I hadn't had to take those kids to school, then I could have turned over and gone straight to sleep again. But sadly, that was not the case. So here I am, awake. Wide awake. How am I going to lose myself for a while?

I drive around the streets. Most of the shops are closed. I look at them hoping to find some inspiration, but I don't find anything that calls to me. After I do two circuits around the shopping street, I decide that since I am now wide-awake, a coffee at the second-hand bookshop would be the best idea. I love coffee and I could lose myself in a good book. In fact, I would be quite happy to drink coffee and read all day long. That would work for me.

I park my car outside the bookshop and listen to the radio as I wait for the shop to open. The morning has a slight chill to it and so it is lovely sitting in the car with the warm summer sun shining in on me. It will be very hot soon enough.

When the door to the bookshop opens, I go inside and peruse the bookshelves. The only thing that seems to appeal to me is a generic crime book. The style of writing seems easy enough to read with not much concentration needed and the story seems intriguing.

I order a coffee and get lost in the plot and the sweet bitter taste of my cappuccino.

"Hello, my slippery fish."

I look up as a creepy, shabbily dressed older man sits down next to me. He grabs my wrist and holds it firmly. I want to pull away, but I am powerless to do so.

"I have to keep a good hold on you this time, so that you can't slither through my fingers. I am tired of chasing you, little eel. It is time that we had a talk. I have been chasing you for so long. I have never had to deal with so slippery a fish before. Don't make me again"

He lifts his watery, dead blue eyes to the ceiling as he thinks. His face is lined and leathery. His grey hair is plastered to his head by layers of filthy grease. A slight sickly sweet smell wafts up from his unwashed skin. He is dressed in a creased blue shirt and khaki pants. I want to pull away, but it feels like I have lost all the strength in my body. I feel weak and terribly afraid.

"Yes, I have never, ever had a problem like you before. You are unusual."

I want to scream for help.

"I wouldn't do that if I were you. You really do want to hear what I have to say and I am tired of chasing you."

I stare into those dead, mocking eyes.

"Good. I am assuming you don't know what has happened to you. I assume this, because your behaviour has been so bizarre."

"I am dreaming all this. My name is Richard Carter and I am lying in bed right now in hospital and I can't wake myself up."

The man chuckles and then starts shaking with laughter. It scares me, because the laughter seems so wrong, so inappropriate. Eventually he stops and stares at me levelly again, as if he had never cracked a smile in his life. The change is very unsettling.

"Yes, poor dear Richard. He was a good choice. Despite your lack of intelligence in every way, you are good at picking your victims."

"What do you mean?"

"I mean Richard, was a good choice."

"I am Richard."

"No, you are not Richard. Richard is has nothing more to do with you than these clothes I am wearing have to do with me. You were wearing Richard for a while. Was he delicious to wear? I got a brief taste of him and it was exquisite."

I stare at the man blankly for a while until my brain kicks in and I realise that this man is seriously bad news and I need to get away from here. I try to pull away again, but I can't. I want to scream for help.

"That's not going to help you. I will find you wherever you go. Now listen to me!" He hisses at me like a snake.

I stop struggling and look at him.

"You are dead. You have been dead for some time now. Usually I meet people, when they exit the flesh, to explain to them what they are, what they have become, but you, little fish, escaped before I could speak. This has never before happened, but there are firsts for everything in this world. You were very fast. And because you were new, I did not get a strong enough taste of your essence. I had to smell you out, so to speak, in order to locate you. It was the faintest of traces and so it took a long, long time to find you. I sent out my servants to locate you. They found you many times, but you ran away again and again. You have made this so much harder on yourself. You have made it harder for me. I will never forgive this."

"I don't know what you are talking about, but I am not dead and you are crazy. I would not be able to drink a cup of coffee if I were dead, now would I?"

He smiles at me – a slow sinister smile.

"How can so much power be given to one, who is such an imbecile? Let me prove it to you." He lets go of my wrist and just leaves his forefinger touching my skin, "Pull away."

I can't.

"That doesn't prove anything. Maybe you hypnotised me or something."

"I suppose it doesn't prove anything to you, but remember it, because I will always be more powerful than you. You may not understand that now or grasp what I am saying, but just remember that I am far superior to you and you will always have to obey me. Not that I am terribly demanding. You are completely free to do as you wish, but if I ever need a favour, you are to remember that you are ranked below me and you are to do my bidding."

This man is completely insane, but I'll have to humour him.

"Why do you say that I am dead?"

"Because I helped to cause your death."

"Excuse me?"

"Human beings have different energy levels. When they are happy or in a positive mood, they have a high energy level. When they are sad or depressed or negative, their energy levels are deliciously low. We feed off low energy levels in humans. It's a sort of symbiotic relationship, so to speak. But delightfully, it can become a parasitic relationship when the human's energy is excessively low. Then their energy is so ripe, it's difficult to resist. We often end up inadvertently aiding the transition to this side, so to speak. That is what happened with you."

"You killed me?"

"Not exactly, little fish, I was attracted to you. Your energy called to me, it was so sumptuously low and once I started feeding, I could not contain my greed and it became lower still, but you did the deed. And what a deed it was, indeed." He smiles again.

"What do you mean? I killed myself?"

"Oh yes. It was quite spectacular. I enjoyed the whole event. You killed too when you took your life and

268

so that makes you quite special on this side, not that you are worthy of this. You see, killing yourself makes you one of us, but when you kill at the same time or have ever killed, you become more powerful on this side. You will be able to command many servants here."

"You say I killed myself and killed others in the process and now I am like you?"

"Yesssss."

"What are you?"

"We have been called many things over the ages, but I suppose the most current popular term, which you should understand, is a demon. A trifling term for such a grand creature such as I"

"I am a demon, is that what you are saying?"

"Yes, little fish. You are quite a powerful demon and you have killed already. It didn't take long for your true nature to take hold."

"Who have I killed? I haven't killed anyone!"

"Did you think you were dreaming?"

"Yes."

Oh no. Could I have killed the hobo and the office guy? It was dream, surely?

"But I dreamt that guy was standing on the window edge when I…."

"When you possessed him and helped to give him that little push in the right direction."

"So if I hadn't 'possessed' him, to put it in your words, he may not have… he may not have jumped. If it wasn't a dream, but it was."

"Indeed. He may have changed his mind. He may still be alive."

"Is he here with, um, us?" I continue to humour the man. Who knows what he will do to me if I don't? Maybe, if I hear all he has to say he will leave quickly.

"Not all suicides end up here."

"Where do they go?"

"That is not important."

"But it is."

"It is not! You are here and you cannot go anywhere else and so you do not need to know about anything else! It is not important."

"But...."

"You have chosen your fate and you cannot undo it."

"How did I kill myself?"

"That is not important."

"Why won't you tell me?"

"It is not important to know those details. It will not make any difference."

"I really need to know to help me process all of this."

"It is superfluous information."

"Am I a man or a woman?"

"That is the wrong question to ask."

"What is the right question?"

"The right question is: how do you function in this new life of yours? There is no point in dwelling on the past. It is done. It cannot be undone. You need to know how to operate in this world and that is why I have been forced to chase after you to tell you what to do – something I won't forgive."

I am not sure I really want to know, but part of me is curious. I am not sure I really believe this man. On one hand, it is so fantastical it could be true, but on the other hand, it seems so completely ludicrous, it must be a dream. Either way, he seems to want to tell me whatever he needs to tell me. I can't get away from him anyway and the sooner I get this over with, the better. I just want to be alone and for these dreams to end.

"I am listening."

"Keep listening, little eel. There are different levels of demon, depending on how powerful you are. Humans see the low-level ones as shadows or unpleasant sensations. They are very weak and they come and go. That's all they are good for. The high-level ones, like you, slippery fish, can possess humans and take over their minds. Naked, you are able to interact with the human world physically for a brief period of time, before you lose your strength. But then you will need to clothe yourself in human again for a while to regain your strength. You will grow exceptionally weak if you do not enter humans on a regular basis or suckle and sip from their energy. If you do not do this, you will eventually become stuck in one place and you will go mad. You will be stuck there for the rest of your existence. For the rest of eternity. The more you kill and the lower you can get a human's energy to become, the more powerful you will become, slimly one. This is how you feed and this is how you learn. You can decide what you would like to do with the humans. You can decide to keep them as pets. This body is my favourite pet. This man is a truly, deliciously, unsavoury character and whenever I come through this part of the world, I make use of him. I will never kill him. Why would I when I like the taste of him?"

"Like a car?"

"My slippery eel, I like that idea. Yes! He is like a mode of transportation for me. How wonderful! I never thought of that. How delightful! You will find that you can travel anywhere in the world. For instance last night, you rose high above the bounds of the earth, did you not?"

"You were there?"

"Indeed. I pushed you back. Otherwise you would have been lost there, had your energy run out."

"How do I travel?"

"We will get to that in a moment. Do you understand your purpose?"

"To create misery?" I hope he leaves soon.

"Exactly! And that is the whole of the matter. There are little details, but they are too many to innumerate for your poor mind. It can only be hoped that you will learn by experience. You have learnt a great deal already, but, from my observations, there are one or two things that I think you require help with. The first matter is that you tend to meld with your vehicle's consciousness. You need to learn to maintain your own identity and listen to their thoughts. What good is a vehicle without a driver? At present, you and your host are both in control. Your vehicle is driving you. Ridiculous! Pathetic! You need to learn to assert your authority, little eel. The second point is that you need to know how to move from one host to another and out of a host. You have the basics, but perhaps not the understanding of how the basics work. This is to be expected of one, such as you, of course. I shall have to explain. Listen carefully. You can only enter hosts with low energy. You will feel the pull of that low energy and you can attach yourself in any way you please. You can decide that you would like to enter a particular type of person and you will be drawn by your thoughts into their thoughts. For example, you may wish to enter the body of a suicidal jumper and you will find yourself there. Delicious! If you wish not to enter a body, but to be free for a while, like last night, you just think about it. It is important to remember that here everything works through the medium of focused thoughts, my slippery, little fish."

"Great, thanks for the advice. But this could all be a load of bull."

"You are trying my patience, but I am tired of chasing you, so let us try an exercise. Is there anybody here with a low energy? I do not want you to look; I want you to feel it."

I decide to humour him and give this a try; the sooner he leaves the better I will feel. I just need to get back to my coffee and my book and hopefully I will wake up from this nightmare soon. I look around the bookshop and try to feel a low energy. I don't find any.

I notice a man standing outside the bookshop, angrily looking for coins to put in the parking meter. I am instantly attracted to him. I can feel a pull within myself towards him.

"I think I have found one."

"Yes. That is a good choice. But next time use feelings more than your sense of sight, slippery, silly fish. Now, focus on being part of him. It is very easy to do. You have been doing it as naturally as a fish learns to swim."

I focus on being part of the man outside. I feel a sudden rush and suddenly I am standing outside the bookshop, staring at a coin in my hand. I look up, as the creepy one comes out the bookshop.

"Do you believe me now?"

"Wait."

I rush to the bookshop and stare through the window. A bewildered lady is sitting at the table I was sitting at and staring around her. The book, which I was reading, sits in front of her and an empty cappuccino cup is next to the book. I turn back to the creepy one.

"I don't want to believe you. I don't want to believe you! It must be a dream!" This could happen in a dream, couldn't it? Anything can happen in a dream!

"Be careful. You are not dreaming, fish! If you persist in believing that, you will perish. You are not dreaming. Have you ever had dreams like this - that you can remember?"

"I can't remember anything! Fuck you! Leave me alone!" I try to walk away, but he grabs my wrist and I can't move at all. I feel paralysed and I can't make any of my muscles work. I can't even breathe or move my eyes. I notice with a panic that my heart has stopped beating.

"You are NOT dreaming! Within two minutes, you will lose consciousness and this body will die. You will be released and will have to seek another body soon, or you can stay where you are and rot for all eternity. I am losing patience with you, fish. Shall I release you, yes or no? Just think it, I will hear you."

I think 'Yes'.

With a dizzying rush, I feel my body starting up again as the creepy one releases me and I drop to my hands and knees on the floor.

"Well then, little tadpole, I will let you swim off. I have nothing more to say to you. I will let you decide if you want to believe you are dreaming or not. I am tired of this conversation. I will call on you if I need you, which is most unlikely, for why would I call on one such as you? But one never knows, does one?"

"Wait!"

"Yes?"

"If I am dead, then where is heaven and where is hell? Which one is this?"

The man chuckles again.

"Little fish, those are fairytales that human beings tell themselves to make themselves feel better about dying. I suppose they do it to make sense of their silly little lives.

There is no heaven or hell. They don't exist. The only thing that exists is this planet and all the souls that are tied to it as it swirls around in space. We are all trapped here in one form or another. We never leave it. We never go anywhere else. We all just swirl around and around."

"But that can't be right. There must be a point or a purpose."

"There isn't one."

25

I have been walking around for a while now it seems. The sun is high in the sky and I am sweating in my suit and jacket. I can feel the sweat sliding down my skin only to be absorbed in a sticky mass on my back. I don't care though. I don't loosen my tie and I don't take off my jacket.

I eventually find a park. There are a few people here and there eating their lunch. I suppose they are office drones having their lunch breaks. I feel the only sense of purpose I have felt since the creepy one left me. I search for a secluded part of the park. The park is large and it takes a long time until I find what I am looking for.

It is not a very used part of the park. I can't see any bent branches or paths and it looks like no one comes through here much. That is just what I want. I walk deeper and deeper into the foliage until I can no longer see or hear any people. I lie down on the wet ground in the rotting leaves and wait to die.

It takes a long time. I thought that wanting to die would be enough, but it isn't. The body is resilient and the man, whose body I am in, is fighting me all the time. I find this strange, because he wants to die and so why should he resist the process if that is what he wants? I can feel him pushing and struggling to get his arms and legs to move. He desperately wants to get up and get something to drink and eat. Thirst seems to be his main motivator. I can feel it too. It is not a good feeling. My tongue has been stuck to the roof of my mouth for a long time now. My lips dried and cracked a few days ago. The pain of that has dissipated as thick scabs formed over the fissures, trying to keep the little moisture that is left inside. The thirst comes with a feeling of panic. It takes a great deal of effort to keep the body from rushing off and finding water. It seems that every cell within it is seeking it, that every cell is trying to save its own life and is slowly crawling towards water. But I hold it firmly in place.

There has been hunger too, but what I feel more is the lack of sugar in my blood. That helps to counteract the body's desperate drive towards water. The lack of food has made me lethargic. The hungry part of me has given up and it just wants to lie down and rest.

I am sore too. I am sore from not having moved in days. I lay down in a foetal position and I have not moved a muscle since. I have done this so that the pain will help me to know that this is real. I need to know that this is real. That is the most important part of this. If I don't make sure that I feel every part of it, then dying has not been worth the effort. And it has been an effort.

I initially spent my time watching the insect activity around me. I watched the ants carrying debris back home and midges swarming in static clouds. I felt the tickle of flies on my skin. I made no motion to brush them off, letting them do what they would. I felt the sting of mosquitoes in the early evening, and again made no move to disrupt their activities, for what do I care about this body and what happens to it?

I seem to wake up just after the sun rises through the leaves. I watch off and on, between bouts of sleep, as the sun arcs through the sky between the clouds and sets again in a blaze of colour. I enjoy the sunset. I have been sleeping through the sunrise. I don't care much though. Even if I missed the sunset, I wouldn't care. I feel burnt by the midday sun. The skin on my face is probably red and blistered. I haven't bothered to check, but the skin there feels tight. The rest of the body is still covered in a suit, so it has been protected from the sun. At night, the stars come out vaguely under the glare of the city lights.

I know I smell bad. I was worried at one point that someone would come past and smell me and come to investigate, but I think I am far away enough not to be detected. I have not used a bathroom in days. I just let what needed to come out come out. I was pelted by a heavy rain yesterday, which has added a mildewy undertone to the ooze of smell emanating from me. That has been unpleasant, both the smell and the discomfort, but again, that has helped me to know that this is real. As real as I can make it. Or is it really real?

We have spoken, he and I. He has asked why I am doing this and I have told him that this is not real. I have told him it is a dream. I know that I will wake up and he will not exist. I will be the only one to exist. Just as it has been every time I wake up. He tells me that it is real, that I need to let him go and that he wants to live. I have told him that in my dream, he does not want to live and that is how I found him. He has told me that he has changed his mind, that now that he is faced with death he feels differently. He wants to live now. He realises that he loves his wife and his kids. He feels he will get work again. He hasn't looked as hard as he could. He wants to live.

I tell him that this is a dream and I am going to prove it is. I tell him that he will not die, because this is not real. I tell him that he does not even exist. He pushes against me and asks if that is not proof that this is real? I tell him that it is not. I know that dreams seem so real. They seem so real that when you are in them you believe that the fabric that your mind creates around you is real. You believe that it is solid. So solid that if you hit it, you will hurt your hand.

He asked me if I have had dreams that last for days.

He said that dreams are never coherent and that they don't go on for days. He said that there is no such dream as a man lying in a park for days slowly and painfully dying, when he could just get up and walk away. He said that dreams don't work that way. I told him that they do, because I am having that dream right now and I will prove it.

He has been quiet yesterday and today. I think he is tired and we are both more incoherent as time passes. I enjoy those incoherent times. It's like taking drugs. I go on trips and I never know what is going to come into my dehydrated brain. I think that, as the synapses slowly atrophy, the chemicals do not release properly and reality gets distorted. It makes the time pass in a more interesting way.

I had one trip where the ground seemed to buzz around me and I felt the shadowy hands of a hundred creatures on me, while they drew in their ghastly breaths. Another time, I was by the sea as waves of pink and purple slid silkily over a beach made of shiny stars.

I have had many trips where a young woman stares at me. Her blonde hair is pulled back from her face and she stares at me from eyes of red radiating pain. Her breath is shallow.

Now, I know dreaming about breathing is part of me dying. If I am really dying. I will see soon, I am sure. It is my brain clutching onto the only thing that is keeping me alive. It is grasping onto the only nourishment it is getting. It is encouraging the body to keep breathing, to keep bringing air in. It is telling the body not to give up. That there is still hope. That if it keeps breathing, maybe other forms of nourishment will be on their way and things will be better. The mind is a liar. I know this more than anyone. There will be no nourishment and soon the body will have to give up. Then I will see. Then I will see what is really happening.

I have been a victim of my mind's deceit for many days now and finally I will be the master of it. I will no longer be its cowering slave. I will no longer wait for salvation. I am taking this into my control. I am now in control. I need to wake up and this is the only way to do this. I know it.

I am fascinated by the trips though. I wonder if they have any significance at all. I asked the man, but he gave me no answer. I think he must represent my unconscious mind and, I guess, if it were easy to access the unconscious, then it wouldn't be called the unconscious.

It is strange, because the man is no longer lucid at all. In fact, he is quiet delirious. I think I merge with his thoughts and that is when I have the trips. So what must be happening is that I must be slipping into my unconscious and witnessing some kind of archetypal activity I suppose. But I am in control. I can be lucid if I want to. I am bored, so the trips are a brief distraction. But I can go out of them and into them whenever I choose to, so this is further proof that I am dreaming.

I have considered that this may not work, that I may end up lying here for a long, long time and that nothing may happen. It is possible, because anything seems possible. But there does seem to be a definite deterioration in the body, so I will wait and see what happens. I know it is a dream. I watch as the stars spin silently around the sky.

This morning things have definitely deteriorated. I was asleep, but when I woke up my eyes were open and stuck in a dry stare. This is annoying, because I can't look around. I seem to be stuck in a fixed blurry stare. My breaths are so shallow that at first I did not notice that I was breathing at all. But they are definitely there, though shallow. My heart rate has gone up. It is a very unpleasant feeling. It isn't pounding. It is fluttering at a high pitch in my chest. My ears feel like they have been stoppered full of wax. I can't really hear much anymore. Sounds are very vague and very far away. I can't feel the rest of my body. The pain of inactivity has gone. It is a relief not to feel pain, but at the same time I am disappointed, because I need the pain to know that this is real. Right now, I am not sure if I am still lying on the leaves on the ground in an unknown part of a park. I could be in another dream. And since my vision seems to have gone, it is hard to see.

I concentrate and make out the jagged corpse of a branch I have been looking at for the past few days. It definitely looks like the same branch through the blur and the smells are the same. Not that I am able to smell much. I have just noticed that. I don't have much of a sense of smell anymore. It seems that all my senses are slowly fading. Maybe this is a sign of the dream slowly starting to lose its grip on me and maybe it is fading back into unconsciousness where it belongs and I will rise once more to my conscious state. I will be awake at last!

I hope this will take place soon. I need an answer. I don't know what is happening. If this is a dream, I will wake up when it ends. If this is reality, the man I am inhabiting will die. I am betting this is a dream. Life does not work this way. If I were some kind of demon, surely people would talk about that. Surely, I would have heard about stories and when I mean stories, I mean common stories. Not those fantastic demon-possession horror movies they show, but real life stories. Like don't you remember last month when Joe was possessed by a demon? He really had a bad time of it, but not quite as bad as when Penny was possessed. Do you remember?

But people don't talk about stuff like that. They talk about weird dreams and they talk about their boyfriends and wives, their children and the good movie they went to last night. They do not talk about being a demon. They do not talk about possession. People only talk about reality. This is not reality. This is a dream. People talk about dreams. They don't talk about dreams they cannot wake up from for days on end. I will be the first. I know this is a dream, though.

This part of the death dream is quiet. It is comforting. Acceptance brings peace. The man knows he is dying. I know I am dreaming. We are both at peace. It feels so good. I watch shadows and light play through the blur. My breathing and heart rate don't bother me anymore. I am absorbed by the play of light. It is totally absorbing and peaceful. I feel content.

The light gets brighter and the shadows' contrast gets starker. The light softens and the shadows smudge until it gets darker and darker. The velvet blue light of twilight covers the world. I can barely see at all. It is the most peaceful I have felt in days.

I have stopped breathing. I just noticed that. I listen to make sure. No, there are no more breaths. I try to make myself breathe, but I can't. I can still feel my heart fluttering faintly like the gentle whispers of a tiny moth inside a jar.

I gasp. I take in one last lungful of air. It is an intake of air that fills my lungs to capacity. It has to feed the last flutters. I watch the body die. It slowly shuts down. There is some brain activity, because I can hear the man thinking, but his thoughts are rotting into fragments. The thoughts are eroded. They are half-thoughts or sometimes half-words or shattered remnants of images. The man is still there, but he is not aware that he is thinking.

There is no bright light at the end of the tunnel. There is no guardian angel coming to fetch him or me. There isn't anything. If I were truly dying isn't that what is supposed to happen? But no one comes and that is why I know this is a dream.

There is silence. No brain activity. No blood circulating. No heartbeat. Nothing. No sounds. No sights. Just nothing. He is here. I can feel him. He is lying inside the body. I am still lying in the body. When will I wake up?

We both lie there. It is hard to judge time. I am not sure how much time has passed exactly. Maybe it is minutes. It could be days. I feel disorientated. The body is dead. Definitely. But I can feel the body buzzing with an alien primordial life. It is almost vibrating with it, but it is a vibration, which I cannot tap into. I finally realise that bacteria have taken over. I think they took over the moment the body died and they are slowly starting to eat the host that kept them under control for so long.

We both lie inside this rotting corpse. Neither of us talks. We don't move. I am waiting to wake up. I suppose the man, who is my unconscious, is waiting to wake up too. Nothing happens.

Eventually I get tired of waiting and I feel tired. Some of my energy has gone. I did not notice this until now. Maybe now it is safe enough to move and wake up? I sit up. I am sitting in the corpse. The eyes are staring cloudily out at the leaves covered in night. The mouth is open, frozen in its last breath. I can see the shadow of the man beneath the dead skin. He is not moving.

I stand up and walk out of the body. The leaves rustle as I walk, but when I look down at myself, I see only darkness – a darkness that is only slightly darker than the darkness around me.

I look around. I am still in the park. Everything looks the same as when I first lay down here to die. The body is where I put it. It looks macabre. The man is still inside. Should he not have left the body by now? It is dead after all. He can't move it. He is curled up inside it like a small child inside a blanket, but this is not a blanket. It is a rotting corpse.

"Get out of there!"

He does not respond.

I sit down. I can see and I can sense things, but everything is very dulled. My senses are muted, like touching through a pair of gloves. It is strange.

I sit and watch him.

26

We don't talk. I have tried, but he ignores me. He just lies inside the rotting corpse as flies buzz giddily around their newfound treasure and maggots feast on their grotesque bounty. He doesn't seem to notice. He doesn't notice the stench that invades my dulled senses in a sickly sweet vapour.

We sit like this for days. I can feel myself get weaker, but I don't care. I was meant to be dreaming. This was not meant to be real. But here we are the murderer and the murdered, sitting side by side in a forest looking on as a body decays.

I did not wake up. I am where I have been for days now. I think I have been here for two weeks now. I think it has been that long, just lying in a forest, dying in a forest, and now sitting in a forest. This is not a dream.

I am too sad to move. I can't think about what has happened to me. I can't think about what I have done. Or what I am.

It is hard to see the man inside the body during the day. He is very vague in the harsh sunlight, but as the light diminishes and it gets darker, I can see him better. He is just a shadow after all and shadows don't exist in the day.

I asked him if I was also a shadow, but he has not spoken to me since the two days before he died. I have so many questions for him about me and about him. I don't want to be alone in this experience, but he is not talking to me so I can't share it with him. It would make me feel better to share things. I am sure it would make him feel better too, but he won't talk.

I can wait though. I have all the time in the world. I am dead. I am not dreaming. I wish I were dreaming.

Now there is nothing to wake up from. There is nothing to make this better. This is my life, if you can call it life, for the rest of eternity. But it is not life. It is not a way to exist.

I don't want to think about this right now. I just sit and watch. There is not much else to do other than watch. I am too depressed to move and I feel my essence slowly fading.

27

I hear laughing and a rustling of leaves not far from where we are. It is hard to make out what is happening, but I feel a slight tingling of energy in me. That is interesting. It is very slight, not much. It feels like something I need, but just a little taste of what I need. It is not enough. I suppose it would be like receiving a drop of water when I was literally dying of thirst a few days ago. It was what I needed, but by no means enough of what I needed.

I am intrigued, as sitting here has been boring, but I am not motivated enough to get up and see what is happening. Nothing really matters, so what's the point? I am not even sure that I can move. I haven't tried.

The laughing and rustling gets closer and I guess that people are walking towards us through the foliage. I can now make out what they are saying.

"Stop that!"

"Come on, let's do it here."

"No. I don't want anyone to see us, let's go in a little further."

"What about here?"

"A little bit further. I promise it will be worth your while."

I hear some giggling and the rustling continues.

"Oh my god! What is that smell? Can you smell it?"

"No. What smell?"

"I don't know what it is, but it smells bad! Can't you smell it?"

"No, where is it?"

"I don't know. Let's get out of here. I don't like it. You are not getting laid here. It stinks."

"Wait a minute."

More rustling.

"Where are you going? I don't want to stay here. Let's go. Please. This place is creepy."

"I can smell it. Definitely. It's really bad."

"I am glad you believe me now. Can we go, please?"

"No."

"Why not? I am seriously not having sex with you here. You can stay here on your own if you like. I'm going."

"Wait. Okay? I know this smell. Something died here. It smells a bit like the time a rat died under the floor boards in my kitchen."

"Are you serious? So then why do you want to stay here?"

"I just have to see what it is."

"What on earth for? You are creeping me out. Do you like to look at dead animals?"

"Not particularly. I just get a feeling I should look and make sure everything's okay. Stay here. I will be back in a minute."

"If it's dead, it's not okay, you idiot! Wait! I am not staying here by myself."

"I think you should. Just stay there. I'll be back in a minute."

"No way! I am coming with you."

I hear them walking towards us as the leaves and sticks squelch and crunch under their feet and as the branches yield around their moving bodies.

Then I see them. A young man and woman. The man's eyes are scanning everywhere until they rest, in slowly registering alarm, on the dead body. He turns around quickly and tries to force the woman back along the path they have come along. But he is too late. She catches a glimpse of the body.

"Oh my god!" she breathes out and turns and runs. He runs after her. I hear their flight quickly fading away leaving me, the man and the evidence of what I have done, alone in the forest.

Stillness returns. It's early afternoon, so I can't see the man very clearly. He has finally moved and is sitting on the same tree branch, which I was staring at, while we were dying. He is looking at his body. He doesn't move and he won't talk to me. I guess I wouldn't talk to my murderer either, if I were in a similar situation. I can't see his facial expressions even in the dark, because he is just a shadow. He feels sad though. I can sense that from him. He feels very sad.

His sadness is reflected in our situation. He is too sad to move and I am too depressed and drained to move. There we are the three of us, two shadows and a rotting corpse, nestling in decaying brown leaves, alone in a small clearing surrounded by thick green trees. An impassive grey sky stares down at us. And all is silent.

All is silent.

"This way."

I hear more trampling. Bloody hell! Can't they leave us alone? I chose this place because of its isolation.

The young man comes back to the clearing followed by some policemen and detectives. The young man points to the rotting body and answers some questions. He is rather evasive about what he was doing in this part of the park. He said that he wanted to walk through the woods and found the body by accident. Most of it is true, except that he didn't want to walk through the woods. But that is neither here nor there. He leaves and the police go about their business.

To me they seem like rather obsessive dung beetles. They are meticulous about gathering up every scrap that pertains to the body and then they wrap it up and prepare to take it out of the woods. What strikes me is that the body is the least important thing here. They don't notice us. Not one of them notices the man or me.

They don't notice the man crying and begging them to leave his body here. He does not want them to take it away. He stands in front of them and begs through his tears. They can't hear him. He throws himself on top of the body to prevent them from moving it, but that makes no difference. You can't even see the impact of his body on the sheet covering the corpse.

"You are wasting your time. They can't hear or see you evidently."

"Leave it alone! Leave it here. It's mine!"

"Why do you care so much? It is going to rot away anyway and then you will have nothing to stare at."

"Please, please. Leave it here. Leave me here. Leave me alone! It's my body. It's mine!"

He runs after them as they carry the body out of the woods on a stretcher. He suddenly stops, as though he were attached to a chain that he had forgotten about, and is pulled up short. He flings himself again and again after the retreating detectives, but he does not seem to be able to move past some invisible barrier.

Maybe he is as drained as I am. I have no energy to move. All I can do is speak and watch. But I wouldn't be able to fling myself around like he is. I wonder what is keeping him here. I look around, but I can't see anything at all. Interesting, and at the same time it doesn't really matter, because nothing matters.

The other police officers and detectives are doing a final sweep of the area and, as one young man comes to stand next to me, I feel the most delicious rush. It feels sweet and heady and delicious. It is a strange feeling and at the same time a very seductive feeling.

I can't really resist it. It is so intoxicating. I find myself moving towards him, almost without trying.

I look out through his eyes. He feels sad. He has been sad for a very long time. He doesn't like his job much. He was told that he would get used to death and murder. He was told that he would toughen up, that it wouldn't bother him, but it still does. It has never changed. He feels there must be something wrong with him, because he is the only one who seems to get affected. His nights are filled with the grizzly grins of the dead. And when he wakes after a night of terror, he does not want to go to work, but he has to. This is the job he has chosen for himself. He spent years and lots of money to get to this position and now he hates it.

He doesn't even know how to meet women anymore. He used to be fine with that. It was never a problem for him, but now it is. Now when he sits down at a restaurant table for a date, the dead stare at him and he cannot talk about what he does for a living. He doesn't think the living would enjoy what he knows about the dead. He gave up dating a few years ago.

It is interesting to listen to his thoughts. I didn't know I could do that. I think this is the first time I haven't taken over. It is quite nice. I feel like I am nestled in a warm comfortable taxi. I will go where it goes and I will be fed. I do not have to take control. I really don't feel like it. I just want to sleep.

I stretch out into his body. I run my arms along his arms and my legs into his legs. It is such a snug fit. I feel like I am cocooned in thick velvet and fur. And I can feel myself starting to drift off.

I guess dying and sitting around has taken its toll and I feel very sleepy.

"Detective Johnson, are you coming?"

"Are we done here?"

"Yes, sir, unless there is something else you need to look at."

"No, I think we have done a thorough sweep of the area. We can go."

"Very well, let's move out. Don't leave any evidence bags behind like last time, Andrews."

We turn to notice a young woman blush a deep scarlet and bow her head as she walks past the policeman and me.

As Johnson turns to walk away, I suddenly remember the man I murdered. I can't see him at all. I wonder if he is still here in the woods. Johnson is turning away from the spot where the murdered man was sitting so I can't see him.

Fuck! I guess I owe it to him. One last effort and then I can go to sleep. I take over Johnson's body and turn back to the tree stump. It takes a few moments, but slowly I make out the silhouette of the man sitting slumped over on the old tree branch.

"Why don't you come with us? This feels really good. I promise you. It's the only way I can make things up to you. Please won't you come and try it. Maybe you can come in here with me? Won't you try it?"

The murdered man raises his dark head and appears to be looking at me. He doesn't move.

"I was murdered here."

"I know that, but you need to come with me. It will be better than sitting here and feeling sorry for yourself."

"I was murdered here," he says in a subdued voice. He slumps over again and doesn't move.

"Suit yourself. Are you going to stay here and feel sorry for yourself forever?"

He doesn't answer me.

I feel annoyed. I am trying to help him. I feel bad about what I did and if he would just listen to me, he would see how amazing this feels. I walk over to him so that he can also get a sense of this great energy, but he doesn't move or acknowledge my presence.

"Please come with me. Please. I feel so bad about what I did to you. This is the only way that I know of to make it up to you. Please. Please don't sit here all alone. Please try. It will be better. I don't want you to stay here all alone. I am so sorry for what I did to you. I am so deeply sorry. I thought it was a dream. I really and truly did."

"It was real."

"I know it was and I know you told me that and begged me and begged me to listen, and I didn't. I didn't know it was real. I promise you, I didn't know. I have been so confused. I have been confused for such a long time. I didn't really mean to kill you. I thought that I would wake up and that you wouldn't exist and that I would be me in real life. I don't even know who I am."

He does not respond.

"I am really trying to tell you why I did it and who I am and why this happened. Please forgive me. I am so, so sorry. I know you can't be alive again, but please don't stay out here by yourself."

"I was murdered here."

"I know. I know. It was me. I did it to you. Please come with me. Please. Let me make it up to you somehow."

"I was murdered here."

My body startles, as I feel a hand on my shoulder. I turn around. The policeman is staring at me.

"Are you all right, Johnson?"

"What? Yes! Yes, I'm fine. I'm fine. Thank you for asking."

"Who were you talking to?"

"The man on the branch here."

"What man?"

"This one sitting here."

"I don't see anyone sitting on a branch."

"Don't you?"

"No."

"Oh."

"Where were you two weeks ago? Where were you Saturday evening two weeks ago?"

"Why do you ask?"

"I am asking, Johnson, because you have been standing here talking to this tree stump very close to where we have just found a dead body and you have just confessed to killing him."

"I did?"

"Yes you did. I am afraid you are going to have to come with me."

"You heard me talking."

"I heard you loud and clear."

"Oh. Did you hear him talking?"

"Did I hear who talking, Johnson?"

"The man on the tree stump?"

"You are going to have to come back with me. I will arrange for your superior and two of your colleagues to be present when I question you. Please come with me now, sir."

I look back at the man on the tree stump. He is not paying attention to us and is sitting forlornly looking at where his body used to lie. I realise that he is not coming with me and the policeman has taken me firmly by the upper arm and is leading me away.

I tried. Maybe I can come back some time and convince him to come with me, but for now I am too tired to try anymore and it seems that I have got Johnson into a terrible situation. He will be fine though, because they will find no evidence of foul play. The man wasn't tied down or fatally wounded or poisoned. He just lay down to die a long and unpleasant death and they will not be able to pin that on Johnson. So, it will all be all right in the end. I release my hold on him and he startles.

As I get all snug again, I hear him ask what happened and listen as the policeman tells him that he just confessed to murder. Johnson is upset and says that he cannot remember the last few minutes. He says that he must have blacked out. The policeman assures him that he was quite lucid and continues to lead him firmly out of the woods.

I slowly fall asleep rocked by the rhythm of Johnson walking and by the sound of his voice, which gets fainter and fainter, as I slowly drift off into sweet oblivion. Maybe for once I will get some much-needed rest.

28

I slowly surface from my sleep. I feel so good – just relaxed and content. I stretch out with sticky toffee ease inside Johnson. Lovely. I could drift off again in the nebula of sleep, but there is a noise that is making me wake up. What is it?

It sounds like a high-pitched drone. Is it from a dream I was having? I try to think, but I don't remember dreaming. It must be an alarm clock signalling an end to blissful contentment and a day of work for Johnson. Not me. Once he switches the damn thing off I am going back to sleep and he can go to work. I don't feel like moving Johnson's arm to turn it off and he isn't turning it off. Maybe it will switch off on its own. Some alarms do switch off eventually even if you don't turn them off. I'll just wait. I don't feel like moving.

Why won't it end? It just goes on and on and on. I just want to go back to sleep. Why doesn't it bother Johnson? I listen. I can't hear his thoughts. That is very strange. Fine. I will have to move him. I try to take control of his body. I try to open my eyes and move my arms and legs. Nothing. What the hell is going on? The noise is starting to die now. Well, that's good.

Ah, I can go back to sleep now. I will worry about why I couldn't make Johnson move later. Maybe some people are more difficult to control than others. Maybe. I don't care right now. All I want to do is sleep. I snuggle down again.

I am awoken by bright light and coldness. What the fuck is going on? All I want to do is sleep. I have endured enough. I just want a little rest. A little peace. Just a few hours. Is that too much to ask for?

A rush of noise hits me with such force that I fall off

the bed. I look up to see two men in white carting Johnson's body away.

What's going on now? Just when things were starting to make some sense to me - now there is a new development.

A man walks into the room and walks over to an elderly woman. He looks like a doctor.

"I am sorry for your loss, Mrs Johnson. We did everything we could, but in the end, I think it was for the best. I know that is not easy to hear right now."

"No. It isn't, but I know you tried your best Dr. Bailey. Thank you for everything you have done."

"Are you going to be all right to drive home on your own?"

"Actually, I don't think I have the strength for that."

"Is there a relative or friend I can call for you?"

"My daughter could come and fetch me after she has dropped her children off at school, but I just really want to be alone right now."

"Would you like me to call a taxi for you?"

"Yes, thank you. I'll fetch my car tomorrow."

"Would you like to wait down in reception and I'll get them to call a taxi."

"Yes, thank you. I just want to pack up his things."

"Take care, Mrs Johnson."

"Thank you, Doctor."

I watch as the woman opens the stark bedside table and the wardrobe and packs a few items into a small, well-travelled bag. She clutches the bag to her chest as she walks out of the room.

I'd better follow her. How could Johnson have died? Surely if there was something wrong yesterday evening, I would have known about it. I would have felt it in his body, the same as I did with the man I murdered.

I walk after the woman and realise that I can do that quite easily. This is great. I have so much energy, I feel like I could run around the world a few times and still have plenty to spare. It's a fantastic feeling! In fact, it's the best I have felt in a really long time.

I am so happy, that even Mrs Johnson's sad, stolen tears do not sadden me. She wipes them away quickly, after they appear at the corners of her eyes. She walks down to the lobby and presently a taxi comes to fetch her. She slams the door on me, but I don't take offence. She can't see me after all.

Can I pass through a solid car door? This is going to be interesting. I need to be quick. She is giving her address and the taxi is going to leave any moment. I just dive into the seat next to her.

We both shiver as I pass by her. I don't know why she shivered, but I shivered, as going through the door of the taxi felt a bit irritating. It didn't hurt and didn't feel like a barrier. It felt like passing through a low-level vibrating force field. It made me tingle everywhere at once and not in a pleasant way. I think I will avoid that as much as possible in the future.

The taxi driver doesn't talk. She is obviously aware that people leaving hospitals alone with a bag are probably doing so because a loved one is gravely ill or has died. Mrs Johnson looks out the window. Occasionally a tear leaks out and she dabs it with a scrunched up blue tissue. I am sorry for her loss. I can now feel how sad she is. At the same time, it feels kind of tingly and I feel very drawn to her. I would love to get inside her, but I resist the impulse. I have lots of strength and energy. I feel stronger than I did yesterday in the park, where I could barely move. If Johnson hadn't come past, I have a feeling I would still be stuck there amidst those trees with the sad, murdered man. The man I murdered. I will never do that again.

We eventually arrive at our destination and I rush past Mrs Johnson as she opens the door. I don't want to have to go through another door again. She shivers once more. I realise that I am the cause of her shivers. She pays the cab driver and walks up to her house. I make another dash for it as she opens her solid white wooden door. I have a feeling that passing through that may be more unpleasant than the door of the taxi.

She shivers again. I watch her closely. She obviously senses me on some level, but at the same time doesn't know I am there. She shakes off the shiver and puts Johnson's bag down in the entrance hall.

I follow her as she goes to the kitchen and makes herself a cup of tea. Her kitchen is light and airy. Floral curtains drift delicately on a cool breeze. I drift after her to the living room.

This seems to be full of photographs and I notice a few recent ones of Johnson. I know it is him, because I recognise his face from yesterday. I wonder how he could die so suddenly and so easily. If he was in an accident or was shot, surely I would have woken up? And I didn't notice much wrong with him when I entered him, other than that he was unhappy with his job and his life. Otherwise, according to the creepy guy, I wouldn't have been able to get inside of him.

There must be another way though and that is why I am staying away from Mrs Johnson. I am not going to go inside her no matter what. That little sleep was what I needed. I just borrowed Johnson for a little while and now I feel great! Maybe that's all I need to do. Just have a little nap and then be on my way, no harm done.

There must be a way to manage this. I don't feel evil

and so why would I have to be evil? No, I am sure that the creepy one was wrong. I will find a way. But I do need to find out about Johnson. I want to know what was so wrong with him that he died so suddenly. I need to know, so that in future I don't go into people who then die on me. That is very inconvenient, as I need someone who won't die on me while I am napping. I want to wake up when I am good and ready. I also need to find out what I did not pick up on about him. That is very strange. Normally I know everything about a person when I go inside. According to the creepy one, that was my problem. I lost myself and became them. I didn't do that with the man in the park and I didn't do that with Johnson either. I need to know what I missed. I am sure when Mrs Johnson's daughter arrives they will talk about what happened. They must do. I would if someone I loved was fine one day and was dead less than twenty-four hours later for no apparent reason.

Mrs Johnson has picked up her mobile.

"Hello, sweetie. Um, I don't know how to say this better. Your brother died this morning. I know. His heart just failed him. He would never have recovered. It's for the best. I am all right. Are you all right? No, I am at home. I took a taxi. I know you would have, but I just need to be alone for a little while. Maybe you and Ben can come over this evening and we can discuss the funeral. I just need some time alone. Are you all right? Do you need me? Will Ben be able to take time off work? The only thing that consoles me is that he is with your father now and I am sure he is taking good care of my boy."

She breaks down into sobs.

"No really, darling, if it's all right, I would prefer to be alone. I'll see you this evening. Bye sweetie."

Mrs Johnson puts the phone down on the table and

puts her head in her hands and sobs. I want to put my arms around her and tell her that I am so sorry for her loss. I feel every wave of sadness coming off her. I ignore the pull it has on me and I concentrate on her. Even if she could see me it would be a little awkward, because she does not know me and I don't know her. I am sure she would not want to share this moment with a stranger. Her grief seems so intensely personal. I feel I should not be witness to it. She obviously doesn't want anyone to witness it. I tell her I am sorry for her loss. She doesn't show any indication that she heard me. I leave the room.

I feel bad about walking around her house uninvited, but there is nothing else for me to do. Her house is not big. There is a main bedroom and a small guest bedroom. I am guessing it's a guest room, as there is no sign of life in it. The main bedroom has a fluffy pink dressing gown draped over a plush wooden chair and the bed has been made rather hastily. There are some books on the bedside table.

I reach to pick one up and am very surprised to find that I was able to lift it. I didn't know I could do that, but then again, I haven't been outside a human body before, so I am sure that there are many things that I do not know I can do. I will have to wait to find out what else I can do.

I put the book down again and walk into the en-suite bathroom. A tube of toothpaste has been left by the edge of the basin. I guess Mrs Johnson brushed her teeth in a hurry. I screw the cap back on and place the tube neatly beside the green toothbrush in the mug.

Not much else to see around here, so I walk down the passage again. There is another bathroom. It seems to be for guests, as it is very neat with no signs of washing, hair brushing, or teeth cleaning in it. It's a little dull.

I walk out again and find a closed white wooden door. A firm, polished brass handle beckons me. I reach out and turn it. I leave no imprint on it. It looks like it was never touched. I quietly open the door and of course, it creaks terribly. I hope she didn't hear it through her crying. I cringe as the door creaks again when I close it and it's worse this time. I tried to be careful and so protracted the creak.

I hear her footsteps coming towards me. My instinct is to hide and I climb under the dark wooden desk, careful not to bump anything. She opens the door. I don't hear anything. I crawled under the desk on my hands and knees and I went in headfirst so now all I can see is the back of the solid desk. I don't dare move.

"Paul?"

We both wait for an answer. Silence.

"Paul is that you? I know you are here. I felt you in the cab with me and I felt you when I came into the house. I love you so much and I miss you so much already, my darling. Please give me a sign to show me you are all right. Are you with Daddy? Is he there with you?"

I hear her walk into the room and sit down on the sofa. Nothing happens. I wonder if Paul is Johnson? I didn't really hang around in his head long enough to pick up his first name. I presume it is, since Mrs Johnson assumed that he was with his father when she was speaking on the phone to her daughter and she is mentioning it again now. She must mean Johnson. I don't think he is in the room with us. I didn't notice anybody else around. I think it was me that she heard. Yes, she definitely heard me. It was the door creaking. Now what? I feel really bad for her. Her voice sounds sad and hopeful at the same time. It couldn't hurt if I gave her a sign. She wouldn't know whom it was from and she would feel much better then and I would be doing something good. Wouldn't I? And it would be really nice to do something good for a change, especially after what I did to the man in the park. It wasn't my fault, but I did it anyway. So this would be a little tiny step to making up for that. And we would both feel better, Mrs Johnson and I. I decide to give her a sign, but first I want to check if Paul is actually here, because maybe he could do it himself. That would be better. Maybe I can help since I have been around a bit longer than he has. He just died today. I am sure he hasn't learnt the ropes yet.

I take a chance, crawl backwards very carefully out from under the desk, and stand up. I turn around expecting Mrs Johnson to see me, but she seems to be staring fixedly at a photograph of Paul. I suppose she expects it to move or something. Maybe that would be her sign. I look around the room very carefully for any shadows. I don't see any.

After some hesitation, I ask aloud if Paul is there. I wait in a state of anxiety for Mrs Johnson to jump up and run away after she hears me speak, but she doesn't. She is sitting staring placidly at the photograph.

We both stare at it and nothing happens. After a while, she sighs and stands up. I should have made that photograph move. I know I can and that would be a sign wouldn't it. I make up my mind. I walk over to the photograph and put my fingertip very gently against it. I wait for her to look up. She is staring at the floor. Then I hear her start to cry again.

"Please look up, Mrs Johnson. Don't be so sad."

But she doesn't hear me. She cries for about five minutes. I keep wishing she would look up. Eventually she stops crying and looks at the photograph.

"I wish I had heard you open the door and walk into

this room, but I suppose I imagined it. I feel like my heart has been ripped apart."

I take this opportunity to nudge the photograph.

She stares hard at it.

"Paul?"

I nudge it again.

"Paul! Paul! I knew it was you! Oh my boy! Are you all right? Are you with your father?"

I nudge it twice.

She comes rushing to the photograph and I run away. I don't want her to get the shivers again. She hugs the photograph closely to her chest and sobs.

"Thank you! Thank you! Now I know you are all right. No more pain. No more pain, my baby. You rest in peace."

She stands there for a long time. I really wish it had been Paul and not me, but it was a good thing to do and she seems to feel comforted. I feel a bit better about myself. I am going to figure this whole thing out. I am going to make this work. I can't die again so there is no way out of this situation, but I can make it work.

Eventually Mrs Johnson puts the photograph back. She caresses Paul's face and walks back to the door. She turns around and comes back. She picks up the photograph and carries it out with her. She closes the door.

I feel much better about myself and wait a little while. I am sure that Mrs Johnson has gone to sleep, as I heard her footsteps moving towards the bedroom. So it will be a while before I have the opportunity to find out what happened. I look around the room. It seems to be a study. There is a soft green couch nestled between two bookshelves and a big mahogany desk with a computer and reading lamp on the top. It is a pleasant room and this lady obviously has money and likes to spend it on the finer things in life.

I decide to while away my time by reading a book. Strangely, I find it a bit difficult to make out the writing on the spines for some reason, but if I really try hard, I can read the titles. I pick out a book by Charles Dickens. I think I like him. It's called 'A Tale of Two Cities'. I sit down on the couch and open up the book to the first page. The words are blurry. I look around the room and I can see perfectly. I look back at the book and the words are blurry. It makes no sense at all. I look at the couch. I can see the grain of the green velvet perfectly. I can see each fibre if I look very closely. I look back at the book. It is blurry. Why? Why? Why? Does this make any sense at all? No. Why can I see everything else clearly, but I can't read the book?

I stare at the book and squint at it. I can make out words if I try really hard, but it takes a lot of effort. Well, that is very unfortunate! Now I can't even spend my time reading. I put the book back carefully on the shelf. I run my hands over the spines. The sensation in my fingertips is dull. It feels like I am touching the books with a glove on. Something else that it not great. I am learning a lot about my situation it seems. I can't read; I can't feel very well; I can move things. If I sleep in someone, I feel better. And I am dead. It's not a lot to go on! I don't even know my own name and I don't know what it means to be a 'demon' really. It didn't come with a handbook and if it did, I probably wouldn't be able to read it. There's irony in there somewhere.

Well, I guess Mrs Johnson is going to sleep for a while. She looked very tired. Watching her son die must have taken a lot out of her, especially since it was so sudden. I need to wait to find out what happened to him and why I was unaware of it. I have a lot of time to kill. Mrs Johnson's daughter is coming over this evening. I will have to get through the rest of the morning and the whole afternoon. That is unfortunate.

I look around. Not much to do in here. I look at the computer on the desk. I wonder if I can turn it on. I push the main power button on the tower and the computer beeps. I freeze and listen, but resounding silence greets me from the rest of the house. I quickly pull the cord out from the back of the tower, which leads to the speakers. I wait for the computer to start up. It is slow, but I suppose I am not in a rush. Eventually it starts up.

I can't really read the words under the icons on the screen. I look at the keyboard. I can see each letter just fine. How strange. How am I able to see the individual letters, but I am unable to see words? It makes no sense to me.

I start typing, but nothing comes up on the screen. Oh, right. This is the start-up screen. How do I know about computers? I must have interacted with them when I was alive. Oh, yes, and I used one in Claire's office, didn't I? Let me think. I think the green thing at the bottom left must be the menu thing. I navigate for a while through the various menus on the computer in a semi-blind and very frustrating way. It is annoying, but it does keep me occupied for a long time. Eventually, after much trial and error, I find a programme that allows me to write text. I start typing slowly.

"Hi mom. This is Paul. I am fine. Don't be sad. I love you."

I felt I should write that just in case she walks in to find her computer on. I wouldn't want her to die of a heart attack. I would feel very bad if I made her feel worse. So that's why I wrote what I did – just in case she comes back into the room. But the reason why I am typing on the computer is to see if I can read my own words. I can't. Well I can, but with a great deal of effort. Maybe the font size is too small, however I can't read anything on the screen to help me figure out where the font size menu would be. That might be the problem. Maybe I had really bad eyesight when I was alive and that is what is manifesting itself now. I am not sure.

I try one more thing. I type a letter and push the space bar a few times and type another letter and push the space bar repeatedly. I look at the screen. I can see the letters perfectly. I can read them all with no problem. I try writing three letter words like 'run' and 'cat'. I look up. I can't see them properly. This is odd. Well there is nothing I can do about this clearly. I will have to wait and see if I meet someone like me, who can explain it to me.

I switch the computer off. There is nothing for me to do and I am trapped in this room. I don't want to open the creaking door again, as I will wake Mrs Johnson and there is nothing of great interest to see in her house. I have explored it already as much as I want to. There is not much that holds my interest in this room. I would quite happily lie on the couch and read a book, but since that does not seem to be an option that is open to me, I walk to the window and slowly open it. I go back to the couch and lie down. It looks comfortable, but I can't really feel if it is or not. I watch the trees and birds outside as the day journeys from light to dark.

"I had a sign from your brother. Right here."

I jump up and run to a corner as Mrs Johnson comes into the room with a younger man and woman. She stops and stares at the window.

"Look at that!"

"What am I looking at, Mom?" asks the woman.

"The window. Look at the window. It was shut when I left this room this morning. Now it is open."

Oh dear. I should have shut it when it became dark outside. I forgot.

"Mom, I am sure you left it open and forgot about it."

"No I didn't! I always keep this window shut, because I don't want dust getting onto my books. Your brother always loved fresh air. It was him who opened it. I am telling you. And he moved this photograph when I was talking to him this morning. He is sending me signs to tell me that he is all right."

Mrs Johnson walks back to the shelf to put the photograph of Paul back in its place. I see that the young woman wants to say something, but the man next to her touches her arm and shakes his head. She closes her mouth.

"Let's go and sit in the lounge, Mom. Ben would you make us some tea?"

"Sure."

Mrs Johnson and her daughter walk back to the lounge. Ben walks over to the window to close it and I take this opportunity to sneak out of the room to the lounge.

Mrs Johnson and her daughter seat themselves on the sofa. The light in the room is bright. It is a warm and elegantly furnished room.

"Come here," the young woman pulls her mother into a comforting embrace. "I have been worried about you all day."

"I'm sorry, sweetie. I just wanted to be alone. I am so tired. It's been a long two months."

"I know. I know it has. It has for both of us too and the kids. You know how much they loved their Uncle

Paul."

"I know. He was so good to them. I wish he had had a chance to have a family of his own. He would have been such a good father. Now he will never do that."

"He is with Daddy now and he isn't suffering anymore. I am sure they are both here with us now and they are looking down on us."

I look up and I don't see anything other than the ceiling. I don't see any shadows up there and I don't feel anybody else around. It's a nice thought though. I think people say that so that they feel they are not alone when people die. The question for me is why am I here? How come I am here, but Paul is not? He is dead too, but he is not here. The man in the park stayed around after he died, but I haven't seen Paul anywhere. That is very strange. Why is he not here? What has happened to him?

"Maybe you should come and stay with us for a few days, Mom. You know, just to be taken care of for a little bit. You have been at that hospital every day now for the past two months. I am worried about you. I don't want you to end up ill as well – you are exhausted."

What?

Paul hasn't been in a hospital for the past two months. What are they talking about? I saw him yesterday. I drift closer to them. I don't want to miss a word of what they are saying.

"Thank you, sweetie, but you have to get on with your lives and I don't want to impose. I think I also just need some time alone. Time to think about your brother. So much has happened in such a short time. I can't believe he is gone. I just don't understand it. Such a healthy man. He always was. Never was sick as a child. Never. Why now?"

"I don't know, Mom. Things happen all the time -

things we don't understand. There was nothing any of us could do. It's not your fault. He is gone now and we all need time to grieve."

"I know. You are right, sweetie, and I wish I could just cry. I just don't understand why my healthy son became so sick and died. I don't understand it. It doesn't make sense. It's not fair! He is... he was a good boy! I want him back! I don't want this to be happening! This can't be happening to me."

As Mrs Johnson collapses in tears in her daughter's arms, I slump on a chair opposite them. I have been asleep for over two months? I thought it had been just over twelve hours. I think I have just killed another person. I feel like the room is imploding in on me, as the realisation hits me. I didn't mean to kill him. I didn't know that that would happen. I was just sleeping for a while. I just needed to rest.

"Here's your tea, Mom"

"Just pop it on the table, honey. She is too upset to drink it now."

Ben sets their tea down and goes back to the kitchen to fetch his cup. Mrs Johnson and her daughter are embraced in mutual sorrow and I am suffused with horror. The scene seems to stay like that. We are all caught in our own misery.

Ben returns and sits down on the sofa next to his mother-in-law. He gently strokes her back as she sobs. Tears leak from his eyes too and he makes no move to wipe them away.

I am the cause of this. I have no right to be in this room. If it weren't for me, these people would not be in so much pain. They would still have Paul and they would be all right. Instead, I stupidly killed another person. Again. That is all I do. All I do is kill and kill and kill. I must be evil. Why did I do that? Why did I sleep in someone? I must have taken all of his energy and that's why I feel so good, because I sucked the life right out of his body, until there was nothing left. I want to leave and get out of here, but I feel I need to stay and see what I have done. I am a killer. I need to see the sorrow and anguish I have caused. I need to witness it. But even that is not enough of a punishment.

"He can't be dead. He can't be. It makes no sense. He's not dead. My boy is not dead. No! No! No!"

"Mom, I think you should take something – just to get through tonight. Ben, please give me the tablets."

"I don't want any tablets! I want my son back! I want my son back!"

"Mom, these are going to help you and Ben and I are taking you home with us. I am not leaving you alone like this. Please swallow this."

"No! If I take that then I am betraying Paul!"

"Mom, you don't have to get yourself into a state to prove you love Paul," Ben gently says to her, "Let us take care of you. Please take this pill, so you can rest. It has been too much for you. It has been too much for all of us. You are not alone though. Let Nancy and I take you home with us. Please. There is no sense being alone at a time like this. You are overwhelmed right now and that makes perfect sense. This is going to help, just for tonight."

Mrs Johnson takes the tablet from him and swallows it down with a sobbing sip of her tea.

"Ben, will you stay with her while I pack her things?"

"Sure."

Ben picks up his tea and leans back into the sofa with his arm around Mrs Johnson. Nancy picks up her tea and leaves the lounge. Ben and Mrs Johnson don't talk. Both of them sip their tea in silence. Mrs Johnson seems a little calmer.

I don't feel calm at all. I am so angry. I want to tear this room apart, but that will only make things worse for them. I have murdered yet another innocent person.

I need to get away from people. I just cannot be around people any more. I need to get as far away from them as I possibly can. I can deal with my feelings about all this as soon as I have made sure that I can no longer do any harm.

I am going to have to borrow someone for a little bit again. I need to find out where I am and I need their eyes to look at a map. I can't use Mrs Johnson, because they would stop her and I can't access Ben. His energy repels me. I get up and search for Nancy. I find her in the main bedroom packing her mother's belongings in a small suitcase. She is crying. Her energy is also not good. It pushes me away, but I think I can get in there. There is a little gap. It won't be easy though. It may drain me. I just have a feeling that might be what will happen, but I don't really care. I decide to give it a try.

I push hard into her. Yes. I am in! I take control of her body. I push her mind aside and I walk to the study. I can see the book spines with great clarity now. I scan them and find a road atlas on the bottom shelf. I pull it out and flip it open. I access Nancy's mind briefly for the location of this house. Right. It looks like we are near the sea and I see that the road curves around near a cliff. I need them to get me there. I hope this is a map of the area I am in. There is only one way to find out, however if it isn't, I will have to think of something else.

I put the atlas back in the shelf, turn off the light and look around. No one is around. I walk back to the bedroom and put Nancy in the position I found her in. I don't want to use her for too long. I leave her body and watch to see what happens.

Nancy shudders and looks at the bag for a while. Then she looks around and shudders again. She looks uneasy. She quickly walks around the room packing things.

I feel drained. That took a great deal of energy out of me. It was not like being in other people. They seem to feed me. She seems to take energy away from me and I really had to hang onto her. If I hadn't, I would have been expelled. I am going to have to time my moment just right.

Nancy finishes packing and takes the suitcase to the lounge after switching off all the lights in the house. Mrs Johnson seems to be dozing. Ben gently shakes her and the three of them go outside to the car.

I manage to slip out of the house and into the car without anyone feeling me. I sit in the back seat with Mrs Johnson. Her head lolls as the car gently pulls off. Ben is driving, which is good for me. I can't access him. I can't access Mrs Johnson, as she is sedated. So I can only access Nancy. If she were driving, I would cause an accident when I left her, and I have taken enough lives, without adding another three to my tally.

I let Ben drive for five minutes before I enter Nancy. I don't want to spend too much time inside her. I need all the energy I have for this. Then it won't matter if I have nothing left. Maybe I can die after all. I am going to try to find out, because I do not want to live like this anymore. I don't want to kill any more.

Taking over Nancy requires much more effort this time. I don't think I have very long. Please let me be by the sea and let it not be far.

"Ben?"

"Uh-huh?"

"Could we go past the sea?"

"Why?"

"I just feel I need to."

"Shouldn't we get home? Your mom needs to go to bed and the kids are upset too."

"I know. I just need to. It's not far."

"No, but….."

"I have a long couple weeks ahead of me and I just need to see the sea. It will help. Please, Ben. Paul liked it. I need to connect with him."

"Do you want to go past the vantage point?"

"Yes. Thank you."

"You are right. It is going to be hard. I am going to miss him so much. Let's go."

We drive in silence. I hope it is not too far. I feel my grip on Nancy is slipping. I hold onto her with every ounce of energy I have. It is draining me fast. With relief, I see the sea ahead of us.

"How long do you want to stay?"

"I just want to drive past."

"I thought you wanted to see the sea?"

"Yes, just see it. Then we need to get back home. As you said, mom and the kids have had as long day, as have we."

"Okay."

I wait for it. Ben turns into the road that snakes along the sea. I wait until I see a bench on the side of the road. I take a chance that this is the vantage point. I surmise that the bench would be located by the cliff in order to afford a good view. I hardly have any energy left. Nancy is pushing me out. I wait. We are almost there. Just a few more seconds. I just need to hold on a little bit more. Yes!

I jump. I hardly have any energy left. I hope I land at the base of the cliff and not at the vantage point. If I land at the vantage point, I will find myself sucked into the first person, who comes there. I don't think I have enough energy left to walk to the edge of the cliff if I miss.

This has taken all my energy and I have nothing left. I drift through the dark night air and hope.

29

I have absolutely no idea how long I have been here, but I have found some semblance of peace. I am far away from the allure of humans and I can no longer do any harm. That is all I want. Nothing more. Nothing less.

Falling from a great height did not result in death. It did not result in my body being shattered on the rocks. I just landed and all my energy was gone, as I suspected it would be. But it was worth it and I don't need energy. I am not going anywhere ever again.

I am staying put. I can't move at all. I did try to go for a walk along the small crop of sea-encrusted black rocks I landed on, but I have been unable to move since I landed on them. I think I have turned into a blob. Well at least it feels that way. I can't turn my head or my eyes. I can't move my hands and feet and I don't feel like I have a head, hands or feet. I don't think I have eyes for that matter either. But I can see.

I can't see much. Everything's blurry around the edges, but I can see the waves thrashing against the rocks, slowly and constantly, wearing them down. I wonder if I will exist forever here and if I will see the rocks eventually worn down to nothing more than shifting, grainy sand.

I can also see the sunrise. The sky slowly starts to lighten from midnight blue, heralding the coming of the sun, which soon follows the path of light. The sunlight illuminates the beach and I stare at the rocks and waves as the sun continues on its journey above me. Then it sets. It is a bit painful before the actual sunset. Well, as close to pain as I can get. Maybe it's more accurate to say that it is discomfort that I have to endure. When the sun is just above the horizon, it shines directly into my eyes. The world goes white. But after this, I am rewarded with a glorious, fiery sunset. Each sunset is different and I look forward to appreciating each one in its uniqueness for the rest of eternity.

I watch as the light slowly fades as it follows the ever-travelling sun on its journey to the other side of the world. The sky slowly darkens and the shy stars blink faintly; the waves become silver-flecked and ethereal, but pound the rocks just as furiously as they do during the day.

The occasional sea gull cries out as it wheels past. Sometimes they land on the lower rocks to see if any stray fish have been caught there when the tide went out. More often than not, they leave empty beaked and scream their frustration as they fly off. Well, if they want to be so picky then I guess they must endure their frustration. Smaller birds seem to be quite satisfied by what the small catchment pools offer up and the crabs are eternally busy scurrying to and fro in their sideways fashion. I do wonder how they manage to see where they are going. I haven't seen a crab trip once, which surprises me, as they seem to be determined at looking forward as they travel sideways. Whoever invented crabs had a wonderful sense of humour! But the crabs have managed to get on with it none the less.

It is always windy down here on the rocks. The wind blows in constantly from the waves. The air is never still and I like it. Sometimes I don't notice the wind if I am focused on something else, but at other times I can feel it gently stroke me through my dulled senses. I find it comforting and can drift off to sleep.

I do sleep, but not for very long, or maybe it is long. It is hard to tell, because I may think I have been sleeping for a short while when in fact I have been sleeping for days. It doesn't really matter. I don't seem to dream. In fact, when I wake up, I think for a long time to see if I did dream about anything, but nothing comes to mind.

I have dwelt upon my lot. Of course, I have. I have thought about my journey here from where it started with that little boy on the farm. I have thought about the people I have killed. I feel so terrible about it and it eats away at me. I wish I had not hurt any of them. I wish I were not me. How did I become so evil? I really didn't think I was evil, but surely, that must be evil at its worst, when evil does not recognise itself. That is what I am - pure evil. I really thought that I could not hurt Paul. I would never have gone into him if I'd known that I would end up killing him. Poor man. He must have suffered so much. He suffered because of me. Had I not entered him, he would be alive today and maybe his life would be far better than it was. His family seemed to love him very much and maybe they would have helped him to find a better job. Maybe one day he would go to the shops and bump into an interesting woman in a queue. The two of them would start talking about how long the wait was and find that there was something about each other they liked. They would go for coffee afterwards. He would find that he could talk to her about his job and she would be able to bare the uncertainty of it. They would fall in love and make a life together. But that won't happen. That will never happen, because of me. Because of me, Paul will never have a better job and he will never find happiness.

And what about the man in the park? What about him? He didn't want to die after all, but I made him lie there, because I did not believe the creepy one. I thought I was dreaming. The man in the park told me it was real. He begged over and over again for his life, but I did not listen to him. I thought he was my unconscious mind. But it was real. All of that was real. All of this is real. I made him die a horrible, horrible death. I don't even want to think about what I did to him. But I can't stop myself. I made him lie there, while the blood started to pool on the side of his body he was lying on as he lay there trapped. It hurt so much that there must have been sores there. It felt like it. He literally died of thirst. It was the most terrible feeling imaginable. It felt like every part of him was heaving in a dry scream for water. He was hungry too. He was so hungry that he became delirious. But it was not the hunger that he died from. It was the thirst. I will never ever forget his desiccated body shrieking for water.

He was so scared too. He was so terribly frightened. He didn't want to die. I think he was depressed and had thought about dying, but when it came down to it, he didn't really want to die, but I made him die and the more frightened he became, the more power I had over him. The stronger I became, the easier it was to hold him down. It was so easy to keep him there, fixed to the ground in those festering leaves, slowly choking the life out of him. I am evil. I paid no heed to his pleas. I could have let him go at any time. I could have left him there and I could have let him go. But I did not. I held him under his own death and let him smother in it. Me. I did that.

A lightning storm. I watch as the sky splits in electric cracks and as the rain falls down in a shaded sheet of streaks. Drops bounce up violently and the waves thrash under the lashing they receive. I enjoy the feeling of the drops gently tapping me. I am sure if I were flesh and bone it would hurt, but through my dulled senses, it feels like a gentle tapping everywhere. It's lovely.

What about the derelict man? What about Joe? Did

he feel his bones snap when the car hit him? I did. I felt it. I felt the sickening pain. I thought you were not supposed to feel pain that intense, that your mind shuts off at that moment. Or maybe you forget about it afterwards, but I felt it. There were no words to describe that moment. It was just a moment, a fleeting one, but a moment of sheer red-radiating, intense agony. I hope he did not feel it. Maybe I felt it, but he was spared?

Would his life have changed had I not stupidly blundered into it? More than likely, because anything can happen. Maybe a social worker or a philanthropist would have met him and helped him to change his life. Maybe he would have come to a realisation on his own and tacked his life onto a better course. Maybe none of these things would have happened and he would have died a bum in a stinking alley, but he would have been able to make that choice for himself. Instead, I possessed him. I made him run onto a highway. I made him get hit by a car. I did it.

And Jack? When faced with the idea of plummeting through the air to shatter on the pavement below, would he have actually taken that little step off the window ledge? He may have changed his mind. Just like the man in the park. He changed his mind when faced with actual death. Jack may have as well. He may have changed his mind. He may have realised in that moment that death was not the right answer and he may not have jumped. Or he may have thought that it was the only way open to him. But it would have been his choice. Instead, I came along and I took that choice from him. Me. Me. Who am I to make these decisions for other people? I have no right to make them and yet there I am giving them that little shove to push them over the edge. I introduced them to the death they were toying with meeting. I am a killer.

The sun beats down on me. The dry white sand swirls in a hot mist around me. The waves fling themselves tirelessly into the unyielding rocks.

The children knew who I was. They knew exactly who I was and so did that old lady in the village. They all knew what I was. They were not fooled. Why did I not pay attention to them? Why did I not listen to them?

I know why I didn't. I didn't listen, because I am stupid. I thought I was dreaming. I thought it was all one big dream that I was having and I didn't pay attention to the fact that those so-called dreams were too vivid to be dreams. They had all the earmarks of reality. Reality is mundane. You don't brush your teeth in dreams. You don't go to the toilet in dreams. You don't do things in a logical sequence in dreams. But no. Did I pay attention to any of that? No, I did not. Instead, I went on to kill two more innocent people. That's what I did. Why? Because at the heart of all this I am evil. It is my essence. It is the very fabric of my existence.

And the little boy? Thinking about him brings on so much pain that I cannot sustain it. He would have known how to survive his situation. I did not.

It is dark tonight. It is overcast and the clouds selfishly block the stars and moon, preventing them from shedding any light on the earth below. It is too dark to see anything at all. I can still hear the waves roaring.

I am the same as a shark that trolls the deep dark ocean. The shark trolls for prey. It kills savagely with its gory, blood-soaked maw. It will kill its own kind as easily as it would kill another. That is what it was meant to do. This is what I do. I drift through the fabric of time and space. I kill my own kind. I feed off them, savagely tearing into the fabric of their existence until there is nothing left but a sad broken corpse. Then I move on in search of more.

But I can stop this. I have put a stop to this. I did not choose this life, but I can choose not to have this life. I can't seem to die. What I am able to do is put myself in a place where no human being will come. I have protected them. I can keep them safe. I can keep them safe - from me.

The waves bash into the rocks. I can hear them roar, "Murderer. Murderer. Murderer."

30

The mist is thick and grey. The rain sparkles through it in flecks of silver. A cold crab slowly walks over to me to pinch my nose, but it misses and goes right through me.

A little crabby crab. Grumpy-bumpy crab. Walking sideways on robotic legs. Stalk eyes. Stalk eyes looking at me with dead eyes that see into my soul. Go away! Go away! Stalky-walky crab! Leave me alone. Get away from me. Stop looking and shopping. What are you shopping for crabby-wabby?

I need cereal and flies today, I think. Does the cereal fly? Look at that! It is flying and flying around the lounge. Don't hit the chandelier of light. Don't hit it. Dizzy cereal. Shooting and spinning and whisking away. Round and round and round. Dizzy-making. Smash! Crash and ka-bash! Falling flecks of chandelier light. Falling like pitter-pattering. Falling chandelier light and cereal flakes. Falling and falling onto me with pins and needles. Ow! Ow! It hurts! Get it off! Get it off me! No more! It hurts too much!!!

My hands are scrabbling on an iron carpet of pins and needles. They sting me. They sting all the time. They sting my skin and they sting my eyes with their sharp lights. Sharp pinpricks of light. Stabbing and pinpricking me. It won't end! It won't end! They are everywhere. They are raining down on me in jabbing sticks. They want to take my blood. Mosquito needles jabbing and sucking. Sucking out all my blood. Deflating me. Hurting me. I hurt. I vibrate. Every part of me feels like pins and needles. Zzzzzzing. Hummmming. I am as small as a pinprick of light. A tiny little light. No more pain. Just a little pinprick of light.

Stop. No! Stop! Please stop! The pinprick of light that is me, is getting bigger. Slowly and it hurts. No. No. No. No. Don't grow like a cactus in a desert full of sharp biting black spines. Spines sitting on a succulent sappy leaf. No. No. No. It hurts. Hurting and stabbing. Stabbing like a knife into a splattering lettuce leaf. Crunch. Splat! Splatter. Splintering. It feels like splinters under my nails. Get them out! Get them out! Now! Yellow, rough, barby splinters digging in, in fierce sharpness. Breaking off in shards of rotting light. Still growing. Can't stop growing. I am drawn like a spit-moistened thread into the eye of the needle. Into the eye of the raging storm.

The sun slides across the silent sand in shadows and warming glows, as the clouds drift through the blue sky.

I am rocking slowly on a boat in the water. To and fro. Rock-a-bye-bying. Slap. Slap. Slap. Slap. Water licking the briny boat. Lick. Lick. Lick. Lock. Tick. Tock. Tick. Tick. Tick. Tick. A tocking tick. A ticking tock. Tock. Tick. Lick. Lock. Tick and tock.

A peaceful wishy-washy. No dishes to sludge in water. Just pretty pearly puffs of foam. Floating bubbles in tight balls of colourful joy. Bursting into more colours and more and more. The sky is alive with filmy, metallic bubble colours. A soapy sky. A filmy sky. A sticky sky. A smothering sky. Sucking me into the water. Deeper and deeper. Drowning in dishes. Dirty white dishes. Sludgy, mouldy dishes. Cluttering in my ears.

The dishes drift away in the crumpled dark blue water, as I go deeper and deeper. The water crunches in my ears. Deeper and darker I go. Thoughts scream past me, as I go deeper.

I am being sucked down the drain of the stained enamel sink. Me and the dishes. They are back. Where did they come from? Swirling around the dark vortex. Will I be smashed on the filthy grating?

The whirling water changes hues with every spin. First, it is white, then pink, then blue, now green. The drain has gone. The dishes have gone. I am sliding on a giant green briny whirlpool out at sea. I am being sucked closer and closer to the dark centre. With every turn, I get closer. The cloudy clouds spin and crash above me in angry roars of thunderous teeth. They want to eat me. The whirlpool is eating me.

I am being eaten alive and I will be eaten either way. The fang-lined clouds or the slurping whirlpool. I scramble up the slippery sides of the whirlpool. I am only prolonging my fate. I can't keep this up forever. I run and run.

I am running in a flashy wheel in a hamster cage. Running for my life from the big dark eye that stares at me. It is as big as the cage. It takes up the whole world. I run inside the wheel. I run and run, but I go nowhere. The eye sucks me into its pupil. It sucks me and the cage and the wheel. There is no point in running. I keep on running.

I have reached the bottom of the whirlpool. I scrabble up the sides of the slick dribbling walls, but it is no use. Any minute now I will fall. I try to hold on. My fingers scream with effort, as I clutch onto churning water. There is nothing to hold onto. There is nothing tangible. Anything I try to grasp runs through my fingers.

I fall in a scream. My feet are heading towards the open mouth of a monstrous atavistic sea beast. It stares at me with hungry primordial eyes. There is neither reason nor cognition in those eyes. Nothing. Nothing at all. Just hunger. Just anticipation. It does not care that I am a higher organism than it is. It does not know that it should be the other way round. This does not make sense. I should be the one to eat it.

I can see pieces of decaying death hanging onto its needle teeth. Gory death. There are pleading hands and screams of terror hanging off its uncaring teeth.

I cannot stop my fall. I am being sucked straight into its mouth. It is in control of all that is. It controls the world. It controls the dishes and the soap, the whirlpool and the filth. It controls it all. It wants me. It wants to devour me. I cannot stop the inevitable. Its teeth close on me with a bone-shattering crunch.

It is night-time. The sea seems slightly calmer tonight. The waves crash a little more quietly upon the rocks. Perhaps they are tired after their day of heaving. Perhaps they get tired after putting in so much effort and getting so little result. The stars blink like newborn babies in the velvet sky.

The leaves are carrying me along the floor of the forest. I can hear them crunching as they scrabble on the dried earth. Scrunch. Crunch. So much noise. I wish it would end. The noise of the leaves is crawling into my ears. I try to dig the noise out with my fingers, but it is going deep inside. Deeper than I can reach. The scrunching crunching is inside my head now. I cannot get away from it. I thrash on the scuttling carpet of leaves, as it weaves through the dark mournful forest. The leaves crawl over me and into me and we move as a heap of crunching.

It's silent. No noise. Just quiet, but it's a loud quiet. A quiet that makes you feel uneasy. I roll over and come face to face with the corpse of the man in the park. We are lying there together on the rotting forest floor. Mould scratches softly on the leaves, as it slowly digests them. I stare at the man's eyes. A maggot hangs out of each pupil.

His hair is matted and greasy. His skin hangs off the bones of his face. His mouth hangs open in slack decay.

"Why did you kill me?" he asks wetly. Each syllable comes out with a wet schlucking sound.

"I didn't mean to kill you. I did not know that I was killing you."

"Why did you kill me?" Schluck. Schluck. Schluck.

"Why did you kill me?" I look up to see the hobo hanging from the tree. His skin is just barely holding the decay inside. I can see that his bones and flesh have been pulled down by gravity into his legs. He is hanging with his head caught in the V of a tree branch. The skin of his torso is stretched to breaking point.

"Why did you kill me?" he asks through a mouth full of broken bones and shattered teeth.

"I thought I was dreaming."

His skin bursts and gore rains down on me in a sickly slosh.

His broken head falls down from the tree and lands on my chest. He looks at me with dead eyes.

"Why did you kill me?" His mouth opens wide and I see broken bloody bones and teeth.

"Why did you kill me?"

I roll onto my left hand side. The hobo's head tumbles off me and lands with a thump on the forest floor. I see Jack lying on his stomach. The bottom half of his body is completely flat. It looks like he is half buried in the earth. He looks at me with one eye. It is shattered. All the veins under the skin in his face are shattered in splatters of decaying brown.

"It wasn't real. It was just a dream."

His eye rolls around in his head and comes back to stare bloodily at me.

"Why did you kill me?"

We lie together on the ground, me and the three men I have killed. We are all dead.

The forest floor comes alive underneath me. The leaves start rustling again and maggots rain down on me from the trees above.

"Why did you kill me?"

I try to sit up, but the corpses throw their dead arms over me and keep me down.

"Why did you kill me?'

I am screaming and trying to brush and shake the maggots off me.

"Why did you kill me?"

I am being eaten alive by maggots and the leaves are digging the earth out from under me. I am being pulled down into the ground to sleep forever beside the three dead men.

"Why did you kill me?"

I try to breathe through the rain of maggots, earth and leaves that are being thrown on me. My arms and legs have been pinned down by the corpses and I can't move. I am drowning in death.

"Why did you kill me?"

The light is bright and hot today. The waves crash and the sand is still. It bakes quietly in the heat. Waves of energy buzz up from the sand and wave in the air.

A pair of grimy black boots appears in the hot sand in front of me.

"Hello little fish."

I scream in silence.

31

"I see my little fish has flung itself out of the water and is lying flopping around on the hot sand. Have you had enough yet?'

"Enough of what?"

"Enough of staying here?"

"No."

"I am so sorry to hear that, my slippery eel."

I watch as he walks to the side of me. He sits down beside me and I see from the corner of my eye that he has stretched his legs out in front of him. He sighs. I imagine he is looking out to sea. He doesn't say anything and I don't want him here, so I am not going to make conversation. We sit like that for some time.

"I have come to take you from this place."

"Why?"

"Because I have to do it. It is for the greater good."

"What greater good? You are a liar. You just want me out there killing people again."

"Yes I do."

"So how does that serve the greater good? How does killing innocent people and making people miserable serve the greater good? Please do explain to me in your twisted logic how that is going to make the world a better place? If you wanted to serve the greater good, you would kill me now."

"Believe me, if I could I would. Nothing would give me greater pleasure."

"So then why don't you?"

"I am unable to kill you."

"Are you unable, or you just don't want to do it? I think you don't want to do it."

"Well you must have learnt a great deal more in your

short time here than I have in that case. So please tell me, fish. Please enlighten me, me who is eons older than you and a great deal smarter than you. Please tell me how am I supposed to kill a mind that is eternal?"

"Well, maybe because there is no mind in the first place. There is no mind without a body and I don't have a body. So there's a little crack in your logic there."

"Sadly not. Mind does not exist in the body. It seems to exist in the body for a short while and then it exists outside the body for eternity. Trust me, it makes me sick to think that I have to share eternity with the likes of you. Had I known it would turn out this way, I would have left you alone when you were alive.'

"Well, that's a thought isn't it? Why the hell did you come after me when I was alive? I would probably still be alive and much, much better off than I am right now. And you came here seeking me. I was nowhere near you, so why should it bother you that I am here? Don't moan at me that you have to share eternity with me. I stayed well out of your way."

"You are right I did seek you out and maybe you would still be alive if I had left you alone."

"So why the fuck didn't you leave me alone?"

"Now or when you were alive?"

"Both."

"I couldn't leave you alone when you were alive for the same reason that you haven't been able to leave any of these people alone, little fish. For exactly the same reason."

"Well, you see there is the difference between you and me. I am leaving people alone. No one around here, is there? I can't hurt anyone now. So I am better than you are. You just have no self-control and you couldn't give a shit."

"I am afraid you are very wrong, little fish. You can do far more damage here than if you were still around people."

"You are so full of crap. Do you think that I am going to believe that?"

"You are going insane."

"So what? It is my affair."

"It's not your affair. If you go insane and a human comes across you here and, let me assure you, it's only a matter of time before someone comes across you, what you and that person will become is far worse than you can imagine. I cannot let that happen."

"Worse than what has been happening already?"

"Far worse."

"But you said to me that if I chose to go insane it would be my own choice and you didn't care if I did it or not."

"Yes, I did say that to you. I was irritated with you. But unfortunately, I cannot allow you to go insane. I have left you here as long as I was able to. To give you some space and also because I didn't feel like dealing with you, so I put it off as long as I was able. But it is time now, slippery one, to get back into the water, because you are not meant to live on land."

"I have one question."

"Yes?"

"How long have I been here?"

"Where?"

"Here in this place. On these rocks."

"Oh, well you are not the first and foremost matter that concerns me, fish, but I suppose you have been on these rocks for about two and a half years now. Nobody walked past you in that time, and if they had, you would have been sucked into them like water into a sponge, but they didn't. So I had to bring someone down today, because if I leave it any longer it will be too late."

"You brought someone here for me?"

"Yes, I did. I think you will find this specimen quite irresistible."

"Is it this man you are in now?"

The man sighs, "I told you, this one is mine. I brought you one of your own. He is tied up a little way from here. I will go and fetch him."

"I don't believe you."

"I will bring him now to show you, insolent one!"

"No. I don't believe you that I will go insane and that I will be worse than I am right now and that someone will find me here. I have been here for two and a half years, according to you, and no one has come here in all that time. It is unlikely that someone will come past here. I think you want me to be just like you and that's why you are making me do all this all over again. I don't care if I go insane. You don't care about me, so why should it matter to you? Just leave me alone! Go away! Leave me here. I want to stay here. I am happy here!"

"You didn't believe me either when I said you were dreaming, did you little fish? But I was not lying about that and I am not lying about this."

"But are the chances really that high that someone will come past these rocks? I think it is very unlikely."

"I was able to get here very easily."

"How?"

"There's a beach to your left and people walk along it. It is only a matter of time before someone comes to these rocks to fish or a child comes to explore here and then a monster will be born."

"Nothing could be more monstrous than me."

"Oh, I am afraid, little fish, there can be things far

worse than you."

"Wait. Wait. Let me think for a minute."

"No."

"Please, just one minute."

"Very well then. One minute."

"Okay, here's an idea. Would it not be possible to put me into a box, a metallic safe, and throw me into the ocean?"

"No."

"Why not?"

"Because I don't feel like putting you into a metal box, fish."

"Listen and hear what I have to say."

"My patience is growing thin and I am in no mind to listen to the ravings of an insane imbecile, such as you. I am going to fetch the man."

He stands up.

"Please listen. You don't like me. I am a nuisance to you. I don't want to be a so-called demon. I don't care if I go insane. If I go insane that would be a problem for everyone, because I would become something worse than I am right now, if that is at all possible, which quite frankly I find very hard to believe. So if you put me into a box and threw me into the deepest darkest part of the ocean no one would find me. I would not be able to harm anyone, so I would be happy. You would never have to see me again, so you would be happy. And the people out there, who I would end up possessing, would be fine, because I wouldn't be around to possess them. I think it would work perfectly!"

"No."

"Why?"

"Why? Why, little fish, why? I'll tell you why!" He hisses at me as he talks, "Because you would be found!"

"How would they find me and who would find me?"

"The humans would find you, imbecile. And how? They would be drawn to you. They would find a reason to go to the exact part of the ocean you are in and they would drag up that rusted little box, because they would be so anxious to see what was inside. They wouldn't be able to stop themselves and they would use whatever means there was available to them to get into it. And once they opened it, you would greedily devour them and become what you would abhor – more than what you abhor now. And do you know why they would find you, little fish?"

"No."

"They would find you, because you would be calling out to them. You would draw them enticingly towards you. They would not know what they were seeking, but they would find a need to seek and they would find you, just as you will want them to. Just as if I leave you on these rocks, you are going to start calling out to them and eventually one of them will come to investigate, or to fish, or to paddle and then you would pounce."

"I'll go insane if you make me go back! So there's no difference."

"Probably not, but I'll take my chances. Don't swim off, little fish, I'll be back shortly." He chuckles.

I can't move! I try to get up. I try to crawl. I try to claw my way along the beach, but I can't move. I can't move anything. I can't even move my eyes.

I see the man coming back towards me. He is dragging another man behind him by a rope. The man's hands have been tied together. The man looks scared and he is trying to resist, but the creepy one is stronger.

As the man comes towards me, he starts screaming, "Please God! Please where are you taking me? There is something bad here. I can feel it. What are you going to do to me? There is something evil here. No! No!"

He falls down and refuses to move, even though the creepy one is kicking him and trying to drag him. The man seems to prefer the beating than to come near me.

It hurts so much. It hurts to know that he is so terrified of me. It just confirms what I am. There is nothing else here to scare him, other than me and the creepy one, and he seems more scared of me than him.

"You see you were lying. He is so scared of me that he doesn't want to come near me. You liar! You want me to be just like you. That is the only reason you are doing this. That's why you spun those lies about me being worse if I did not possess another human."

"I don't care what you say, fishy fish! The point is that you can't move and so you have no choice but to do as I say. You have no control over this situation. I do. It is only a matter of time before a person comes here and I am not interested in your lies anymore."

"Excuse me? My lies? No. I am not the liar here."

"Well from where I stand I see things differently."

"Are you trying to mess with my head?"

"No, I think it is you who is trying to mess with my head. It was you who suggested you stay here on the beach and it was you who suggested I throw you into the ocean in a metal box, was it not?"

"Yes. And how is that messing with your head?"

"It's because the process of transition has started and now you want it to finish. You want to become what you have started to become and you do not want me to interfere."

"What? You think I am going to fall for that terrible logic? And you are supposed to be my superior? I am supposed to do your bidding? Surely then you should be far more intelligent than me?"

"I am not going to fall for that either, eel. That is why I am sorting this situation out right now. That I think is a sign that I am wiser and more intelligent than you and when you return to normal it would be prudent to remember that."

"Oh don't you worry! I will remember this for the rest of eternity! I will remember what you have done always!" I hiss.

"Do you think I am scared of you, little demon?"

"What are you talking to? Leave me alone. I knew there was something evil here. Why are you taking me here? What have I ever done to you? What have I done to deserve this?" The man is begging.

"Shut up! What have you done to deserve this? You have done nothing to deserve this. I am graciously giving you an opportunity here."

"Don't listen to him. Run! Run away!"

The creepy one laughs, "He can't hear you yet, demon, so shut up!"

"I am not going to shut up."

"I didn't think you would. Come on!" He pulls hard on the rope and manages to drag the man a few feet.

"You asked if I thought you were scared of me. And I'll give you the answer, before you got distracted. Yes! I think you are shit scared of me."

"Rant. Rant. Taunt. Taunt. You are a fool. I am a demon myself. I am not going to be fooled by you, fishy fish. Keep talking if you want. I know there's nothing you can do. You can't move. So I am not particularly scared of you, no, not really. What are you going to do to me? Nothing. So talk if you want. Talk all you want. This is not going to take too much longer and then I won't have to listen to your inane dribbling anymore."

"Oh, dear God! Please help me. I beg of you. Save me from these demons" The man is screaming now.

The creepy one stops dragging the man for a moment. "God? God? Are you asking God to help you? That amuses me. Where is this God you are talking to? Let me look around. In the water? No. In the air maybe? No. Walking along this beach with you? No. No God. You fool! So shut up!"

"Well if you do this to me, I'll just come back here and you can come and fetch me again. That seems to be your issue not mine. So we can have a little reunion every two or so years if you want."

"I leave that entirely up to you. If you want to come straight back here or drown yourself in the ocean or sit on top of the highest mountain, you go on and do that. I or one of the others will come and fetch you again and again and again. If that's the way this is going to play out then so be it, but today this is what is happening. What you do after this is up to you, fish."

They are coming closer and closer and I can't move. I feel so frustrated and angry. Why? Why? Why won't he just leave me alone? I am perfectly harmless here. And I don't believe his lies. Demons lie. He is lying. I would not become worse.

"I've finally figured it out. You made me and now you are trying to make me just like you. You can't admit that you made a mistake picking me. I am not like you and you won't admit that. You want me to be an evil, soul-sucking bastard just like you!"

"You must be a species of super intelligent fish I have never come across before. That's exactly what this is all about. I have always wanted a moronic idiot to follow in my likeness."

"That's why you made me in the first place."

"That is true. That is the only truth you have spoken today, little fish, but sadly you followed it with a lie. That is very far from the reason why I am doing this now."

Slowly and steadily, the creepy man drags the sobbing man towards me. Inch by painful sobbing inch they come closer to me. I feel trapped. I can't run away. All I can do is stare in horror, as the inevitable slowly encroaches upon me.

When they are about two meters away from me the creepy man bends down and hauls the sobbing man to his feet. He is a pathetic specimen. His beard is long and scraggly. Snot drips into it from his nose, as he sobs in terror. His skin has been sucked dry by the wind and sun. His long matted hair flies out in a grotesque halo in the sea breeze. His clothes are tattered and grazed with beach sand.

"Here, demon! Here's something for you to feed on. And best I don't have to come after you again for a very long time. I am tired of you!" With that, he flings the terrified man towards me.

For a moment, we stare at each other eye-to-eye only inches apart. What I see reflected in his eyes is naked terror.

Then I am shaking, staring at the sand, as I crouch on my hands and knees. It takes only moments before I orientate myself and I am suffused with a powerful rage.

I stand up and charge through the beach sand after the creepy one. I see him as I come round the corner. I fling myself at him and land face to face with him on the grainy sand. He is on his back. I straddle him and start pummelling his face with my fists. I smash his face until I hear teeth and bones crunch and then I continue.

Through the haze of my fury, I slowly realise that he is laughing. He is laughing at me.

"What the fuck are you laughing at?"

"I am laughing at you."

"Why?"

"Do you think this is hurting me?"

"Yes."

"You are duller than I imagined."

He continues to laugh at me as I look down on him. Then he stops. His eyes grow cold and dead. He stares back at me.

I am thrown backwards with great force and land, with the wind knocked out of me, in a cloud of sand.

"You will not do that to me again. I will not tolerate such disrespect from you ever again," he says quietly as he stands up. All the time he is staring at me through his ruined face. He spits out the broken teeth, straightens his jacket and walks away.

I realise that I have once again hurt another human being. The creepy one is walking away from this untouched, but the man he is inside is going to have to go to hospital.

I lie back in the sand, with my bound hands, stare up at the sky and cry.

32

Eventually I stop crying and I get up off the sand. I feel hungry and thirsty and I don't want this one to die from either of those right now. I walk along the beach. He was right. After about a kilometre, I come across people walking along the beach. They were not far from me at all. I thought I was so far away. It was a desperate effort to get away from people. I did not put a great deal of thought into my plan. All I wanted to do was get away from people as quickly as I possibly could.

I feel so much better now. I am able to think clearly and I am feeling so energised. There is a part of me that wants to explore and walk for ages and eat and drink and just partake of simple physical pleasures, but there is another part of me.

I am so angry and I feel so revolted. I feel so revolted with who I am and what I am. How can I be such a creature? How can I exist? I don't want to exist. But it seems that I cannot be destroyed ever. I can only get worse. I can't get better. I can't die. I cannot cease to exist. I kick the sand angrily. How is this fair? I am going to spend eternity possessing people, because if I don't I will call to them and become some kind of monster more terrible than I am already.

As much as I loathe the creepy one, he has not lied to me. So, I suppose, everything he has told me so far must be the truth.

What am I supposed to do now?

How must I continue when everything I have to do is evil? Where every action I will take from this moment, stretching out into the endless reaches of infinity, must be an act of malice. How do I do that?

A feeling of sharp isolation engulfs me. I have no one

to talk to about this. I have not met any other entity that is like me and the creepy one won't tell me. He said I need to learn from experience. Does he think I am a child with a new toy that I am delighting in figuring out? Because there is no delight at all in what I feel. None at all.

I flop onto the ground. Waves of terrifying vertigo swarm over me in ever-dizzying waves as I contemplate my fate. Any action I take, any and every action I will take, will result in harm. Anything I do. Just sitting inside this man right now is doing harm. Right now, I am causing harm to a person. Just by sitting in the warm, golden grainy sand watching the ocean breathing in and out, just by doing this, I am causing harm. I am eating this man's energy and, by doing that, I am sapping his life force. And that is going to result in his death eventually.

I crawl onto my hands and knees and retch foul-smelling bile and bits of bread. I vomit until nothing comes out any more and then I continue to dry heave. I wish I could vomit myself out of existence. I wish I could cease to exist.

Eventually I am too tired to continue. I fall onto my back, away from the foul puddle and stare at the sky. My throat is burning, which makes me feel even thirstier. I suppose I should go off and get something to eat and drink, but I am so depressed that I physically do not have the energy to get up and start seeking.

I stay where I am until the sun starts to set. I don't think at all.

With a great deal of effort that leaves my head reeling, I stand up. It is peaceful in my head, because I have pushed the man back into the far reaches of his own mind for now. He won't remember any of this. He won't remember from the moment he was pushed towards me.

Poor thing. He is not going to know what hit him. I wonder if he will realise that he was possessed?

I spend a frustratingly long time wiggling and flexing my hands and wrists and using my teeth on the bindings until I eventually free my hands. I let the rope fall to the ground.

I stagger off towards the main road. Lights shine in the twilight towards my right and so I head off in that direction. The walk is made longer by my thirst and hunger. My low blood sugar is making me feel quite faint, but I push myself on. I could leave this man for one who is in a better position, but I feel bad about what happened to him, so I keep going. The least I can do is get him something to eat and drink. I feel around in his pockets for any money. They are empty. He is clearly a homeless man, unless he likes to do this kind of thing for fun, but I am presuming that is not the case. I could find out, but I don't feel like accessing his thoughts and memories right now.

Eventually, I arrive at the main road and walk along it. It is lined with dark closed shops and restaurants that are just beginning to get busy. I look in through the restaurant windows. There are people dotted around tables inside, having drinks and ordering food. I stare at them all and then move on until I find what I am looking for.

It takes a while, until I come across a fine dining establishment that the likes of this man could never enter. I see, sitting at a table inside, a very evil man. I can feel the waves wafting off him enticingly towards me. Being inside him would be far better than being inside my current host. That man is so evil that I would have enough energy to last me for weeks. I am not sure what he has done to become what he is. I don't really care. If I entered him, I am sure I would find out, but that is not my mission for tonight. If I leave the man I am in at present, he will run away and I need to get a decent meal inside him. It's the least I can do. And that man inside the restaurant deserves a few misfortunes coming his way. Not that what is about to take place is a huge misfortune, but at least it will be something bad that happens to him. Well, maybe not bad, more inconvenient, but it's something.

He hasn't ordered yet, so I walk away, as I see a waiter eyeing me uneasily. I walk around the back of the restaurant and wait for a while. I don't have a watch, so I try to guess the time. After what feels like half an hour, I go back to the front and peer through the window.

This is my lucky day. He has a lovely steak with vegetables and potatoes steaming up from the plate before him. There is also a glistening bottle of white wine in an ice bucket next to him.

I am going to have to be quick. I run into the restaurant straight towards the man. I grab the wine and the ice bucket. I upend the ice bucket into his lap and I grab his plate of food. Then I run out of the restaurant, past two very shocked waiters. I run a few blocks. It is not easy with the plate of food and my exhaustion. I am so scared that I am going to get caught and that this will be for nothing. I run a few blocks and find an alley leading to the back of some buildings. I hide behind one of the buildings.

It is hard to hear through my heavy breathing and pounding heart rate if anyone is pursuing me or not. I wait. Eventually both my breathing and heart rate normalise. No one comes. I take this as a good sign. I sit down with my back against the wall and proceed to partake of one of the best meals I have had ever. I am not sure if this is because I haven't eaten food for over two years, or if it is because this man I am in hasn't eaten good food for a long time. Maybe it is because the restaurant food is very good. I feel quite pleased with myself for having ripped off such a high quality restaurant. And here I am eating like a king. I find myself chuckling in delight.

It's dark by the time I stagger drunkenly out of the alley. I am giggling to myself. I am not sure about what. I walk out onto the main road and realise that I have to go quite badly. I fiddle with my trousers and find a handy zipper. I relieve myself with great relief on the road.

"That's so disgusting!"

I turn around to see a middle-aged couple staring at me.

"Ah…." I shoot out a last few spurts.

"You can't do that here. I need you to move."

I turn around again and see a waiter staring at me. I turn around further see I am outside another restaurant. I think if I ate anymore, I would be sick, so I turn blearily back to the waiter. He is standing there with the middle-aged couple, staring at me.

"What did you say?"

"I said that you are not welcome here, please move on."

"Why am Ish not welcomes here?"

"You are disturbing the people in the restaurant."

"How am Ish disturbing them? Oh. Oh. Ish shee!"

I look down at my dick, which I am still holding. It is massive. Wow! That is the biggest schlong I have ever seen in my life! I feel quite proud of it. My ex wife used to quite enjoy it as far as I recall. I chuckle.

"Yesh. I agree it is quite disturbings. Not many men have whats I have. Listen heres. There's enough here for alls of you. I can take youse all at the same time if you wants."

I stagger into the restaurant. "Who is hungry for shome shausages? I can shares with alls of youse. Who'sh first?"

I find myself being firmly escorted to the door. I look to see a male waiter on either side of me.

"Both of youse? Who wants to go first? That'sh okay. I don't mind the men or the ladiesh."

I find myself face to face with the pavement, but it doesn't hurt.

"Froms beeshinds? Um, I thinks Ish likes to gives rather than resheeve."

I try to get up and get pushed down again.

"You aren't going anywhere sicko. We've all just had about enough of you. The people round here have been lenient, because we know you've had a rough time, but we are tired of this continual sexual stuff. You are bad for business."

"Itsh my firsht time. I schwear. Ish this your firsht time? I'lls be gentlesh."

"I wish it was your first bloody time, Ed. How many times a day do people catch you with your pants down? I can't even count any more. People have ignored you and we have tried to be tolerant, but it's enough now."

"You'sh jsht jealoush. Mine is ginourmoush!"

"Ed, you drink so much that it doesn't even work properly anymore."

"Osh dearsh. Thens I can'ts helps youse outs tonightsh."

"I think I will learn to live with the disappointment. You were a great guy once, you know? Do you remember? Now you are the poster boy for 'don't do drugs and alcohol. It will fuck up your life!' What a waste.

Your old lady really tried to sort you out, but you weren't having any of it were you? Well at least she's happy now. You stupid old fucker."

"Ish am not Edsh!"

"Oh, because I am having this little chat with you, you don't want to hear it, is that it? Don't worry, Ed, I wasn't pinning my hopes on this being the talk that sorts you out, but a few nights in a jail cell with no alcohol and smack to lubricate your brain might just be the thing. We should have done this a long time ago."

"Ish notsh Edsh. Ish an evil demonsh."

"That's the first bit of sense you've made tonight, Ed."

"Yeesh! Sosh yoush knows Ish an evilsh demonsh? Cansh yoush shee mesh?"

"Yip! I can hear that evil demon speaking, Ed,"

"Atsh lasht! At lasht! Pleash helpsh mesh!"

"Are you serious?"

"Absholutely."

"Hey, James, get out here."

"What? I've been covering my tables and your tables! This better be good."

"Ed here wants to go to rehab."

"Really? That's great, Ed! We've all been worried about you. That's a brave step!"

"Nosh. Isha demonsh."

"Isn't that great? He is eventually admitting that he has a problem with substances."

"Nosh yoush foolsh. Nots alcoholsh! Ish a demonsh!"

"Fuck it, Marc. He's still talking about his sex shit again. He doesn't want to go to rehab. I'd better get inside again. You going to wait with him till the police come?"

"Yeah."

James goes back inside.

"Fuck you, Ed."

"Shorry Marcsh. Ish trying tos shtell you Ish a demonsh. Ish needsh helpsh."

"I tell you what I think, Ed. Why don't you shut the fuck up till the police get here?"

I start giggling. I roll onto my back and giggle and giggle. I am not sure why I am giggling. Maybe it's the alcohol I drank? I can't stop. It's kind of funny rolling around on my back on the grey concrete with the restaurant window full of staring faces. They look so funny! So shocked and revolted. Some look sympathetic. The sympathetic ones look even funnier. I didn't know people's faces could look so funny. People do such funny things with their faces. Facial expressions are strange things. I burst into another fit of giggles and roll around.

"Oh God! Can't you do something, Marc? Put it back in his pants for him."

"No way, Mr Cooper. No way. I'd rather lose my job here than touch that thing. No way man!"

That's so funny! I struggle to breathe, as another fit of giggles overtakes me.

"Put it back in your pants, Ed."

I am thrashing around, as I am laughing so hard. I can't seem to stop myself and every time I try, another fit erupts. This is the funniest thing ever!

"Ed, I am asking you nicely. Please do up your pants."

I try, but I am laughing too hard. I sit up and my eyes are blurry from all the laughing tears. My hands fumble and I flop down again into another quiver of giggles.

Suddenly, I am face to face with the pavement. I

realise that someone must have kicked me over onto my stomach. I can see little speckles on the pavement and they look so funny. I start laughing again. Me and the speckles having a private joke.

I vomit again. I think it was all the laughing. I start laughing again, because it is funny that I laughed myself into vomiting.

"Up you get. Come on, Ed. And if you feel like vomiting, you'd better tell me, because I don't feel like having to clean it out of my car afterwards."

I am pulled to my feet by two sets of strong hands and handled to a police car. My head is pushed down as I am guided into the car. The door is shut and locked. I try to open it, but I can't. An annoying grill separates me from the front of the car. I feel trapped in here.

I bang on the windows, but the policemen ignore me. They are preoccupied with talking to the people at the restaurant. Some of the patrons have come out of the restaurant now. I guess they feel safe to come out now that I have been locked up. Cowards. They come to stare at me like people looking at animals in the zoo.

I snarl and fling myself at the window and glare at them. They all jump with fright and move back. That's so funny! I burst out laughing again. They should be frightened of me. They have no idea what they are dealing with. I am a demon! I am the scariest thing they will ever meet. I stare at one woman, who looks particularly timid. She is holding onto a man's arm. I presume it is her husband. Does she think he protects her from me? He is a puny human. I am a powerful demon. I stare at her coldly. She shrinks further into the man and he pats her arm reassuringly. I stare with every ounce of my being. I can feel her delicious fear. It makes me feel giddy again and I want to start laughing with the intoxicating joy of it.

I want more and so I go for more. I point at her. I point at me. I make a slicing motion across my neck and point at her again. She is absolutely terrified now. How lovely. I drink it in and fall back on the seat laughing hysterically again.

Eventually the two policemen get back into the car again. The car sways like an unbalanced boat out at sea, with their weight and the slamming doors. It makes me laugh again to think that this ungainly tub should hold a powerful being such as me. It is not worthy of one such as I, which I tell them both.

"Yeah well, maybe the holding cell will be more worthy of you, your esteemed greatness," says one of the cops.

"Just don't puke back there, Ed. Let me know if you need to go and I'll stop the car."

I look into his eyes in the rear-view mirror and I stick my filthy finger down the back of my throat. I start retching.

"What the fuck? Stop it, Ed!"

I vomit out the rest of my dinner. Sorry Ed. I make sure it lands all over the back seat. I try again and manage to bring up some more, which I ensure lands inside the sliding mechanism of the main seat. I try again, but there is nothing left. Damn! I sit up and stare levelly at the cop.

He stares back at me and we almost drive up the curb. He swears and corrects his steering. I continue staring at him and chuckle quietly.

The other cop turns to me, "You are a nasty piece of work, aren't you Ed? We all pitied you, you know, but not anymore. I don't pity you anymore Ed and if you pull anymore stunts like that, I will make sure you pay."

I lunge towards the grating, making the other cop swerve again. My face is just inches from him.

"And how are you possibly going to make me pay?"

"Sit back, Ed," he says nervously.

"No, I don't think so. You told me you were going to make me pay and I really truly want to know how you are going to make me pay."

"Just sit down, Ed. You are drunk."

"I was, but now I feel very sober and clear-headed. Please tell me how you are going to make me pay?"

"Just drop it, Ed."

I scoot up behind his seat and push my face into the grating. I breathe heavily on the back of his neck. I start chuckling, because I can feel the waves of terror flowing off him. It's such a lovely feeling; I fall back onto the vomit soaked seat and collapse in a fit of giggles.

It passes as his fear passes. I feel his relief. He really is annoying. How dare he talk to one such as me like that? I chose to sit in the back of the car, because I felt like it. He can't make me stay here. I feel like seeing how this is going to pan out. Because why the hell not? There is nothing else to do right now and this is amusing me. So let them take me to the police station. I will leave when I so chose. I sit back quietly for the rest of the ride and stare at the back of their quiet heads.

When we arrive at the station, the cop pulls me roughly out of the car and turns me around. He slaps some cuffs on me. The other cop is watching this whole procedure warily, in case I do something. His hand rests on his gun.

The cop spins me around and pushes me towards the entrance of the brown brick station. I let him push me. We go inside and they book me. I am supposed to keep my face still and impassive when they take a mug shot of me, but since all of this means nothing to me and it means a great deal to them, I can't stop laughing at how seriously they take their insignificant jobs. They fingerprint me and don't bother to wipe the ink off my hands. They did ask me to do up my pants, but I didn't feel like obliging. I am enjoying their discomfort and curiosity too much.

The cop pushes me into a cell while his partner stands there, ever ready, in case I do something and his friend needs back up. The gate slams behind me with a metallic clang.

"Put your hands through the bars."

I back up to the bars and slide my hands through. The cop slides the key into the cuffs, careful not to make contact with my skin. When the cuffs come off, I turn around and stare at him levelly.

"Boo!"

He jumps back and stares at me.

"Fuck you, Ed. I'm not scared of you! Now do yourself up."

"Oh, I think you are scared of me. I think you are very, very scared of me. And when I feel like it, I am going to give you a delicious taste of terror."

"Come on, Frank. Just leave him here."

I chuckle again in anticipation as they leave. I just need a little nap and a slash and then I will deal with him later. It's hot in this cell so I take off all my clothes and throw them out through the bars. I urinate in the steel toilet and lie down on the bed to sleep.

33

"Put your fucking clothes on, Ed. Here's your breakfast. I hope you are sober enough now to behave yourself properly."

"Um."

I roll over and go back to sleep. When I eventually do wake up it's very bright in the cell. I squint up at the window and the sun catches me right in the eyes. Ow! I think it must be about midday. It's hot.

I rub my eyes and swing my legs out of the bed. I feel pretty good. I pad over to the table, which is fixed into the wall, and sit down to eat my now cold breakfast. It consists of some greasy bacon and powdery eggs. The toast has turned soggy and stale and my tea is cold. I don't really care. It is food and I can eat whatever I want and whenever I want. I reckon this is the best food Ed has had in a long time, apart from last night's dinner, which ended up all over the cops' backseat. I laugh as I think about the two of them mopping up all that expensive puke. I am glad the bacon is greasy. It helps the rest of the parched food slither down my sore throat. The tea also helps it go down better.

There's not a lot to do in this cell, but I don't feel like leaving just yet. I lie down again and scratch my balls. Roger doesn't seem too keen to stand to attention. I raid Ed's mind for some good fantasies.

The slimy old dog has a thing for a lady in the nail bar. He has often walked past there just to look at her. It seems that he walks past every day. Wow. That is what I would call an obsession. She hasn't paid him any attention other than a cursory glance that quickly turns into dismissal and loss of interest. She goes back to applying nail varnish carefully onto the nails of some posh. Poor

Ed. He is hopeful though that one day things will change and that she will give him a chance. I could tell him right now that he doesn't stand a chance. Really, from what I can see in his memories, she doesn't seem the least bit interested in him.

But that hasn't stopped Ed from fantasising. He is a flesh and blood man after all, even if he is doped up to his eyeballs and drunk to his gills. His favourite one, and it is a well-worn fantasy, is about going into the nail bar when it is closing time. All the customers and other staff have left and his girl is there on her own. He gives her a rose. No one ever said Ed wasn't a romantic and she just can't resist him. She ends up on her hands and knees on that polished white floor with Ed taking her from behind. Her large tits sway with each thrust.

Nope. Roger is still dead. I guess too much alcohol does have its disadvantages.

"Stop wanking, Ed and get dressed."

My clothes land with a thud in the cell. I see a portly middle-aged policeman fumbling with his keys, whilst balancing a tray with his other hand.

"I just ate."

"Oh well, too bad. The government pays for you to get three square meals a day, so here is your next course and for Pete's sake, Ed, please don't do that while I am here."

"Why?"

"Because it is highly inappropriate and it's disgusting. Here's soap and a towel, why don't you shower and clean up. Maybe it will help."

"Well, thank you kindly. I think the soap may well do the trick. Unless you want to lend me a hand? I don't seem to be doing so well on my own."

"That's quite enough, Ed."

The policeman backs out of the cell and locks the gate.

"Don't worry, I wouldn't have gotten you from behind. It's not working properly. Mind if I ask you a personal question?"

"Yes I do."

"You seem to be a man who has a love for larger. Does it affect your performance?"

"Just eat your food and take a cold shower, Ed."

"What's a man supposed to do in here? It's dead boring. There's nothing else to do. No reading material. Hey, that's an idea! Why don't you go on and get me some nice girlie mags, Tubby. That should do the trick."

The bastard walks off and ignores me. I feel like possessing him just to get something to read, but I want to bide my time until my friend from last night returns.

I try the shower and the soap. Neither of them helps in the way they are reputed to. I dry myself off and pull my shirt over my head. It smells so bad that I throw all my clothes out of my cell with disgust. I wrap the towel around my waist and sit on the bed.

I pass the time singing and swinging my legs, while I lean back against the wall. I know he will come in and check on me tonight. He is too macho not to. He won't want to admit he's scared and he will come back. I could find him easily right now if I wanted to, but I have a plan. It's meaningless really in the greater scheme of things to have a plan, but it amuses me to have one. It amuses me to wait a while and delay the gratification. Once it is over it will be over, so the anticipation is what counts. That's why I am in no rush to leave. The build up is the most important part. That's the part I can drag out. The release is over too soon. I am learning deep and important lessons from Ed's mind. Thank you Ed, oh great and wise teacher. Who would have thunk that a man such as you was the purveyor of such great wisdoms? Inside this scrawny squeezed out body and shaggy head, lies great wisdom. And people just think you are a bum, Ed. How wrong they are.

As night draws its dark curtains on the world, I pick up his scent. Lovely. He is on his way. Soon I hear his car pull up. His scent becomes much stronger as he walks into the station. They are going to have to release me soon. I don't think they can hold me here indefinitely.

I hear a gate open and close and footsteps coming towards me down the stark passage. I look up, after he has been standing at my cell door for a few moments. I want him to be rattled and I want him to know that I am not rattled. Nothing scares me, because I am the scariest thing on this earth. And if I am the scariest thing on this earth, there is nothing for me to be frightened of, especially this puny wretch.

"Good evening, Officer. What can I do for you tonight?"

"I am checking up to see that you have sobered up, Ed, and that you are behaving yourself now."

"Oh, I am sober, but I am not behaving."

"We have to let you go, Ed, but I can't let you go if you don't behave yourself."

"Why are you so scared of me, Mr Policeman?"

"I don't know what you are talking about. I am certainly not scared of a piece of shit, homeless nobody, like you."

"Oh, but you are scared of a worthless piece of shit like me, because I can smell it on you."

I stand up and look at him. He looks at me. Then I charge. He falls back against the wall, his eyes wide with terror. As I reach the bars, I leave Ed's body and enter the cop's body. Ed screams, hits the bars, and hits the floor, unconscious. I push the cop's mind aside and chuckle, as I adjust my belt around my waist.

"Sweet dreams, Ed and leave that poor woman in your dreams alone, will you?"

I swing my keys, as I walk back out the holding cells.

34

"What the hell happened back there, Frank?"

"I don't know. That mangy nut saw me, went crazy and threw himself at the bars of his cage headfirst. Knocked himself out. He's lying there out cold on the floor."

"And you just left him there?"

"Yup."

"Is he hurt?"

"Nah. I'm sure he's fine."

"You didn't check?"

"No way, man. I'm not touching him with a two-foot pole."

"Fuck, Frank. We could get into serious shit about this. I'm going to check on him."

"Knock yourself out. I'm sure he's fine."

"For your sake I hope so, Frank."

The officer brushes past me on his way to the holding cells. I smile; the little things that seem to worry people. Well, Frank is not going to worry about little things. I am going to give him some big things to worry about, the stupid asshole.

"Hello Frank."

"Hello, Goodwin."

"You ready?"

"Yup. Let's go. My turn to drive tonight?"

"Yes. Here you go."

It's a quiet evening. Goodwin natters on inanely, while we drive around the quiet streets. I 'um' and 'ah' occasionally, which seems to be good enough for him. He happily continues talking. He comments that I am quieter than I usually am. I tell him that I have a headache tonight and I don't really feel like talking. That seems to satisfy him and he doesn't ask me again.

We stop off at a late night burger joint for some burgers and fries and a rather necessary toilet break. Our radios buzz on our shoulders incessantly while we eat our burgers, sitting on hard, bright plastic under the harsh neon lights of the fast food outlet. I am glad to get out of there. It's nice to drive around the dark city streets.

Since I am in control of the route tonight, I take the opportunity to explore the area and to remember it as well as I can. Goodwin complains that we are not doing the circuit we are supposed to do. I reassure him that if there is an emergency we'll get there quickly. I am a fast driver. I tell him to live a little and to be a bit rebellious. Live on the wild side, Goodwin. He isn't happy about this, but he lets it slide. Maybe he doesn't want to seem less manly, but I suspect he is very much a by-the-book type.

At about 2am, I find what I am looking for. The park. I memorise the route and make my way slowly back to the station. Our shift ends at 3am. Strange time for a shift to end. It makes no sense why it should end at that time. It should end at 5am. Maybe people want to sleep when it is still dark outside. Who knows? Or maybe it's when our nine hours are up. I did go on duty at six o'clock yesterday evening. I am sure that some person, who enjoys having the illusionary power afforded by a high up position, decided that this would be the best time for police officers to work. Who knows? Who cares? Not me. I am not going to be residing in Frank for very much longer. I am going to teach the arrogant prick a lesson tonight and I am going to enjoy it. I have been looking forward to this since last night in the car. I have been thinking about it all day, just waiting for him to come to work.

The tension has built up to such a degree in me that I can't wait to put my plan into action now, so I can see the end result. I wonder if I am normally like this. I wonder if I was a person who liked to anticipate future events and if I enjoyed waiting for them to come about. Or maybe I still have a bit of Ed's disgusting mind clinging filthily to my being. It's really difficult to tell the difference. I suppose what makes it particularly difficult to tease out is that I don't have a fucking clue as to who I am. If I knew who I was that would be helpful. Then I would know what is mine and what is theirs, but since I don't know, I have nothing to anchor myself on. Nothing at all.

It's so frustrating not being able to remember who I was before I died. All I remember was waking up on the farm as the little boy. I thought I was him. I don't remember anything from before that time. I took on all his memories and so it seemed to me that I had always been him. There was nothing from before that time. It's just dark and blank. It annoys me and puts me into a worse mood. Now I really want to punish Frank.

I change into my plain clothes in the locker room and put my uniform back into the locker. Frank can wear it again tomorrow. He will smell a bit, but he deserves it. I hand in the patrol car keys and say good night to the guys and gals still on duty. Goodwin gives me a manly pat on the shoulder as he leaves the station.

I should check on Ed just to see how he is fairing, but I have changed into plain clothes now and I am sure that the other officers would make a fuss about me going down there. Frank didn't do anything to Ed. I did. But they don't know that and they all suspect poor Frank of some foul play. Good.

I locate Frank's car using the remote. The lights flash and I get into an old beat up husk of a car that smells of beer drenched sweat with a hint of cigarette smoke. I open the glove compartment and sure enough, there is a pack of smokes. I read the packet: Smoking kills. Well, too late for that, so I light up and have a satisfying drag. I smoke the whole thing before leaving the car park. When I eventually drive off, I feel fantastic. This could work out for me. I can abuse all kinds of substances without ever having to suffer the side effects. As soon as my vessel starts to ail, I'll just leave the fucker and move onto the next sucker. This may not be so bad after all.

I make my way down the quiet streets towards the park. When I get out there's a bit of a nip in the air and it is very dark. The night is lit by a sliver of moon and some distant stars. I fumble around in the glove compartment and don't find anything. I am looking for a torch. I don't feel like tripping over things on my way into the forest. I feel around and find a lever for the boot next to the driver's seat. I go round to the back and heave all the shit he has in the back of his car out onto the ground. I pull up the back panel and find a torch. Excellent. I am annoyed with Frank, though. Why keep a torch in the boot in the spare wheel well? That makes no sense. He should keep it in the glove compartment. I need to teach him a lesson tonight. I need to teach him a lesson, just because he is stupid and he annoys me. He thinks he is a big man. He thinks he can do whatever he wants. We'll see about that.

I crank up the radio to maximum volume and I turn the lights onto bright. I leave the driver's door open, so that the interior light stays on. Then I pocket Frank's car key and pick up his jacket and torch. I make my way through the park, enjoying the thought of Frank finally finding his car, after being lost in the dark, and not being able to go anywhere, because the battery will be dead.

Delicious.

It takes a good half an hour to find the woods. I find them more by feel than by memory. I wasn't really paying attention when I walked into them a few years ago, but I can still feel what I thought I would feel. I am surprised and I am not. It's disappointing, but I suppose I haven't really moved on in the two and a half years either.

I make my way through the dense foliage. It is much denser than it was a couple years ago. I suspect people avoid this part of the park. Angry unyielding branches scratch at me as I pass through. I can feel blood trickling down my bear arms, but I don't care.

When I find what I am looking for, I take off my shirt so that I am bare-chested. I really want Frank to feel vulnerable. I take off his trousers and trainers. I leave his socks and boxers on. I am not completely heartless. I bundle them up in his jacket and I fling them as far and as high as I can out into the forest, away from the path I came on. I turn the torch off and fling it after the clothes. I hang onto the keys as I walk into the small clearing.

"Hello. It's been a long time."

"Get away from here! This is my place."

"Don't you remember me? We found this place together?"

"I was murdered here. This is where I died."

"I know. I murdered you."

The shadow on the tree stump raises its head and looks at me.

"You murdered me? You murdered me? They took my body away. They took it from me. It used to lie here." He points to the ground in front of him. "It was mine and they took it away."

"Have you ever left here? It's been over two years, you know."

"I was murdered here."

"Yes. I know that. Stop whining about it. Why haven't you moved away from here? Why don't you go out there and get inside some people?"

"I was murdered here."

"Well, I have brought you a tasty morsel. It's the least I can do. He's all yours. Just wait a little bit before you enter him. I want to teach the arrogant fuck a lesson. So give him five minutes and then you can get inside him. I promise, you'll love it. It feels amazing. You will forget all about this. I let his car run down. Again, I wanted to teach him a lesson, but when you get to it, you can just enter someone. I am sure there will be a park hand or someone you can get into, if you don't feel strong. Otherwise, you need to focus on someone you really want to enter. I suggest someone very depressed or suicidal. It's so easy. All you need to do is just think about it and then there you will be. Right. So we have a deal then? I am going to jump out of Frank now and after about five minutes you can jump in. Here we go."

I pull myself free of Frank and watch him. He shakes his head and drops to his hands and knees. He looks at the ground and then he looks up at his surroundings. His pupils have dilated to encompass his entire iris and his heart rate and breathing have gone up. He looks quickly down at himself and establishes that he is not wearing any clothes. He looks around again. I can feel the delicious fear vibrating off him. He opens his clenched hands to find the car keys. He grips the car keys tightly again.

He stands up and walks blindly around. He is so scared that his movements are jerky and a little uncoordinated. He walks past the murdered man, who is still looking at the ground and he shivers and quickly walks away. He doesn't speak. I think he is too scared to speak. I stand by the trees I walked through with him and watch. Whenever he comes near me, he recoils and walks back again.

He looks like a terrified animal in a cage with a dangerous predator lurking in the shadows. And I am a dangerous predator and so is the murdered man. It's only a matter of time before he is devoured and he knows this. He doesn't know how to get out of here. He tries one part of the forest, but it is particularly dense part. He gives up and comes back into the clearing.

He is so scared now his teeth are chattering. That's right big Frank. Not so tough are you now? No. Not so tough. I am enjoying this. But I must set things right.

"Okay, thanks. I have had my fun now. It's your turn."

I walk towards Frank and push him towards the murdered man. Frank screams. The murdered man stands up and screams, "Get away from me. This is my place! You cannot take my body. Get away! Get away! Get away!"

Frank gets up and runs into the forest screaming. He goes right through the trees and branches and stubborn bushes. He is so scared that he doesn't seem to notice.

The murdered man sits down on his tree stump again.

"Why didn't you take him, you idiot?"

He looks up at me.

"I know you. You are the one who murdered me. Please leave. I was murdered here and they took my body away from me. It was the only thing I had left and now it's gone. Please leave me alone."

"Why do you want to stay here?"

"I was murdered here."

"Don't you want to leave and go somewhere else?

Don't you want a life?"

"I had a life and you took it from me. Now all I have is this."

"You are right. I did take it from you and I am so, so sorry for that. That is why I brought him to you so you could leave this place."

"I don't want to leave this place."

"Why not?"

"This is all I have left. This is where I was murdered."

"So you are going to stay here forever?"

"Yes."

"I will leave you to it! But first, I have one question. You said you had a life before this happened. Do you remember your life?"

"I remember it. I remember it with tearing sadness. But you took it from me. Now all I have is this."

"If you wanted to could you get up and leave here or are you too weak?"

"I can leave, but I do not want to leave here. This is where I was murdered."

"Fine. I have said I am sorry. I have tried to make your life better, but you won't do anything about it, so I am going to leave you here on your own. I will never come back and visit you."

"Now why would I want a visit from you?"

He stares at me. I can't see his face, but I can feel the intensity of his stare.

"Leave me alone!"

"Fine with me!"

I concentrate on finding a little old lady who is in a nice home where all her needs are taken care of and who has everything done for her, because she is unable to do it for herself any more. She needs to be suitably depressed of course. I decide that this is where I want to be for now. I need time to think and that would be the best place for me to think. I feel a tug throughout my being and I leave the forest forever.

35

I spent a week or so pondering my situation. I found what I was looking for. I am in a frail wisp of an old woman. She is sad and lonely. These often seem to be the companions of tottering old age. She is depressed, as she is unable to do things for herself. She is also blind and hard of hearing. She should be grateful that I have chosen her. She has a whole week off from her emotional and physical misery, thanks to yours truly.

After I am bathed and fed, I listen to classical music until my next feeding and toilet session. Then more classical music. Then lunch followed by another toilet session. Then tea and then another toilet session. Then dinner and the toilet. Then bed. Not what makes for an exciting existence, but certainly, what makes for a good place to sit and think.

I have been thinking all week and I am angry. I never chose to be a demon. I did not ask for this life. Who made this decision on my behalf? Who had the right to make this decision? And what kind of world is this, where evil entities enter into people who are already having a hard time? They do not need to suffer more than they are, but here am I and the only purpose of my entire existence is to cause additional suffering to those suffering already. Is this not madness? If it is not, then I am not sure what exactly would qualify as madness.

And I was just left to my own devises like a toddler in a room full of the most precious china. I was left to wreak havoc. No one tried to stop me. The creepy one said that he had tried to find me, but that is one being. How is he supposed to accomplish that all on his own? Why didn't someone meet me and tell me that this is what has happened to me. Why were the rules not explained to me? And it seems like there are rules, as I was not allowed the freedom to choose to rot on the beach for eternity. Now I need to accept that I am an evil entity? No.

So there I was trying to wake up from a dream that I was never in and how was I supposed to know any different? I killed real people when I believed that it was all imaginary. And I was a person once, or so it seems, so I am not so keen on killing my own kind, although they are not my own kind anymore.

Who was I? I really need to know who I was and what I did to become this way. The creepy one won't tell me. And I suppose, after I insulted him by attacking him, he will never tell me. How come I cannot remember? It's all blank before the little boy on the farm. Nothing existed before then. I don't have any feelings that pertain to the time when I was alive and no memories. What is the point of that? There can be no meaning to this life if I cannot remember who I was and what I did before I died. Then this is all meaningless rubbish. Life and death both hold absolutely no meaning. You can't grow, because you can't remember. There is no journey and it seems that I am a demon and a demon I will remain for the rest of eternity. For the rest of eternity? I am going to be like this forever? At least life is finite. You are not stuck in it forever. I am stuck here forever and I don't think I can handle it.

I don't think I can handle the fact that in order to survive I have to live off souls. In order to exist I have to feed off the life energy of other human beings. I may not be a human being anymore, but I was one not so long ago. And I don't think I was a cannibal in that life. I am one now. That's what I am. Doomed to haunt people's miserable lives and steal their souls and suck from their lives, so that I may live and not become something far worse than I am - if that is at all possible. This world is sick.

This world is sick and there is nothing good in it. Nothing. And I am evil. Every action I take results in harm. I have tried, since I became conscious, to look out for myself and to be a good person - when I thought I was a person. I have tried to not harm people when I realised I was a demon, but I guess that is what I do. I am evil and I carry out evil deeds. That is the be all and end all for me. If you wanted a description of me, it would be: Pure Evil. The creepy one was right. I am stupid. There I was trying my level best to be good and do good. How inane was that? I cannot do good. There is nothing good about me. Nothing at all.

So why bother trying any more. I am going to be who I am. I am going to be who I was created to be. If this world created me to be evil then it will get evil.

I have been thinking about where I want to go next and whose lives I want to destroy. I have thought about it for a while now and I have come up with the perfect scenario of what I want to do. I am going to wreak terror and despair and I am going to do it well.

Good-bye little old lady. Enjoy your suffering. And know that when you die, more awaits you. Sweet dreams.

36

I find myself staring at a building. I look down at myself and establish, through various checks, that I am a man. That's fine. I wasn't sure how this would play out, as I wasn't too specific as to whom I entered. I creep into a corner of his mind and watch as his day unfolds. I hope that my plan turns out as I wanted. If it doesn't I will just have to try again.

He is terribly unhappy, which makes me feels giddy with pleasure. I don't take control of him. I hover just inside him and I make sure that I don't fall asleep. I wouldn't want to kill my new toy, now would I?

I establish that he is an architect. He does not enjoy his job as much as he believed he would when he started studying. He thought he would be a rich hotshot architect, who designed buildings, which would be stared at in wonder by hundreds of thousands of mortals, who in turn would feel so privileged to live part of their lives within the confines of his creations.

Instead he designs office blocks, which are tailored to meet the expectations of his boss and his customers, none of whom are vaguely interested in hearing about his thoughts and ideas. In the beginning, he used to go home and design his own creations. He would first draw them out and then he would render them on his computer. He even built models. He believed that he would get a chance soon to show someone what he could do. Slowly, his dream died from lack of opportunity and interest shown in his creations. He no longer buys drafting paper for his own use. The office supplies plenty. He hasn't logged into his three-dimensional rendering programme at home in years and his models lie squashed under piles of forgotten possessions in his attic.

He is perfect. I will have to see, when he goes home, if the rest of my plan will work. I can wait. I have all the time in the world. All the time in the world. Nowhere to rush to. Nowhere to be. I watch him closely, as his day goes by, taking little exquisite sips of his energy.

Eventually, after a soul-numbingly, unfulfilling day, he cleans up his desk, says goodbye to his co-workers and heads home. What little gift awaits me there? I can't contain my excitement and he drives fast because of it. I hope my gift to myself is just as I expect. If not, I am going to be very angry and I think James here is going to have to suffer for it, since there is no one else around. He will suffer one way or the other. It makes no difference to me. He suffers anyway. I am just here to make it a little worse.

He pulls into his garage with a sigh and barely has enough energy to slam the car door shut. He grabs his briefcase from the boot and makes his way inside with sodden feet. He really doesn't want to come home. This is too good to be true.

"You are late. Your supper's in the oven. I ate already. I wasn't going to wait all night for you."

My heart (If I had one) skips a beat with joy. There she is! I am the master of all. This is working out so well. I jump out of him and into her. I need to learn all I can about my prey.

She walks, completely unaware of me, into the lounge and flops down on the couch. She stares at the TV set and, after a while, turns it on. She flicks through the channels until she finds a soap opera that she likes and then gets absorbed by it. I can't really read her thoughts, because they are all about the soap opera and I don't really want to possess her fully just yet, because I want to learn more about her from herself. The soap opera is hideously boring and the desire to possess her, just to push the off button on the remote, battles with my resolve to keep quiet and watch and learn. Her energy is also lovely and I nibble on it. I have a great deal of energy myself from both of them and I will be able to exist quiet happily, alone, without them for a while, which I intend to do later.

Eventually the awful rubbish finishes. She gets up and forces herself to walk past the kitchen without going in. She is tired of fighting, but a part of her still wants to have a go at him. He wasn't like this when they first met. He had so much spunk and he was so enthusiastic about life. Now he never wants to do anything. He will go and watch TV after he finishes eating. She doesn't feel like being in the same room as him now.

She goes upstairs and has a shower. She washes her hair and then spends hours in front of the mirror blow-drying it. She is sitting in front of a mirror. I do not see anything much really, because I am on the periphery of her mind. All I really get are her thoughts. Her thoughts have told me she is sitting in front of a mirror and that she is blow-drying her hair. She then sits on the bed and removes the old nail polish on her toes and fingernails. She selects a ruby red nail polish and proceeds to apply it. She is not thinking about anything other than what she is doing. That is why I know about it in such great detail. Her mind is emptier than James's is. When she is finished, she lets the nail varnish dry. She admires the way her hands and feet look and puts everything away before escaping into a horrible romance book. This woman really has horrible taste! Sadly, as I am privy to her thoughts, I get to hear the horrible sordid little tale from her thoughts. I will try and expunge it from my mind later. I have to remind myself again that I am here to learn. I know she longs for romance, even though she may not know it. Why else would she watch the soap opera and read this trash?

For a moment she registers that he has come into the room and then she goes back to the book. We hear him showering in the background and then we feel his weight, as he gets onto the bed next to us.

"Are you still angry with me?"

"I am trying to read."

"Fine."

We feel him turn over and turn out his light. She can't figure out why he wants to sleep in the same bed as her. He probably just wants to punish her. Why doesn't he go and sleep in the study? She should go, but she doesn't want to give him the satisfaction. So she reads for a little longer, so that he won't be able to sleep, because he can't sleep with the light on. She knows that he is still awake and she can see he is annoyed from the set of his shoulders. This just spurs her to read ten more pages. She is determined that it will be ten pages. It is a nice round number.

She snaps the book shut and makes a lot of noise and movement to annoy him further, before settling down for the night. She turns her back towards him, and then switches off the light.

As she drifts off into her dark dreams, I slip out of her and stand by the bed. I can see her sleeping peacefully. I watch for a while as she breathes in and out deeply. She is an attractive woman in her late twenties. Her brown hair curls around her white cheeks as she slumbers. I walk to the other side of the bed. James is breathing heavily. His skin is dark and he seems to be of some kind of mixed race background. His hair is shaven closely to his head, just leaving a centimetre of length. His full lips are parted as he snores softly. He is a big man. He has broad muscular shoulders and arms. I guess he must work out, although he didn't when I was in him today and he didn't think about it at all during the day. Oh well, lots of time to find out all about both of them.

I let them sleep peacefully. They do not know what I have in store for them. They do not know that I am here yet and the anticipation is the greatest part of the pleasure. I settle myself in a chair across from them and watch them sleep.

37

I decide that I will enter the one who gets up first, just to make things a little interesting and random. Put a little chance into my otherwise tightly thought out plan. I need to enter one of them to get some energy, otherwise I will collapse here in a puddle for eternity, which seems like an option that I may well pursue at some point. I think, since I have to exist for eternity, I would rather be mad, but I will keep the creepy one off my case for a while. I will have to fill my time with other pursuits in the meantime. Then I will find a place that he will not be able to get to and then I will happily go mad. It did bother me initially about doing more damage than I am doing now, but damage is damage. I don't think one kind can be worse than another. So that is my long-term plan.

I see the woman is waking up. She turns onto her side and then sits up. She gives James a disparaging glance and swings her legs out of bed. I guess it will be her today then. Time to learn more.

Over the next week, I learn about James and Sandy. They aren't married, but have been living together for close on six years now. In the beginning, it was amazing. They both found each other exciting and fell madly in love. They seemed to just click. James was at the beginning of his architecture career with endless possibilities before him, as any career wantonly promises and then never delivers.

Sandy was finishing her last year of college. She then embarked on a career as a teacher in a school in a bad part of town. She always wanted to work with children who had problems. She felt that as she had come from a good background and had never wanted for anything, she would help those less fortunate than herself. She would educate children from dysfunctional families and help them to have a better life.

She had entered her new school fresh and eager, only to be ignored with a cold shoulder. The children didn't seem to want to have a better life. Instead, they refused to listen to her and seemed keener to cause havoc than anything else. The children were rude and uninterested. The few who were keen to learn didn't seem to get it, no matter how many courses she went on and then tried to implement, and no matter how many resources she had in the classroom. As the years wore on, she found herself screaming at them every day to keep them in line and only focusing on the one or two children in her class who were able to learn.

After work, she would come home, tired and drained and counting the school days until the holidays arrived. Then she could replenish her reserves, before having to go back there and face them again. Why didn't people who needed help the most want to take it?

The parents were even worse. They didn't want to do extra things to help their children. They wouldn't attend meetings or do homework with their kids. They would shut the door on social services, instead of inviting them in and working with them to make life better for themselves.

And all she ever wanted to do was help them.

Their relationship in the beginning was wonderful and it helped to counterbalance their ever-spreading disillusionment with work. They would joke about their days together and go on fun outings and holidays and make passionate love and it kept the bad at bay. But bad always eats at the soul and it slowly ate away at theirs, until they were taking out their frustrations on each other.

They both still clung to the good times and they do

still love each other. That is why they are still together. They hope that they will get through it all and that things will change and they will be happy and that a better future is somewhere in the future. They both hope that something will happen and they will get a break or a surprise, or that life will change course slightly and it will all turn out for the better.

I know all this, because I have studied them carefully for a week now. I know their wishes and their dreams. I know they both have hope. I am going to shatter the little that remains.

38

I decided to start with Sandy. She is more receptive to my presence than James. James tends to ignore whatever does not make sense to him and proceeds completely to forget about it. I find it quite insulting and I will get my revenge.

I have brushed past him. He will shiver and then get on with what he was doing as if nothing happened. I have slammed a door and he looked up from the TV and then went back to watching it again, with little interest in what had just happened. I even took a book out of the bookshelf and dropped it on the floor when he was working on the computer. He looked up, saw the book on the floor and continued working. Later he got up and put the book back. It is infuriating! I will get to him though, because I am a being that is far more evolved than he is and I will make him pay. I do not like being ignored by him!

Sandy is a different matter. She is more jumpy. I just need to walk past her and she will shiver and look around and then move to a different room. That is all I need. I am going to haunt Sandy.

I did accompany both Sandy and James to work when I was observing them, but now I stay at home during the day while they are out. I quite like it. At night, I drink from one of them, so that I have enough energy to last me the whole day. The next day, I potter around the house and garden. I am used to passing through walls and doors and all manner of matter now. It is still a slightly unpleasant experience, but it is bearable and if it gets me where I need to go then I can endure it.

The reason why I don't go with them to work anymore is that I need a break from the two of them. I am not that fond of either of them. I feel like their home has actually become my home and they are annoying interlopers. I enjoy my time away from them, but then again I do so enjoy my time with my pets too. I look forward to my evenings when they come home and I look forward to putting my plans into place.

39

The front door opens and Sandy walks in. This pleases me, because I want some time alone with her. If James is here, she will feel safer. I watch as she walks upstairs and puts her bag down on the study floor. She walks to her bedroom and kicks off her heels. She goes down to the kitchen and starts preparing supper. I brush past her.

She looks up from what she is doing and looks around. She hugs herself briefly and then continues making dinner. When she has finished cooking, she serves the food up on two plates. She puts one plate in the warming oven and walks to the lounge to watch TV while she eats, as she always does. I follow her and quickly rush past her to turn the TV on before she sits down.

She jumps as the TV springs to life, and spills some of her dinner on the carpet. She stands there staring at the TV for a while and then seems to pull herself together and gets a cloth to wipe up the mess. She sits down and changes channels to watch something else.

James comes home and grabs his plate of food from the kitchen. He comes to join her in front of the TV.

"James?"

"Yeah?"

"I think there is something wrong with the TV set. It turned itself on."

Good, I am glad she is still thinking about it.

"I am sure it's nothing. Probably just a surge or something. Has it done it before?"

"No. It's the first time."

"Nah, I'm sure it was a surge."

*

Sandy comes home and goes through her normal

379

routine. While she is preparing dinner, I turn the TV set on. She walks through to the lounge to see what has happened and turns it off again. When she is back in the kitchen, I turn it on again. She comes through and turns it off again. I do it again. She walks into the TV room and angrily switches the TV off on the set by depressing the power button. I can no longer turn it on using the remote. I can turn it on by pushing the button too, but I leave it for now.

"James, please take a look at that TV set."

"I'll get to it after dinner."

"You always say that and nothing happens. You'll end up staring at the computer again for hours. Please look at it."

"Fine."

Sandy continues cooking and James walks into the lounge and turns the TV on and off a few times. He walks back into the kitchen.

"There's nothing wrong with it."

"You're sure?"

"Yeah. What's for dinner?"

"Pasta."

"Fantastic. When will it be ready?"

"Five minutes. James, that TV turned itself on three times tonight. Is that normal?"

"It seems fine, Sands. Just power surges. They happen more often than you think."

"But it hasn't happened before. Just yesterday and today."

"Who knows what those guys are getting up to at the power station? I'm sure it will get sorted out. Give it a couple days. If it doesn't come right, maybe it's time to buy another TV set."

"Yeah?"

"Yeah. Just give it a couple days. Maybe it's faulty. I can't see anything wrong with it, but maybe it's faulty or something. How old is it now?"

"Three years?"

"Yeah, something like that. You know these things only have a lifespan of about two years. Maybe it's time we moved on. We have loads of savings now. So why don't we splurge on a nice big plasma?"

"You serious?"

"Why not? We can afford it. We both love TV and it would be fun."

"Yeah? This weekend?"

"Yeah. How about this Saturday, you and I go shopping for a nice large plasma screen with all the trimmings?"

"I like that idea!"

Sandy gives James a kiss and they sit down for a more amiable dinner. They have been getting along better this week, but it won't last for long. I can't wait to get my hands on the plasma.

It is convenient that Sandy comes home before James. If he were more receptive to me and came home after her, he would not feel as afraid, because he would have her there with him. But Sandy is alone for an hour before James gets home. He would like to get home early, but his firm has long hours. I chose them well.

I go into the lounge and push the button on the set to turn the TV on. This is my last opportunity with this particular set, because tomorrow they are going to buy a new one for me to play with.

Sandy comes through and pushes the button. She pushes hard and looks at the TV afterwards to make sure it is off. Then she goes back into the kitchen. I give her five minutes and turn it on again. This time it takes her a while to come through to the lounge. When she does come through, her steps seem timid and I feel the fear washing off her. This is the first time I have managed to elicit such a huge fear response from her. She walks up to the set and switches it off. She turns all the lights on in the lounge. She switches the ceiling light on and the two standing lamps.

I could turn them off, but I am enjoying myself too much. This has to be a slow and gentle process to ease her into a continual state of terror. I wait ten minutes this time before I turn the TV back on. Sandy does not come back to the lounge. I waft along her waves of terror to find her cooking determinedly in the kitchen. I chuckle to myself.

James comes home and she runs to him and embraces him.

"Hello? What's wrong?"

"James, that TV set is turning itself on, even though I have turned it off on the actual set. I physically pushed the button. It did it three times again."

"Sweetie, it's power surges. Okay? I promise you. Don't get so worked up about it! What do you think is turning it on? Ghosts? I promise you, there's no such thing as ghosts. It's clearly faulty and we are going shopping tomorrow."

"I guess you are right. It's just that it is always three times and it always happens when I am alone at home. It doesn't happen when you are here."

"And that is because the ghost is playing tricks on you and not me. Don't be silly, Sands. You always come home at the same time and the power company is obviously sorting stuff out at that time of the day and there are power surges. Maybe by the time I get home, they are finished with whatever they are doing. There is always a rational, logical explanation for these things."

"You're right. I'm being silly. Work has been stressful."

"You should leave that job, Sands, and get something else."

"You say that, but what else am I qualified to do?"

"Skills are transferable and I am sure there are plenty of things you could do. You need to look."

"Yeah. It's not as easy as it seems, James. Otherwise you would be doing the same thing, wouldn't you?"

"Okay, we've had a good week. We are getting a new TV tomorrow. Please let's not fight tonight? I'm sorry, you are right. Okay?"

"Yeah. I don't want to fight either. So what brand are we getting?"

Later in the evening, I have lovely drink from Sandy. Her unease, which is still there, energises me. It feels lovely. I leave them alone for the weekend and part of the week to enjoy their new acquisition and the pseudo-closeness it has brought them. They bought a snazzy DVD player as well and spent the weekend setting it all up with their surround sound speakers. They seem to have spent a great deal of money on something that they are both soon going to loathe. I watch as the two of them snuggle up and watch DVD's on the couch.

I also needed to observe how this new contraption works so that I am able to turn it on and off myself.

I wait for Sandy to come home and start cooking and then I turn the TV on and slowly turn the volume up so that it reaches a deafening level. She can't ignore this.

She rushes into the room and frantically looks for the remote control. When she finds it she turns the TV off and, with trembling hands, she turns it off on the set as well. She rushes around the room and turns on all the lights. She stares around the room and walks, stiff with fear, back into the kitchen.

I turn the set on again, while holding the mute button so that it doesn't alert her to the fact that it is on. I flick through the channels to find something that will be particularly scary. I don't find any horror movies. I suppose it is too early in the evening for those. I find a channel with poor starving children somewhere in the third world. I watch for a little while. They may be my next victims. There's plenty of suffering and misery there for me to feed off.

I put the remote down in a different place. They always leave it on the coffee table. I carry it over to the side table. I push down hard on the volume button and pump it up until it's full volume and wait.

It takes a few minutes before Sandy comes to turn it off. She can't find the remote control and her hands are trembling as she searches for it with frightened eyes. Eventually, she runs to the set and turns it off. The doorbell rings and she jumps. She runs to the door and opens it.

"Hey, Sandy. How are you?"

"Fine thanks, Mike. How are you?"

"I'm good thanks. Um, I hate to bother you, but I just wanted to ask you if you'd mind keeping the TV volume down a bit. Um, you know, with the new baby and all."

"I am so sorry, Mike. I don't know what's happening with it. It seems to turn itself on. It was happening with our old set, so we bought a new one. But the same thing is happening with this one. James says it's power surges."

"Could well be. You want me to take a look?"

"Please, Mike. That would be great thanks. If it's no trouble?"

"No trouble. Through here?"

"Yes. Do you think it could be power surges? Have you had any at your place?"

"Um, yes, it definitely could be power surges, but we haven't had any. No. Strange. You would think that it would affect us too, but you never know how they wire these places up. They really do a crap job. Put them up in a matter of days and then it all falls apart. And we are the ones who suffer."

He turns the set on and jumps, as he is hit full volume from the surround sound speakers. He quickly turns the set off again.

"Dawn is going to kill me! I hope I haven't woken up the baby. Where is the remote?"

"Um, I don't know. I usually put it down on the coffee table here. We both sort of agreed on that, so that we wouldn't lose it. I'm sure I put it down there, but I can't see it."

"Good idea. I often lose the remote. Usually it's stuck under the sofa cushions! Really irritates Dawn. Ah, oh, here it is."

"Oh, I don't remember putting it there."

"Okay, let's see."

He turns it on and holds down the mute button. He lowers the volume. He turns it on and off a couple times, both with the remote and then with the switch on the set. James comes home in the middle of this.

"Hey Mike, what are you doing here? I thought you and Dawn were enjoying the little one."

"Hey James. We're all good. Just came over here, because there was a problem with your set. Sandy says you think it's power surges?"

"Yeah. Is it happening with this one too now?"

"Seems so. Volume was right up. That's why I came

over."

"Huh. I don't know what to do. I am sure it's a temporary thing. I'll call an electrician over tomorrow. Is Dawn home during the day?"

"Yeah, poor thing. I think she is keen to get out. You guys should come by and visit again. She would love the company."

"We didn't want to intrude," says Sandy.

"Oh, no, you wouldn't be intruding. She is going stir crazy on her own there."

"Do you think she would mind letting the electrician in tomorrow?" asks James.

"I don't think she would mind at all. We've still got your keys. Just give the guy her number and I'm sure she'll be happy to sort you out."

"Thanks, Mike, and tell Dawn we say thanks and I'm sure Sandy will be over. Maybe tomorrow evening?"

"Any time. Take care."

"Take care, Mike."

Sandy cuddles up to James. She is still scared, but seems to feel more reassured now that the electrician is coming by. She hopes that he will sort it out. I drink from her, as she slumbers with her arms wrapped around James.

I watch the electrician discover that there is nothing wrong with the set or the wiring. Sandy is not going to enjoy his report on the situation. I don't get to terrorise her this evening, because she orders take-out and takes it over to Dawn to say thank you for helping them out during the day.

James comes home and turns on the set and Sandy sits with him when she gets home. She asks about what the electrician found out and James tells her he found nothing wrong. He maintains that it must be power surges. Sandy says that she is going to phone the power company the next day to find out if that is the case. I look forward to her coming home tomorrow night.

Sandy arrives home later than she normally does. I think she must have phoned the power company and found out that there were no power surges and now she is afraid to be here alone without James. She has brought take-out with her. She puts it in the kitchen and goes upstairs instead of cooking as she normally does. Does she really think that is going to change what happens?

I go into the lounge, turn the set on quietly and surf through the channels for something ghastly. I find what looks to be a documentary about the inhumane treatment of animals in farms and abattoirs. And I am evil? I take the remote and stand behind the sofa. I turn the volume way up just in time to hear the blood curdling screams of a cow. I drop the remote on the floor behind the sofa. I really wish I was upstairs and could see Sandy's face, but I can feel how frightened she is.

She does not come downstairs at all. Eventually the doorbell rings. The button is pushed several times before she hears it and comes downstairs. Mike does not look too happy when she opens the door. He indicates that he would like to come inside and she stands aside to let him pass. He walks straight to the TV set and turns it off.

"I don't want to make an issue, Sandy, but could you keep the volume down?"

"I didn't turn it on."

"Okay, I know you are having a problem with this set, but why didn't you come down and turn it off? It was blaring for ages. It woke the baby. I don't want to fight with you about this. We're friends."

"The electrician said there was nothing wrong with it."

"Yeah, I know. So it's surges. Maybe keep it unplugged. Would you mind if I unplugged it?"

"No."

Mike unplugs the set.

"It isn't surges."

"What?"

"I phoned the power company and it isn't surges. They said that they haven't had any power surges at all this month. It isn't surges."

"Well, until you guys figure out what is wrong with it, would you mind keeping it unplugged, unless you are watching it. Then if it happens when you are watching at least you can turn it down or off or whatever?"

"Yes. We'll do that from now on. Sorry Mike."

"Sure."

I can feel that Mike is still angry and I can hear the distant wailing of the baby through the walls. Sandy stands with her back to the door for a while and stares into the lounge. I don't do anything. When nothing happens, she walks upstairs again. I leave her to it. I sit down on the sofa and stare at the TV set. I am not going to be able to turn it on with the plug out. I could put the plug back in, but I wonder if I would be able to turn it on without the plug in the wall. Would that be possible? I wonder. It probably is not possible at all. But it's worth a try. Why not? I have the whole day tomorrow to play around.

When James comes home, Sandy tells him that it has happened again. She tells him that there have been no power surges at the power company and reminds him that the electrician didn't find anything wrong either. She tells him about Mike coming over and unplugging the TV set.

James thinks it's a good idea that the TV set was

unplugged. He tells Sandy that just because the electrician didn't find anything wrong, doesn't mean that there isn't something wrong. He reminds her that people make mistakes and that not everyone knows everything about everything. He maintains that there is something wrong with the wiring and that she shouldn't freak out about it and that they will keep it unplugged from now on and then it cannot turn itself on. And does she feel better about that idea? She does. James says it's better anyway, because they will save electricity. He reminds her that things draw electricity all the time and it all adds up, so they would be saving money and the environment by making sure their appliances are unplugged.

I spend hours trying to make the TV set turn on by itself when it is unplugged. It takes a great deal of my energy as I try to charge myself up and channel it into the TV set. I can definitely feel that there is something there, but it doesn't work. It takes me a couple of days to finally figure out how to do it and Sandy is not as terrified now as she was on the night Mike angrily unplugged the set, so that leaves me with less energy to play with, because I am not getting fed as much as I would like. As they are both in a slightly depressed state at the moment, I have to draw energy from both of them, but it is not quite as fulfilling as when Sandy is scared.

I set myself up very carefully and wait for Sandy to get home. She goes into the kitchen and prepares dinner as usual. I wait until I hear her serve the food onto two plates and put James's food in the oven. I have to do this now.

I trail my essence from the wall socket to the plug, which is lying next to it and I charge myself up. I use the remote, which is lying on the floor in front of the TV, to switch the set on. The volume is barely audible. If I have it at high volume, it takes too much out of me. I wait for Sandy to come. I hope that there is nothing to delay her, because then I will have to wait until tomorrow night to try this again and I am getting more and more drained as time goes by. I may have to resort to a different plan if this doesn't work. And I am loathe to do that. I really want this plan to work. I have put a great deal of time and effort into it and I know that the results are going to reward me well.

I hear her walking slowly towards the lounge. Why is she walking slowly? Please don't let the phone ring. These two don't often talk on the phone at night. They prefer to do it during the day when they are at work. I suppose to waste time. But they have made occasional phone calls at night and the phone has rung on occasion too. If it rings tonight, and she goes to answer it, I am going to have to forgo this plan for a while, if not forever. I have been building up and working towards tonight. I didn't know they would unplug it, but it has played into my hands better than I ever could have imagined.

I lie on the floor with electricity buzzing crazily through me, hoping that she will come into the lounge and see that the TV is on.

I continue to hear her slow - and now I can feel it – frightened footsteps. She stands in front of the TV set clutching her dinner plate and stares at the set. I look up at her from the floor. She looks at the plug, which is not plugged in. She stares at it and looks at the TV. She looks back at the plug. She drops her plate on the floor and runs to the wall to switch the light on. She switches the floor lamps on. I lose the connection, because I need a drink. I sip from her and then run to the lamps and turn them off. I turn the main light off.

She is absolutely terrified. She is shaking so much

that she cannot move. She stares in terror at the light switch, which is too far away to reach. I brush past her again and she faints with a thud on the floor. I enter into her and drink deliciously.

40

James comes home a while later to find Sandy lying on the floor next to a broken plate of bleeding food.

"Sandy! Sandy! Wake up. Are you all right?"

"Uh. Mm."

"Come on, sweetie. Sit up. What happened to you?"

"Oh James. Please hold me!"

"I'm here. I'm here. Shh. What happened?"

"The TV set was on."

"You know that happens. That's why we are keeping it unplugged. This is really getting to you. What's happening?"

"James! No. Listen to me. The TV set was on and it was unplugged. Look it's still unplugged."

They both look at the plug lying sinisterly on the floor.

"I'm sure you imagined it."

"What? What? How would I imagine a TV set being on?"

"You've been under a great deal of stress for a long time and maybe it's getting to you."

"Let go of me!"

She angrily pushes James away and stands up shakily. He makes a backing off gesture and stands up too.

"TV's don't turn themselves on when they are unplugged, James! I did not imagine it. I ran to turn on the lights. All three of them and then something turned them off. I could feel it, James. I could feel it in this room with me and it turned the lights off. I could feel it walk past me."

"Sandy. I am telling you that there is always a rational explanation for these things. Always. Okay? So please listen to me. I know you are upset. There are no such things as ghosts. You and I are both well-educated people. Granted we are not experts on everything...."

"Exactly!"

James holds up his hands, "Wait. Please listen to me. Just hear me out, Okay?"

Sandy nods.

"We don't know everything, but don't you think it would make the front page of every news programme, magazine and newspaper, if they had discovered that ghosts exist? I know we are still learning things, but with all this quantum physics stuff, don't you think by now they would know? Remember that experiment we spoke about with the electron that was fired through a slit and two points arrived on a screen? Remember that?"

"Yeah, vaguely."

"We used to talk about stuff like that when we first got together. My point is that if they have discovered things like that, which is some pretty crazy mind-blowing shit, right?"

"I suppose so."

"Right? Well if they have discovered stuff like that, then they would have discovered ghosts, if they really existed. They don't exist, Sands. They really don't. People imagine ghosts, because we don't want to accept that when we die we die. There is nothing left."

I should be so lucky!

"So I think you are stressed. I agree that the TV has been turning itself on over the last few weeks. It happens. Stuff like this happens all the time. I don't think it could have turned itself on tonight. It was unplugged. The only way it could have happened was if you forgot to unplug it, got freaked out and then unplugged it. Or you imagined it. Don't get cross. I am not blaming you or saying that there's something wrong with you."

"But you are, James. If I imagined all this, then there must be something really wrong with me. That's what you are implying."

"I am just saying that you are stressed and weird things happen to people when they are stressed. People see things. They hear voices. They get paranoid. All those things happen."

"And who makes you the expert on all this, James?"

"My aunt, Esther, went a bit nuts after my uncle died. You know that."

"I am not Esther. And maybe she was seeing ghosts and no one believed her. I am not stressed James. I would know if I was!"

"Sandy, you have been unhappy at work for years. For years and years. You are stressed."

"Maybe you are right."

"I am right, honey. Maybe you should take some time off work?"

"I can't. It's the end of term and I don't want them to think I'm crazy."

"You are not crazy, baby."

"James, you just told me that I imagined the unplugged TV turning itself on and the lights turning themselves off, after I just turned them on. Of course I am crazy!"

"Hang on. There is a long line between crazy and stressed. You have two weeks left before school closes, right?"

"Yes."

"Okay. So you just need to get through these two weeks and then you need to rest. Promise me!"

"I promise."

"Will you get something for anxiety in the meantime?"

"I don't want to take pills, James!"

"Just a temporary thing. Just to get through to the end of the term and then you can rest and I think you need to look for another job. We have enough money to get by on my salary for a long time. I want you to be happy and you are not happy where you are. Please think about it."

"Okay. I'll go to the GP tomorrow and ask for a prescription."

"Good girl. I would suggest watching TV, but I think we'll leave that for now. Why don't we go up stairs? I need to work anyway and you can sit on the couch and read. You always say that relaxes you."

"Okay."

Oh, and this is just the beginning. Anxiety pills are not going to help you, Sandy.

41

I leave them both for a while. If I do too much too soon, it will destroy the whole thing. Subtlety, I am learning, is the most important ingredient in creating a stew of terror. If you don't want the mixture to explode prematurely, you need to add the ingredients one by one and slowly. Then you stir for a while, before you add in another ingredient, which you introduce bit-by-bit. In the beginning, you can distinguish one ingredient from the next. You can taste each one, but in the end, when it is all mixed together, you cannot taste the individual components and the mixture transmutes into a different substance - something all its own. I am going to see if the ingredients and my cooking techniques are going to produce the meal I had planned to make. Time will tell.

Sandy did get those pills the following day. I watched her as she stood in the kitchen and reluctantly swallowed them. I did not play with the lights or the TV set. Sandy felt a little down about taking the medication, but at the same time, it did help with her stress and anxiety. She and James have been getting on better and this makes her think that the reason for their deteriorating relationship may well lie in her hands.

The risk, as always, for me, if I wish to continue to stay with James and Sandy, which I do, is not to let them get too happy, as that will mean I cannot feed from them. I need them to have some respite though, because it makes the game I am playing so much more enjoyable. Just when they think they have discovered, through their cleverness, the solution to their maladies, I will come along and show them that in fact that is not the case and they are back where they started. In fact, they are in a worse place than where they began. This only serves to break them down and increase terror, because things are going to get a great deal more terrifying for Sandy and the situation is going to get a lot worse for both of them. And then I can get drunk on their despair and their terror.

This is what I am.

42

I do not have the strength to do my TV set trick anymore and so instead, I turn my mind to other things. Also, I need to show these two mortals the true extent of my powers so that they know that they are mere playthings to me.

I decide to try a few very subtle things, which will cause moments of panic but are easily dismissed. Sandy will think that it is to do with her 'condition' and that the medication is taking time to work, or that she is experiencing a side effect. If she does not come to that conclusion on her own, I will try to plant the idea there by using James. I am sure he will come up with the idea on his own anyway. If I were a betting entity, I would lay my bet on James telling Sandy on his own, as the most likely outcome, but it is quite likely that Sandy will come to the conclusion on her own. I will see how this leg of my plan plays out.

Sandy is asleep. She is breathing deeply and quietly and is turned away from James, who is in turn facing away from her. These two do not move a great deal while they sleep and I have been waiting two nights now for them to be in this particular position. I wonder, if what I am about to do, is going to work.

I creep up to her sleeping form in the darkness and hover over her, my mouth just a breath above her ear. Then I shout her name.

She jumps up and stares into the darkness. I dance around by the side of her bed. Terror always makes me feel giddy with joy. I am also most delighted that my plan worked! Her terror subsides and she turns over and curls herself around James, but it takes a while for her to fall asleep again.

Sandy is walking towards the lounge. The room is dark and she has not yet turned on the lights. She will when she enters the room. I stand in the doorway so that she has to pass through me as she enters the lounge. She shivers and walks out again rubbing her arms. She does not go back into the lounge for the rest of the evening.

Sandy is cooking and she has been using a measuring cup repeatedly to measure out various ingredients for a dinner party she is giving this evening. She is concentrating intensely on what she is doing. Sandy loves cooking and she likes her meals to turn out perfectly. That is why she does the cooking and not James. It is one of her passions.

I watch as she measures out ingredients and places the cup back in the same position next to her cookbook, which she consults regularly. I wait for the moment when she has gone over to the sink to wash courgettes and then I carry the cup over to the kitchen table.

Sandy walks back to the counter and proceeds to chop the courgettes up in quick slices. These tumble off the chopping board into a fragrant pot of boiling water. She consults her cookbook once more and then looks around for the measuring cup. It is not there of course.

She looks around the counter, moving things out of the way and getting frustrated as this is wasting her time.

"What have I done with it?" she asks with annoyance.

She eventually gives up searching the counter after releasing her stubborn refusal to believe that it is anywhere else and stamps over to the sink. It is not there either. She turns around to scan the kitchen and eventually spies it on the kitchen table. She knows she would never have placed it there. She walks hesitantly towards it and picks it up. She pokes her head out the kitchen door into the rest of the house, but doesn't hear anything.

"James?" her voice is quiet and hesitant and it is greeted by the quiet house. She returns to her cooking and quickly forgets about the whole episode.

The dinner party initially is a success. They are all laughing and enjoying Sandy's cooking. It makes me feel ill. So I decide that I am going to ruin it. I float over to the oven and find it difficult to read the numbers on the dials. I always find this skin-crawlingly frustrating. I wish I could just read. I am in half a mind to possess James and get him over here so I can read these stupid knobs, but I refrain from that for now. I decide that if I turn them both to the very left, that should do the trick.

I know that Sandy set the timer so she won't be in for a while. I hang out in the kitchen as the happiness in the other room jars my nerves. The only consolation is that my cooking is going to turn out better than Sandy's.

Sandy comes running into the kitchen.

"No!"

She yanks open the oven door, tries to pull the baking tray out with her bare hands, burns them, swears, grabs the oven mitt and pulls the dried, burned food from the oven. She stares at the slightly charred carcass and then looks at the knobs. She stares hard at them. She reaches to turn them off and burns her hand again as the heat from the oven has risen to roast the knobs. She swears again and puts the mitt on to turn the oven off.

The timer has not yet gone off. She must have smelt the food burning and that is why she came running through. I sniff the air. It is hard to make out with my dulled senses, but I do get a hint of burnt flesh in the air.

Sandy is poking at the meat and vegetables. I walk over to inspect my handiwork and am quite pleased with the result. The food is charred badly. Sandy grabs a knife and prods the food. The underneath looks fine. She proceeds to cut away the burnt crusts and slices a bit of the pink meat underneath. She puts it in her mouth and chews it thoughtfully. Tears slowly leak from her eyes.

She pulls herself together and wipes the tears carefully from her eyes, so as not to smudge the make-up she fastidiously applied earlier. She draws in a deep breath and walks back to face the guests with her failure weighing heavily on her shoulders. They end up ordering take-away food.

Sandy and James clean up the meal after their guests have left, while tears leak slowly down Sandy's face and I lap up her sorrow in great licks.

Sandy is fast asleep and James is working late in the study. The light from the study fades as it stretches towards the bedroom, just leaving a dull glow. I decide that it is time that Sandy saw me. Again, I am not sure if it will work as I have never done this before, but at the same time, I know that it will. It seems that there is a core of knowledge about myself that I can access if I try hard enough. I know that Sandy will see me if I want her to.

I stand on her side of the bed and scratch my fingers along the surface of the bedside table. It seems to make a noise. I can vaguely hear it. I hope it is not loud enough to bring James out of the study. I don't want him to know of my presence just yet. I have to scratch a few times before Sandy stirs. She makes an annoyed grunting sound and turns away from me.

I don't stop and she eventually turns around again. She opens her eyes with difficulty, looks up at my face and says, "Please stop it, James, I am trying to sleep!"

Well that didn't work too well.

The next day, she confronts James about disturbing

her. He says that he was in his study until late and that he ended up sleeping on the couch, as he did not want to disturb her. She feels freaked out and he assures her it was a dream and that the medication she is on may have side effects, or that she needs more time on it before she feels stress free. The holidays are coming up in three days time and she will be able to relax fully then and then she will really see a change.

I know my pets well and, if I could have access to money, I would be very rich indeed.

43

I continue with little subtle acts, which can be easily dismissed as mere forgetfulness or mindlessness on Sandy's part. But if I continue too much longer she will become like James and ignore everything I do and I cannot have that.

At the beginning of Sandy's holiday, James has to go away for two days to a business conference. He assures her that it is a good time for her to rest and it will be nice to have the house to herself for a few days. She agrees and plans to read and sleep late and watch TV. They continue to unplug the TV when they are not using it. I do not need it anymore as I have decided I am not going to be with them for too much longer.

I am getting bored with Sandy and James. I need to create and play new games. This one is almost completed.

James and Sandy say their farewells. His conference is only a half hour drive away, but the company wants everyone to stay there for both days, as it is some kind of team-building endeavour. I don't think it is going to help James much, but he has no choice but to go along.

I leave Sandy alone during the daytime. She is much more likely to get frightened at night, I have discovered. It is strange how humans fear the night more than the day. Maybe it is because they are daylight animals and not nocturnal ones. If they were nocturnal, maybe they would fear the daytime more, as they would be out of their element, so to speak. At night, their animal instincts come into force, where they seek safe shelter from night-time predators, even though they are top of the food chain now. Well, they were on top of the food chain until I came along.

On the first night, I try not to scare her too much, as

I want her to stay in the house for the second night. If she did leave I could follow, but I don't feel like it. I don't have a home of my own and this home feels like mine, although I will have to leave it soon.

I wait for her to fall asleep and then I float over her body and breathe in ragged breaths staring down into her sleeping face. Sandy wakes up, but she does not move. I know she is awake, because I can sense it. I think she is trying to pretend that she does not hear me and that she is still sleeping, but I know she is awake and so I continue.

I am angrily disappointed to find that she passes out on me. I rip the covers off her prone body and prod her a few times. There is no response and, what makes it even worse, is that she acts like nothing happened the next morning. Did she think she was dreaming? Now I am angry. For the first time, I am really angry with Sandy. I will have to do something worse to her tonight. I scheme all day long.

This time, I wait for her to go to bed and turn off the light. Before she can go to sleep, I tread heavily along the carpet. She turns on the light and looks around. I don't make a sound. That got your attention, didn't it, you bitch?

She sits dead still in her bed with the light on and then pops one of her anxiety pills. She is obviously tired as she drags her novel off her bedside table and fumbles with the pages to get to her spot in the book. She looks up every now and then and glances uneasily around the room as she turns a page, but I don't do anything. I am delighted that she is still a little anxious, though that tablet is dulling the effect quite a bit.

Eventually, she puts the book down and slides under the covers. She looks around the room once more and then she turns out the light. I walk up to the bedroom door and slam it shut.

The light flashes on again.

"Who's there?"

She has the blanket tucked around her and is staring around the room with huge frightened eyes. Eventually she climbs out of the bed, every fibre of her being thrumming with terror as she walks towards the door. I drift past her and switch off her bedside table light. She is plunged into darkness.

I can hear the rapid beat of her heart through the waves of terror and adrenaline that pulse from her. I float past the terrified statue again and open and slam the door shut. This seems to galvanise her into motion and she runs back to the bedside table and fumbles to turn the lamp on. She hurdles over the bed and turns the other bedside lamp on. She opens a bedside table drawer and grabs a flashlight, which she turns on. She walks hesitantly towards the door; I suppose she is expecting it to swing open again and she carefully turns the main light on and opens the door. She swings the flashlight around, its beam highlighting objects, which now have become sinister for her. She proceeds to run around the house and turn on all the lights. She spends the night under a blanket in the study staring at the door.

When the dawn breaks, she gets dressed and leaves the house. She does not return until the evening when she expects James to be home. What she does not remember is that I took control of her briefly to tell him to pick up food on the way home, so he will be home later than she expects.

Sandy climbs into the shower and lets the water ease the tension out of her body. I wait until she feels a little more relaxed. It seems that she is less frightened after a day away from the house and knowing that James is coming home.

I climb through the shower door and enter the shower with her. I focus all my energy into my fingers and I scrape them down the shower door making ten clear tracks through the condensation.

Sandy turns at the squeaking sound and stares at the tracks going down the shower door. I can't see her face, but I can feel her exquisite fear. When I am done, I turn around to look at her. She is staring at the tracks, the hot shower water sliding off her naked body unnoticed.

"Hello, Sandy."

She screams and tries to open the shower door, but I put my foot against it so she cannot pull it open. Then I start to scratch her until pink welts rise off her skin in harsh stripes.

"Sandy? Sandy!"

James runs into the bathroom and pulls open the shower door to look at his girlfriend, who is sitting cowering and scratched in a corner of the shower. He climbs into the shower and pulls her up.

"What's happening? What's happening? What have you done to yourself?"

"There's something in here, James! There's something evil in our house! I want to get out of this house! Please. Please take me away from here. There is something bad here!"

"Okay," He carries her out of the shower and covers her in a towel. He is dripping wet and the shower is still running as he carefully dabs her dry. He examines the welts and determines they are not too bad.

He scoops her up and she tucks her head into his neck as he carries her back to the bedroom. He places her carefully on the bed, caresses her face and turns to leave.

"Don't leave me alone!"

"I need to turn the shower off. I will be back in a second."

He turns the shower off and comes back to the bed. He strokes her head as she clings to him once more. His eyes alight on the pills on her bedside table.

He reaches over and picks them up.

He pockets the pills and tucks Sandy back under the covers.

"Where are you going?"

"I am going to the study to make a call."

"No, James."

"You are going to be fine. I am not far away. There is nothing here. I need to make a call and I'll be back as soon as I can. If you need me, just shout and I'll be here. Okay? Everything is going to be fine."

I stay with Sandy as James leaves the room. We can hear him mumbling softly on the phone in the study. Sandy is still terrified, but she feels safer now that James is back. She cuddles into the covers and closes her eyes.

James comes back into the bedroom.

"Okay. I phoned the hospital and told them what happened to you and they say that this medication can have a particular side effect for some people. It can cause people to harm themselves and to have hallucinations."

"What?"

"Yes. They advised me to take you off the medication immediately. It should wear off over a couple days."

"What does that mean?"

"It means it could happen again."

"No, James."

"I think you should stay with your parents this week and they can keep an eye on you. You know we have this big project at work; otherwise I would take the week off. It's just such bad fucking timing."

"I can't go to my parents."

"Why not?"

"I can't let them see me like this," She raises her clawed arm, which is zigzagged with scratches. I admire my work.

"I am too worried about leaving you at home like this, baby. I can't be with you and you need to be watched. If it happens again, you could really hurt yourself. The hospital said that I could bring you in for observation. Maybe that's a better idea?"

"No, James. I don't want to go to hospital. I don't want people to think I am crazy."

"It's not your fault, honey. It's mine. I made you go on these pills and now look what I have done to you."

"You didn't know. You were trying to help."

"I can't leave you here alone."

"What if I text you every half an hour to let you know I'm okay? We could try that. And if you don't hear from me then send the ambulance over. Please, baby. I don't want to go to hospital. It will get out, it always does. I don't want people to think I'm crazy."

"Let me think a moment."

James stares at a spot in the carpet and Sandy looks at him expectantly.

"Okay. We will try that tomorrow. Every half an hour. If I don't hear from you, I am going to call the ambulance, right? And you are either going to hospital or to your parents. I would prefer your parents. I don't like this one bit though. I really don't, but I can't make you go against your will."

"What do you mean?"

"I asked the hospital if I could book you in, but they

said not without your consent."

"You would have committed me to a mental institution?"

"Calm down, it's not like that. But see it from my point of view. I come home to find you screaming and scratching yourself in the shower, only to tell me that there is something evil in the house. What would you do if it were me?"

"I see your point."

"So we have a deal?"

"Yes."

"I love you, Sandy. I don't want anything to happen to you. It's my job to protect you."

"I love you too."

"I am going to have a shower. I will make it fast. You shout if you need me."

"Okay, sweetie."

The following day I leave Sandy to sit in self-pity amid her florid scratches and go with James to work. Possessing him is lovely. I have not done this for a very long time. I manage to make an excuse for him so he can have an hour for lunch. I claim that I have a headache and that I need to go to the pharmacy. They let me go reluctantly. I speed back home.

I open the front door and find Sandy sitting in the sun in the lounge.

"What are you doing home? Did you get my texts?"

"Yes. I just wanted to check on you."

"Oh, sweetie, that's so sweet of you. I didn't think they would let you off work though."

"I made an excuse that I had a headache and came over to check on you."

I go over to her and kiss her. I kiss her mouth and she responds. I end up making love to her on the floor. I must say that it does not compare at all to the rush I get from feeding off her terror. It really is neither here nor there. But this is what I have been building up to.

"It's a pity James isn't here to enjoy this with us," I say as I lie on top of her.

"James, what are you talking about?"

"I'm not James."

"Stop kidding around, James. Get off me!"

"No." I keep her pinned underneath me.

"This isn't funny anymore, James. Get off!"

"I am not James." I chuckle mirthlessly and stare hard at her.

She is quite and stares back at me. I was hoping she would scream and fight, but her terror is growing.

"I loved how scared you were in the shower last night. James thinks you did it to yourself. I don't think he will believe you. He's not going to remember our little moment of passion either. What a pity. He's not going to believe you about our little tryst today. He will think it is the medication too. That you imagined it all and you are going to end up in a loony bin after all. That's what you fear most, Sandy. I wonder where that fear came from? I didn't delve into your mind long enough to find out. You are not that interesting. Your terror is delicious, though. I can feel it. It is making me hard all over again. Did you really think you could get me to leave your house by swallowing some pills and turning on the lights? I am here to stay, you bitch. We can share many more moments like this. Just you and me. James will never know."

Eventually when I am ready, I take her again. The two of us staring into each other's eyes – the predator and the prey. When I am finished, I zip up my trousers and take James back to work, leaving Sandy lying on the floor. She doesn't move at all.

I can't wait to see what happens tonight when he gets home. He won't understand why she is suddenly so afraid of him. She won't know when he is himself or me. Then we will see who is arrogant after that…..

44

I drive back to James's work. I go into the bathroom to splash water over my face and run it through my hair. I need to look like I am recovering from the aftermath of a headache. I look into a mirror for the first time. I am not sure why I am doing it.

I can see James's face and I am well aware that it is not my face. It is hard to look at yourself in the mirror and you know that the face staring back at you is not your own. I stare for a long time and then I see me for a brief moment. I look again. I stare right into my eyes and then, as if the world is shifting between me and the mirror in a sliding motion, I see myself staring out of James's eyes.

I feel like I am staring at a deadly predator and I cannot move. Eventually, I pull myself away from the mirror. I finish up in the bathroom and vow to never ever do that again.

I take James back to his desk. I answer questions about going to the pharmacy and feeling much better now. I tell everyone that I'd prefer not to talk about what happened. James is not going to remember driving home and I don't want anyone to ask questions or make comments, which will make him think anything other than that he has been sitting at his desk this whole time. Once I sit down at his desk, I leave his body.

He stares down at his hands and then looks at the papers on his desk. He quickly glances around the office and ascertains that no one can see that he does not know what is going on. He seems to recover quickly and continues working.

When he does not get his text messages from Sandy, he starts to worry about her. He looks at his phone and puts it down. Half an hour later, he picks it up again and looks at it. He does this three times in the next five minutes. But still nothing from Sandy.

He slips his phone into his pocket and goes into the men's room. He calls her, but clearly gets no answer. He leaves a message for her to call him immediately. He walks back to his desk and tries to work, but I can see he is not concentrating. He dials her number again, but she does not pick up. He thinks something has happened to her. He does not know that he happened to her. He packs up his desk and awkwardly makes an excuse to his boss saying that his wife phoned and is not well. His boss is clearly not impressed, but lets him go. He seems to have decided not to call the ambulance.

I ride in the back of the car as James drives home trying not to drive too fast, but trying to get home as quickly as possible at the same time. He clearly thinks that Sandy is having another episode. I wonder if I will find her in the same position I left her in.

We arrive home and James bursts through the door calling for Sandy, but there is no answer. He checks every room. She is nowhere to be found. I wonder where she went. James finds that her handbag is missing and swears. He runs back outside and flips the remote for the garage door. It grinds open to reveal gaping emptiness. I feel very triumphant now. Sandy has left James and now I am going to start terrorising him. We will see if he will manage to ignore me now.

He calls her again and again receives no answer. He leaves an angry message punching into her voicemail, grabs a beer from the fridge and sits down to watch TV. I leave him for now. I have plenty of time to terrorise him tonight when he is all alone at home, worried and angry. For now, I just feed. I ponder about what I will do next. I am not quite sure, but I am sure something will occur to

413

me. After the horror I will create, I will leave and find new prey.

He tries her a few more times over the course of the afternoon. He gets angrier and angrier. As the twilight steals into the lounge, James and I hear the groan of the garage door. James makes a move to get up and sits down again. He cranks the TV volume up a bit and stares at the screen stubbornly.

"Please come inside." It's Sandy and she has brought someone with her. Someone, who looks vaguely familiar to me. Is it one of their friends? It gnaws at me and I try to figure it out, but I cannot. I let it go. I can't wait to see what happens next and cannot be bothered with little trifling thoughts about who this familiar stranger is.

Sandy walks into the lounge and James is staring at the screen. He glances over at the woman with Sandy and returns to stare at the screen.

Sandy does not seem at all comfortable around James and stands close to the woman.

Still staring at the screen, James asks, "Where were you? I have been texting you and calling you all day long. I have been worried sick about you and you could at least have let me know you were okay. We agreed that you would not go out today and yet you've been out all afternoon. I have been here since two thirty and you arrive home now. Do you know how busy I am at the office? Do you know that I left in the middle of a busy day to come and find out if you had had another breakdown? No. No, you were out shopping I suppose and hanging out with your new friend here. Could you not have had the courtesy to let me know? To answer my goddamn calls?" James throws the remote across the room.

"James, please, we have a visitor."

"I don't give a damn about your visitor! I am stressed. I have worked the whole day today without a single break, because that is how bad it is right now at the office. I miss an afternoon at work in one of the busiest times of the year to come home because you did not stick to our agreement. What the fuck is wrong with you? Do you know how worried I have been?"

"Do you remember coming home at lunch time to check on me, James?"

"No. I worked through lunch, Sandy. Stop playing games. You were the one who did not stick to things. Why would I have come home at lunch? I worked through lunch just like I do every goddamn day of my life just so I can get ahead."

"You don't remember?"

"What?"

"Coming home at lunch time?"

"I think you must have imagined it. I don't know who you are, lady, but be careful, my wife is crazy."

"Call Peter."

"Why?"

"Call him and ask him if you came home during lunch."

"No! I am not calling Peter to ask him a crazy question like that. You want them to think I am crazy too?"

"Call him now, James!"

"No."

"Right, then I will."

Sandy dials a number and puts her mobile phone onto speaker. She does not move closer to James.

"Hey Sandy, how are you feeling? Heard you had a bit of a rough day. James said you are feeling ill."

"I am feeling a little better, thanks Peter."

"What can I do for you?"

"I was wondering if you know what time James left work today?"

"He left at about two o'clock I think. Why? Did he not come home? Is everything all right, Sandy?"

"His phone is off. I can't get hold of him. He went to the pharmacy to get some drugs for me."

"Wow. That is a long time to be gone."

"Has he been all right today at work?"

"Actually, no. He went out at lunchtime, for about an hour, which he never does. Well, as you know, none of us ever do. Deadlines looming and all. He said he had a bad headache. He came back, said he was feeling better and then said he got a call from you, saying you were ill and then he left again. Sandy…."

"Oh, thank god! I hear the garage door opening now. He is home. I am so sorry to worry you, Peter."

"No problem, Sandy. Sounds like the two of you are coming down with something."

"It seems so. I am just glad he is home safe and sound."

"I think you both need to go see the doctor. Let me know if I can do anything and tell James that I need him back at work as soon as. I don't want to sound like a bastard, but we have huge deadlines."

"I will. Thank you, Peter."

"Take care, Sandy."

"Bye."

Sandy pushes the button on her phone firmly to end the call and stares triumphantly at James, who is looking at her in bewilderment.

"You don't remember, do you?"

"No. I thought I was at work the whole day. I was gone for an hour? A whole hour? I can't remember. You say I came home? I thought......"

"Do you remember what you did to me, James?"

"What I did..... No. No, I don't remember anything. What did I do?" His face is ashen.

"You raped me, James."

James stares at her and all the blood seems to have left his face. His mouth hangs open and his eyes reflect bewilderment and fear.

"No."

"Yes, James."

"I would never. I would never hurt you. Oh my god. I don't remember. Was I drugged? Oh my god."

He sits down heavily in the armchair facing Sandy and the lady. He just stares at Sandy in horror.

"I know you would never hurt me, but I had to make sure."

"But you just said I....."

"It wasn't you. This is Chandra, oh I forgot, I was not supposed to use your first name. This is Ms Palmer. I have asked her to help us. I know you are going to think that I am crazy, but I believe that there is an evil entity that has been living with us for a long time now and I believe it possessed you this afternoon. I do not want that to happen ever again. So let me do this, James, whether you believe in this or not."

James looks at Sandy and nods his head numbly.

"I am so sorry, I forgot, am I supposed to use your surname only."

"It is fine. It gives them a little more power over us, but I can handle this."

"Is it here?"

"Yes. It is sitting there."

Chandra points directly at me. She is looking directly at me, which startles me. No one has seen me so far.

"Can you see me?"

"Yes, I can see you, demon."

I get up and start walking towards her. No one has seen me or spoken to me before.

"You will stay where you are."

I try to walk forward, but I am unable to move.

"I just want to ask you something. I have so many questions. How is it...."

"Stop your trickery, demon! I am not interested in your deceptions. You will be leaving this house soon and you will leave these two people alone."

Chandra proceeds to turn her back on me and take things out of her bag. I so desperately want to ask her questions, but she won't let me. I am angry.

I rush around the room and start smashing and throwing things. This is the first person who can see me and she will not listen to me! With each thing that flies across the room, with each thud, with each object that smashes into sharp shards, I feel myself becoming angrier and angrier.

"Please God, make this stop!" Sandy is clinging to James. They are both standing near Chandra, staring as their belongings fly through the room in a rage.

"God? God? There is no God. Don't you understand? If there were a God, I would not exist!" I hurl a book directly at the two of them. James bats it away and holds Sandy again.

"Do you believe me now?"

"Yes. I am so sorry, Sandy. I am so sorry for everything."

Well at least he acknowledges me now, but that victory feels so impotent and hollow.

"Stop ranting, demon!" Chandra is facing me and she is holding a pot of foul-smelling smoke, which curdles in the air. Does she think she can stop me with that? She thinks she can stop me with a jar of smoke? I am all-powerful! She should be cowering before my wrath! I throw a vase at her. She dodges it deftly and it smashes against the wall behind her.

The doorbell rings.

Good. More people to throw things at, maybe I'll hit a few of them!

James runs to open the door. Mike is standing there.

"What the hell is going on here, James?"

"Come on in and take a look. You won't believe me otherwise."

I stand still. I am not giving James the satisfaction of showing Mike that I exist. I want Mike to think that James has been tearing this place apart.

Mike looks around at the battered room. He looks questioningly at the three people.

"Um, well, it seems to have stopped now."

"What has stopped?"

"Um…"

"It's laughing at you, James. It knows that it is making you look like an idiot. My name is Ms Palmer and you are?"

"My name is Mike. Next-door neighbour, with a new baby, who is not getting much sleep lately. Me and my wife are getting a little fed up with all this. I don't like to make a scene and I really like to be on friendly terms with all my neighbours, but this is going too far. I am not sure what is going on here, but I would like it to stop. I have shown nothing but consideration for you both and I would like the same courtesy returned to Dawn and me. I am afraid the next time I am going to have to take this further and it may get to the point where the two of you are asked to leave. I am sorry that we are getting to this point, but we can't continue living like this, especially with a new baby."

I chuckle. I always win. This smoke-blowing lady is not going to do anything. I will throw things around again tomorrow night and then they will have to leave their home. There will be more misery for you two yet!

"Stop your laughing, demon! There is nothing to laugh about. You think you have won, but you have not. You will not be returning to this home ever again. You will not be able to hurt Sandy or James again."

I look at Mike's face, which is a picture and I burst out laughing again. He thinks she is completely insane. I am not going to give him any reason to think otherwise. I keep still and I don't throw anything. I stare triumphantly at the woman.

She starts to mutter things under her breath and I feel that I am being pushed back slowly. It doesn't hurt and it is not violent. It is a gentle, persistent pushing. I feel I am moving further and further from the knot of people on the other side of the lounge. I push against it, but it does not work. I try to push through it, but I cannot. I fly up to the ceiling and through the ceiling into the next apartment and try to enter their apartment again, but it doesn't help. I go through the roof and try the other side of the block, but I cannot get in. A circle of energy seems to be radiating out of Chandra and pushing me away.

I fly back into the lounge and find there's little space left. I am so furious! How dare she do this to me? I pick up what I can reach and try to throw it at her to knock her out so she will stop. She seems completely unphased by me and what I am throwing at her. She continues to mumble under her breath and dodges anything that gets too close to hurting her.

"You see, Mike. You see it don't you?" James looks

at Mike intently and pleadingly at the same time. Does he want Mike to believe him, so that he does not get them thrown out, or does he want Mike to see it too, so that James has a witness and does not feel like he is hallucinating now?

"I can't believe my eyes. What's throwing stuff at us?"

"It's a demon," says Sandy, "It's what has been turning the TV set on and turning up the volume so loud. No one would believe me and I thought, in the end, that I was imagining it all."

"I honestly would rather be imaging this. This is the scariest shit I have ever seen in my entire life." Mike looks at the point, where things are being thrown from. He clearly can't see me, as he is looking wildly from one corner of the room to the other. None of them can see me, except for Chandra, who keeps her eyes fixed on me.

I am backed up against the wall. Any moment now and I will be pushed out of this apartment. I squeeze my way between the apartment wall and the wall of energy to a side table in the corner of the room.

"Don't worry. Mike, is it? I am going to make sure that this demon has no access into this apartment from the sides, the sky, or the ground. You will be protected as well."

"Thanks……" Mike is staring like a stupid goldfish at the table, which is being dragged along the end of the room, scraping its way along the wall.

I manage to position the table where I want it. Most of my body is now either in the wall or outside in the garden. I feel terrible - too many sensations at once, but I won't give up. I thrust my head into the room. My arms are still inside. I scrabble to get purchase on the ground outside with my feet and then by the time I do, my head has been forced out of the room. All I can see now is the slow aching energy of the bricks in the wall. I am not giving up! I saw where Chandra was standing. I have it firmly in my mind. I lift the table, which now feels far heavier than it was a few moments before, and try and hurl it at her.

But the table thumps into the wall I am being dragged through and this interrupts the flow of my throw. It tumbles frustratingly to the floor as I am pushed out of the house, never to be able to enter again.

I throw myself repeatedly against the barrier, as it grows and expands through the garden. I am alone in the dark garden and I cannot get back into the house, no matter how hard I try.

Eventually the energy field seems to stop and does not grow any more. I am far away from the apartment block. I fling myself against the barrier in a surging rage, but it does no good. Eventually I stop. I float back down to the ground again and sit down to think, which is difficult, because I am so angry.

The only thought in my head is that I am going to get Chandra. I am going to make her pay for what she has done.

I fly up over the house again and hover over the parking lot. I cannot land, because of the barrier, but it does not take much energy to hover in the air. I don't know which car belongs to Chandra and I would not be able to get to it in any case, as I cannot access the parking lot anymore. But I am patient.

I wait a very long time for her to appear. They are probably thanking her profusely inside there. Mike doesn't even emerge from the house. I wish I could hear what they are saying. I would love to hear it all. I try to merge with James, Sandy, Mike and Chandra and absolutely nothing happens. I am left hovering in the air and I don't move a fraction closer to them. It is highly irritating.

Oh, thank you, Ms Palmer. You're the best Ms Palmer. Now we can live in peace and quiet again, Ms Palmer. I can just imagine the conversation. Blah blah blah.

"You were miserable before I came and you will be miserable after I leave!" I shout at them. It is not very satisfying, because none of them can hear I word I am saying.

I am going to get her.

Eventually I see her and Mike exit the apartment. Sandy and James come out and shake hands with everyone. Mike enters his apartment and shuts the door, while James and Sandy watch Chandra walk to her car. She puts her belongings in the boot and pulls the driver's door shut. I watch her little car spring into life, as she pulls off with a wave from Sandy and James. I wish them both mountains of ill fortune as I follow Chandra out onto the road.

45

I try to enter Chandra's car, but I am unable to. I try to possess her and again I am unable to. Both of these serve to make me feel angrier. I have to settle for sailing along in the air above her and this takes a great deal of energy out of me. I clearly am not designed for travelling through space like this. I seem to be better at jumping through space into bodies. That does not take as much out of me as this does, but I continue. My anger fuels me.

We travel through the dark, quiet night together. The occasional car passes us, but otherwise the streets are quiet. Chandra does not seem to be in a rush and takes her time getting home.

She parks her car in her driveway and climbs out. She takes a deep breath of the night air and locks the car door. She walks in the dark up to her front door, which is set in a quaint front porch. Her house has been painted white, but, in the dark, it looks pale blue. Her porch light does not come on as she nears the door and she does not seem at all bothered by this. She seems to find the keyhole easily and slips the key in and turns it. I am standing next to her. I am waiting for my moment to enter the house.

Chandra does not open the door, however. Instead, she turns around and looks at me.

"You are wasting your time, demon. You cannot enter my house."

"You've known all along that I have been here."

"Yes. The journey over here must have tired you. I drove slowly to make sure."

"You knew I was following you?"

"Of course."

"How did you know?"

"I can feel your presence. Actually, I was thinking about you on the drive over here. You missed our little conversation after I banished you from the house."

"How did you do that?"

"That is not important. Even if you knew how I did it, you would be able to do nothing to stop me or anyone else from banishing you. We have to have some type of defence against your sort. And I am too tired to sit down and chat to you about the whole procedure. And, as I don't particularly like you, I am in no mind to chat to you at all. What you do need to know is what we spoke about after you left. Now that is the interesting part, demon."

"Fine, tell me about this fascinating conversation."

"Well, the fascinating part is that that young couple you were haunting were having a great deal of trouble in their lives. I suppose that is why you went there. You wanted to make it worse. The strange thing is, I think you actually brought them closer together. You see, I told them that only people who have problems, or who are depressed attract entities like you and they have decided to work on their issues. So, all that hard work that you put into destroying them and their relationship seems to have had the opposite effect. I am going to have a good night's rest now, knowing that. Why don't you leave this town and go somewhere else, or go back to whatever realm you came from. Oh, and by the way, you won't be able to get into my house. Good night."

I try to follow her, but I can't get in the door. Again, there seems to be some type of invisible barrier there, which keeps me out. I walk around the house and fly up onto the roof. I can touch the house, but I am unable to enter it. As I try to penetrate the walls, doors, windows and roof, I encounter a force field. I run around the entire house, looking for some kind of weakness, but I can't find one.

She has not bothered to protect her garden. I can wander freely around it and I can touch her house. But I cannot enter it. I try her car, but I cannot gain access to that either.

She mentioned going up through the ground. I give that a try. It is a very unpleasant process. I feel the slow hum of the earth vibrate through my entire being and it makes me feel disorientated and sick, but I am determined to get into her house. I search under the house and eventually squeeze out of the ground near the back of the house and lie on the ground exhausted. That took a lot out of me. There is absolutely no way in.

When I feel a little recovered, I fly up to her bedroom window. I guess it is her bedroom window before I even get there. It is the only light on in the house. The window is open and the curtains drift gently in the breeze.

Chandra is lying under her blankets in her lilac bed reading a book by the warm glow of her stained glass bedside table lamp. A fluffy ginger cat lies asleep on the bed next to her and she absently rubs its fur while reading a book.

I watch her impotently. The window is wide open and yet I cannot enter through it. It makes me feel so frustrated. I really want to teach this high and mighty bitch a lesson. How dare she come in and kick me out? Am I not the most powerful entity on this entire planet? I also feel hurt. I feel angry that she is totally unafraid of and disinterested in me. And I feel hurt that she did not even want to speak to me. Finally, the first other creature on this entire planet that can see me, sense me and interact with me, does not want to talk to me even for a few minutes. The creepy one did not seem to want to talk to me either. Why will no one talk to me? For the first time, I feel truly sad.

I am all alone in this world. I am destined to cause pain and suffering and there is no one, who will talk to me. The ones who fight me and the ones who are the same as me - neither of them will talk to me and I do not understand why that is.

I don't know why I cannot possess Chandra, because I can certainly feel the waves of depression and loneliness emanating off her. I feel like a prisoner starving in a jail cell with a feast before me, which is a hairbreadth's length out of reach for me. I know I can feed off anyone I choose, but I want her. I want her, because she has defied me. She has beaten me and one of the few joys I have in this life is winning my own games.

She has now become my new game and I will have to figure out how to defeat her in order to win it. There must be a way to get to her and to get her to drop her defences against me. I will make her allow me to possess her.

She eventually closes her book and turns off the light, before shifting her body under the covers. The cat wakes up with a moan at being disturbed. The cat puts its head down to go to sleep again and then raises it and looks at me with fathomless eyes. It seems to see me. I lift my hand and move it across the window from one side to the other. The cat watches my hand. That is interesting. The birds and crabs on the beach did not notice I was there.

I am weak and don't have much energy left, but an idea does come to me about a possible way to get to Chandra a little bit. I grab the window and slam it shut; I am too weak to make the glass break. I run my fingers down the glass in teeth-curling squeals.

The cat stands up on the bed and arches its back in a

show of jagged fur. Its eyes widen and it opens its mouth in a sharp white hiss as it digs its claws into the bed.

"I am not sure why you are still here, demon. You are different from other demons. Most of them give up, but not you, it seems. You have been here for a few hours now, trying to get in. You are wasting your time. You cannot enter my house and you cannot possess me. Now we would like to get some sleep."

With that, I feel the barrier around the house grow slowly until I can no longer touch anything.

I am too tired now to be angry. I visualise myself entering a bum somewhere in the town, where I can recharge and think. I think I might quite like the homeless for this, especially if they are prone to sitting around all day and not doing much. It will give me time to think. If I were to take another person, who had a family and a job, I would not be able to do nothing all day long without disruption and inquiry.

I find what I am looking for. I stare at the fire in front of me and take a swig from the grimy bottle in my hand. I sit and think for a few days, only taking time off for necessities. Eventually, I develop my plan of attack.

46

It takes a long time to find Chandra's house again. The problem is that I cannot imagine her and project myself directly into her body. I physically have to find her house again. I could use a human to do it. I could possess one who owns a car and drive around for ages to find her house, but I don't feel like spending all that time looking for it. It is easier if I fly over the neighbourhood until I find something that looks familiar.

It takes a while before I accidentally come upon James and Sandy's apartment complex again. The barrier is still there, unfortunately. I try to look into their windows from afar, but it does not look like anyone is home, not that that would do me much good in any case. Chandra made sure I would not get near them, wherever they are.

But finding their home does help me orientate myself and I can now find my way back to Chandra's, as I just need to remember the route we took from their house to hers. As I fly along the street, landmarks come back to me and trigger memories. I do make a few wrong turns, but when nothing looks familiar, I turn back and try a different direction. Eventually, I find Chandra's small double storey house sparkling white in the sunlight. I can still enter the garden, but I cannot get near the house. Her car is gone. She must be out.

I decide to come back in the evening, when she is more likely to be home. I retrace my steps back to the bum in the alley. It is quicker this time, as I know the route better. That is important, as the less time it takes me to get there, the more energy I will have at my disposal. I flew higher on my way back to the hobo, so that I could get a better sense of the direct route I need to take. I think this evening I will be able to fly directly to her house.

When I arrive at Chandra's house, I can see the car in her driveway. It is dark and I watch her progress through the house as the night travels on. She starts off in the kitchen. Then she makes her way to another room. I am not sure what she is doing in there. Perhaps she is eating her dinner. She then lets the cat out into the garden. I retreat so that neither of them senses my presence. She shuts the door leaving the cat outside.

This is going to be a first. This is something I have never tried before and I am not sure if it will work or not. But it is part of my plan of attack and I have to see if it is an avenue to get to Chandra.

I focus and then release myself.

I stretch myself out and stare into the distance. I am aware of all the little things flying around me. A moth passes me and I track it with ease and precision. I feel my claws come out and an unstoppable desire to catch the moth. I spring into the air in a graceful arc and I grab the moth in both my paws. I feel it fluttering frailly between my paws. I find this sensation fascinating and keep it there for a while. I release it to see what it does. I watch as it beats the air with erratic wings. An overwhelming urge to eat it surges through my jaws and I find myself crunching on the tasty moth. It leaves dust coating my mouth, but I forget about that as I wonder off in search of other prey.

After a long night of hunting, I suddenly realise that I am possessing the cat when we arrive back at the house again. I have an urge to jump up on the windowsill, wind my way through the dark house and snuggle next to Chandra. Well, let's see if I can get into the house this way. I bound up to the house only to find myself lying on the grass while the cat continues its journey to the windowsill. I watch as it stops, turns around, hisses at me and then winds its body around the narrow gap.

I fly dejectedly up to the dark bedroom window. I can barely make out the outline of Chandra in the dark. I see the cat jump softly onto the bed and curl up next to her.

I make one last effort to project myself into the cat. I find myself rushing through the air towards the window. I encounter the barrier and fall onto the ground in shock.

Clearly, I am able to possess the cat, but I am unable to get through the barrier while possessing it. I was hoping to use it as a type of vehicle with which to breach the barrier, but I cannot do that. The other plan was to try and possess it in the house, but I cannot do that either. I seem to be thinking about this barrier as an actual barrier. I suppose I have been thinking about it in that way, because it feels sort of physical. I certainly can feel it when I bump up against it.

But maybe it is not physical. Chandra has her bedroom window slightly closed tonight. I look around the garden and find a stone, which I am easily able to lift up. I hold onto it as I float as close to her window as I am able to. It is time to see if physical things can pass through this barrier if they originate from me. I heft the stone and hurl it at her window. The stone passes through the barrier without any difficulty and smashes a loud, jagged hole into the glass.

That is interesting. It seems anything can come through the barrier except for me. It seems designed specifically for keeping me out. I wonder how that works?

After a little while, I see Chandra's shadow peering round the corner of the window. Well at least I made her scared, which makes me feel better. I am starting to get to her. I watch as she scans the garden. Then her eyes alight on me. The fear is replaced with a feeling of anger and the barrier starts to grow again until I am no longer able to enter her garden.

I pick dirt off the pavement outside her house and throw it into her garden in furious fistfuls. Everything I try with her is thwarted. Well, at least she will have to pay to have the window of her precious house replaced and I could tell she was angry about that. So, I may not get to her in the way I want, but I am getting to her.

I sail home to the man in the street. I enter him and decide on the next step I will take.

I wake up as the dawn starts to break. I won't let the man sleep in the cardboard box he usually climbs into. I covered him in newspapers and an old smelly blanket and slept under the night sky. I wanted the dawn light to wake me up. I need to get to Chandra early in the morning.

I hover high over her house in the hope that she will not see me nor sense me. She does not appear to and I fly along watching her as she drives herself to a quiet street in the city. She parks her car in a familiar-looking street and goes to a little shop. She opens the door and goes inside.

I come closer and walk around the street, keeping my distance so that she does not sense I am there. This street looks very familiar. I walk around for a while and eventually it comes to me. This was the street where I possessed the lady in the supermarket by accident and Chandra was the lady who invited me into her shop. She said I could come back to her when I was no longer lost and she would see if she could help me. She doesn't seem to want to help me now at all.

I find the coffee shop a couple streets away, where the creepy one found me. That lady must live around here somewhere. The murdered man is in the park around here. And so is Ed. He must be living on the streets near me, but I haven't seen him in the vicinity I have been living in. I could possess that woman again. But Chandra seemed quite wary of her. So maybe not.

I walk back to Chandra's shop and look at it from a distance. She said that I would be able to enter her shop. I wonder if I still can. I have an idea that might guarantee me entry.

47

Yapping greets me. I look around the room and find a small dog staring at me and yapping. Its ears are pinned back against its head and it looks frightened.

"Shut up! Or I'll make you shut up!" I yell at it. It runs from the room with its tail between its legs.

I get up on stiff legs and look around. I hope that I have possessed who I wanted to possess. I was quite specific about what I wanted. I access her memory and remember where she keeps her car keys. I locate her handbag and the car keys and drive to the street where Chandra works.

I can't find parking near the shop and so I have to park a couple blocks away. The walk back is not so easy, but, as I continue to walk, my joints seem to ease up and it becomes easier.

I enter the shop and see Chandra talking to a customer. Her back is towards me. I walk towards her but am barred from moving past the small entrance hall into the main area of the shop. I remember that she barred me from entering further than I have and that is why I am possessing this woman. I retreat a little and look timidly at the shop.

Chandra rings up the purchase for the other customer, who walks past me. Chandra looks at me.

"Hello, dear. I was wondering if you would be able to help me up this little step. My legs just don't work the way they used to and I forgot my walking stick at home. Old age tends to make us look like fools, I'm afraid. I feel very embarrassed about this," I implore in my frail old voice.

She looks at me, but does not move.

"I need your help with a problem I am having.

Please could you assist me, so I can tell you about it?"

"What is the problem you need assistance with, Ma'am?"

"I feel a bit foolish about it and even more foolish about telling you from the doorway. Someone may come in and I would feel terribly embarrassed."

"People come in here with all kinds of difficulties. There is no need to feel embarrassed."

Chandra steps from behind the counter and walks towards me. She stops in the middle of the room.

"Well, dear, it's just that strange things happen around me. I thought at first that it was just my mind going. That does happen at my age, but then my little dog would notice it too and start barking. He looks like he is looking at something that is in the room with me and he just barks. I have felt very foolish about talking to other people about it, so I have tried to ignore it, but I am scared. Tell me I am not imagining these things. I can feel it with me now."

"No. You are not imagining it at all. I can feel something's here."

Chandra walks towards me, but stops a meter away from me.

"You walked into this shop unassisted?"

"Yes, I did. I can walk along flat ground. I am a little stiff, but it is manageable, but I need my cane to help me climb stairs. I feel so foolish about leaving it at home. I am terribly sorry. I am embarrassed about asking for your assistance."

Chandra walks up to me, "I apologise for being so rude, Ma'am. Here, let me help you. Here take my hand."

I reach out towards her and am stopped by an invisible barrier. I cannot touch her. I try not to let the surprise show in my face. I thought I would be able to reach across it.

"Sorry dear, I don't think that angle will work for me. It makes me feel quite insecure. Do you think you could stand next to me and hold my elbow? It works better that way. You can help lift me up and I can use the wall here for support on the other side."

She doesn't make a move.

"Oh, oh. Now I feel so embarrassed. Sorry to trouble you, dear."

I turn around and make as if I am about to leave the shop.

"It's with you now."

"What dear?" I turn around again.

"I said that the thing you are scared of is with you now, I can feel it. That is why I am hesitant, also there is something familiar about it."

"Where is it?" I ask alarmed, darting my eyes around the small space. I hope I am being convincing.

"It's okay." She reaches out and touches my arm.

I grab her arm and try to pull her into the entrance hall with me. Unfortunately, she is much stronger and is able to pull loose. We both fall backwards, but in opposite directions. She stares at me in horror.

"Let me into your shop, Chandra Palmer!"

"No!"

"Then you leave me no choice!"

I exit the old lady and stare down at her. She is sitting on the floor with her back against the door, barring her own escape. She looks around in bewilderment.

"Where am I?"

And then she screams. She screams, because I start scratching at her face.

Chandra rushes towards the old lady just as I wanted her to and I try to swipe at her face, but I can't get near her. Instead, I focus once again on the old lady and am satisfied to see my red scratch marks on her face. Ignoring them, Chandra grabs the old lady and drags her into the shop.

I fling myself against the barrier and scream in frustration.

Chandra and the old lady are huddled together on the floor, staring at the space where I am. Only Chandra can see me though.

"Where am I?"

"I am sorry, Ma'am. Are you all right?"

"No. I am not all right! I find myself in this strange little shop being scratched by something. How did I get here?"

"You were possessed by a demon. It brought you here to get to me. I am sorry, Ma'am."

"This is your fault. None of us like that you have a shop in this town. We knew it was bad. Some people at the church have signed a petition to get you out of town. I am going to tell them exactly what happened here."

"It is not my fault that you were possessed."

"Not your fault? Excuse me, young lady, you just told me that this demon thing possessed me to get at you! You just apologised, not a moment ago. Not your fault? Indeed!"

"It is my fault that this particular one brought you to my shop and what it did to you. It wants to get to me, because it possessed a young couple and I made it leave. But it is not my fault that you were possessed. That blame lies with you."

"Excuse me! I am a devout Christian. There is no way I could be possessed."

"But you just were."

"Well, that is because of you. You are some witch or

something."

"I am not a witch! And being a Christian has nothing to do with getting possessed or not. Demons are drawn by your low energy. They are drawn to people who are worried, depressed, lonely or sad on a continual basis. Religion is not going to help with that, Ma'am. Only you can help with that."

"Excuse me!"

"If you are happy and content, they cannot come near you. But I will help you. I will help you, even though you don't want my help or understand my help. I will make sure that this demon will not come near you again."

"How dare you be so rude? I don't want your hocus-pocus, mumbo jumbo, thank you very much! I will talk to my pastor."

"You may not want it, Ma'am, and normally I charge for this. And believe me, I don't really want to help you, but I am going to anyhow. So demon, you can stop laughing. You are not going to go near this woman again."

She mumbles under her breath again.

"You really should stop mumbling. Are you embarrassed about what you are saying? Don't you want other people to hear you?" I taunt her.

She looks up at me and I can see there is hurt in her eyes. I am right. I laugh.

She looks at me angrily and continues mumbling.

The old lady looks at her in revulsion. Chandra is aware of this, but ignores her.

Let me help you up, Ma'am," She says when she is finished.

"I don't need your help!" The old Lady says crossly. But she can't get up from the position she is in and takes Chandra's hand reluctantly.

"You are free to leave the shop now, Ma'am. No demon will be able to come near you now."

"I tell you, I am going to make sure the whole town knows about the evil you practice!"

"I am sure you will tell everyone, and no thanks needed for the help I have just given you."

The old lady leaves in a huff. She is a little frightened as she passes through the entrance hall, but she feels braver as the shop door closes behind her and then the anger and indignation come. I can't touch her.

I lock eyes with Chandra. She walks towards me and locks the shop door. She turns the sign over so that it now reads closed. She fetches a chair from behind the counter and carries it over to the centre of the shop. She sits down on it and stares at me.

"I am not sure what you are. I have never encountered anything quite like you before."

"Are you scared of me?"

"No, not really."

"I will find a way to get to you, unless you let me possess you."

"Well, that doesn't make any sense at all. If you are going to find a way to get to me, why would I let you possess me? It seems that you are going to get me in any case."

"That's right."

"But the thing is, you are not going to get to me. You see, I am now going to banish you from my shop. And I am going to make sure that you cannot come near this shop from a very good distance. So, you are welcome to possess whomever you like and make them do whatever you like, because I am not going to know about it. So, knock yourself out."

"I can possess your cat. You are not a very good

mommy to your kitty cat are you? You haven't protected him."

"Cats are interesting creatures. Some cultures believe that they are the vehicles for spirits and I am not able to protect him from spirits the way I protect myself. So, it does not surprise me that you can possess him. The thing about my cat is that he tends not to stray from my garden and as my garden is now protected, I am not worried about you doing anything to him."

"Why did you not protect your garden like your house?"

"Because I had no need to do that before."

"I find that quiet flattering then."

"You can take it any way you choose, demon. Now, I am going to banish you from my shop and the surrounding area. And I look forward to never seeing you again."

She starts mumbling under her breath again and I feel the barrier growing and starting to push me towards the door of the shop.

"Why don't you say it out loud? There's no one to hear it now but me. Have all these years of shame affected you this much?"

She ignores me and continues. She stares fixedly at me as she does so.

"I have a question. Wait! Just listen to me. I have one question to ask you!" My back is now against the door.

She stops mumbling.

"Why did you tell me I could come into your shop?"

"I don't remember telling you that, and if I did, it was clearly a mistake, which I am fixing right now."

She goes back to mumbling and I let the barrier push me away from her until it stops moving. I stand where I am, far away from her shop. I cannot see it from where I am anymore. I could see it if I flew over it, but not from the ground. She has achieved what she said she would. There is no point in possessing someone here and making a scene. All it would do is make that person look crazy and she wouldn't know a thing about it.

She has thwarted me once again. I enter the homeless man in the alley and sit and think. I am far more intelligent than she is and I want to get her back for being such a know it all. I want to show her that it is I who is powerful, not her.

I sit and feed and think.

48

It's dark and quiet tonight. I have everything I need in a backpack, which is slung over my shoulder. I have checked the house to see if they have any dogs, but they do not. I climb over the high wall and land in the garden behind some trees. I walk quietly along the wall, keeping it on my left hand side.

I come to a clearing next to the wall, where I am exposed. I can see the light on in the house and the flicker of a TV screen. I don't see anyone in the room. The other windows of the house are dark and I stare at them to see if anyone is looking out of them. I don't see anyone. I chose this man for two reasons. He has good eyesight and he is strong.

I creep along the wall until I see what I am looking for. I look around again to make sure that no one has seen me and then I scramble up the high wall. My feet grind against the wall and I am sure that the sound can be heard for miles.

I perch on top of the wall and look around in all directions. I sit and wait and watch, but no one seems to have heard me. It is very difficult to walk along the wall. I do not have much space and I don't want to fall down and hurt myself, because that would mean that I would have to find another person to inhabit to do this, plus the people in the house may become aware of intruders once they had already found one.

Eventually, I reach the big oak tree, which I saw while flying overhead this morning. I touch its rough bark. It is very tall, which is why it is ideal for my purposes, but it also makes it very difficult to climb. This is going to be the hardest part of the evening.

I steady myself against the tree, making sure my

footing on the wall is secure, and remove the rope from my backpack. I unwind a length of rope and sling the rest of the coil over my shoulder. After a couple of tosses, I manage to get the rope over a sturdy branch. I tug the rope to make sure it is strong enough to hold my weight. Very awkwardly, I start to wind it around the tree trunk in a spiral and make loops, which I tie off as handholds. I knot the end securely and cut off the rest.

Now for the hard part. I grab the rope and start to pull myself up the tree. I reach the branch I was aiming for and grab it when I have enough height to pull myself up onto it.

It is perfect. I can see the ground at a dizzying distance beneath me and I have a clear view of Chandra's bedroom window. Her light is on and I can see her reading her book in bed with her cat.

I hold onto the tree and pull the backpack off once again. I take out the remaining rope and sling a length of it over the branch above me. I make a slipknot and pull it tight so that a length of rope is hanging down in front of me. I tie the end into a noose, which I slip around my neck. I let the backpack fall with a thump to the ground. I no longer need it.

"Chandra Palmer!"

She looks up from her book and out the window.

"Come to the window now, Chandra Palmer. If you do not, you will have this man's death on your hands."

She climbs out of bed and I see her put a jersey over her nightie. She comes to the window and opens it wide. She looks at me.

"If you do not let me come into your house. I will hang this man right here outside your bedroom window and every time you look out your window you will see this tree and you will be reminded that you killed this man."

"I am not killing him. You are."

"Well, technically I am, but I won't have to live with his spirit hanging around on a tree outside my bedroom window. You will. And the only reason he will die is because of a choice that you are about to make. If you let me in, he lives. If you don't, he dies. So, in a sense, I may be forcing the choice on you, but you will still be playing a role in his death. It's up to you. On the count of three, I am going to jump and snap his neck like a dry twig! One….. two……"

"All right! Just come down from there. Bring him into my house."

With a satisfied smile, which permeates my whole body, I pull the noose off. I have won. I am more powerful and superior than she is. Climbing down the tree takes a while. I would let the body drop to the ground, but I don't think she will let me in then, so I climb carefully.

"What are you doing in my tree? You are trespassing!"

"No need to get your panties in a twist, sir. I have a little issue with your lady neighbour. I'll be hopping over the wall to her house right now and you won't have to fret."

"Chandra!"

"Thanks, Teddy. It's okay. Sorry to disturb you."

"You sure it's okay? You don't want me to call the police."

"No. I'm sure it's fine. He's a client, who has been desperate to see me. I told him to make an appointment. He is persistent, but harmless, I assure you."

"I don't feel comfortable about this, Chandra."

"I promise you, Teddy. It's fine. He will be leaving

shortly. If he does not leave in five minutes you can call the police, if you'd like."

"I like the sound of that idea better. I am going to my gate and I will see you leave in five minutes, buddy, and no funny stuff." He looks up at me meaningfully. I lift both my hands in a show of defencelessness. I enjoyed watching the two of them shouting over the wall.

I jump onto the ground and come to stand facing Chandra.

"Well, my house is not protected now, otherwise you would not have been able to jump into the garden. Will you please take this man outside? Did you drive here?"

"Yes."

"Good. Please take him to his car and let Teddy see him drive off. Then you may come inside. I will be waiting in the lounge. You will find that I have created a path for you to go along so it will be easy to find."

She turns and walks back to her house.

"You'd better not banish me once I have left your property, because I will hang people all around your property if you do."

"I will be waiting in the lounge."

Once I have seated the confused man back in his car and Teddy and I have both seen him drive off, I find Chandra sitting with her feet curled up under her on a soft couch in her lounge. I project myself into her, but I cannot enter her. Instead, I sit down in a chair opposite her.

"So, tell me demon, why are you tormenting me? I have never experienced anything quite like this before."

"I want to possess you."

"Why?"

"Because you are sad and lonely and I should be able to, but you won't let me. You are the only person I have met that I cannot possess."

"And when you possess me, what will you do?"

"I will kill you."

"That sounds appealing. And why would I let you kill me?"

"Well, it's that or I will kill a lot of other people and leave them for you to find and you will know that it is because of you that they died."

"So, you want me to sacrifice myself in order to save the lives of others?"

"Yes."

"And if I do this, you will never kill again? Never?"

"Well, no, because that is what I do. I am a demon and I kill."

"I am confused. It makes no sense for me to sacrifice myself. It seems pointless. And the thing is, I can banish you from this whole town. I would never have to see you again and, if you killed more people it wouldn't matter to me, because I would not know about it and you would do it anyway."

"So why did you let me into your house if all you wanted to do was play tricks on me, again?"

I get up and I want to fling something at her. I spot a vase and go to grab it.

"If you throw that at me, I will banish you from this town immediately. Sit down right now!"

I haven't been spoken to like that before. I am a little shocked. I look at her and replace the vase. I sit down again. Being banished does not help me right now.

"Well, if you are so powerful, why don't you banish me right now?"

"Because I have never met a demon who was so determined to get to me."

"You have met others like me?"

"Yes. I have met many like you."

"What do you do when they come to you?"

"Well, you are all quite scary, so I banish you."

"But you didn't banish me when we first met."

"I banished you from Sandy and James's house. That was when we first met."

"No, it wasn't. We met a few years ago. It was in a supermarket. I possessed a lady who had been for a reading with you the previous day and I crashed into a shelf of cans when I possessed her. You took me to your shop and you told me that I would only be able to enter a short distance into the shop. You said I should find you when I was no longer lost."

"I remember now. That was a long time ago. I had never seen anything like it before. I had never seen a person being possessed like that in the middle of a shop and you didn't seem to know what had happened to you. You scared me, so I knew you were a demon, but you were so strange. It didn't make any sense to me at all. I have seen people being possessed, four times in fact, and every time the demon knew what they were doing and took control of the person. They knew all about the person and the people in their lives. But you seemed so confused. And that confused me. I thought maybe you were something I had never encountered before, but now I see that you are just a demon."

"I thought I was dreaming."

"Excuse me?"

"I thought I was dreaming when I possessed that woman. I did not know that I was a demon. I thought I was a man in a mental hospital, because I had been possessing him for a long time. I thought I was him. I did not know I was possessing him. I was being chased by a demon, but I thought it was all in my dreams. I just

447

thought that I could not wake myself up. I thought I was awake when I was in the psychiatric ward, because my psychiatrist told me that I had been dreaming before. In fact, possessing that man was the only thing that woke him up. I didn't know any different. That demon eventually caught me after I met you, when I was inside that woman. He told me what I was and yet I thought I was still dreaming, so I possessed a man and made him die, because part of me wanted to believe that I was dreaming. I killed him and he was not the first person I killed. I had killed others when I thought I was dreaming. I was so tired and weak that I possessed another man and went to sleep and that made him die too. I realised that my very nature was pure evil and I did not want to be pure evil. I tried to get myself away from people. I managed for two and a bit years and then that demon found me again. He said that I could not stay where I was, as I would go mad and lure people. When I possessed someone in that state, I would be worse than I am now. I just wanted to die, but I can't because I am already dead. I am going to be like this forever. So I decided that I should just be what I a clearly am. I do evil, because I am evil. In order to exist and be able to act freely, I have to feed off people, and I cause those who suffer to suffer more."

Chandra looks at me for a long time. As she seems to be listening to me and I have been alone for so long. I slow down and tell her the whole story from the start.

When I finish my story, Chandra asks me, "So do you still want to possess me?"

"Yes."

"Why?"

"Because the only thing I have left is winning. We played a good game you and I, but I am going to win."

"I suppose you have won. I seem to have no choice. I need a week and then you can possess me."

"You don't get to chose. I will possess you now."

"No, if you want to possess me and win as you put it, you can possess me in a week's time. Take it or leave it."

"I'll be back in a week and if you try something you will regret it."

"I won't try anything. I will see you in a week."

49

I stand outside Chandra's house. She'd better not try anything. I will make her pay if she betrays me. It has been a long week. I was tempted to come back and possess her, but I didn't think it would work. I am sure she would have put something in place to stop me. I worried about whether she would keep her end of the bargain or not. I don't want to be played for a fool.

Nothing stops me entering Chandra's house and I find her seated in the living room. She looks at me when I enter.

"You didn't change your mind then?" she asks.

"No."

"I hoped you would."

"I win, Chandra."

"I don't know if you do."

I feel annoyed. Of course, I win. "Let's get this over with. Stop trying to change my mind."

Chandra stands up and mutters something under her breath as she looks at me. When she is finished, she is shaking as she tells me she is ready. That, and the look of terror in her eyes, makes me feel immensely powerful.

"Say goodbye to your life, Chandra!"

I push myself into her body with all the force I can. I am in! I look at my hands. They are Chandra's hands. I skip up to her bedroom and look in the mirror. I see myself staring out of Chandra's eyes. I am inside you, Chandra Palmer. You lose! I win!

I look at her neat bedroom and start to throw everything around. I try to rip her bedding, but the fabric of her sheets is too strong. I find books on her bookshelf. Some of these books are well worn. They must be precious to her. I pick one up and start to tear the pages out in fistfuls. I pick up the discarded pages lying on the floor and scrunch some up and tear others. I pull the rest of her books off the shelves and throw them around her bedroom. There is nothing you can do to stop me!

I walk into her bathroom and open up her cabinet. There are expensive-looking creams inside. I gouge the cream out and smear some of it over the mirror in her bathroom. I throw the rest of it down the toilet.

Chandra has another small bedroom upstairs, which she seems to be using as a study. There is a small desk with a computer monitor on it and more bookshelves filled with books. She has a single bed, which I presume is for guests. I open the wardrobe and discover it is full of clothes. I pull them out and fling them onto the bed. I take the chair and smash the computer screen with it. The sound of shattering glass is immensely fulfilling.

I wander downstairs and look around her sitting room. I push one of the armchairs over before walking into her dining room. Her dining room is very simple. There is a wooden table and six chairs and a painting on the wall. I lift the painting off the wall and smash it on the chair until there is glass and ripped painting everywhere. I hope it was precious and sentimental to her.

I make my way into the kitchen. I open cupboards and look through them. I find a vase in a cardboard box at the top of a cupboard. I am sure it is important to Chandra. I take it out of the box and drop it onto the floor. I look through her small pantry and take note of the food there. It is very well organised and she has not bought anything in excess. I notice a bag of half-used cat litter on the floor in a corner under the bottom shelf. Where is that cat?

That will really hurt Chandra. I walk around the house calling for the cat. I look under the beds and the sofa. I look in the cupboards and wash basket. I search the house thoroughly and methodically and I can't find the cat anywhere. It must be outside. I walk around the garden and look under all the bushes and shrubs. I cannot find the cat. Then I remember cats wander where they want. I am sure it will come home soon.

I walk back into the house and sit on the sofa to wait.

I get bored after a while, so I get up and make a tuna sandwich, as I am hungry. I hope the tuna will draw the cat back home. Maybe it will smell it and think there is food. I go back to the sitting room and turn on the TV and watch a reality show about dancing while I eat my sandwich. Still no cat. I feel thirsty and look through the kitchen cupboards until I find some tea. I make a pot and take it back to the sitting room. I flick through the channels. Nothing really takes my fancy and I end up watching a football match.

I wake up with a start. I am not sure what woke me up. I look around and realise it is dark outside. Maybe the cat came back in and that is what woke me up? I get up and turn the lights on in the house as I look for the cat again. I still can't find it.

Cats don't stay out that long do they? I can't remember. I am not sure if I have ever had a cat. Not that I remember. Maybe I could put some food out in the kitchen for it and wait there. I have more energy from my nap. I should be awake for a long time and I will get that cat.

I walk into the kitchen and look for the cat's bowl. I can't find one. I imagined that Chandra would have a bowl for her cat. Maybe she feeds it out of her own bowls? I don't really care. I open a cupboard and take out a bowl. I look for the cat food. I look everywhere. I look in the fridge, the cupboards, each shelf in the pantry and even in the front hall. There is no cat food. She really must love that cat. I wonder if she cooks human food for it? I open up the freezer. Sure enough, there are frozen cuts of fish in one drawer and the others are full of frozen vegetables. I take out a frozen piece of fish and put it in the microwave to defrost. Does it eat raw or cooked fish, I wonder? I am guessing Chandra would cook the fish for her cat. I bet she is that type of person. Do cats eat fried fish or boiled fish? Maybe it has to be grilled? I am getting annoyed! I take more fish out of the freezer and defrost it in the microwave so that I can fry one piece and boil the other. I take more bowls out of the cupboard and lay them down in a row in the middle of the kitchen. I put the fried fish in one and the boiled fish in the other. I take the defrosted fish out of the microwave and put some in the grill and another piece in the frying pan for myself. The smell of cooking fish makes me hungry. I save a bit of uncooked fish and place that in another bowl on the floor. I boil up some veggies as well and make another pot of tea. Once the grilled fish is done, I put that in the last bowl on the floor. I take my meal to the dining room and position myself so that I can see the cat flap in the backdoor, as well as the bowls on the kitchen floor. I sit down to eat and slowly remember that cats like milk and there is plenty of milk in the fridge. I get up and fill another bowl with milk and place it on the floor.

I eat my meal slowly and drink the entire pot of tea in small sips. Still no cat. I need the toilet desperately. Too much tea. I reckon that even if the cat comes back while I am on the toilet, it will take some time to eat the food and I won't be gone too long. I should still be able to catch it. I run upstairs, relieve myself and run back down again. No cat. Maybe it snuck in and went out again? I'd better check. I open the back door and squint out into the darkness. I don't see a cat. I try to call the cat by making a hissing sound and then a meowing sound. Still no cat.

That's fine. I am patient. It will come back to eat. They always do. I sit down in my chair in the dining room and wait.

50

I wake up with a start. My neck really hurts. I must have fallen asleep with it at an odd angle. I try to stretch it out, but it doesn't help. I get up stiffly. The sun is streaming through the windows in the kitchen. I walk to the bowls of food. Everything looks untouched. The milk does not look like it has been drunk. I open the back door again and look around outside. I see no sign of the cat. It occurs to me that maybe the cat flap is not working properly. I test it. It's working fine. There is still time for the cat to come back.

I make myself a bowl of cereal and another pot of tea and go back to my spot in the dining room to eat it. Cats can disappear for a day at least. They find other people to feed them or eat rats. I can't sustain this sitting arrangement though. It's too uncomfortable. I pull an armchair into the dining room and get a book to read. I make another pot of tea and settle down to wait. I have all the time in the world.

After a while I realise I have spent a lot of time lost in my own thoughts and I have not heard any of Chandra's thoughts. I also realise that I have not actually accessed any of Chandra's memories. That is very strange. I did not experience this when I possessed other people. I try to access Chandra's thoughts. Nothing. No matter what I try, it seems that I am on my own in her body.

For a little while, I like that feeling. I feel like I have my own body and I am alive again, but it doesn't feel quite right. I feel that I could slip out of my body as easily as slipping out of a silk gown. I don't think that people should feel that way in their bodies. If they did, they would leave them all the time. It feels unnatural and not satisfying. It's just a borrowed body. It's not mine and the whole point of this endeavour was to win. I wanted to beat Chandra at her own game and now it feels like a hollow victory. What is the point of possessing someone if I can't torment them?

Where is that damn cat? That will make her speak to me. I am going to make that cat suffer! I walk around the property again, check the bowls and look through every wardrobe, under the beds and chairs and in the washing hamper. There is no cat to be found. I return to the untouched bowls. Surely the cat would have wanted to eat by now? It would have come back by this stage.

I am hit with the realisation that Chandra has sent the cat away. There is no sign of a cat living in this house except for the bag of mostly-used cat litter. She must have known I would hurt that cat. Again, I try to access her thoughts and memories, but there is nothing there except for me.

Fuck! This is not how it is supposed to happen! I am going to find that cat. I walk into the garage and get into the car. I can't start it. Where are the keys? I don't know where the car keys are and I can't access Chandra's memories to remember where she put them. Can I hot-wire the car? Do I know how to do that? I don't think so. I pull leavers and the bonnet pops up. I open it to have a look. Maybe I can start the car from there?

There's something wrong with the scene under the bonnet. It takes a while before I see that the car battery is missing. Annoyance flares up and crawls over my skin. The bitch has taken the car battery and hidden it somewhere. Why would she do that? Did she know that getting in the car would lead me to her cat somehow?

Well, if that is what she feared, maybe sitting in the car will help me to remember where the cat is? I slam the bonnet down and sit in the driver's seat. I sit and I sit. No thoughts come. Nothing! Not a damn thing!

I storm out of the garage. I can't drive the car, but I can walk around and I will find that blasted cat! I stride down the garden pathway and as I walk through the gate, I find I just can't get my body to move any further. No matter how hard I try, I cannot move it. I scream with frustration. She has trapped me in her house. I know she has! I try to climb over the wall to the neighbours and again the same problem - I cannot make my body go any further.

I walk back inside and have an idea. Chandra must have called a friend to ask for help with this. I could probably find the last number she dialled and get that person to come over here. That's a great idea! I could get them to bring the cat and then I could torture both of them. That would make Chandra come out of her shell.

I look around and cannot find a phone of any sort anywhere. I eventually find a telephone jack in the sitting room and I find another one in the study. As I look at the carpet under the desk in the study, I trace the outline of a computer tower with my finger. She had a computer and it has been moved recently.

Chandra has trapped me here in her house with no way of leaving, unless I leave her body, and no way of communicating with the outside world. The fridge and freezer are full of food. There is enough food to last me a long time. She prepared for this.

I am Chandra's prisoner as much as she is mine.

51

The only solution I can think of is to hurt Chandra physically to make her talk to me. I go upstairs to her bedroom and face the mirror. I look deep into my reflected eyes. I see me and I see Chandra in them. This is the only way. I brace my hands on either side of the mirror and start to bang my head as hard as I can into the mirror.

The pain and the blood in my eyes makes me stop. I am in agony. I blindly make my way into the bathroom and fumble around until I find the toilet paper. I hold it against my throbbing head and lie down on the bed. The pain is all consuming and it is only after a while that I remember that this was meant to bring Chandra out. I search in my mind to see if I can locate her, but again there is silence.

The pain is intense. I wish I had not done this. Part of me feels happy to have hurt Chandra's body, but she does not seem to be around to experience it. The one who is suffering the consequences of this, is me.

After a while, I fall asleep. When I wake up, I feel slightly better. The sharp pain has turned into a dull throb. I look at my face in the mirror. I have a swollen nose and a huge swollen gash on my forehead. No reaction from Chandra.

I gingerly make my way downstairs. I am thirsty and hungry. I make myself a cup of tea and a sandwich and go and sit in the lounge. I have tried everything to get Chandra to talk to me. She has let me do what I wanted and has not fought me. She did not try to stop me when I destroyed her precious belongings, or when I ruined her face. She has trapped me here and seems to have given her body to me in its entirety. Isn't that what I wanted?

I won. But it does not feel like it. What else is there to do? I can sit in this house and ruin it and her body. I can watch television, eat the food, until it is gone, and sleep. I could starve her to death as I did with the man in the park. Will she beg for her life like he did?

That is the only way. That will make her talk. It is a horrible way to die. I am not leaving this house until she starts to talk to me and I can feel her suffering. My victory will feel hollow otherwise.

I put the tea and sandwich on the table and sit on the sofa, staring at the food. I feel hungry and very thirsty, but I resist the temptation to eat or drink. I look at the plate and cup continuously. I want Chandra to beg for them.

I become increasing bored and sore as time goes by. I let my mind wander and think of other things while I wait.

I wake up with a start. I feel strangely better for my sleep. I don't feel hungry at all or thirsty. The cup and plate are still untouched. I touch my head and feel a bandage over my forehead. When did I do that? I look down at my clothes. I am not wearing the blood-splattered clothes I was wearing earlier.

I don't want to get up, because that will defeat my plan of making Chandra feel uncomfortable, but I have a horrible feeling that that plan isn't working anyway.

I walk around the house. It has been cleaned up. The computer monitor is still broken, but the bits of glass have been swept up. The mirror in the bedroom is gone and the torn books have been taken away as well.

I look at my face in the bathroom mirror. The blood has been cleaned off and the wounds have been attended to.

When I go downstairs, I find a pot, a plate, a cup and

some cutlery drying in the dish rack and the faint scent of a meal long-gone lingering in the kitchen.

No, I will win this! I sit down again in the chair and will myself to concentrate and to keep control.

It is very hard to keep my mind from wandering off. Again and again, as time goes by, I wake up after unintentionally losing control and find myself fed, bathed, dressed in different clothes and rested.

I also feel calmer, which is strange. I can't recall ever feeling calm. Even though my plan to torture Chandra is not working, I do feel calmer and more peaceful. It doesn't make any sense to me.

I look outside and the sun is shining. It feels warm in the house and I have a sudden urge to garden. It is better than sitting in the house all day long. Clearly, my plan to force Chandra out is not working. Maybe the urge to garden is hers? I will see what happens.

The sun on my skin feels lovely and I lose myself in taking daisy plugs out of their container and carefully replanting them in a flowerbed. I water the garden and rake up some dead foliage. Once I have put everything away, I make a cup of tea and sit down on a garden chair on the back porch.

"Wasn't that a nice day?"

"It was lovely."

Who said that? Chandra?

52

I sit back in my deck chair and watch the insects buzzing in the garden in the late afternoon sun. I drink a glass of water and feel utterly content. It is a feeling I have become more and more used to over the last few days and, in fact, I have been craving it. I will get up in the morning and go out to garden. I discovered that Chandra has a large patch of ground at the far end of her garden where she is growing all kinds of fresh vegetables and fruits. There is not a lot and certainly could not sustain her for very long, but I enjoy tending to it and eating the ripe produce. I have found that when I am busy in the moment, I seem to know what I am doing and I don't feel so alone.

I tried to force Chandra out again after she spoke to me, but I could not get her to communicate with me. I found that I could not sustain my control all the time and she had once again attended to her needs when I lost control.

It is strange, but, as I have spent more time in the garden, I have been less bothered about forcing her out. It seems to matter less. I don't really care about making Chandra pay anymore. But I don't want to let her go either. I don't want this peace to end. I feel that, at long last, I have reached the end of my journey. I would happily live here in this house inside Chandra's body, spending my time in the garden during the day, making delicious meals and reading books at night, before drifting off to sleep.

Even though Chandra does not talk to me, I don't feel alone. Maybe it is because I am in her body, or maybe it is because I am happy to garden. I did not know I enjoyed it so much.

I sip from a tall glass of cold water filled with fresh crushed mint leaves and lemon juice. It is so refreshing to drink. I wriggle my toes as I sip it and look out as the garden slowly falls asleep in the late afternoon light. My stomach aches. I have been trying to ignore this when it happens. It has happened on and off over the last few days and seems to be occurring more often and with more severe discomfort as time goes by. I have also noticed some red spots on my arms, which appeared about two or three days ago. I did wonder if that was an allergy to something in the garden. I look at them again. They seem bigger and more livid. If I could leave the house, I could probably get some cream to put on them to stop the reaction. They are a small price to pay for the contentment I feel.

53

I laugh as I fall back onto the ground. I was digging out what I thought was a weed, but when I yanked it out I found potatoes hanging off the roots. I am going to have those for supper tonight. The laughter brings on a spate of coughing. I have developed a nasty chest infection and I have tried to ignore it, as I want to hold onto the feeling of peace and contentment.

It's a bad coughing fit this time. By the time it ends, I find myself lying on my side exhausted. I rest a while and then slowly get up. As I stand up, my nose begins to bleed badly. I take off my sweater and bundle it up under my nose to stop the blood from dripping everywhere. I go inside and get some ice from the freezer. I wrap it up in a towel and hold it over my nose. It takes a long time to stop bleeding.

I feel very tired and short of breath, so I brew a cup of tea and make my way up to the bedroom. I strip down into my pants and t-shirt and lie down under the covers. I should not have gone outside today, but the potatoes were a lovely discovery! I am looking forward to eating them tonight.

I sip the tea and feel another coughing fit about to take hold of me. I put the teacup down as carefully as I can and then succumb to such an intense dizzying series of hacking coughs that I find myself catapulted to the other side of the bed. I am looking at myself.

I am not sure what is going on. I have been feeling very dizzy for a while and maybe this is a really bad episode. I wait for the coughing to stop, watching my body heaving weakly with each spasm. Eventually it stops and I watch as I sink back into the pillows with my eyes closed.

I wait a long time, but the dizziness does not seem to end as I am still out of my body, standing at the foot of the bed looking down at myself.

"Hello, demon."

"Who said that?"

"I did."

"Chandra?"

"Yes."

"What has happened?"

"I pushed you out of my body."

"Why? Why now? Could you do this any time?"

"Yes."

"Why did you wait until now?"

"Because it is time. I am dying. And you are ready."

54

"I have cancer. It's incurable. The doctors gave me about a year to live. And I saw a lot of them - doctors. They all told me the same thing. There is nothing anyone could do for me. Well, apart from helping with the pain. Helping me cope with the symptoms."

"A year? When were you told this?"

"About four months ago."

"But it has not been a year then? Why are you so sick now?"

"Because of you."

"No!"

No. No. No. No, I don't want Chandra to be ill because of me. I don't want to have done this to her. I can't even look at her. She looks terrible - so small and frail and ill. Why did I not see this when I was in her? Why did I not look at her and realise what was happening? I thought I wanted to hurt her and I should be glad I have done this to her, but I feel terrible.

"Talk to me."

"No. I can't. I can't believe I have done this to you. I am just evil. I told you I was. I told you that I am pure unadulterated evil. You see, Chandra, I win! I will always win!"

"Whether you want to or not."

"Yes, whether I want to or not, I am here to destroy people's lives. I am here to destroy people's lives for eternity."

"Stay, demon! Don't make me make you stay here against your will! I don't have the strength left."

Chandra has another violent fit of coughing.

"Why should I stay? What is the point? My work here is done. I have destroyed your life. That is what I set out to do and that is what I have accomplished!"

"Then why not stay to see the bitter end? Why does my suffering bother you so much if it is what you wanted?"

I stare at her. I don't understand that. It doesn't make sense. I should be happy that I won.

"Listen, demon. We don't have a lot of time left. There is no point in you and me not speaking to each other. Tell me what is on your mind. If you don't, it will be too late for both of us. I don't want that."

I look at Chandra. She has tears in her eyes. She takes a tissue and carefully wipes a tear that has escaped out the corner of her eye.

"I don't feel happy that you are dying. I feel responsible for you dying. I know I caused it and it should make me feel happy. It should make me feel triumphant, but I don't feel happy or triumphant. I feel terrible. I feel evil and dirty and I want to die. I want to be able to just die and leave people alone!"

"I know."

"The earth would be better off without a thing like me in it! What kind of world creates something like me? Or allows something like me to exist? I feel like I am in a never-ending, sick nightmare!"

"These last few weeks have not been a nightmare."

"No, they were false. They were an evil, cruel illusion that masked the truth!"

"They weren't an illusion for me."

I look at Chandra. She is clearly so ill that she is deranged.

"I think you are a very sick woman and you aren't thinking clearly."

"You are right. I am a very sick woman, but I am thinking clearly. They were a wonderful few weeks. After you stopped beating me up and destroying my house."

Chandra looks at me with a twinkle in her eye.

"What do you mean?"

"Peaceful. Just peaceful, contentment, relaxation and no worries. Thank you. It was something I had not anticipated when I allowed you to possess me."

"Thank you?"

"Yes, thank you."

Chandra smiles at me.

"I took a chance letting you possess me. I knew it could go horribly wrong. I don't know anyone who has willingly let it happen to them and I didn't know what would happen. I knew I would get sick, but I also thought it would be scary and horrible beyond anything I could imagine. It wasn't."

"Why did you let me possess you? Why wasn't it scary?"

"It wasn't scary, because you aren't very scary."

"I think I am scary! I have killed people! I have killed you!"

"Yes. I'm not dead just yet, though, but yes, possessing people can lead to death, but that's not what I am talking about. I have been scared of being ill and scared of what my life was all about. Scared that my life meant nothing. There is so much I still wanted to do. I am still young. It seemed so unfair to have that taken away from me and not be able to do anything about it. But those days with you in the garden were beautiful. Your joy in just being in the moment erased all my worries and all my thoughts. I felt content. It was an unexpected gift. Thank you."

"But you didn't speak. You didn't have any feelings. I didn't know you were there!"

"I was there. I was there all the time. I was

possessing you as much as you were possessing me."

"What? How?"

"I planted ideas in your mind and then I watched them take shape as I hoped they would."

"You had planned this all along? Wait, this is too much! I don't understand!"

"Yes, I had planned it. When you were so hell bent on possessing me, I thought I would take a chance and let you do it. I knew the risks, but I thought it would be worth the try. I didn't have much to lose. Just a few more months of misery. So, at worst, it would shorten that for me. But I hoped that I would accomplish more out of it. A win-win for me either way, you see."

"I don't see. And how come I didn't feel you there?"

"You weren't really paying attention, I suppose. But a part of you was, because I could suggest things to you and you did them. I suggested that you look after me better and you did. In the beginning I had to tell you to feed me and wash me and give me enough sleep, but in the end you did that on your own. I did not have to think about those things. It was nice to be taken care of. I suggested that we garden. I have always found being in nature peaceful. I hoped that you would too and you did. In the end, you were happy to go out and garden and you got so much enjoyment and contentment from it that you did that on your own too. Again, I could let you take control and I just enjoyed feeling what you felt and being in the moment with you."

"You possessed me?"

"Yes."

"I gave you those good feelings?"

"Yes, and that is why I am grateful. They did not come from me in the end. They came from you. That was you possessing me."

"I was possessing you still, but you were possessing me also?"

"Yes, and you were possessing me in a good way. You made me feel better."

"I was possessing you in a....."

"Say it. Say that you were possessing me in a good way."

"I was possessing you in a good way."

"Without you I would never have felt those feelings. I would not have enjoyed life so much. I was so focused on dying and suffering and being sick, that I forgot that life could be good too. If it wasn't for you, I would not have felt that!"

"But I am responsible for you dying now. For dying sooner than you would have! How is that good?"

"Well, that brings me to the point of why I allowed you to possess me and the risk I took. When I asked you to give me a week to prepare myself, I spent a lot of time preparing for this and that included finding out what information I could on demons. As you know, most people don't believe in you so there is not much written, but I did find something that said that some ancient cultures believed that demons could alter a person's mind for good purposes. I didn't think you would believe me if I just told you that and I wanted to see if I could alter your mind. I knew I could get rid of you if I needed to. You would have still hastened my death, but I would have had some time without you there. I wanted to see if I could plant thoughts in your mind to make you feel better and alter how you saw the world and I did. So I know you can do it too."

"Why would you take such a risk?"

"For two reasons, which I thought about a lot. The first was your story. Remember you told me your story before you possessed me? It made me see that there was more to you than you saw. You were not pure evil. You were lost and misguided by someone who was equally lost. That was for you. I could see you were suffering and I thought I could do something for you to stop that. The second reason was for me. I want my life to mean something. I have always been an outsider, with most people thinking I am weird or mad and imagining that I had psychic abilities. It's lonely. I think that's something you and I have in common. Loneliness. We weren't lonely these past few weeks, but that comes with a price. I wanted all of my struggles to mean something, but I was dying with no chance to make my strange life meaningful. Then you came along and you gave me that chance."

"You see, demon, you have a choice. You can possess people and destroy them by making their lives miserable and sucking out all their energy until they die, or you could do things differently."

"You could enter a person's mind and help them to experience something different, something better. You would not have to be there long to feed and then you could move on."

I look at Chandra as I let her thoughts sink in.

Chandra looks at me and starts to cry softly.

"I don't have long, demon. I am going to die very soon. Please don't let me die in vain and please don't let me die alone. Please find my friends, Annie and Tim. You know them, trust me. Please bring them here. They have my cat. Please bring them here with my cat, so I don't have to be alone when I die. I can't make you do that. I can't make you do what I intended you to do. I know I tricked you into it too. But I hope you do. I hope I don't die in vain."

Chandra is weeping and this starts making her hack.

Her face turns a blotchy red colour as she is strangled by one hacking spasm after the next.

I run away.

55

I fly up and up until I can see the stars spread out before me beyond the earth's atmosphere. The sky is infinitely black with swirling stars wherever I look. I want to stay here forever. I wish I could. I feel at peace here. It's just me all alone, all alone with the universe.

But I know I can't leave and the Earth is there at my back. I am tethered to it. I pretend it is not there for now. It is too difficult! What is the purpose of all this?

Chandra would say the purpose of this is to change people's lives for the better. Maybe she is right? I didn't make her life better. I have killed another person. I have killed my only friend.

I am going to be all alone again. I am evil! I warned her and she should have banished me instead of taking such a stupid risk. Maybe they would have found a cure for her, or at least she would have been able to live her life on her own terms instead of having to deal with me.

But she said that it was a gift. Has her mind been destroyed by me and her illness, or did I really make her life better?

I hurt her. I physically hurt her and I ruined her house. I would have hurt her cat. If she had let me leave her house, I would have done my best to ruin her life even more. I would have ruined her reputation; I would have even made her commit murder.

Chandra.

I have to go back! I can't leave her alone to die! I don't know how long I have been up here.

56

It's easy to possess Tim. It's harder to convince Annie that we have to go to Chandra. I get it all wrong in my desperation to get them both there. I have the cat in my arms. He is hissing at me and trying to get away and Annie looks at me as if I have something wrong with me. I have to get this right! If I don't, Chandra is going to die alone.

I don't know what to do! I can't possess them both at once! I'm running out of time. I have read from Tim's mind that it will take forty minutes to drive to Chandra's house. I don't know how long I was up there. I don't even know if it's the same day since I left Chandra. She could be dead already!

I am going to fail at even this simple task. I consider threatening Annie or tying her up and dragging her there, but I have a feeling that won't work in the end. She will get away as soon as we get there and she certainly won't be in any frame of mind to support Chandra. Nor will Tim for that matter! Stop hissing, cat!

I can't possess them both. I can only possess one person at a time and while I am in that person, the other is free to do what they want. I consider threatening Annie again. It would work better if I threaten Annie while I possess Tim, as he is taller and stronger than she is, and I would have the physical advantage. Again, it won't work out the way it should for Chandra when I get them there.

I wish I could just stand in front of them and shout at them this time. I tried talking to them by hopping out of Tim for a bit, but that didn't work either. He was confused and Annie didn't hear me. Maybe if I shouted that would work? Maybe they would both hear me then?

I don't know how to get them both there! How do I

convince them to both go to Chandra? And then the realisation hits me!

Frame of mind.... only possess one person at a time.... maybe.....

"Annie, listen to me. I have a bad feeling. Please listen to me. If you don't, we could regret this. Please, let's go and see Chandra."

"No, she told us not to go. Under no circumstances. We promised. We knew it was goodbye. And you are acting really strange. You are scaring me. Even the cat is scared! Put him down, Tim!"

"No, we need to take the cat back to Chandra!"

"Are you listening to me? We promised her we wouldn't!"

Now! I look at Annie and tell Tim to listen to Annie. I put the thought into his head. I hope this works!

I jump into Annie.

"All right, I think we should go to Chandra."

"I'm listening."

"I agree with you. I am also getting a bad feeling about this. Let's go!"

"What are you talking about? What bad feeling?"

This is harder than I thought. Maybe it won't work. I can't do this! Tim looks at me.

"Hello?"

"Wait! I'm thinking!"

He looks a bit taken aback. I ignore him.

He did listen, didn't he? Yes, he did! He said he was listening. What did Chandra say? I need to help them to think differently.

I close my eyes. I try to merge my thoughts with Annie's. I have no idea if I can do this, or if it will even work. I listen and wait. Then it comes; I can hear Annie's thoughts.

Why is Tim looking at me like that?

He is worried about Chandra. I am too.

Oh, that's right. But we promised her we would stay away even though we didn't want to.

I have a feeling she needs us. If we don't go to her, it will be too late and we will regret that forever. What if she is dead? What if she is very ill?

She might need our help!

Yes! She might need our help.

But she might be very angry with us for breaking our promise. She is very particular about that and I don't want to betray her trust.

Sometimes people should not be allowed to make decisions like that! We were stupid to agree to something so bizarre!

Yes, it was stupid. Something must be going on! We should check up on her!

I feel Annie taking control away from me, as she makes her body take action. I jump into Tim.

"I agree with you. Let's go to Chandra!"

"Oh, that's great! Let's get going!"

"Leave the cat. He's spooked!"

Damn it, I should have spoken about the cat when I was in Annie.

"He's spooked, because I am. I don't want to leave him here. Please let's take him to her. We can always bring him back."

"Fine, but put him in the carry box. I don't want him jumping on us when we are driving."

I can't believe it worked! I am so relieved, but the feeling does not last long, as it seems to take forever to drive there. Annie is driving. I wish I had told her I would drive, but I don't want to spook her again and I did not think possessing them while they are driving would work too well. We might have an accident and then Chandra would be alone again. I keep quiet and wrap my arms around myself to stop myself from shaking.

After what seems like hours, we arrive at Chandra's house. It is dusk. I hope we are not too late. The house is dark. I can see no lights on or sign of life. I run to the back of the car and get the cat out of the boot. He starts hissing at me again.

Annie is standing by the car, looking at me. I try to smile at her as I take her hand. We walk around to the back of the house. I never bothered to lock it while I was living in Chandra and I hope it is still open. The door is open.

"This doesn't look good," Annie gives me a meaningful look.

"I know."

We walk inside. I can't see her downstairs. I can't run up the stairs. Part of me wants to, but part of me is scared that it is too late. I am scared that I messed this up too.

It's dark and quiet upstairs. The bedroom door is closed. Did I leave it that way? I hang onto Annie's hand for support and put the cat box down on the floor. I put my hand on the door handle and turn it, dreading what I will see.

I'm too late. Chandra is lying, just a small broken thing, under her blankets in the dim dusk light. She is deathly pale and not breathing. I let go of Annie's hand and start sobbing.

I crouch down at the foot of the bed, my head in my hands, trying to take comfort from Tim's physicality, from being able to hold myself with his arms. I have never felt so sad in my life. I have betrayed Chandra twice. I have failed her twice. I wish I had never met her! If I had never met her, she would have had a chance of being all right.

"Tim! Tim! Stop it! Get some water!"

"I don't want any!"

"Not for you! For Chandra!"

I look up. Annie is looking at me in exasperation. I look at Chandra. Her eyes are half-open. It looks like she is trying to focus on Annie. She's alive!

She's alive!

I want to gather her up and hold her and hug her, but I run downstairs instead to get the water. I am a mess. I am feeling so many things and I realise all of a sudden that Tim is too. I become aware of him wanting to get the water and take it up to Chandra. I let him go.

Tim looks around for a glass and fills it with water from the sink. I watch as he runs out the kitchen. I stay in the kitchen for a while, before I rush back to Chandra.

She is propped up on a pillow, looking weak. She is sipping from the glass of water. Annie is supporting her head and the glass. Tim is sitting on the edge of her bed, looking terrible.

Chandra looks up at me as I enter the room. She smiles fraily at me, "Thank you."

"It's no problem, sweetie. Just drink. Tim, please organise some food for her."

"I'm all right."

"You are not! You need to eat!"

"Annie, I am dying."

"I know, sweetie, but you have to have something. Tim, see if you can find a can of soup or something."

"Okay."

"Tim, did you bring my cat?"

"Of course."

"Can I have him?"

"Sure. One second."

Tim returns with the cat, which is no longer hissing but looks disgruntled. Tim places him on Chandra's stomach. The cat seems pleased to see Chandra and purrs while he nuzzles her. She seems a little brighter and I back away as far as I can, as I don't want to spook the cat.

"Tim, please get the soup."

"Oh right. Be right back."

Tim leaves the room.

"Annie, I don't want to be any trouble."

"You are no trouble, sweetie."

"I think I would feel better and less embarrassed if I had a face wash at least. I have been too ill to get up and wash. I'm sorry."

"Don't be silly. Would a rub down do? I could fix a bowl of soapy water and a cloth?"

"Thank you."

"I'll be right back. Call if you need anything."

"I'll be fine."

Once Annie leaves the room, Chandra turns to me.

"Thank you."

"I am so sorry. I am so sorry for being so selfish and ruining your life."

"Thank you for saying that. It means a great deal to me that you are sorry. It means I didn't make a mistake with you. You did it, didn't you? You made them think in a different way."

"Only Annie."

"It's a good first step. Now, demon, I want you to promise me two things. The first is that you will not make this a waste. Promise me that you will help people. You know you can do it! And the second thing I want you to promise me is that you will stay until the end. You are my friend."

"Friends don't kill friends!"

"We are special friends. Our relationship is different. Promise me."

"I promise."

And I stay. I watch over Chandra as Annie washes her down and helps her change into a fresh nightie. I watch as Tim carefully spoons a few sips of soup into her mouth. I watch as Annie and Tim hold her hands as she gets weaker and weaker. I watch as her cat curls up on her for the last time.

The room seems to grow quieter as her breathing becomes so slight it is less than a whisper. Tim and Annie are quiet, apart from the occasional tear. The cat has stopped purring and is curled protectively on her stomach. The bedside table light cannot keep the dark gloom, which has crept in with the night, at bay.

Then I see her go. Chandra opens her eyes and gasps once and then she is free of her body. She is a bright white light. She hovers over Annie and then Tim. She hovers over the cat, which starts purring again and then she comes to me. As she touches me, I am filled with light and a feeling of ecstasy, which courses through me and then all goes dark.

Chandra is gone.

57

I stayed while Tim and Annie mourned. I stayed while strangers came to fetch her body. I don't think they knew how special she was. Her body looked so small. I waited while Annie and Tim shut up the house and put the cat back into the carry box. I watched them as they slowly pulled out of the driveway. And then I was all alone in the dark house. I sat by her bed for a while. I couldn't be near her when she was dying, because I didn't want to spook the others. I wished I could have sat by her. I touch her bedspread. I wish I could have taken something of hers to keep with me always, but I am not a thing, which is capable of holding something. I looked down on Chandra's house as I floated up into the sky. I will never go back there again. She is not there anymore. She is gone forever. I forced myself to remember every detail of her house so that I could carry it in my memory always. I looked at it until it became a tiny dark speck.

As I stare out at the galaxy with the Earth gently pulling at me. I try to savour the feeling I had when Chandra's spirit passed through me. It makes me feel a little better. I will never forget that feeling. It is what I can hold onto always. It's a way to keep her with me for eternity.

I look out at the sky and even though I know it's not true, I like to think that there is a new star that arrived there tonight. I find the brightest one and call it Chandra. I tell her I just need a little time here with her before I go back to fulfil my first promise.

58

My body feels stiff and unused. I look at the familiar walls and curtains fluttering in the breeze. With great difficulty, I stand up and slowly stretch my arms up.

"Look! The statue is awake! The statue is awake!"

ABOUT THE AUTHOR

Karen Andor grew up in South Africa and now lives in England. She is a psychologist and psychotherapist.

31556005R00275

Made in the USA
Charleston, SC
22 July 2014